THE LAST FLEET

THE LAST FLEET
BOOK 1

JOSHUA T. CALVERT

FOREWORD

Dear Reader,

For the present novel I recommend that you read the timeline in the appendix at the beginning, which you can find from page 405. It takes you from the present day to the 25th century, so you'll feel right at home in the main plot. But of course you can also start right away with the prologue and catch up with the timeline later. In the appendix there is also a detailed glossary and a list of characters.

Sincerely,
Joshua T. Calvert

PROLOGUE

"Freighter *Ushuaia*, state your destination and cargo," Manuél Ferreira heard a bored voice calling from the coms.

You have my transponder codes on hand, Cabron, he thought, shaking his head. He had paid a lot of money for the fake codes, and worse, he had flown all the way to Black Haven for them, for which he still felt dirty.

"This is Capitán Ferreira of the *Ushuaia*. We have loaded energy matrix relays. Our buyer is *Tromso Electronics LLC*. The exact assignment to one of the logistics hubs will not be made until we enter the inner system," he said with carefully maintained patience.

"Figures we'd end up in the sample again," grumbled his partner, Huelga, who sat at navigation, studying the charts like a fortune teller studies her crystal ball.

"Bad luck," he grumbled, raising his hands in a gesture of resignation. He knew, of course, that since the disappearance of two *Mammoth* Freighters from the sector, inspections were stricter and spot checks more frequent. Still, he had hoped to have some luck for once.

"*Ushuaia*, your energy emission is eighty percent below the value that is usual for a *Light Hauler*," the space flight control informed him.

At least Manuél was prepared for that. "That's correct, two of our three radiators no longer extend properly, so we were forced to shut down non-essential systems en route. Perhaps you can recommend a space dock for us?"

Huelga gave him an *are-you-serious*-look, and he raised his hands in resignation.

"Proceed, *Ushuaia*." A short beep signaled that the connection had been terminated.

"That's it?" he asked incredulously, laughing with relief when the com continued to be silent. "Told you!"

Manuél thumped her upper arm and returned her satisfied grin with an even broader one.

"We've only just jumped into the system, and at the outermost planet," she pointed out after a moment, but he didn't let her typical pessimism get him down and waved it off.

"Then we'll just fly another day and..."

"Two days. We're flying on economy, remember?"

"Well, two then. I can think of a few things we could do in that time. Celebrate, for example! In forty-eight hours, we'll be rich, and we can settle down on New Eden or Aquarius. *Si claro*?"

"How are we supposed to celebrate when only one fusion engine is active and the entire ship is without power, except for our cockpit?" she asked with a somber look. "We haven't been able to shower in two weeks, you smell like a dead polecat that's been on a radiator for two months along with some blue cheese. That plus your rectum and..."

"Yeah, yeah, I get it!" he interrupted her, grimacing.

"All I'm saying is that this is our worst job yet and we..." That's as far as she got, because all at once the power went out in the cockpit. Immediately it went pitch black before the emergency power supply kicked in and bathed them in red light.

"No, no, no," he cursed, looking at the data from the automatic emergency system check running on the only remaining display. "Not this close to the end!"

"What does it say?" Huelga wanted to know.

The last fleet

"An energy fluctuation in the dorsal superconductors. The on-board computer automatically shut down to prevent an overload in the secondary systems."

"A fluctuation? With only one active reactor?"

"I don't know why; the thing is completely new."

"*They* put that part in for us," she reminded him of a fact he was only too happy to forget. No captain liked to see hooded men taking his ship apart and putting in a critical component that even as the owner he could not get access to. Maybe the whole thing had been a stupid idea after all, since the energy matrix crystals would provide emergency power for the next two days - enough for life support, but not for course corrections or even a turn and brake maneuver. So far, he had not complained about it, as their foray into the Seed Traverse had nearly cost them their lives. The bastards had come aboard, jammed all the sensors and put temporary overrides on his on-board computer. It had felt like a deep betrayal - of him and his ship, but also on his own part.

"Uh, Manuél?" He heard Huelga say, and the sudden tension in her voice made him sit up and take notice.

"*Que?*"

"Take a look at the mass data. I'm pretty sure our total mass at departure was 1,433 tons and 474 pounds. As a physicist, I can tell you that the mass of a closed system cannot change."

"I know that myself, thank you!" He uttered an indignant curse. The *Ushuaia* had supposedly grown 660 pounds heavier. According to the system log, the mass increase had occurred at the same time as the energy fluctuation. "Impossible."

"Yes, damn it, impossible!" she agreed with him, unbuckling herself from her co-pilot seat. "I'm going to check it out."

"I'll go with you." He unfastened his own straps and immediately began to float.

"No. Keep an eye on the logs, I can do this on my own." Huelga grabbed one of the breathing masks from the wall next to the door to the central corridor and then squeezed into one of the survival suits hanging just below it.

"Forget it. I can't do anything here anyway, and I'm not leaving you alone. You know the rules. No man goes out alone."

"Good thing I'm not a man."

"I'm the *capitán*," he said, slipping into the second rubbery suit, which glowed such bright yellow that even the meager emergency light made it pop. Then he took a breathing mask of his own, which automatically conformed to the shape of his face. He pressed the square oxygen pack, connected to the mask by a small tube, with the Velcro side against the corresponding panel on his chest.

"Ready?" he asked, hearing the echo of his own voice through the mask.

"Ready," came her muffled reply.

"As soon as we go through, all atmosphere is gone. The suit will keep us warm, but we won't be able to talk."

"I drained the atmosphere from the rest of the ship myself, remember?" she reminded him, but grabbed him by the shoulders and pressed her forehead to his. "Let's go."

Manuél nodded and took a deep breath before pressing the button for the cockpit door - and then again after a warning lit up on the control panel that there was a vacuum on the other side and acute danger to life.

The central corridor was something like the main artery of his 200-yard-long *Light Hauler*-class freighter. Around it was the various cargo modules, of which only one was currently in use. The others were loaded with empty containers. Four hatches opened directly in front of the cockpit, behind which were the sleeping quarters, a small kitchen, and a hygiene room. At the far end of the corridor was the propulsion section with maintenance access for engineers and mechanics.

The corridor was relatively narrow and round like a tube, surrounded by honeycomb wall panels that made it look even narrower. The armored door to the propulsion section was nothing more than a small dark dot in the far distance.

It became dead silent as the vacuum also took the tiny cockpit and all the air trapped inside.

Manuél moved forward before Huelga could beat him to it

and floated out into the corridor. He shivered, although the survival suit did not indicate any malfunction and kept his body temperature constant at 97.7 degrees Fahrenheit. The sparse light began to flicker under the reactor fluctuations. At times it was pitch black, at others glaringly bright, as if it were a cheap party effect from a club on New Berlin.

He shimmied forward on the interspersed handholds, gliding through the weightlessness like a fish. His every move was intuitive - since the age of twelve, he had spent far more time on spaceships than in gravity wells.

"Twenty more yards," he said, having to remind himself that his co-pilot and wife couldn't hear him. Just this one more job and they would be able to afford transducers, hardly prone to failure and implanted. But that left him alone for now with just the echo of his own breath. The mask fogged in front of his mouth with each exhalation and cleared again with each inhalation. Thus, the ground beneath him seemed covered again and again with a mystical fog, which only intensified the unpleasant tickle on the back of his neck.

The cargo compartments were arranged along the corridor which connected the cockpit and propulsion, like precisely fitted burrs which could be unlocked and replaced during loading and unloading. Each was forty cubic yards with their current configuration and met the cargo standard to which all docking drones were designed. Number twenty in row two of four was the one that housed their only cargo on this trip. Huelga and he hadn't even had to spell it out, as they both knew that this compartment alone was in question when it came to a cause for the fluctuations - and the increase in mass that, after all, could only have come from a misreading of the sensors.

The corridor seemed to stretch on and on, like an alienating lens effect. As a child, Manuél had often dreamed of walking along a road whose end disappeared further and further into the distance the harder he tried to reach it. He didn't remember what he had chased in the dream, but the feeling was similar enough to bore uncomfortably into the back of his mind.

"Twenty," he whispered as he finally arrived in front of the narrow hatch, which was painted with a capital two and a zero. Huelga, arriving right next to him in the vacuum that tolerated no sound, and catching herself on one of the handholds, tapped her chest with a finger.

"No." He shook his head. "I'm going in first."

She drew her brows together in disgruntlement and pointed to the panel for the door control. It only worked with fingerprint or DNA matching.

Of course it did. He wanted to scream.

With one foot, he hooked into one of the handholds to keep from floating away, then tapped away on his wrist terminal to activate remote access to the on-board computer.

But there was no connection.

"Emergency power," he said to himself, cursing his situation. To show her what the problem was, he shook his head and pointed first at his wrist terminal and then toward the ceiling. "No non-essential systems have power." As the light flickered again, and the periods of darkness in between were longer this time, he added, "If we have any at all any time soon."

Then he remembered something. Like on most freighters, the hatch's locking mechanism was a magnetic device that didn't work without power. However, each one had a battery that provided up to twenty-four hours of the small amount of power needed to keep it locked in the event of a total failure. Companies were careful when it came to protecting their cargo.

Manuél clasped Huelga's head with both hands and pressed his mask to hers. Aloud he said, "Reverse the circuit! Then we can reverse the magnetic field and open the hatch!"

When she merely shook her head in confusion, he shouted the words, hoping they would carry over the vibrations of their masks in a semi-intelligible manner.

His wife's brow remained furrowed in deep creases, but behind her eyes it seemed to be working. Finally, she looked past him and whether she understood the right snippet of words or had come up with the same idea at that moment - she nodded in understanding and got to work.

First, she removed one of the white honeycomb panels and

then began to tinker with the wiring behind it, while he continued to try in vain to contact the on-board computer on his wrist terminal. Only after what felt like an eternity did a connection briefly flash between two energy spikes coursing through the superconductors.

What he saw in that scant ten seconds did not encourage him: all three reactors had powered up and were fusing helium-3 pellets at a record pace that came close to the maximum of what heat the magnetic containment chambers could contain.

"This can't be!" He protested at the readings that were displayed to him and immediately disappeared as a fresh spike of energy coursed through the superconductors, causing secondary systems to shut down.

A movement in the corner of his eye made him wince. By the time he saw that it was the hatch suddenly shooting upward into its socket, it was already too late for relief. Adrenaline shot into his bloodstream, making his ears rush and his hands shake.

Before he could react, Huelga pulled herself into the cargo bay and disappeared through the narrow entrance inside, from which a bluish flicker penetrated the central corridor.

"Wait!" he shouted, cursing as he tried to chase after her but got caught on his hooked foot and dangled back like a pendulum. Hastily he freed himself, grabbed the handles to the right and left of the hatch and pulled himself inside.

Huelga hovered directly in front of him, but she was no longer the Huelga who had been beside him a moment ago. She had turned her back on him and bent him over strangely. Her arms hung limply at her sides as if normal gravity prevailed. Two dark red wings had formed on her shoulder blades and were flowing away from her tenaciously like quicksilver.

Only it wasn't wings, but blood.

He wanted to scream her name, but instead only a stifled gasp escaped his lips. Like a prisoner in his body, he drifted to the left, past the horrific image of his wife bleeding out before his eyes. There was something obscene about the angelic figure she seemed to represent in her death that destroyed everything sacred in him that had bound him to her for twenty years. Silent tears streamed down his cheeks and his mind could barely grasp what was happening there in front of him when Huelga's corpse no longer blocked the view of the cargo module: the cargo, a coffin-like box made of a strange material that looked like a ship's hull encrusted with shells, stood open. Floating above it were three spheres, large as medicine balls and unadorned except for the occasional blue flicker they gave off.

Behind the three objects stood a giant figure that seemed to have sprung directly from a nightmare, and at the same time was of such beauty that Manuél began to weep. The rapture he felt, although everything in him resisted it, felt like the deepest betrayal towards his wife.

The creature possessed two legs, just like him, but they stuck out at a strange angle, as if the knees were bent in the wrong direction. The skin was pearly and shone like velvety jewels. The torso was slender and V-shaped, encased in a robe that was tight and shimmered in several colors at once, as if it possessed a life of its own. From the shoulders grew two wing-like appendages with multiple joints, deep blue like the oceans of Manuél's home world, Castilliana. They were splayed at the same angle as the wings of blood that flowed from his wife's shoulders. Directly in front of them were two arms made of a morphing substance that was black and looked like liquid pitch. The fingers they ended in were Huelga's fingers, a cruel mockery of her lifeless form that should have made him angry. But he could not feel even such a basal emotion as hatred beside the fascinating horror that held him gripped.

The alien's head was teardrop-shaped and towering, with a narrow mouth and six breathing holes arranged in rows of two, one above the other, above which were two fist-sized eyes, dark as the universe itself. Everything was reflected in them: Huelga, the three objects on which spiraling streaks of light kept glowing, flickering, and fading away. The light that emerged from them seemed ethereal and captivating, as if it were sucking up all the other photons in the cargo module and turning them into itself.

How did you get here? What are those machines hovering over the cargo? What have you done to my wife? Questions flashed through his mind, the answers to which he feared more than anything else.

Suddenly he noticed that the alien had long since locked on to him. Infinite, alien eyes stared at him like black holes that seemed to consume all light and life.

Then he began to scream.

1

Haeron II, third emperor of his house and leader of humankind, circled the long conference table and the admirals, who stood before their chairs and bowed their heads respectfully. Their expressions were serious, their eyes correspondingly tired for the early hour, but their uniforms immaculate as the gold trim around the edges of the table.

Having reached his seat - a slightly larger armchair at the head - he spread his arms and gestured for the two dozen ranking officers of the Star Empire to sit down.

As soon as the rustling and creaking died down, Haeron II gestured towards his brocade sleeping robe and looked around the room.

"So, what can't wait until morning?" His gaze lingered on his chief of staff, High Lord Marius Albius.

"Our listening stations in the Sigma Quadrant have located a Never infestation spreading toward Andal," the Grand Admiral replied.

"A Never infestation?" Haeron II raised an eyebrow in the officer's direction and then looked at the silent faces. Most pairs of eyes were avoiding him. So not every one of them was sitting at this table in the heart of the imperial country estate at four in the morning out of conviction.

"Yes, Your Grace."

"We have not had one of those since Rohol."

"That's right. Apparently, it has gathered itself," High Lord Dain Marquandt interjected after the Grand Admiral gave him a prompting wave. "Because it is clearly larger than it has ever been before."

So Marquandt is the one driving this meeting, the Emperor concluded. *So presumably also the first person to whom the listening post data had been reported. Interesting.*

"What do you mean bigger?"

"Our preliminary data indicates that there are three swarms with the same destination," Marquandt explained in a calm voice that nevertheless carried an undertone of urgency. "And the destination is Andal itself."

"Three swarms?" Haeron made no effort to hide his disbelief. "The Never spreads at random. For a hundred years our scientists have been unable to detect any pattern in its expansion. And now three swarms are supposed to be heading for one target at once?"

"Yes, Your Grace," the High Lord confirmed curtly. His gaunt figure sat motionless, his hands folded in front of him on the ornate tabletop and his gaze fixed. He was not a bootlicker, and Haeron II appreciated that, even if the man was said to have a certain closeness to republican elements in the Senate. But perhaps that was just a fastidiously maintained stigma, so as not to appear dangerous to any of the higher-ranking members of the Admiralty.

When he did not reply, Grand Admiral Albius gestured to Marquandt to continue.

"Emperor, three swarms are more than we can contain on the ground, and Andal is a thriving colony. House Andal is fiercely loyal and is one of the largest financial contributors to the Border Sectors. It is also home to important listening stations that secure the Seed Traverse and shield it from smugglers. If we don't show strength now and protect them with enough foresight, it will play into the hands of your opponents in the Senate - not to mention the many millions of lives at stake."

"So, what do you propose?" the Emperor demanded, continuing to speak before the Admiral could answer, "When I was last

The last fleet

briefed - and that was yesterday - forty of our one hundred fleets were assigned to security, asset protection, and sector missions in the Star Empire. Thirty are guarding the Wall Worlds on the frontier to the Orb." He looked to his chief of staff and opened his hands in a questioning gesture. "That leaves twenty fleets, at least a handful of which should be in the docks in the course of the current rotation."

"Terra's Home Fleets are still free," High Lord Marquandt suggested after his superior glanced in his direction again.

"You are proposing to send my *bodyguards*? For containment of a Never infestation?"

For the first time, the other admirals at the table stirred. Quiet rustling, a cough here, a clearing of the throat there.

"Yes, Your Grace." Marquandt remained firm. "The Border Worlds are among your most loyal supporters, monarchists of the first order who carry great weight in public opinion because of their charisma for colonists of the inner worlds. If you do not provide sufficient protection for them now and we lose one or even more colonies, it will weaken your position permanently. If you send five fleets, that should be enough to stop the infestation with ease before it can spread."

"That's almost the entire Home Fleet!" protested Admiral Takahashi further back. "Besides, Andal is known to have a larger underground of republican terrorists that their intelligence services can't handle."

"That may be. But the point is to set an example. Namely, that we will not abandon the loyal Border Worlds to their fate."

"If they pull their fleets together, they can handle this problem themselves," Takahashi objected. "These are, after all, six closely allied sectors with six powerful, extremely modern fleets."

"Probably," Marquandt admitted, outwardly unmoved, looking again at Haeron II. "But in addition to military considerations such as a feared weakening of the Border Sectors, a shortage of supplies due to overextended spare parts deliveries, and declining morale among key allies, there is also a political dimension: what message are you sending, Your Grace, if the Home Fleet remains here around Terra and - pardon me - rusts away while your most loyal subjects suffer losses and are weakened economically and militarily for years? The Home Fleet is also paid for out of your taxes. After all, the most modern of our ships were not built for ceremony, one would think."

"Have some respect!" Grand Admiral Albius snarled across the table at the High Lord.

Haeron II made a generous gesture with his right hand. "It's no disrespect," he said, giving Marquandt a gracious look. "He's right, of course. All but the first of the Home Fleet will be withdrawn from Terra and moved to the Karpshyn Sector to ward off the infestation. And when the battle is won, it will remain in place to help Cornelius Andal uproot those republican elements in his realm once and for all."

The High Lord leaned back and straightened his uniform. There was no complacency in his eyes, rather something like relief.

"An important political message, Your Grace. Especially in these times," he said, inclining his head. "And an elegant solution to the problem on Andal."

"My son Magnus will lead the First Fleet and four other Home Fleets, and I want High Lord Andal to be given supreme command of the assembled Frontier Fleets," Haeron II decided. "We don't want it to look like we are militarily disempowering them and proving to them that only the Core Worlds can solve their problems for them. Magnus will come as a helping hand, not a punishing one."

"Of course, Emperor." Chief of Staff Albius bowed.

"One more thing." Haeron II stood up and the assembled admiralty also rose immediately. He pointed to Marquandt. "Since this idea obviously came from you, High Lord, you will be given supreme command of the defense of our territory. End the infestation, make the Frontier Lords look good, and get my son the combat experience he needs."

"As you wish, Your Grace." Marquandt bowed. "With your permission, I will deploy the fleets of my Wall Sector to achieve victory with as little loss as possible."

"Good." The Emperor tapped his signet ring twice on the

tabletop and then left the room. "The Orb have been quiet for decades, so hopefully they'll stay quiet for a few more days."

"He's sending his own son?" Grand Admiral Albius rubbed his broad chin thoughtfully.

Dain Marquandt, who had just passed the chief of staff and was the last to leave the conference room deep in the basement of the Imperial country estate, stopped. The words were as obviously meant for him as a red stop sign, although his superior had not addressed him directly.

"Yes," he replied neutrally. "A good sign of strength and personal responsibility, I think."

"You pushed him to do it."

"Pushed?" Marquandt frowned. "As I recall, that was not my suggestion."

"The prince is smart and a good commander, but everyone in the Star Empire knows he shouldn't be leading the First Fleet at the rank of vice admiral." The chief of staff shook his head. Some bystanders could hear them, but that didn't seem to bother him.

"The public knows exactly how to understand the rise of an Imperial descendant in the ranks of the Navy. Contrary to popular opinion among nobility, the commoners are neither unworldly nor stupid."

"Are you suggesting that the heir to the throne is not sufficiently competent, but is instead an elaborately costumed figurehead of the monarchy?"

Marquandt ignored his superior's challenging look and shook his head, disregarding their surreptitious audience. "I'm not implying anything, merely pointing out that the people will appreciate the gesture, not to mention the lords of the Border Worlds."

"Of course," Albius replied laconically. "You'd better ride to a glorious victory, Dain. With so much firepower at your command, you'll be expected to do nothing less than make a defense for the history books - because it was so easy."

"I'll do my best," he replied neutrally, not letting his guard down. The Chief of Staff was an arrogant fellow, and he was welcome to act out his foolishly concealed rage at the fact that one of his subordinate admirals had, against all expectations, gotten his way with the Emperor himself. At least, that's exactly how their little scene would look to bystanders. Dain Marquandt had not risen to be one of the most important fleet admirals because steam came out of his ears at any sign of pressure, no matter how small.

"What about your armored fleet?" asked Albius, when he was hoping the charade had reached its natural conclusion. He disliked such spectacles, important as they might be.

"What about it?"

"You command five fleets in Wall Sector Three. That's only fifty-six hours to Andal."

Marquandt waited for the question that followed and almost smirked at the anger that lit up the Chief of Staff's eyes when he received no answer. How on earth had this man made it to his position?

Bootlicking, corruption, intrigue in the court and the Senate, he reminded himself. *Like all lords with ambitions. And yet I need him, and he needs me.*

Outwardly, he remained neutral and looked Albius expectantly in the eye.

"A fleet admiral does not leave his fleet behind. But the Emperor will not like it if you leave a Wall Sector unprotected."

"A Wall Sector is never unprotected. There are more space fortresses and static defenses there than anywhere else - except Terra, perhaps. Besides, His Majesty has raised no objections."

"That's not how the First Secretary of State sees it, though. You know how seriously Darishma takes the Orb threat and how influential he is," the Grand Admiral insisted. From his lips it sounded more like "how overly seriously he takes the danger from the Orb."

"We shall see. Or are your orders to leave my fleets behind?" he asked.

Albius appraised him with a disparaging look. The Chief of Staff was not happy, but that was not because of the campaign, after all he was an ardent monarchist, but much more because one of his subordinate admirals had gotten his way and he had to support the whole thing as well. For Dain Marquandt, the matter was clear: the top brass had long been cut off from the needs and realities of the enlisted men serving and were more concerned with their own interests than with the naval units entrusted to their care. It was always about their own advantage. About politics. Their audience knew he thought that way. So why not leave them knowing just that? Let them quietly think that Albius was of a completely different ilk.

"No. You will abide by the Emperor's orders." Albius made it sound like an order, though they both knew there was no wiggle room in the matter - for either of them.

"As you wish," Marquandt said with a gesture somewhere between a nod and a bow. "The infestation will be contained before it has begun, Grand Admiral. Do not worry."

2

Gavin Andal, youngest son of High Lord Cornelius Andal, Lord of the Karpshyn Sector and His Majesty's Sector Governor, steered the shuttle directly toward the orbital ring that surrounded his home world like a silver lining. Blue oceans alternated with lush green land masses, dotted with brown and white where mountains rose from the endless forests. Even if the planet had not borne the name of his house, the sight of it would have been no less impressive.

Not that it mattered. What mattered was only the shuttle and his right hand on the flight stick.

"Shit, Gav, the antennas!" cursed Lizzy beside him, pressing her hands against the instrument panel in front of the windshield. She pressed herself into the co-pilot seat as if her life depended on it.

Maybe it even did.

He grinned and jerked the stick hard to the left, sending the arrow-shaped spaceship pitching to one side and hurtling between two long antenna spears. Out of the corner of his eye, he saw the proximity warnings in the head-up guidance system, which indicated eight inches to the left and six to the right.

His grin widened.

"Did you see that?" the young lieutenant gasped, glancing over her shoulder as if there were a rear window like on a car.

"Yes," he said lightly, staying within hair's breadth of the orbital ring's hull to loop along its jagged surface. As he did so, he turned it upside down toward the many windows of the ring-shaped space station, until the astonished and mostly horrified faces behind them could be glimpsed. "Did you know I used to play in those old hangars when I was a kid? Today they've been turned into soccer fields because they've been built over."

"Shuttle XZ-1, this is Space Control," another radio warning sounded after he had ignored the first two. The voice sounded extremely angry. Almost sexy, he thought. "This is your final warning. Correct your dangerous course immediately or we will open fire."

"Gav!" shouted Lizzy breathlessly.

He felt the tingling on the back of his neck increase and turn into an itch.

"They're going to shoot us down! Are you insane?"

Gavin waited a moment longer, savoring the tension fully, then pressed the answer button.

"This is Lord Captain Gavin Andal," he said, taking pains to make his voice sound stately rather than pressed despite the G-forces acting on him. "I hereby give myself flight clearance."

The loop was nearly complete, with less than a yard of mean distance to the armored steel plates of the orbital ring above them. Only then did space control reply, "Excuse me, my lord. We were not notified of your flight beforehand."

He spared himself a reply, completed the loop, and sped toward Andal, passing between two cargo barges that were headed like tightly packed slugs toward one of the transit stations from which goods were shuttled to the surface. It was easy for him to trust his depth perception and the power of the shuttle. It was harder not to stare at Lizzy beside him, to enjoy her shudder, the horror and the relief that set in.

"And that," he said triumphantly as they entered the upper atmospheric layers, "is how you determine the operating limits of a new-generation Triton shuttle."

He engaged the autopilot and spread his arms like a boxer after sending his opponent to the mat.

The last fleet

"Bloody devotion!" the communications officer cursed, swiping a strand from her face that had come loose from her by-the-book bun.

Gavin found that this apparent carelessness made her seem even more attractive. He could see and hear the adrenaline in her system doing its work: trembling hands, quivering voice, restless gaze.

"I thought we were going to die."

"Welcome to your new life." He laughed, took her hand, and pulled her to him. If he had been sure when he left his ship that she had her eye on him, there was no doubt about it now. She threw herself at him more than he had to pull her and pressed her moist lips to his.

The pilot's chair protested with a creak under the sudden extra weight, as Andal's gravity was already acting on them.

"This is definitely naughty," he mumbled between their frenzied kisses, and tore off her uniform jacket. The buttons on the front ripped off, sending them hurtling through the cabin like bullets. Lizzy put a hand over his mouth.

"Shh!"

Then she began to fumble with his pants, grinning as she realized that their little outing was going to have a happy ending.

Ten minutes later, Gavin felt used - in the very best sense. He smiled blissfully, not even paying attention to the fact that he was sitting half naked in scraps of functional clothing in a brand-new shuttle and, in the last half hour, had violated just about every fleet directive that he had ever read.

Which couldn't have been very many, he had to admit to himself. He laughed inwardly at the thought.

"And that," he said with a satisfied sigh, "is how you test the operational limits of the prettiest junior officer in our sector forces."

"You truly do not lack arrogance, my Lord," she retorted mockingly, putting her uniform back on. Skaland was already visible in front of the windshield, looming on the horizon like a white-grey blur. Gradually, the many skyscrapers peeled out of the horizon like dark monoliths in front of the rising sun.

"Healthy self-assessment." He shrugged and, sighing, flicked the switch for the radio link to approach control, which was now sending a third request that they identify themselves.

"Prince's carriage approaching," Gavin said, joining in Lizzy's giggles. In doing so, he forgot to let go of the switch, but he didn't care. Let the few lazy air traffic controllers hear it. Instead of another transmission, he turned on his personal transponder code, which gave him and any vehicle he was in the highest priority and identified him as a family member of House Andal.

"How about two days rest in Skaland?" he suggested as he watched her finish dressing with some disappointment. "We've been on that barge up there long enough."

"That was only two weeks," she remarked, shaking her head.

"Long enough, I say."

"I had to serve six months straight on an ancient cruiser before I even got my admission to the Academy. I'm not surprised that kind of 'fun' apparently escaped you."

"I was at the Imperial Pilot School, locked up with a bunch of guys!"

"Is that supposed to elicit sympathy, now?" she asked, snorting.

"Yeah." He grinned broadly. "After all, it's why I met you much later."

"Is that supposed to be charm?" Lizzy cupped her hands over her mouth.

"Did you not enjoy that flight?" Gavin winked at her.

"You're not a bad pilot," she replied, just as the shuttle lowered for approach, turning a tight circle.

In the back of his mind, he wondered why she was going so fast, but he didn't take his eyes off the officer. When he realized she wasn't going to add anything, he blinked. "Hey, wait a minute! What is that supposed to mean?"

Lizzy, meanwhile, had put on her boots and adjusted her bun. Before she could answer, the tailgate slid open and a gush of cool air blew into the cabin, dispelling the smell of sweat, passion, and a pinch of ozone. A tall figure in a black uniform stood in the square of light, hands clasped in front of his stomach, head shaved and covered in a red tattoo.

"Great," he grumbled as he realized the shuttle had landed on one of the landing pads of their family compound. That didn't bode well. "Wait!"

Lizzy turned around again on the ramp.

"When will I see you again?"

"If I can't find a better pilot for the return flight..." She paused, as if thinking hard. Then she shrugged, winked at him in a manner he knew well from himself, and left the shuttle.

He and Meinhard, his father's secretary, were left alone.

"What a befitting way to arrive," the courtier remarked with a raised brow and a blank stare as he eyed the scattered remnants of Gavin's uniform lying across the cockpit.

"Did you reroute my flight?" He gathered his things and pretended not to mind walking around naked in front of the man who had fed him and rocked him on his knees as a child.

"Yes."

"Who gave you the precedence codes?"

"My orders," Meinhard replied, handing him a stocking on his outstretched index finger that Gavin had been looking for under the wrong seat. He plucked it from his finger and emitted a low grumble.

"How bad is it?"

"Your father is not pleased."

"He rarely is when it comes to me."

"Does that not give you pause?" Meinhard's expression remained composed, but there was something like disappointment in his eyes, which struck Gavin worse than an angry rebuke ever could.

"Is he waiting in the office?" he asked at last, feeling more dejected than he was willing to admit.

"In the dining-room. The family has gathered for breakfast." The secretary grabbed Gavin's arm as he tried to pass him. The grip felt warm. "I've placed a fresh uniform in the guest restroom in the south corridor."

"Thank you, Meinhard."

After a gallant bow, Meinhard let go of him and remained in the shuttle.

How the hell did he know I'd need a uniform? wondered Gavin as he walked across the landing pad toward his family's primary residence. Unlike most families of high nobility, of which there were only one hundred in the entire Terran Star Empire, Skaland Castle was not a sprawling ostentation in the style of the European late Middle Ages, but a fusion of several architectural styles. The cathedral-like main building had something of a Classicist-Baroque about it, with yawning window arches and plain roof ridges. In contrast, the secondary wings, which housed mainly bodyguards and clerks, more closely resembled the French Renaissance: gray and playful with stone ornaments along the roof edges depicting scenes of their home dating back to the Consolidation Wars under the first emperor Tyrus.

From the landing field, a paved path led through shortly cut grassy grounds where, unlike other castles, there were no gardens. Gavin knew from his travels to other fiefdoms that Skaland Castle came across as less ostentatious than many a golf club owned by a lesser senator from the commoners.

The mandatory guards were missing at the entrance to the south wing, a wooden-looking double door that was actually made of fifteen inches of armored steel. He sighed with relief and said a mental thanks to Meinhard before placing his hand on the scanner and slipping through the door. In the restroom, he changed his clothes, stowed the old uniform, mostly destroyed by Lizzy, in the remaining bag, and fixed his hair. Only then did he return to the hallway and walk with measured steps toward the dining room. On the way, he met the two guards in their blue armor, who returned to the door and smiled knowingly at him.

Gavin returned their unspoken greeting with a laconic shrug and finally reached his destination. Liveried servants greeted him with tilted heads and pulled open the door panels for him.

At the round table sat his parents, Cornelius and Sophie Andal, along with his siblings: there was his older brother and titular heir Artas, broad-shouldered and finely coiffed, a typical aristocrat with a serious air and an intelligent look; his sisters

The last fleet

Elisa, just coming of age and with freckles on her nose to match her playful disposition; and Mariella, playing at a holoterminal.

"Ah, there he is, our mad pilot," his father greeted him, gesturing towards the only remaining seat. Gavin wasn't foolish enough to grin and instead sat down with a silent nod.

Servants in blue livery filled his wine goblet and the water glass beside it before Cornelius dismissed them with a wave. Only when the last door had closed behind them did he fix him with a stern look.

"That was your last outing as a teenager!" his father said. With his bear-like figure and soft mouth, he often seemed like a somewhat bearish teddy bear, but not here and now. His voice had a harsh undertone, and his lips were taut with anger.

"I'm twenty-five," the words escaped Gavin, and he glanced out of the corner of his eye at Artas, who was eyeing them both intently, while Elisa looked like she wanted to slide under the table and hide until it was over. "But maybe you forgot."

"If you were acting your age, it wouldn't have slipped my mind."

"How do you want me to act?" He pointed at Artas. "Like him, I suppose?"

"Show a little more respect for your father!" his mother admonished him, now giving him an equally stern look, which was rare enough and thus did not fail to have its effect.

Gavin stifled a venomous remark and felt his anger go up in smoke.

"I'm sorry," he said sincerely, taking a deep breath. "I had a crush on a junior officer, and I was showing off a little."

Elisa giggled, but stopped when her mother looked at her.

"I was young once, too, Gavin," his father countered. "And someday you'll look back on that time and laugh about it. It will give you a comforting, nostalgic feeling to think back to your days as a womanizer. You're a young man with too many hormones in your bloodstream, I understand that. What I have no sympathy for, however, is showing off. It is one of the basest impulses of the human spirit."

"Really?" asked Gavin with a furrowed brow, holding up his

wine goblet. "This." He gestured with the goblet, including the entire room along with the brocade curtains and gold chandelier. "This is all showing off."

"No, son." All at once Cornelius Andal looked old and tired, and all anger was gone from his countenance. "All these are golden chains. There is purely nothing that distinguishes us from our fellows out there, except our birth. We didn't do anything for this and that's why we must earn this privilege every day. It is not a gift, but a burden. Before this day is through, you will understand that."

While Gavin was trying to understand what was meant by this, his father continued, "We rule this sector. We are unjustly above the law, and yet we are mere serfs of a law all our own. We are theoretically allowed to do whatever we want, but what is a theory worth if it has no practical application? We can't go to restaurants; we can't go to movie theaters. No oblivious strolling in the parks of Skaland, no visit to the waterfalls of Fredheim. Nothing without reporters, reams of bodyguards, and the invisible eyes of the public interpreting and picking apart our every micro gesture. We can't make friends because everyone wants something from us. Every kind word toward us is a spectacle of benign intentions. And then there are the political enemies, where every breath seems to be part of an intrigue. Our ship may gleam gold, but it is surrounded by sharks wherever we go."

Gavin thought about it and wanted to object, but whatever words came to his mind seemed childish and shallow.

"I know you've had everything handed to you on a silver platter yourself since you were born," his father said in a conciliatory tone, and the fact that he calmed down so quickly without reprimanding him made him suspicious. Moreover, they never ate breakfast together. Only dinner was firmly scheduled as time together in the family's busy schedule. The one hour of togetherness between all the duties that were imposed on them. "And that's despite the fact that you've done nothing wrong. Maybe your behavior is rooted in that - an attempt to break out. Until now I have turned a blind eye because every child has the right to rebel against his parents and emancipate himself. But that ends here, today. Because it has to."

Cornelius looked at Sophie and gave her a barely perceptible nod.

"Elisa, Mariella?" his mother said, getting up. "Come along, let us leave."

"Not Elisa."

She looked at her husband and eyed him disparagingly.

"She's going to cadet school starting tomorrow. She should hear this too, don't you think?" he asked, waiting for her nod of agreement.

When Gavin's mother had left the room with his youngest sister, Cornelius motioned for his children to move up at the table.

"Our sector is in danger," he got right to the point. Artas wasn't surprised, so he already knew.

Of course he did.

"Has another Mammoth freighter disappeared?"

"The Never is moving toward us and will reach the outer system before the end of this week."

"The Never?" blurted out Gavin. "Here?"

His father nodded and gave Artas a wave.

"Our deep space listening stations relayed the correlating data to us tonight, and the High Command on Terra has confirmed it."

"The high command? Terra?" His head was spinning. He only knew of the Never's infestations from the Feeds - a sinister phenomenon that had originally been classified as a locust-like species of extreme aggressiveness. But that had proven to be wrong. Something about it defied the laws of physics, for what a Never swarm infected and eventually devoured disappeared forever from the known universe. Without a trace and for all time.

"Three swarms."

"But that's not possible. Three swarms? That has never happened before. Besides, the Never occurs only in the Sagittarius sectors and not here with us."

"That's the way it was before. But now there are three swarms heading this way and we don't know why," Artas explained with the professional calm expected of a High Lord's successor. But Gavin had known his brother for twenty-five years, noticed the slight differences in his voice, the slightly deeper crow's feet at the edges of his eyes, and the shadow that lay in his gaze. He was worried.

"Have we alerted the other Frontier Sectors yet? Are they coming to help?"

"Yes," his brother replied. "And not only them. The Emperor is sending the Home Fleet to assist. The First Fleet is led by Crown Prince Magnus."

"The Home Fleet is coming here?" Gavin didn't know if that should frighten him, because the danger was obviously even greater than he had thought. Ultimately, however, his amazement got the better of him. "When will the ships arrive here?"

"Tomorrow evening. I have already given the order to mobilize the sector fleet. You two will help lead the defense," their father said, sighing heavily. "I wish you could have had a few more years before the war comes calling, but apparently even the Border Worlds will not be spared from it."

"How many fleets will we have?" He tried to imagine what the defensive battle against the swarms would look like. The images of the lost sectors, the history of which every school child learned, scared the hell out of him to this day. For a long time, he had had nightmares in which the masses of hideous bodies descended on Andal and ate up everything in their path - until everything disappeared. That's what had happened to the lost sectors, eight colonies, gone forever.

"Five from the Home Fleet, five sector fleets from the Border Worlds that have already pledged their support," his big brother listed, and Cornelius eyed Gavin in response, as if expecting a specific reaction. Artas noticed and quickly continued, "According to current doctrine, that's about the amount of fully operational fleets it would take to intercept and neutralize three swarms. Three per swarm, to be exact, plus an escort flotilla for logistics and resupply. The battles can be very munitions intensive and require a large number of nukes to soften up the clusters."

Their father gave Gavin a look that didn't take much effort to interpret: *You would know that if you had been paying attention at the academy and not just running shuttles and chasing skirts.*

"That leaves you two flotillas short in the bill," Gavin noted.

"Yes. You can compensate by over-munitioning. That's possible if the hangars are cleared. Fighters don't make sense in the fight against the Never anyway, to that extent we could use the stowage space for battery packs and missiles," his brother continued.

"Could? Shouldn't the preparations for that have been made long ago?"

"Fleet Admiral Dain Marquandt has assured us that he will join us with his Wall Fleet. He is in overall command of the entire operation," their father intervened. "He's arriving tonight."

"Marquandt?"

"He is commander-in-chief of the Wall Sectors, though in day-to-day operations he is stationed in the Kopralla Sector. He has withdrawn his fleet there, however, to support us." Artas leaned back and exhaled a long, drawn-out breath. "A Wall Fleet consists of a disproportionate number of artillery cruisers with long-range armament and is three to four times larger than a standard fleet. With its help, defense will be a done deal. We have the numbers and intelligence on our side."

"Still, it's important to be careful on your first combat mission. I'd keep you out of it entirely if I could. But we have obligations and that includes service in the Imperial Navy," his father explained, placing a hand on his arm. Gavin felt shame welling up inside him, especially under the eyes of his brother, who had received his captain's commission with distinction and not, like himself, by virtue of his position. He was a good pilot, but far from a good commander.

"I understand, father," he said. "I am ready."

Cornelius did not answer immediately and instead eyed him closely.

"Your brother will lead our units. Stick to his order and only that. No more showing off to impress any female soldiers. The Never is dangerous, no matter how many fleets we can pull together here." His father's grip tightened. "Do you understand?"

"No," Gavin admitted with a sigh, meeting Cornelius' gaze. The gravity of their situation lay like an oppressive weight on the room, on their world. It was almost physically palpable that this wasn't some distant problem, skirmishes with the Orb at the Wall Worlds, or battles against insurgents and pirates in the inner sectors. This was not a movie, but reality. The monsters of his childhood were coming here. As soon as tomorrow. "I haven't seen combat yet, and the Never is a scary story for campfires for me. But I won't abandon Artas, and I won't abandon our people. Whatever it is, I will do my part."

"Good, son. Good." He had expected his father to be pleased, but he seemed much glummer as he rose, and they followed his lead. Elisa, who had been listening intently the entire time, nodded silently at him as if she had understood something unsaid. "Then prepare yourselves now. Artas, you should be on the Amundsen overseeing the arrival of the other sector fleets. Gavin, prepare your crew and the Glory. You will not be able to return until the end of the defense."

"No vacation on *Pulau Weh*, huh?" asked Gavin in his brother's direction as they rose from the table.

"You wouldn't have liked it that far from any civilization anyway, little brother," Artas said with a warm smile. There was a trace of regret in his gaze, however.

"I've always wanted to see the planet. A place of endless beauty, with no strategic relevance, no resources in its system. Nothing anyone would want," he listed, looking off into nothingness.

"When this is over, we'll fly there, I promise. You'll fly us."

"When this is over."

INTERLUDE: JANUS

Janus Darishma, First Secretary of State of the Terran Star Empire, stepped onto the upper deck of the Rubov Orbital Ring next to his master, Haeron II of House Hartholm-Harrow. Five years ago, Janus would never have thought it possible to even be allowed into this part of the gigantic space station, which was reserved for the Emperor and his family. The atrium was at the heart of a 1,000-acre section that was completely glassed in, allowing a view of the light of the arcologies on Terra during their ninety minutes in the planet's shadow. Most of the North American continent they passed lay there in darkness, while the sealed cities shone like points of light. For the other ninety minutes, the mono-bonded glass filtered the sun's harsh radiation through sophisticated filters until it reached earthly conditions as on the surface, simulating the refraction of light through gas molecules.

The Emperor stood with his arms folded behind his back in front of the great Saphyra tree in the heart of the parkland that spread out before them, curving along the elliptical curve of the orbital ring. Tiny imitation bees buzzed through the air, seeming to hover more than fly at the comfortable 0.3g that Rubov was generating, and gathered nectar, helping to pollinate the fragile ecosystem that had been built up here over the decades. Janus saw birds - not drones, but real birds - chirping and arguing, picking up sticks for their nests or tugging worms out of the spicy-smelling soil with their beaks. A host of gardeners in green overalls were busy tending to everything, taking samples and trimming those plants that were taking up too much space in the complex cycle of life.

"She loved it here, Janus," the Emperor said, craning his neck to look up at the mighty crown of the tree, whose leaves secreted their typical green glow that continued over a fine nest of veins in the bark. The hair at the temples of the leader of humankind was graying, his facial skin just wrinkled enough to express the wisdom of age, and his eyes alert and clear - exactly the image his geneticists had intended.

"It's the most beautiful place in the known universe," Janus said carefully.

"Is it originality or sin that makes it so?"

"Your Majesty?"

"There are only two Saphyras in the entire Star Empire, and the other is on the forbidden planet, away from prying eyes. This one is the only one whose fascinating sight privileged individuals like you and I can enjoy. So is it exclusivity that makes us so devout? Or is it the sin it represents?" the Emperor asked thoughtfully, inviting him with a casual gesture to speak freely, as he often did when they were among themselves.

"I don't think it's either, if I'm honest," Janus said, looking at the one-hundred-foot tree, which was almost the size of a small frigate and whose bark was as hard as armored steel.

Now Haeron II turned away for the first time and looked over at him.

"The Saphyras are unique because they did not come from natural evolution, but from biotechnological processes of an extraterrestrial civilization, whose only legacy they represent. But Earth's sequoias were similarly impressive - if not as complex and enigmatic. Of them, only one remains."

"Yes, it's over there." The Emperor pointed across the canopy of a small oak grove, behind which rose a mighty trunk, its crown scratching the glass dome.

"Nor is sin, because sin is a taint that stains all beauty. Blood cannot paint a painting capable of enrapturing pure hearts. Especially since, on a very practical level, the decision to transplant this specimen was at the express request of the Science Corps, which wanted to study the interaction of the Saphyras with Terran flora and fauna," Janus continued his thoughts, letting himself be carried away by the pulsation of green lights.

"But you said this was the most beautiful place in the universe. Peraia used to say that, too, and I'm trying to figure it out. I feel as if I can only understand her fate if I know what led her to think that." The Emperor paused. "It is the lamentation of an old man, is it not?"

"It is the wish of a loving father who has already lost too much," Janus replied.

"Perhaps. I'm letting myself be driven by melancholy again, sorry. You were going to explain to me why you think this is the most beautiful place in the universe."

"Because of the longing that haunts my heart nowhere so much as here."

"Longing? And this is supposed to be something beautiful? Isn't there always an inherent loss in longing, or at least a sense that something is missing?"

"Yes. But that's the one common denominator that makes everyone the same. The feeling of not being complete. This tree here is an enigma in itself, representing questions that cannot be answered like nothing else in the known universe. There are endless stories about the keepers and their living heritage that has endured through the millennia. None of them will be true, and yet one look at this Saphyra is enough to make us dream and long for the impossible. It is a witness to something that will remain lost forever, no matter how much we strive," Janus said. "In me, that creates melancholy, a loneliness that is somehow liberating. To know that realizations have limits, liberated from the duty of pushing further and further into the shadows. Soon enough, for this tree of millennia in the blink of an eye, we will die and serve as food for its roots and it will make no difference. For the universe."

"And you call that beautiful?"

"Yes, because this melancholy has a twin, and that twin is called hope."

"Ah, the one mental constant of the contradictory human heart. Hope even where there is none," the Emperor said. "Keep going, even when the door is barred."

"If we have any strength as a species, it is that. And perhaps your daughter also clearly saw that light in the shadows, looking up at this marvel of nature and technology."

"I wish she had included me in her thoughts."

"Would you have let her go?" asked Janus.

The Emperor did not answer immediately and thought. Then he shook his head, barely perceptibly, and whispered, "No. Not then. Today, perhaps, so at least I would have known what she was up to and could have said goodbye. Not knowing what fate might have befallen one's child is the worst torture the universe can inflict on a parent."

"That would be greatness. Greatness that you undoubtedly have within you, Your Majesty."

"Looking back, every ramification of destiny proves to be an open book. Anyone can read it who has eyes to see and a heart to understand."

Not for the first time, Janus wondered what would have become of this man if he had not been born into the ruling family as the eldest descendant. A famous thinker, perhaps? A man of letters? A philosopher in the Science Corps? The reason he revered him so much was at the same time the reason he thought him a weak ruler who needed to be told when to tighten the reins, even if the horse neighed.

"You are right about that, your majesty. But these are two things that are not given to everyone. Be it out of simple-mindedness or plain unwillingness. If you will permit me the question," he added. "Why have you summoned me here?"

"I want you to do something for me. Discreetly."

Janus stiffened involuntarily. 'Discreetly' was a signal word the ruler had used toward him only once before. At that time, it had been a matter of relieving his brother of all court duties - of booting him out without the press making discord in the House

The last fleet

of Hartholm-Harrow. However, he did not believe that this time it was about Prince Jurgan and his scandals, especially since he had not uttered a sound on his fiefdom in the distant Dust system for three years.

"Of course, your majesty. Whatever it is," he said, bowing.

"The Admiralty continues to refuse to make any advance into Orb territory, the Senate in any case."

"For good reason, if I may be so bold. The Solar Union fell over the very idea of waging such a campaign, and thus drove McMaster to his coup in the first place."

"I know you think this is all about my daughter," Haeron II countered, stroking his hands over his cloak made of ornate brocade. "But the Wall Worlds consume nearly forty percent of our military budget - for just four alien systems to keep at bay. Many senior members of the Science Corps believe that the technological gap is not as large as it was a hundred years ago, and that with an exceptional decree we can quickly equip enough torpedoes with antimatter warheads to take them by surprise with a massive frontal assault. We would have sufficient reason to do so after so many deaths."

"So it is nonetheless about your daughter, I take it."

The Emperor sparked angrily at him for a moment, but then sighed and nodded. "I know it sounds selfish, but we could kill two birds with one stone. Find out for me who the opinion leaders are in the Council of Admiralty and what arguments or gifts to colleagues they are putting in the field. And where the weak points are."

"For you it's not just about a possible field campaign, am I right?" asked Janus.

"Albius and Marquandt are actually adversaries. Everyone knows that Dain is aiming for the post of chief of staff, but Marius is unstoppable and well connected. That he jumped in at the meeting because of the threat of contamination to the very person who is sawing at the leg of his chair alarms me. Admiralty is more easily controlled if divided, you said it yourself. And we've had an uncontrolled Admiralty before, just before the collapse of the Solar Union."

"I agree with you, your majesty. Marquandt was the first to present the plan for a defense, and the plan is a good one. He is putting himself in the line of fire and taking some of the risk. It's the perfect opportunity to make his mark. Nothing endears you to the people like a defense of the horror that Never inspires in all of us."

"But he's suggesting that Magnus lead the Home Fleet into battle with him - the perfect opportunity to put my son in the spotlight. Why would he suggest standing modestly in the shadows himself, giving way to the crown prince of the Star Empire?" the Emperor asked. "Either he is seeking my and Magnus' favor as my successor, or I do not understand his motives."

Janus had to smile involuntarily.

"What?"

"I guess you're turning into a politician after all, Your Majesty."

3

"He's having a hard time not taking over command himself, am I right?" Gavin sat leaning low in the armchair of the eastern fireplace room while the technicians prepared his shuttle. His mother was answering important correspondences on her private holoscreen and paused for a moment to turn to him.

"Yes, you could assume that. But he knows that at his age, he needs to focus on other things."

"You mean politics."

"Yes."

"But he hates politics."

"Any person with a backbone hates politics," she countered.

"When we get visits from senators or members of the planetary assembly, I'm often not so sure. These lickspittles seem to thrive in the political swamp like mold," he grumbled.

"What's wrong?" his mother asked, turning off her holoscreen to join him. "Are you afraid?"

"Yes." It wasn't hard for him to be honest with her. It never had been. She never judged him.

"It's not the Never that scares you. It's your brother."

"Yes," he breathed. "Artas is everything you could ever want. He's smart, an excellent tactician, fiercely loyal, controlled and thoughtful, and as well-liked by his officers as by the crew as he is by the public."

"He casts a long shadow, yes," his mother admitted, taking his hands in hers. They felt warm to the touch. "But what would be gained for us humans if we lived up to all the ideals? What are they anyway? Every culture has different ideas of what a leader should be like. And that's just the cultural perspective. The big picture. When you're on your deathbed at some point at the end of your life, what mattered most?"

"I don't know."

"Memories that warm your heart, I suppose." She thought for a moment and nodded, barely perceptible. "The knowledge of having lived. Exactly what those factors are is different for each of us, including you and your brother. Artas' greatest strength is his sense of duty, but it is also his greatest weakness because he forgets himself far too often. Only those who take care of themselves can do the same for others. Sometimes I wish I could mix you two up and make it two equal parts. But I can't. Only the two of you can, by learning from each other."

"The go-getter and the procrastinator?" Gavin snorted. "What a cliché."

"Cornelius and I know exactly how lucky we are to have you two. You've refused to grow up, but that will have to change soon. And then you'll be ready to show us who you really want to be."

He thought about this as his wrist computer chirped.

"My lord, your shuttle is ready for departure. The *Glory* has already been notified of your imminent arrival," Soergen, their chief engineer, informed him. The roar of turbines could be heard in the background, mingling with the rush of the wind.

"Thank you, Soergen." Gavin rose and hugged his mother. "Thanks, Mom."

"You take care of yourself and don't do anything stupid, you understand?" She broke away from him and held his head in her hands so he couldn't avoid her gaze. "Listen to your big brother and make sure you stay alive."

"I will."

"Promise."

The last fleet

"Mom, we have fifteen fleets facing the Never. That's more than..."

"Promise," she interrupted him sternly.

"All right: I promise."

The flight to his ship took twenty minutes and was uneventful despite the heavy traffic in orbit. Gavin left the autopilot on and indulged in his thoughts. In retrospect, he felt embarrassed to have acted like a spoiled idiot in front of the men and women of space flight control - after all, Never infestation was imminent, even if he had not known it at the time.

What would Lizzy think of him?

Well, at least he didn't have to wait much longer for the answer to that, because she was already aboard his ship.

Outside the window, several columns of transport ferries moved along like gray coffins, connecting the surface of Andal with the orbital ring and the large supply ships. The latter reminded him of gigantic space whales that swallowed the ferries like swarms of krill. The entire orbit looked like a stung bees' nest and told him that his father had long since informed all authorities and military decision-makers. Now it couldn't be long before he stepped in front of the cameras and informed the population of the system and the sector what the mobilization was all about.

They had to brace for a storm, and Gavin was about to sail right into it.

The *Glory* was on the lower dock ledges of the system's only space fortress, Mjölnir. An attack corvette of the new Arrow class with four fusion engines and antimatter afterburners. Beneath the huge fortress, it was at first no more than a dull black glimmer, next to the much larger cruisers and frigates on the other ledges. But the closer he got, the more clearly he made out the mighty thruster section at the stern, which appeared less fat than it actually was only because of its elongated design. The elongated hull merged into a flattened snout that was particularly heavily armored. Sensor phalanges protruded from it like toothpicks of various sizes. Gavin loved the *Glory* so much that for eleven months he had managed to delay taking over as captain of a frigate by dragging out documents and missing deadlines.

During his approach, he realized that this mission would probably be the only one, and therefore the last, that he would undertake as pilot of the corvette - a thought that filled him with melancholy.

He parked the shuttle in the designated docking bay at Sims 2201 and waited until the clamp grip and pressure equalization were complete before opening the aft ramp. The artificial gravity of the rotating Mjölnir, which was basically a giant drum with an axial tube and one hundred fusion reactors along its end caps, was a comfortable 0.8g.

"My lord," one of the technicians in the orange jumpsuit greeted him, connecting several cables to the shuttle's exposed ports. "Welcome back."

"Thank you." Gavin turned directly to his left, where the airlock to his ship was located, and was about to leave when the technician cleared his throat. Apparently he was uncomfortable about something, but at the same time it was important enough to address him reluctantly.

"My lord, Captain, I uh, wanted to ask you something, if I may." The man, at least ten years older than Gavin, with smudged cheeks and bushy eyebrows more the veteran type, suddenly seemed like a little boy.

"Sure, out with it."

"Excuse me, but I heard we were under attack. But no one from the ground crews will tell us by whom or what."

Gavin pondered why the local officers withheld the information from the deck crews, but felt the fact was unfair.

"It's the Never, Specialist. The Never." He nodded as his counterpart's eyes widened. "But we'll assemble fifteen fleets and kick its butt mightily, count on it."

"Thank you, Lord Captain, thank you." The engineer bowed slightly and wrestled a smile from himself, though he looked like he was going to throw up.

Fifteen fleets really are enough, aren't they?

When Gavin reached the airlock to the *Glory*, the hand

The last fleet

scanner next to the door cleared him and released him into the short neck that connected the Mjölnir and the corvette. Since the ship was docked with the front, everything was upside down, creating a disconcerting impression, as if he couldn't find anything again, even though he had been flying the *Glory* for more than a year. In the cockpit, five yards behind the bow, Lizzy was already waiting for him, about to go through the mission checklist.

"Ah, there you are!" she said, without looking up from her handheld terminal. The fingers of her right hand darted across the projections in practiced motions, making a tick here and there or scrolling hurriedly along.

"I got here as fast as I could." He climbed over the handholds on the walls to his gimbaled pilot's seat and was relieved as soon as he could turn against the gravity direction of the rotating space fortress. All the flight controls and displays - except for the two manual flight sticks on his armrests - were holoprojections that surrounded him like a cocoon of light.

"Followed your approach. Autopilot?" she asked with a grin.

"Yes," he returned simply, meeting her gaze through a projected graphic that showed him the energy amplitude in the fusion engines. When she nodded, there was understanding in her eyes.

"The *Glory* is almost ready to take off. When can we expect mission orders?"

"If you think my brother filled me in before the rest of the fleet, I'm sorry to disappoint you." He shook his head and ticked off the maintenance logs that had been forwarded to him by Space Flight Control for sign-off. By nature, Gavin despised the Republicans in the Star Empire who wished to see the end of the monarchy. Not merely because his own social position would disappear should they take power. No, he also doubted the ability of a democratic society when it came to sustaining a permanent state of war. But they had one argument on their side: every monarchy had a habit of creating a bloated state apparatus that at some point no longer sustained the people, but the other way around. The result was a never-ending bureaucracy. Everyone who was in some small position secured himself with forms or justified his position with something as simple as a single digital stamp. The result was lengthy processes like this departure authorization, which took at least half an hour.

"Artas is as principled as the Emperor himself," he continued, having sent off the document and already skimming the next one, unnerved. "I have great respect for that and at the same time often enough murderous rage in my belly. He just can't turn a blind eye."

"I can imagine." A pause. Another document. "He seems like a born leader. Except for your father, I don't think any officer in the sector has as good a reputation. Did you know that there are motivational memes circulating among the crew ranks of the Frontier Fleets based on a picture of your brother?"

"No, I didn't know that," he grumbled. "What picture?"

"Hold on." She swiped across her handheld terminal and tossed him a photo on the main screen. It showed Artas conducting a troop review on the Harbinger, Andal's carrier ship. About a thousand sailors were lined up in order by their overall colors and functions. His brother had put his hand on the shoulder of a female mechanic with a soiled face (a breach of custom at a ceremonial). With the other, he was smearing dirt on his own cheek - judging by the two light stripes on the mechanic's cheek, it must have come from her. Underneath, in big white letters, it said, "Unity."

"It also comes with the words *equality before the enemy*, *one voice*, *always forward*, and many more," Lizzy explained.

"He just can't do anything wrong. He forgets the rules one time and makes a sign, and it goes viral." Gavin felt a twinge of injustice that was more of a reminder than genuine anger, having already felt far too often that his brother could do no wrong. Even stronger, however, was the warm affection for Artas he felt at the sight of the photograph.

"Don't be offended. You're a passable pilot, after all."

The best in the sector, he corrected her in his mind. Aloud, he said, "Unfortunately, the offspring of the high nobility are not allowed to be fighter pilots."

The last fleet

"This is better than a fighter," she observed.

Gavin turned his chair and gave her a meaningful look. "I might agree with that sentiment."

She grinned and seemed about to say something else when the door to the cockpit opened and two figures climbed in to join them.

"Gino, Max," he greeted their diminutive fire control officer and the somewhat stocky defensive officer.

"Captain," Max called out in a grumpy voice and shifted in his chair at the back of the flak consoles. Geno merely growled like a dog and muttered to himself. The fact that they didn't address him as "Lord Captain" or "Mylord" was something he had had to drum into the two of them for over half a year before they really believed him, that he wasn't just trying to set them up for an encounter with the cane. That probably didn't speak well for their positive image of him.

"All right, get ready, go through the checklists and give me a thumbs up when everything is ready," he instructed them. "Tonight the Home Fleet arrives with Crown Prince Magnus and a few hours later Fleet Admiral Marquandt with his units. By then we must be in the outer system at the rendezvous point. Our goal is clear to everyone, isn't it?"

Max gave a resigned sigh. "To be the first. Of course."

"Someone's been paying close attention the last few months." Gavin grinned, dispelling some of the heaviness in his stomach that hadn't left him since the news of the approaching Never infestation.

"Looking at the system's current situation picture, though, some of the bigger ships already have a decent head start," Defense Officer said.

"We'll catch up to them. And when the fleets arrive, we'll be the ones to greet them. Well, how does that sound?"

"Like stress," grumbled Gino.

"Nine hours of flight time if we properly abuse the *Glory*. We can manage that." Gavin considered simply telling space flight control that they were now casting off, but then decided against it and did everything strictly by the book. He tried not to notice that this fact pissed him off.

"When you sent Gino and Max away, I was actually expecting you to rip my clothes off," Lizzy remarked as they sat in their seats two hours later, looking at the projected starry image on the display wall in front of them. The outer planets shimmered like distant glitter, barely distinguishable from the billions of other stars in the infinite blackness. There was nothing to indicate that they were moving at any appreciable percentage of the speed of light - except for the occasional warning when they collided with a speck of dust and the armor absorbed the energy.

"I wish," Gavin sighed, rubbing his temples. "But this whole thing..."

"You mean the Never."

"Yeah." He threw a video file at the display, which was so crisp it was indistinguishable from a window. "Did you see this?"

"Is that the destruction of Turan-II?" she asked, shuddering when he nodded. "I've only seen the official feeds."

"This is a shot of the garrison troops who led the defense at the time, along with the police forces."

"And this is..."

"Under lock and key, yes." He waved it off. "I guess I can still afford that much rebelliousness." When she eyed him, he asked, "What?"

"Thank you for your trust," she said earnestly.

"Ah. I just want someone to share my nightmares."

"No, I mean it."

Gavin cleared his throat and turned on the recording. It showed the helmet-cam image of a Sergeant Miller, whose name was superimposed in the upper right, along with a series of vital signs and his Marine service number. He was walking through a deep street canyon, ordering a few handfuls of soldiers left and right and yelling at civilians who weren't lining up neatly enough next to an evacuation bus.

"One after the other, goddamn it! Will you hurry it up?"

Miller grunted and shook his head. The civilians obediently complied. Most were families with children clinging anxiously to their parents' pants and skirts. The adults took great pains to shield the eyes of their little ones, obviously so that they would not look up. There was sheer panic on their faces.

"They were the first," Lizzy muttered. "No one knew what we were dealing with then."

"Mmm," he went on. "Back then they still thought we were dealing with Space Bugs, Zerg or Tyranids."

"Excuse me?"

"Ah." Again he waved it off. "I have a soft spot for classic games. More prophetic than you might think."

"See the look in their eyes?" She extended her arm and switched to freeze frame. Miller was looking straight into the face of a father standing at the very end of the column, the only one who had craned his neck to look up at the sky. There was sheer horror in his eyes.

"I see it." He continued the recording.

Miller told the man he had to catch the next bus, number 66, and then walked toward a skyscraper. Through the entrance, he came to a foyer where several platoons of Marines stood around with Gauss rifles and appeared to be waiting for orders. An officer came out of the stairwell and yelled a few unintelligible commands that were distorted by the audio. Movement then came to the three or four dozen men and women and they began to run up the stairs. The patter of their boots was all they heard for the next few minutes, as none of the soldiers spoke. The only source of light was the helmet lamps, whose cones of light made for bizarre shadows.

"Isn't that Tarshan, the capital of the colony?", Lizzy inquired.

"Yes, why?"

"Tarshan was on the main continent after all, I forget its name. It was attacked during the day."

"Yes," he replied, fast-forwarding and returning to normal speed just before Miller and his platoon, breathing heavily, poured onto the roof of the skyscraper like a spilled liquid. Some of them had large boxes strapped to their backs, which they now set down. With practiced moves, teams of four soldiers began to set up the guns packed inside.

Miller walked to the edge of the roof and looked down into the canyon of houses where at least a dozen electric buses were parked. The one in front was just pulling away. Lines of waiting families were still gathered around the rest, at least that's what it looked like from above.

"It was actually daytime," he said.

"But it's pitch black," Lizzy noted in confusion. Bright flashes reflected on the puddles of the roof. Again and again at irregular intervals.

Instead of answering, Gavin pointed at the display.

Miller rebuked one of his subordinates, who was in the process of placing the targeting optics on the gun, apparently in too much of a hurry.

"Easy, Gaucho. Calm the hell down!" Then the sergeant looked up at the sky for the first time. It was almost pitch black. At first it looked like a typical night, except that it lacked the stars and the two moons that had usually been visible over Turan-II. It took a reminder that this was an invasion to understand exactly what was happening. The bright spots against the black were the system defense ships. And the bright flashes of light that kept flaring were explosions from reactor cores where captains had decided they'd rather die with a bang and take as many enemies with them as possible. Noble deeds, if there could be such a thing in a war at all, but in vain, as was now known. At that time, however, the battle took place under unknown circumstances. Miller grunted and averted his eyes only when Gavin could clearly see that the darkness was in fact not darkness at all, but a swarm of nightmarish bodies. They were so numerous that they looked like a coherent mass.

A mass that kept descending. It was impossible to tell how close the first reaches of the Never were. It wasn't until a shadow plunged a hair's breadth past Miller into the street canyon like a meteorite that the sergeant seemed to realize it himself.

"By the bloody heavens!" he cursed, with little pretense, and turned again to the edge of the roof to look down. In the light of the streetlamps, the meteorite could be seen crashing into one of the buses. The screams of civilians trying to flee toward the entrances of the buildings swelled to a ghastly howl.

The bus that was hit began to shake violently, as if in an earthquake. Glass shattered and blood spurted from the shattered windows. Then more entities crashed into the valley of the street, five, six, then so many that they were hard to count. Several monsters shot out of each crater, letting out a bloodcurdling screech and slaughtering everything around them. Wherever they moved, a dark mass that seemed to swallow all light followed them. It covered a bus filled with screaming families, who shortly thereafter fell silent forever as the vehicle was crushed as if by an invisible hand and disappeared beneath the Never mass.

"Fuck!" Miller only now seemed to snap out of his horrified stupor and pointed upward. "Fire, goddammit! Fire for all you're worth, you dogs!"

"Stop," Lizzy said, ending the shot. Her face had gone pale as chalk.

"Now you know why the footage has been kept under wraps. Watching telescope footage of Turan-II just disappearing a few days after the infestation, as if the planet had never existed, is very different from this," he explained, taking a deep breath until his chest ached. "I saw my brother watch the recording after he got his officer's license. Probably my father wanted to prepare him for what lurks in the darkness out there for humanity. We've discovered two species. We know next to nothing about either. The Orbs are technologically far ahead of us and what they do seems like magic. The Never seems to be neither an entity with anything like a mind nor a true species. Truly something that cannot be negotiated with, that simply consumes and destroys. That out there," he pointed to the star field on the display in front of them, streaming in real time from the bow telescopes, "is a cold hell, and the more I think about it, the less I'm in favor of us exploring other regions of the Milky Way. The best thing we can do is stop all expansion immediately and prepare ourselves even more for an endless struggle for survival."

"Now that I've seen it, I wish I hadn't," Lizzy whispered. "I'm damn glad I'm not a Marine. Out here, at least we can blow ourselves up instead of... disappearing somewhere else."

"That's why I'm glad the Emperor didn't forget his backyard and send the Home Fleet. It took four fallen sectors for us to stop the first Never Swarm, and even that took us years of production to recoup the losses."

"Were there actually any survivors from Turan-II?"

"No. Although the conspiracy theory persists. My brother assured me that not a single ship made it out of the sector. Except for the drones that were able to salvage data like this," Gavin said dejectedly, rubbing his face as if to chase away a penetrating nightmare. "It wasn't until the subsequent infestations, when listening stations were optimized to locate swarms, that some could be salvaged."

"But only those who were evacuated early enough."

"Yes. None of those who encountered the Never were able to tell their story."

"The more I hear about it, the more relieved I am that we're in the field on one of the Navy's fastest corvettes," Lizzy countered. "At least then we can get out of the way before that... *something* hits us. At least that's true, isn't it?"

"That a single contact is enough for a ship to be lost?" he asked, nodding. "Yes. Whatever the Never is or does; whatever it touches, it engulfs and ultimately sweeps it into nothingness with it."

INTERLUDE: JANUS

"Nancy, where are you with the annual financial reports?" asked Janus of his secretary, who was sitting across from him at his desk, going through her virtual data lists with an absent-minded look. Her gestures were as quick and precise as ever, except that her expression seemed frozen in alarm.

"I've gone through everything down to the fleet admiral level, First ..."

"Mister Darishma is enough," he reminded her patiently, turning off his datamotes, which had projected into his field of vision a whole separate wealth of data edited into charts, diagrams and lists, and assisted him with all manner of software helpers. His gaze cleared and, as always, his eyes burned afterwards. "Let's hear it, then."

"Of course." Nancy cleared her throat as if preparing for a speech in front of an audience. "So, the twenty fleet admirals in the council invested a total of five hundred million crowns in non-mobile fixed assets last year, and eight hundred million in mobile fixed assets. That's an increase of twenty percent over the previous year. On average, eight investments per capita, spread over three asset classes at the median."

"They all have plenty of money because, without exception, they come from the high nobility and take advantage of their positions at the top of the Navy to get good deals and get even richer." Janus waved it off and rubbed his temples after hours of data sifting. "So far, it's familiar. Also, the occasional favors they buy via the clever use of classified information are an open secret. Are there any outliers?"

"Yes, Admirals Marquandt and Takahashi have invested the least, and Chief of Staff Albius and Admiral Heusgen the most."

"Show me Marquandt's and Albius' investments and make an appointment with the Jupiter Bank representative. Next possible. Best use the imperial data seal."

Nancy nodded eagerly and sent him the desired data with a swiping gesture from her neural memory lacunae to his neural computer.

Janus had her use datamotes to display what Albius and Marquandt had *officially* privately invested in the standard Terran year to date. The word "private" was a difficult term among the heads of the one hundred dynasties that had, under the Emperor, divided the Star Empire among themselves de facto. Each and every one of them had brothers and sisters in the highest positions, as governors of planets, high-ranking officers in the Navy, managers of multi-system corporations, or diplomats in the Corporate Protectorate. Thus, whenever an official investment appeared, it was both a sign of the current momentum and policy of an entire sector, as well as that sector's most relevant connections to other important sectors of the Star Empire. He instructed his datamotes to stream over his desk's holoprojector - with voice output activated. His eyes needed a little rest after the past few hours and his brain some natural slowness.

"So, what do we have with Albius?"

"Investment packages in the double-digit millions in biotech start-ups in the Corporate Protectorate, similar sums in quantum tunneling technology, force field and wormhole research. These operations are similar to those of previous years and are actively managed by the private bank Schofield&Brugger," the androgynous computer voice explained at a pleasant speaking pace. "In addition, there are several exchange traded funds, most of which have been listed on Remus through the JFTSE and on Alpha Prime through the FXTP in the Corporate Protectorate."

The last fleet

"Any funds that were withdrawn?"

"Yes," the AI confirmed. "The largest item was three hundred million crowns, corresponding to all of the Grand Admiral's shares in the Warfield Armored Reconnaissance & Security mercenary group."

"He had shares in WARS?" asked Janus in surprise.

"Yes, as did another five members of the Council of Admiralty."

"What percentage did he hold with that?"

"Five."

"What percentage did the other members hold and what were they?"

"Five percent each. Fleet Admirals Heusgen, Ladalle, Bachelet, Jericho, and Marquandt. The latter had even more."

"Marquandt," Janus repeated. "Why do I hear that name so often lately in connection with the chief of staff?"

"Because there are several correlations in the records, and Fleet Admiral Dain Marquandt, as commander of a Wall Sector, holds an exalted position within the Admiralty and thus necessarily works closely with and reports directly to the Chief of Staff."

"I realize that. Did any of the four also sell or buy shares?"

"Three have sold - all their shares. One bought in ..."

"Let me guess: Marquandt?"

"That is correct," the datamotes confirmed. "High Lord Dain Marquandt bought out all the shares of his fellow Admirals at a preferential price, giving him a blocking minority of thirty-six percent, since he was already the largest single shareholder before the purchase."

"What other investments has he made?"

"One. He had 500,000 shares listed with the Imperial State Bank in the first round of investment for the Terra Ultima terraforming project, that was in January 2397, four years ago. Each year he has raised that share by the same amount."

"So he should hold quite an amount."

"Two percent," the AI explained. "Considering the small

amount of shares issued to private individuals, this is one of the three largest privately held blocks of shares."

"Who owns the others?" he asked.

"The current Senate President Varilla Usatami and Grand Admiral Marius Albius."

Janus grumbled. Something always seemed to bring the two admirals together and apart. It was not unusual for the high lords to collude and listen to the same advisors and informants who gave them more or less good investment advice. He could not fall into the trap of desperately wanting to see something that he might then imagine. But he couldn't afford to look the other way either. Maybe it was nothing, probably even, but if it was, he needed to know. He had decided to get to the bottom of the Emperor's question from the very beginning, knowing that going directly with conversations within the Admiralty would be like trying to teach a wall to sing.

"How are the investments distributed?"

"To four Seed Systems: Ruhr, Alpha, Dong Rae, Luna Mining Corporation," the AI obediently replied.

"Only four?"

"Yes."

"What about the Seed World under Yokatami control?", Janus wanted to know and came up with the answer himself, "The sectors under control of the Albius and Marquandt dynasties both border the Wall systems. Yokatami is still subject to a boycott there since the disappearance of Persephone."

Because they blame Yokatami's sensors and automatic transponder systems for the failure of space control. What else could they do? Admit to the Emperor that they were responsible for one of the worst mishaps in Star Empire history? He thought to himself.

"That's a possible explanation, yes."

"But Varilla Usatami? She's a civilian, doesn't have any feud with Yokatami - not even one that's just a fig leaf for the public." Janus considered. "Let's chalk this up to coincidence for now. Which of the Seed Systems are restricted areas?"

"All except Ruhr, as it is the only navigable access to the Orion Traverse, and the 2398 Decree on Free Research and

The last fleet

Prospecting Traffic stipulates that Ruhr's restricted area status be lifted," the Datamotes AI patiently elaborated.

Terraforming and mercenaries, Janus thought. *What a strange mix.*

"Give me some information on WARS. That's a rather small corporation, isn't it? I only remembered it at all because of the name, which I don't know if it's deliberately trashy or self-deprecating. Maybe both are just wishful thinking, though."

"Warfield Armored Reconnaissance & Security was founded in 2366 by Arthur James Warfield, a former colonel in the Imperial Marines. He positioned his company in the field of security engineering and personnel for ground and vacuum combat, first exclusively in property protection, and later for changing clients in minor border or trade disputes that were resolved by force of arms before they became large enough for the Empire to take care of. After his death in 2395, his son Chester James Warfield took over as CEO."

"The company is still privately held?"

"Yes, a private stock company with fifty-one percent stock ownership in the Warfield family. WARS is a non-permanent member of the Corporate Council and its headquarters is on Alpha Prime in the Corporate Protectorate."

"What margin is it on in terms of its annual profit in the mercenary corporate sector?" asked Janus.

"At position eighty-six out of one hundred and ten," said the AI.

"A pretty small fish for so much investment interest on the part of the Admiralty," he thought aloud. "They probably know things about the corporation and its plans that they learned as high-ranking admirals that remain closed to us."

"Does Warfield have any known customers?"

"Yes. They are in the property protection business for Yokatami. Since the beginning of the year, they have signed a five-year contract to that effect, worth a total of five billion crowns."

"Yokatami?" Janus shook his head in disbelief. "I can't imagine that. Yokatami, like each of the permanent council members in the Corporate Protectorate, has hundreds of thou-

53

sands of corporate guardsmen, augmented to the hilt and well equipped and trained. Why would they hire a third-rate mercenary corporation in property protection, of all things? Where, even?"

"This information is not publicly viewable, even with your clearance."

"How is that possible?"

"The information is not available," the androgynous voice said impassively.

"Are you telling me that this is supposed to be a *verbally* agreed upon assignment?"

"That's a possibility. Or in the form of disks not connected to the Dataverse."

"Nancy?" he called his secretary via transducer. "Something extremely strange has come up here. Is there a representative from Warfield Armored Reconnaissance & Security here on the Rubov Ring?"

"I'll check, Mister Darishma," came the immediate reply. "Yes. A certain Captain Rickard Lowell. He has an office in the diplomatic wing of the Corporate Protectorate. Shall I order him here?"

"No, not necessary. Just send me direct dial to his wrist terminal. I think I need to have a talk with him. And I need you to get me something for the appointment."

4

"Captain Andal," a tall, broad-shouldered officer with two yellow eagles on his epaulettes that identified him as a vice admiral greeted him. His golden locks were, at the very least, borderline long in terms of official regulations, and his face looked far too young to be an admiral. Also, the carefree smile and friendly glowing eyes were certainly not in keeping with the admiral image Gavin had acquired over the years - which probably could have had something to do with the fact that he usually only got to see officers of their rank when they reprimanded him for breaking the rules.

"That's me, sir," Gavin confirmed. *He left out the "Lord". How refreshing.* "I suppose you forgot your name tag when invited to the party?"

His suspicion that his counterpart was either not of the high nobility or had little use for overly strict formalities seemed to be confirmed, as the Vice Admiral laughed and pointed to the corridor ahead of them that once ran across the Mammoth, the flagship of Fleet Admiral Marquandt's fleet.

"I think there will be plenty more tinsel and nameplates waiting for us in a moment. You have to stand out somehow when everyone's dressed like penguins, right?"

Gavin grinned and followed the admiral down the corridor. Behind them, more high-ranking officers arrived from the

Mammoth's port hangar. The other commanders' shuttles were landing on the battleship by the minute, spitting out more and more Navy personnel of distinction.

"What about you? Didn't you bring any aides with you?", Gavin wanted to know.

"Good god, no, I ran from them. They're like ticks if you ask me. Constantly wanting something from me," the admiral replied. Gavin noticed that the corridor in front of them was completely empty, except for the honor guard: Marines in parade uniforms who took a stance as soon as they approached. "What about you, Captain? I understand you were the first ship to arrive here at the rendezvous point?"

"That is correct, sir."

"But that still does not explain why you are attending this planning meeting. I don't suppose you are on your brother's staff?"

"Yes and no." Gavin cleared his throat. "He has requested that I attend his staff meetings and learn for this deployment."

"Ah. You are fortunate to have your brother. He is a good man. I sometimes wish I'd had an older sibling of my own to lend a hand as I climb the slippery peaks of the Navy," the admiral countered, giving him a sidelong glance. "It has come to my attention that you are an excellent pilot."

"I'm honored, sir."

"That you were modest was not part of the rumors."

"I'm here to learn," Gavin replied, and the admiral laughed.

"Very good, captain. Very good. Feel free to contact my office when this thing is over. Next year I'm recruiting the best fighter pilots in the Star Empire for my personal fighter squadron. This will probably be your only chance, as the son of a High Lord, to have a career in the cockpit of a *Stingray*."

"The *Angry Aces*? Sir, that's..." blurted out Gavin, and for a moment he even forgot that with the Never, the galaxy's cruelest threat was approaching and they were on the verge of a battle. A personal fighter squadron? No one maintained a personal fighter squadron. Except...

He was about to say something else, but by then they had

The last fleet

reached the entrance to the briefing room, a huge room with a long table and high-backed chairs. There was nothing ostentatious about the décor; the only sign that this was a place for privileged fleet personnel was the sheer size of the place.

Most of the seats were already occupied by admirals in black uniforms with gold trim, each with two aides standing behind them holding data pads. As they entered, they all rose at once and bowed.

"His Majesty Vice Admiral Crown Prince Magnus Tiberius Albeth of the House of Hartholm-Harrow, second of his name, Duke of New Eden and Prince of Neuenstein," one of the two Marines at the door called out. Everything drained from Gavin's face as his interlocutor approached the table with a light-hearted smile and, with a placating gesture, motioned the assembled admirals to be seated again.

"Your Majesty," said a gaunt fleet admiral with broad cheekbones and raven-black hair, who could only be High Lord Marquandt, since he had been sitting in one of the two chairs at the end of the table. Next to him was a young woman with a stern look and short-cropped hair who looked enough like Marquandt to be his daughter.

Gavin heard a clearing of the throat behind him, and he cleared the way for the rest of the officers who didn't want to be late for battle planning under the eyes of the Emperor's son. Out of the corner of his eye, he saw a beckoning - his brother, standing relatively far forward at the long table.

"Making friends with the crown prince, huh?" asked Artas, smirking. "Once again, quite the lucky guy."

"I didn't know that he..."

"It's all good. I also only know him from the news feeds and wouldn't necessarily have recognized him. I guess that's because you don't expect to run into the second most important man in the Star Empire."

"He invited me to join his personal guard squadron," Gavin whispered excitedly.

Artas blinked in surprise, then smiled joyfully. "That's wonderful, dear brother. Really wonderful."

"But father will hardly..."

"I'll go out of my way to get him to agree. You can count on it." His brother patted him on the shoulder. "I told you; you'll find your way. The Guard Squadron, huh? You do realize you'll be a Navy superstar, right? After this, I'll have to look at digi-posters of you every other cabin inspection."

Gavin grinned and was about to say something back when a chime sounded and all conversation around the table fell silent.

All eyes turned to Marquandt, who was the only one still standing, along with Crown Prince Magnus. Gavin settled down on one of the two chairs behind Artas and nodded to his aide Roger, who, however, was busy typing away on his terminal.

"Your Majesty, distinguished commanders," the fleet admiral greeted them. "I want to get straight to the point, because we don't have much time: as you all know, we are dealing with three swarms of Never that have recently appeared on the sensors of our deep space listening stations. They may be much larger than the ones we have dealt with so far. Although the last infestation occurred over two decades ago, we know what to do and will ensure that a disaster like the one on Turan-II never happens again."

Approving tapping on the tabletop began, but Marquandt quickly halted it.

"We are especially honored that the Emperor, in his wisdom and allegiance to his most loyal supporters, has sent the Home Fleet under the command of his own son, the Crown Prince, to our aid. The most modern and powerful ships of the Navy are gathered here today to join us in defending the backbone of the Terran Star Empire, and I tell you we will not lose a civilian to that abomination out there!"

Again, approving knocks. The Crown Prince indicated a bow and sat down, leaving only the fleet admiral standing.

"Our reconnaissance has revealed that the three swarms extend over several light minutes and are currently estimated to consist of eight hundred trillion cells." A murmur went through the assembled admiralty. Marquandt continued impassively, "But

The last fleet

they will pass through the eye of a cosmic needle, presumably to pick up charged hydrogen."

A hologram appeared above the endlessly long conference table, showing the Andal system. Then the clip zoomed in on the outermost planet, which was orbited by a dozen large moons.

"This is the gas giant Kolsund. Of particular concern to us is its largest moon, Bragge." The image froze, showing the blue ball of excited hydrogen and helium that was his home's coal mine, with hundreds of floating refineries extracting helium-3 around the clock. Their crews had long since been evacuated and were en route to the inner-system home world.

"With their current course, the three swarms will merge at Kolsund and Bragge," the fleet admiral continued, and a red dot appeared between the gas giant and the moon. "We will not get a better opportunity to intercept the infestation. The battle plan calls for the Border Worlds fleets, under the command of Fleet Admiral Sinclair, to defend the gap between Kolsund and Bragge. The honor of manning the center of the formation will go to Rear Admiral Artas Andal."

Approving murmurs and appreciative glances toward Gavin's brother, who bowed his head in gratitude.

"Crown Prince Magnus and Home Fleets One through Five will take up positions in the shadow of Bragge and, after the onset of initial hostilities, will circle the moon and flank the Never in order to bring the swarms under fire across as wide a swath as possible and provide ideal coverage. I myself will take position with my Wall Fleet behind Kolsund and lead it around the equator after the first contact to attack the other flank. Due to our more than adequate firepower and the extremely favorable position of the defense point for us, we expect low casualties and an outright victory." This time High Lord took more time before ending the rapping of knuckles on imitation wood with a curt gesture. "Nevertheless, I demand clear discipline, a meticulous adherence to the battle plan and the individual orders that are being transmitted to all the on-board computers of each ship at this moment. Timing will be critical, so do not indulge in cockiness, we have a job to do and we will do it like lords of the Imperial Navy."

The knocking was even louder this time, sounding almost like anticipatory victory.

Then a couple of admirals came forward with very specific questions about the distribution of logistical units and resupply routes for ammunition or the removal of wounded and tugs for badly damaged ships. Answering them was apparently not Marquandt's responsibility, but his deputy - the one with the stern look at the high lord's side - who turned out to be his daughter Akwa.

"*That* is what we all came to the flagship for?" asked Gavin incredulously as the meeting dispersed a short time later and they waited to find space in the stream of uniformed personnel to return to their shuttles.

"These meetings are more of a tradition and are expected before any major deployment. At least, if time permits," Artas explained, turning his palms upward as if to say, '*What can we do?*'

"This doesn't make any sense at all. Such meetings could be held virtually with holograms. That would save a lot of fuel and time," Gavin found.

"Our Navy thrives on traditions and rituals. It's part of the discipline and the ethos we exude. I'm guessing more than a few young men and women stand outside recruiting offices because they crave order, cohesion and clear structure."

"*The Navy is my family. With it by my side, I will want for nothing,*" Gavin quoted a phrase from his *Imperial Navy Sailor's Encouragement Textbook*, which every member of the Space Force was handed when they were sworn in.

"Something like that."

"Anyone who believes that probably also takes the legendary page two hundred at face value."

"*If you detect a hull breach, expect immediate decompression of the affected compartment. If you have been sucked into the vacuum, hold your breath, narrow your eyes to slits, and move with swimming motions back to your ship."* his brother quoted this time, and they both chuckled as if they were back in high school. There was a fleeting moment of levity before Artas' look turned serious. "Listen."

He took him aside and waited until two admirals from the neighboring Akkrulu Sector walked by and greeted them respectfully. They returned the gesture, then Artas continued in a lowered voice, "Stick to the battle plan and the instructions from my ship. This is not about glory and honor, but about survival. Afterwards, we can celebrate the victory together."

"Don't worry, I'll be good," Gavin assured him, but Artas was already speaking further.

"You don't need to prove to anyone what you can do. The Crown Prince himself has practically already appointed you to his personal *Stingray* squadron. The *Angry Aces* are a legend. That's about as good as it gets if you really want to sit in a cockpit and live the life of a star."

"Don't worry," he repeated, trying for a serious expression, although he found his brother's vehemence almost amusing. "I'll keep my feet still and do as I'm told. Most Serene Lord Rear Admiral, sir."

At last Artas seemed to loosen up a bit and smiled, even if it was not a joyful smile. But he nodded and gave the impression of being satisfied.

"If a shipmaster's daily routine consists of bureaucratic nonsense like this, I'll gladly pass with thanks," Gavin said as they finally found room to move with the flow toward the hangar. "I don't know how you stand it."

"Patience and a sense of duty."

"Ah, that's why I can't understand it," he said laconically.

"You'll find your place among the stars yet, little brother." Artas squeezed his shoulder one last time as they entered the hangar and had to separate to get to their respective shuttles, where the pilots on duty were already waiting. "I know what you're made of, and so do Father and Mother. They are parents and understandably feel they need to turn you in the right direction, but they love you as much as I do. Consider your assignment to my units a vote of confidence from Father, for it is nothing less than that."

"Thank you," was all Gavin could think to say.

"Good." Artas nodded. "Good hunting, dear brother!"

"Leave me some targets!"

"After all, the good thing about Never is that there are always enough targets for everyone." His brother put on his cap with the yellow eagle on the front and turned to his shuttle.

As a corvette, the *Glory* had no hangar or docking bay where a shuttle could remain permanently docked, so Gavin flew with one of those that took off several ships, making him the only commander among staff officers and aides.

By the time he was back on his ship, Lizzy, Max and Gino knew more about the battle plan than he did, even though he had been sitting in a far too illustrious circle of key commanders as a mere captain.

"We're assigned to what?" he asked incredulously when Lizzy brought him up to speed.

"Reconnaissance behind the battle lines," she repeated calmly. "What did you expect? Your brother is commanding our section of the defensive formation."

Gavin thought about the speech Artas had given him, understanding now that he had merely been preparing him not to get angry once he heard the details of the plan.

"All good?"

"No," he grumbled. "He wants to keep me out of the fights."

"It does make sense to use us for reconnaissance. We are a reconnaissance corvette, after all," she reminded him with undisguised sarcasm.

"Thanks for the reminder."

"Did you hear anything important at the nobility meeting? Or is this really just a tea party with a golden spoon?", Max wanted to know behind him.

"Worse, there wasn't even tea," he replied, confirming the orders with a fingerprint. What a bore the wait for the actual battle would be without all the red tape.

The last fleet

"That's what I thought. Uniform parade."

"Anything else in the stuff I just confirmed as 'fully read and accepted'?" asked Gavin in Lizzy's direction.

"Little things. There are a couple more civilian ships behind the lines forming up right now. Six of them in all, and for some reason they couldn't get out of the restricted area fast enough. Three of them had engine failures and were evacuated. The tugs will soon take them away. The other three still have crews on board, probably smugglers faking some kind of malfunction, hoping they won't be bothered before the battle starts, before they get lost in the chaos and disappear."

"Small ships, I guess?"

"Yeah, the biggest one is a *Light Hauler*-class freighter with a really weird energy signature. The amount of heat that thing is radiating is significantly higher than it should be with its reactor configuration. That's probably why no Marines have been sent aboard yet."

"Fooled their drive and got the receipt at the worst possible moment," Gavin surmised, shaking his head. "If they get contaminated, they had it coming."

"We're supposed to keep an eye on them, too," Lizzy said.

His gaze jerked to her again. "Excuse me? We're supposed to babysit some stranded civilians while our sister ships take the rap?"

"Does it bother you that we might be mocked as babysitters, or that their lives might be in danger without us?"

In reply, he merely grumbled.

"Could be Republican terrorists," Gino mused, "sneaking up behind the formation and then blowing it up. Wouldn't be the first time they pulled some sick shit like that."

"If that's supposed to be a pep talk, you failed," Gavin said.

"So what do we do now?" Lizzy eased away from her holographic consoles and gave him a dismissive look.

"We follow orders."

"Oh." She looked surprised, then visibly relaxed. "Good."

"I wouldn't go that far. But it could be that I just talked to the Crown Prince and he offered me a place with the *Angry Aces*."

"What?" she asked, puzzled. Max and Gino showered him with similar expressions of disbelief until he grinned and told them to shut up.

"I didn't know it was the Crown Prince, I swear!"

"How can you miss the Emperor's son? Every school kid knows his picture because it hangs next to the Emperor's in pretty much every room!" snorted Max.

"It's the VIP effect," he defended himself. "In everyday life, you don't expect to meet a VIP, and then you don't recognize them."

"I wouldn't call this *everyday life*, but let's go ahead and title your mental derangement the *VIP effect*. You just made that up, didn't you?"

"I'm happy for you," Lizzy interrupted them, "honestly."

"Thanks. But first we have a battle to fight - I mean, of course: keeping an eye on a few civilians and watching our comrades fight off three Never swarms," he said with a sour expression.

At the mention of the Never swarms, the mood immediately became more subdued. So far, they had been concerned with getting to the rendezvous point quickly, then hundreds of incoming subspace rifts had ensured that they had plenty to see. Now, however, only a few hours separated them from the start of the battle. The first reaches of the swarms had already reached the outer system and were rapidly approaching. On the sensors they looked like galactic dust clouds of a sickly brown that might have been of a morbid beauty had it not been for the many specks in them. Several strands went off from the main arms like tentacles, sometimes growing larger and then smaller.

The monster was standing in front of the door and it would open shortly.

INTERLUDE: JANUS

Janus sat on one of the simple wooden benches of the Imperial State Garden in the audience wing of the diplomatic section of the *Rubov* Orbital Ring, listening to the robotic birds chirp. The park was nowhere near as impressive as the Imperial Family Atrium, but was still a sign of the Ruler's progress and power, with a view of Terra that was most beautiful just now, as the Terminator shifted westward and the surface was once again plunged into darkness. Old-fashioned lanterns in the style of Victorian gas lamps lined gravel paths that led through spruce groves and meticulously manicured grasslands. In the center loomed the orbital audience chamber of the imperial family.

"First Secretary of State," a man greeted him who was of difficult-to-estimate age, typical of someone who had already had multiple telomere extensions performed. He possessed knobby muscles that stretched beneath an expensive but not ostentatious suit and a broad face that seemed to merge directly into his barrel-shaped chest. Clipped to his lapel was a lapel pin, presumably that of his company, Warfield Armored Reconnaissance & Security.

"Ah, Mister Lowell," Janus said, rising to shake the newcomer's hand. "Or would you prefer *Captain* Lowell?"

"Mister Lowell will do just fine. After all, I'm not on duty anymore."

"You're not?"

The diplomat hesitated.

"Well, you know what they say," Janus continued, seemingly in good humor, and waved it off. "Someone who has served once always stays in the service. You can take the person out of the military, but you can't take the military out of the person."

"There's certainly something to that," Lowell admitted, nodding as Janus motioned for him to sit down. "To what do I owe the honor of meeting you here, then, Lord Darishma?"

"An honor," he repeated, as if he had to taste the word *honor* on his tongue like an ancient wine. "You know, it still is for me, too. Even after all these years as the Emperor's right-hand man. This garden is only open to the most important confidants of Haeron II. Not as restrictive as the family gardens, of course, but still only accessible to a narrow circle. Why do you think that is?"

"No electronics of any kind are allowed here. In diplomacy, we also call these gardens forbidden zones." Lowell's face parted into a practiced smile.

"We're constantly surrounded by so many helpers, our neural augments, and any number of gadgets that we quickly forget how liberating it can be when all of that is not working and turned off, am I right? Just thoughts and words. Simple and direct, the way conversations happened between us humans when we were still roaming the prairies of Africa and relying on each other."

Lowell nodded. Janus didn't have the impression of talking to a born diplomat, but even this man was probably able to understand what he was trying to tell him.

"How did you come to join Warfield, anyway? You were a captain in the Navy before," Janus abruptly changed the subject. "You'll have to excuse me, I'm afraid I never served, but Warfield ARS does specialize in ground operations and starship combat, not fleet services."

"Ah, that's a longer story. The short version is that I was in charge of logistics during my twenty years of service, and made a good network within the Admiralty along the way."

"That little fork of special catering to friends, huh?" Janus winked as if he were joking.

The last fleet

"Yeah, right." Lowell obviously fell for it and nodded with a smile.

"I guess you can't blame anyone for that. *Small gifts preserve friendship*, my mother used to say. What kind of gift did Warfield give you in return for setting up the deal with Yokatami?" The fake birds chirped around them, deceptively real and all at once felt very loud.

"Yokatami deal?" asked Lowell, so obviously concerned with buying time to think that it seemed clumsy. Janus could see the gears turning behind the former officer's brow as he tried to figure out what this meeting was really about and how to get out of it without losing his job. Because that was exactly the look his eyes had taken on.

"Relax," he suggested, putting on a lighthearted expression. He patted Lowell on the shoulder as if they were old friends, and left his hand there for a while longer, while his interlocutor forced a smile. "After all, we're here among ourselves, just chatting. There's no one here who cares about us. Isn't that relaxing?"

"Uh, yeah."

"So, you weren't responsible for setting up the deal," Janus finally continued, opting for another reverse suggestion, "I believe you, don't worry."

"Am I in trouble?"

"Oh no, not at all," he assured his seatmate, but did not smile. "I'd just like to understand how a - pardon me - not-so-big security corporation gets hold of a contract from a permanent member of the Corporate Council, who has an army that could take on the Wall or Border Worlds. It simply does not make sense to me, and I am paid to shed light on the unknown for the Emperor."

Lowell looked at him warily from the side, presumably to gauge how problematic this conversation really was for him and what suspicions were in the air. What was certain was that this man was hiding something, for that Janus did not even need to rely on many years in court and in the diplomatic corps of the ruling family. And he was afraid.

"I can't help you, Lord Darishma," he said finally, when he

apparently thought he had recovered his poker face. "I was not entrusted with the contract negotiations or their initiation. Even though, of course, this matter has represented a great success for our group."

"What do you know about this deal?"

"Uh, it is worth five billion crowns and is in the area of property protection."

"Just as it says in the official documents. I wonder if there's even room for other customers there. After all, such a high volume of capital will surely involve a large part of your forces in the cooperation."

"Yes, about eighty percent for the next five years," Lowell replied with growing unease.

"Who is leading the project?"

"Lord Darishma, may I ask where this interest is coming from? Is it an official survey? If so, I'm wondering why you didn't go through the official tax or compliance channels?"

Ah, he must be getting nervous, he's already looking for a way out, Janus thought. *I must be close to the mark.*

"I'm the First Secretary of State," he lightly reminded the corporate man. "I think you're a genuinely good diplomat. I might even make a motion to put you under my Corps. We can always use capable people."

Now Lowell turned white as a sheet. Pulling professionals from the private sector into the Imperial service was rare and considered politically annoying, but it was not without precedent. What the consequences would be for the former captain, of course, only the former captain knew, but judging by the expression on his face, not good ones.

"That's... very kind of you, First Secretary," he said.

"We can just be friends, too." Janus winked as if he were joking. "What do you think? Good contacts in the palace never hurt."

"That would be very kind of you," Lowell repeated himself.

Janus remained silent and looked at his seatmate, waiting. It took a few seconds for the latter to finally understand.

"I'm afraid I have upcoming appointments," he began, licking his lips. "But I think your best bet is to speak with my colleague, Colonel Dimitri Rogoshin. He was in charge of project planning at the beginning of the contract period."

Finally throwing the dog a bone, Janus thought. *What a difficult delivery.*

"Ah," he mused. "Then I've merely wasted your time, please forgive me. I will turn to Rogoshin. Thank you for being so patient anyway, and for sharing this magnificent view with me. And the peace and quiet."

When Lowell left, Janus used his privileges as First Secretary of State, the only one besides the Emperor who could access his augments and open secure links to the outside world.

"Nancy?"

"Yes, Mr. Darishma? How did the meeting go?"

"Enlightening. The man was scared when I approached him about the project. Something is up, so my sniffer was good. He gave me the name of a man to talk to, a certain Colonel Dimitri Rogoshin, who must have been in charge of project planning initially and is now assigned here - for who knows what."

"Should I make an appointment?" his secretary asked.

"No. I think we need to approach this differently. Get in touch with IIA, we'll have to use indirect means to get somewhere here. Have them send one of their agents to my office. No fuss."

"Of course, Mr. Darishma."

5

The battle began with a single, invisible laser beam. It was the communications laser of the *Fouchault*, one of the cruisers under Artas' command, a low-frequency, highly focused signal of focused photons whose reflection allowed distance measurement to within a millimeter of the foremost reaches of the Never swarms.

The gigantic space clouds of bizarre bodies, which seemed to be unaffected by the hostility of the vacuum, wafted like an elongated tumor in the direction of the gas giant Kolsund, which shone like a blue ball on the screen of the *Glory*. The planet looked almost inviting, like a lush ocean. There was nothing to indicate that there were storms there of several thousand miles per hour, larger in extent than some celestial bodies of the inner system.

But the real storm was the Never, which seemed to be subject to no laws of physics, except for the constant of the speed of light. The individual entities of the swarms, monstrosities of the most different form, of which none resembled the other, moved on with furious speed - without any sign of a drive. There was no emission of excited particles, no plasma clouds, the interferometers of the *Glory* did not even indicate gravitational waves.

Immediately after the last of the *Fouchault*'s one hundred range measurements, his brother gave the order from his flagship, the *Amundsen*, to open fire with the range weapons. His fleet and the four attached from neighboring systems under his command for the battle hovered 125,000 miles behind the orbital gap between Kolsund and its moon, Bragge. Arrayed they were in a tightly woven web of forward and rearward deployed units.

As they launched their volleys of MK-VIII nuclear torpedoes, a jumble of red dots appeared on Gavin's tactical display, from which a clear pattern only gradually emerged. The MK-VIIIs were the main long-range weapons of the current generation, successively replaced by the new MK-IX series of nuclear weapons. But there were still far too few of these for the mass of firepower needed to repel the swarms.

Each of the total 24,000 torpedoes fired in the first salvo by the five defending Border World fleets trailed a half-mile-long plasma tail on the telescopic images. Gavin's visual data display looked like it had a pixel error that trailed streaks from right to left.

"So here we go, and we get to sit behind the front line and watch," he grumbled. His mood worsened as the adrenaline level in his bloodstream rose. He imagined the destructive force that had just been unleashed there and how little it would change the overall situation. The Never swarms stretched from the orbital constriction almost to the edge of the heliosphere, longer than the distance between them out here and the central star in the middle of the system.

"What an inferno," Lizzy murmured almost reverently as minutes later the first flowers of fire flared up and the first spurs of Never burned in nuclear fire. The explosions were very short-lived, consisting of extreme heat and light, spherical waves of gamma and X-rays racing away, eating through the vacuum.

"Take that, you fucking monsters," cheered Gino behind them.

"0.0000001 percent of the swarms," Gavin said.

"What?" asked Max.

"That's how much of the total mass that salvo destroyed."

Silence fell again in the cockpit until all that could be heard was the beeping and whirring of life support.

"We haven't really gotten going yet either," Lizzy stated, pointing to the tactical hologram in front of them. It showed the Wall Fleet under High Lord Marquandt's command - over two thousand ships in tight formation, hiding in the shadow of the gas giant, piecing together their situational awareness by means of drones arranged like a ring around Kolsund's Terminator, providing a steady exchange of signals. On the other side, a somewhat smaller but still impressive number of ships from the Home Fleet waited under the command of the Crown Prince, just realigning themselves in the shadow of Bragge to prepare their flanking maneuver.

"You got that right." He contemplated the ever-shrinking distance between his brother's fleets and the Never, and the next volleys fired at predetermined intervals to achieve the perfect density of effect calculated by the tactical computers. Then, in accordance with their mission - which they shared with six other corvettes - he focused on the swarm movements. The mysterious structure of non-autonomous creatures was in constant motion and by now so tightly intertwined that the swarms were indistinguishable from each other. It was clear to see that they were contracting to pass Kolsund at the narrows.

To pass, he repeated in his mind and instructed the computer to run a short simulation. The quantum computers at the heart of the ship took less than half a second to spit out the result to him.

"So they didn't come here to slurp hydrogen," he stated aloud.

"What?" asked Lizzy absently.

"The swarms." He slid the result of the simulation onto her main screen by hand gesture. "Marquandt's tactical reconnaissance was wrong. The Never isn't targeting Kolsund's precious atmosphere, but the Narrows themselves."

Lizzy looked at the yellow vector lines indicating the most likely directions of the sinister entity's movement, extrapolated from their current orientation and velocity.

"Hmm, the Never shows no signs of intelligence or tactical action, but this is really stupid. Why would it maneuver itself into such a strategically disadvantageous position if it didn't have to?"

"I don't know, but they're flying right into the meat grinder, and in an hour that meat grinder will have so much firepower that this thing will be over faster than it took to fly out of here." He forwarded the simulation results to Marquandt, the Crown Prince, and Artas as the respective commanders of the three fleet units. Presumably, they had long since received similar data or had made it themselves, but the rules were clear. Report, report, report.

When that was done, he looked again at the narrowing distance between the forward reaches of the Never and his brother's unit. The forward gunships, which were basically nothing more than a battery of torpedoes with thrusters, were already withdrawing to rearm and begin the rearguard action. The plan called for the Borderworlders to move out backward to keep the distance wide and force the swarms completely into the narrows before Marquandt and Magnus initiated their flanking maneuver.

"Keep it nice and wide," he whispered, looking at the gigantic Never cloud. It was getting narrower and narrower, possessing a spread of just over 180,000 miles in its forward third.

"Uh, Captain?", Max spoke up, and something about the sound of his voice made Gavin uncomfortable.

"Yes?" he asked, downright cautiously.

"I've got something weird on the screen here."

"Can you be more specific?"

"Not really. The *Light Hauler* with the energy fluctuations ..."

"The *Ushuaia*?"

"Yes. It just dropped off two objects that are roughly the same size as Sentinel reconnaissance drones, but can't be identified by the sensors," Max explained.

"That's not possible. Start a new scanner sweep. The fleet databases have every human-built piece of technology listed," Gavin ordered.

"I know, but this thing is either brand new pirate tinkering and therefore has never been scanned by a Navy ship, or..."

"We'll be first, then," he interrupted his defense officer again, trying to divide his attention between the tactical battle display and a live image of the *Ushuaia* drifting behind the lines like a long-drawn cigar 50,000 clicks away. The two objects Max had been talking about were marked by the on-board computer with flashing red brackets.

With rapid gestures, he zoomed in on them and looked at them closely: spheres the size of medicine balls, charcoal gray and a little brighter than the universe around them, so that they stood out with the help of the software's brightening. Bands of bluish pulsing light flickered across the surface, though there were no irregularities like joints or other depressions.

"If this is supposed to be a drone, where are the cameras and probes?" he thought aloud. "And why is this thing even flying? It doesn't have propulsion."

"What are you guys talking about?" Lizzy inquired, tuning into the sensor feeds.

"The Ushuaia is doing strange things. I'm trying to hail them." Gavin opened a channel to the light freighter, though several efforts had already been made by other ships. "Freighter *Ushuaia*, this is Lord Captain Gavin Andal of the *Glory*. Respond."

No response. He tried again without success and then gave up.

"What about my second scan?" he asked in Max's direction.

"Same result. Unknown object. I'm just saving the data for an entry in the databases. We're going to be famous!"

"That can wait, I want information!" he impatiently admonished his defense officer.

"Perfect spherical shape to the nanometer, diameter thirty centimeters. Minimal heat radiation. Either insanely well shielded or not particularly powerful. No detectable particle fluctuation in the immediate vicinity - however it's moving, it has no propulsion of its own. I'm guessing a launched projectile."

Gavin frowned and called up the *Light Hauler*'s design plans, compared them to the *Glory*'s sensor data, and shook his head. "The *Ushuaia* doesn't have any launch mechanisms," he said.

"Well, in any case, the thing is flying. If it wasn't fired, some guy on the ship has a really impressive throwing arm," Max returned.

"Where is it flying?"

"Toward Bragge. More specifically, just past it toward the L2 of the moon."

"What's that thing want at the L2?" Gavin frowned and looked questioningly at Lizzy. He was a pilot, not a navigation expert.

"Bragg's gravity dip won't be enough to get it significantly off course. The on-board computer will have already factored the minor deviations into its calculations," she replied without looking up from her holodisplays. She shared the navigation display with him and they stared at it silently for a few moments. Then Lizzy drew a total of four lines on the three-dimensional display, all emanating from Lagrange point two. The area between the lines, which together formed a kind of pyramid, pretty much covered the Crown Prince's fleet and at the same time a relatively large portion of the Never swarms.

"Wait a minute," he muttered. "Are you thinking what I'm thinking?"

"A spy drone." She nodded with a somber expression. "But from whom? It's certainly not one of ours, and it's certainly not one of the Never. The Never doesn't use technology."

"Just because this thing moves to a place where we would place a spy drone doesn't mean it is one," Max pointed out. "Could also be a coincidence and a misinterpretation."

"It's round and glows blue, now don't tell me its function is blue glow!" scolded Gavin, cracking the knuckles of his fingers. The sound they made sounded hollow and unhealthy. "I'm going to report it to the *Orion*," he said.

"The Crown Prince's flagship?" asked Lizzy, half surprised, half startled.

"Yes. I'd rather end up being laughed at for a false alarm than flogged for a missing report." He connected with the huge battleship that stood out like a leviathan from the Home Fleets behind Bragge.

The last fleet

"Lieutenant Bakeesh, Battle Coms, Orion. I read you, Lord Captain," a female voice sounded in her cockpit.

"Lieutenant, we have an unidentified object on our screens here, heading toward the L2. We can't rule out the possibility that it's an enemy reconnaissance tool," Gavin said, and a brief silence followed.

"Thank you, Lord Captain. I will pass this along. Please send further information over the Battlenet."

When the connection was broken, he slumped back in his chair with a sigh, only to be thrown back by the pulse. The straps of his gimbaled seat caught his inattention again.

"She basically laughed at me," he summarized.

"In the most polite way, after all. If it wasn't for your name, she probably would have yelled at you to keep the damn channel clear," Max agreed with him, chuckling.

"Gee, thanks." Gavin looked at the progress of the battle. His brother's units were retreating according to plan - right on schedule - while continuing to fire from all guns. By now, a sustained wave of heat and hard radiation had built up, against which the Never charged, pushing the surf further and further toward the Terran front. Looking at the tiny ships, though numerous, they seemed but a collection of small rowboats in the face of an approaching tsunami. The shoals seemed so huge and unstoppable, like a cosmic force. But the bombardment was having an effect, especially now that the railguns of the Border Fleet were spewing their tungsten bolts at five-digit-mile distances. At relativistic speeds, they chased thousands upon thousands into the Never, shredding flesh that was none, and milling many miles deep into its mass.

"Uh, that thing just disappeared," Lizzy said.

"What do you mean, disappeared?" he asked in irritation, calling up the data from the sensor he had tasked with tracking the mysterious object. Sure enough, the software searched for the target point, which was nowhere to be found.

"Just gone."

"I see it. But I don't accept it. We're pulling sensors from front-line surveillance. I think this is more important," he decided.

What the hell is going on here? He wondered if it might be a secret Navy project, something from Luna's secret research labs that were said to have all sorts of miraculous abilities. He had dismissed most of it as conspiracy theories, especially anything to do with stealth technology. Rumors about it had been around for decades, and to date, all official projects on it had failed, devouring trillions that the Star Empire didn't have to spare. The permanent state of war - even if it was a mostly cold war with the Orb and one could hardly speak of a war with the Never, rather of a natural disaster - had caused the financial margin to become smaller and smaller. The rate of mankind's technological progress had stagnated for almost half a century. All money had flowed into recruitment, maintenance, production and defense. He couldn't imagine that a secret breakthrough project would be pulled out of a hat and used in a battle with an extremely uncertain outcome - and in such a bungling manner, to boot. If the Navy had been involved, it would have deployed a ship of its own, not pulled off a farce like those smugglers from the Ushuaia. All it would have taken was a spotter like her to drop off the three drones and mark them in the database as something other than what it really was. A recruit could have easily planned that.

"This is different," he thought aloud. "What about the others? Do we still have them on the screen?"

"Yes. One is headed toward Kolsund and a third is headed in the opposite direction from us." Max paused and seemed to do some math. "It's heading toward Andal."

Gavin blinked in irritation. *Andal*? His home world? The second drone made sense, assuming they were dealing with enemy technology; after all, one was now heading for the Crown Prince's formations and one was heading for those of the Commander-in-Chief, Marquandt. But why was the third flying toward Andal? The world was irrelevant to the battle, especially since all of its supplies came from the shipyards and production facilities on and in the moons around Svylla, the fourth planet in the system.

The last fleet

"We're intercepting it!"

"The drone? Which one?" asked Lizzy. A jolt went through her body as she straightened up.

"The one flying into the inner system," he said.

"But we have orders not to leave our current position," she protested.

"The situation has changed. So we have to improvise." When she didn't budge, he snapped at her, "NOW!"

"Understood, Captain." Her fingers were already beginning to scurry across the holographic keys. Gavin, meanwhile, opened a direct channel to his brother on the Amundsen, which was running its guns hot in continuous fire behind the forward units and launching torpedo swarm after torpedo swarm. He also sent an automated warning to Marquandt's flagship.

"Gavin," Artas reported after a short time. In the background, the muffled confusion of voices could be heard on the bridge, which, unlike that of the Glory, was as large as a theater auditorium and held ten times the number of personnel. His voice sounded focused, and if he was surprised or annoyed to hear from Gavin on, of all things, that channel meant only for absolute emergencies, he certainly didn't let on.

"Artas, we have three strange objects on sensors here that don't show up in any database and are acting decidedly strange. One is just on its way to L2 behind you and recently disappeared from radar. Even the optical telescopes can't get a lock on it in any spectrum," he informed his brother, speaking so quickly he almost slurred his words.

"That sounds strange indeed." There was a pause. "Our sensors don't indicate anything like that."

"I swear to you, it's there."

"Hmm." He knew his brother was trying to gauge whether he was just dealing with the Gavin who liked to play to the gallery, or this was one of those situations where your own preconceptions could bite you in the ass.

"I didn't make this up. I can send you the data right now if you accept the request."

"No, that's all right. I believe you," Artas said. "We'll keep an eye on the L2. Where are the other two heading?"

"One toward Marquandt's Wall Fleet behind Kolsund, the other toward Andal."

"Good then, you are hereby under official orders to investigate. We'll be fine here, everything is going according to plan."

"Thank you." Gavin understood that this meant he could decide for himself which of the drones to go after, and nodded accordingly to Lizzy, who immediately powered up the engines and turned the ship one hundred and eighty degrees. As the engines accelerated her hard, he was pressed into his seat so hard that he lost his breath.

The *Glory* shot away from the battle like an arrow toward the inner system. Max and Gino groaned behind him as their Flynites lined up along their vascular walls, widening them to keep them from stroke at 12g acceleration. Gavin himself hated the feeling when his entire body felt like it was being poured out with liquid fire. The impression of being able to feel every single vessel in his body was something that was probably simply impossible to get used to.

"How's it looking?" he asked over the transducer network, which turned his thoughts into an electronic version of his voice and sent it directly to the others' neural computers. Moving his mouth would have been an impossibility with the infernal forces that made his body twelve times heavier than his own weight.

"We're catching up. Very slowly," Lizzy reported.

"Blast four o'clock!" exclaimed Max, "seventeen thousand clicks!"

"What happened?"

"I think one of Marquandt's ships shot down the drone that was flying toward them."

"Did the fleet admiral send a message out to the rest of the units?" wanted Gavin to know.

"No," Lizzy answered in Max's place, confirming what he already knew anyway. There were no such notes in Battlenet.

"Why is he shooting it down if he doesn't even know what it is? If he thinks it's dangerous, he should report it."

"But he didn't."

Gavin squinted his eyes and drove away all thoughts of Marquandt to focus on the drone speeding away from them, heading toward his home and his family's residence. It was almost within range of their two railguns and only weapons.

Five clicks.

Four clicks.

Three clicks.

Two clicks.

And it disappeared. Gavin had to blink to make sure he could trust his eyes.

"Target's gone," Gino stated the obvious.

"Shit!" he yelled, pounding his fist on his armrest in frustration. "Lizzy, we..."

"What?" she asked, but he paid no attention to her. Instead, he turned his full attention to the tactical display to his right. Keeping his eyes open was difficult with the current acceleration readings, so he took control, throttled the ship down to an acceptable 6g, and turned her around a tight corner that made all the gimbal pressure points creak. Then he looked back at the display with its myriad green, yellow and red dots, circles, triangles and dashes and switched to a second display to add the live images the bow telescopes were providing them. Much of the Never, which stretched from the orbital region of Kolsund to many hundreds of thousands of miles beyond and had just looked like a contracted bundle of morphing tentacles, was now completely changed. New arms had formed - six in all - that were no longer traveling on a straight course, but were bulging out toward Bragge. They were speeding up, weaving back and forth, but there was no doubt: they were breaking away and beginning to circle the moon.

"Look at that," he breathed, his mouth dry.

Lizzy didn't answer and, gesturing wildly with her hands, began to reconfigure her tactical displays and calculate something.

"Don't bother. I am ready to bet they're headed for the L2," he said, entranced.

That she said nothing back was answer enough for him. He opened a channel to the flagship of the Home Fleet, the Orion, and by means of his precedence code, which he possessed thanks to his status as the son of a high lord, got through to the first officer.

"Admiral Levine," he greeted the captain curtly, dispensing with the title 'Lord' as was customary among the nobility. "I believe the Never will attack your formations."

"We see nothing of the sort, Captain," the officer replied in wonder.

"That's because you can't see it. We are a trailing reconnaissance unit and are at the right angle to see it."

"But no such observation came from the fleet admiral. We have not received any data."

"That may be so, Captain, but the Never is coming directly to you. You must withdraw," he pressed the officer. "Talk to the crown prince."

"Hold, please," Levine said, and Gavin was about to breathe a sigh of relief when the captain continued, "We're getting a message from Fleet Admiral Marquandt right now."

"You can't waste any time! If..." A click in the connection signaled him that he had been put on hold. "You've got to be kidding me."

"They must be transmitters or something. Signal transmitters that attract the Never," Lizzy said incredulously. "Look at it!"

Two vectors appeared on the tactical map, and sure enough, out of the three swarms that had merged into one, two of roughly equal size now peeled out. The center of one was connected by a line to the L2 behind Bragge, and that of the other by a line to Andal far away in the inner system.

"You're right," he stated, biting his lower lip until it hurt. Then he tried to reach Marquandt's flagship, the *Mammoth*. But his connection request was blocked unanswered. "Did you see that?"

"I see something else," Lizzy said. "We're getting automated commands loaded onto the ship's computer right now."

"What, from who?"

"From the *Mammoth*."

"Was that part of the battle plan?"

"No, it certainly wasn't. Besides, they were non-rejectable and coded using his personal precedence code. There's absoutely nothing we can do." She raised her hands as if to show how powerless she was.

Gavin looked at the orders and turned white as a sheet. Immediately, he opened a connection to Artas - through her direct channel.

"Really bad timing, Gavin, it's really heating up here right now. Where are the flanking maneuvers by the Crown Prince and von Marquandt?" reported Artas, audibly tense.

"Listen to me. There's something wrong with the Never. The Home Fleet is under attack, you can see for yourselves how the swarms are splitting. And Fleet Admiral Marquandt is sending us orders right now that will disable our jump drive. You need to reboot your systems now so you can be spared. I don't know what's going on, but I'm sure it's not good," Gavin explained frantically. His heart was pounding up to his throat and only relaxed when Artas, to his relief, shouted appropriate instructions that were relayed to his fleets.

"Captain," Lizzy said, and the way she emphasized his rank made him shiver.

"What now?"

"The Wall Fleet."

He glanced at the tactical map. One symbol of Marquandt's fleet disappeared, one by one, from the system.

"They're jumping away," he said, aghast. "They're just taking off."

The cockpit suddenly seemed claustrophobically cramped, as if all air had escaped in one fell swoop and the space had been cut in half. The displays seemed to glow more brightly, the life support buzzing louder.

"Artas, you need to leave, now!"

"Our jump drive is offline. Sensors are shutting down," Max reported, and one of Gavin's displays went black. In the middle, it said in red letters, *Offline*. Communications also shut down.

"Shut down reactor," he ordered, and fortunately Lizzy didn't hesitate. She placed a hand on the virtual confirmation field, and when he did the same to himself, the computer asked for a final confirmation.

"If we do that, we're screwed if...," Max tried to reason, but Gavin was already verbally confirming the command, and it abruptly went dark and dead silent.

Then the battery kicked in, bathing them in diffuse red twilight.

"Or we could just do it and see what happens," Max sighed surrendered.

Gavin ignored him again and restarted the reactor using the toggle switch on its mostly bare armature. At first nothing happened and he was already getting nervous when finally a chirp sounded, followed by the familiar whine of the four fusion reactors interlocked with their respective thrusters.

"Lucky bastard, lucky bastard."

"Intuition, my dear," Gavin contradicted his defense officer, exhaling quietly so no one would notice how tense he had really been. "Lizzy, systems check."

"Communications are still offline, sensors offline except for telescopes, we can still look manually but the software can't process the data. Everything else above and below the optical spectrum is gone because software controlled," she read out. "Jump drive still offline. We were too late; the damn code has already written its commands into the firmware."

"Marquandt," Gavin growled. "A bloody traitor."

"That doesn't make any sense. Why would he want the Never to infest the whole system?" Lizzy looked apologetically at him, apparently remembering what that statement meant to Gavin. "I'm sorry, I..."

"He's letting us walk into the knife."

"And the crown prince. Plus almost the entire Home Fleet," Max added. "They're not going to make it. A third of the fighting force gone, the advantageous battle position gone. The moon is even a hindrance now, cutting our forces off from each other."

Gavin fixed his eyes feverishly on the telescopic images, seeing

The last fleet

the many explosions where the Home Fleet defended itself with everything it had. But even the most advanced ships in the Star Empire, with the best crews, could not resist the tide of Never. But retreating was not possible either, and so it would only be a matter of time before they were destroyed and disappeared.

To whatever hell the Never sent them when it tore them from this universe.

Please get out of there, he thought, looking at the flashes and flickers between the gas giant and the moon, which could only be the group of Border World fleets that his brother led - at least officially. It was clear to everyone that he had been given an honor because this was the home system of his house. What had become of it now?

"We can't help them," Lizzy reminded him, her voice admonishing. "We should get the hell out of here. Remember, we're not getting any more proximity warnings in. The first reaches of this cursed horror might even have already overtaken us and we wouldn't know it. Without jump drives, we're doomed."

"She's right, Captain," Gino agreed with her, almost pleading as he continued, "The only advantage we have is our position behind the front. But that advantage is getting smaller and smaller."

"They are lost, the Crown Prince and the Home Fleet," Lizzy continued to press him. "You warned your brother. If he was fast enough, he jumped long ago and got to safety, if not, then..."

"He didn't jump," Gavin said, feeling all at once as if all life energy had left him. "He wouldn't do that. He'd follow his orders and take as much of that thing as he could."

"Sorry, man," Gino exclaimed with growing panic. "Really. But we're still here. But not if we're just going to sit around and wait to die."

"He's right, Gav." Lizzy spoke quietly from the side now and put a hand on his arm. He almost slapped it away reflexively, but something in her voice got through to him and he nodded, dazed.

With mechanical moves, he took over the manual controls and put them on a direct course to Andal. He selected full acceleration at 13g and enjoyed the pain of the brute force inside him as he was pressed against the seat. It showed him that he was still alive, while leaving little room for his agonizing thoughts of Artas and the fact that most of his home's military had just been destroyed. Now nothing stood between the Never and his home.

His family.

INTERLUDE: JANUS

"Agent Walker," Janus greeted the nondescript woman who sauntered into his office.

"First Secretary of State," she returned the greeting in a voice that sounded like that of a local politician whose speeches could never be remembered because nothing had any recognition value. "You have something for me?"

"Sit down, please." He gestured to one of the two simple aluminum chairs in front of his desk, then turned on the white-noise generator. The effect felt as if his ears had suddenly become plugged or the air became thicker. Silence enveloped them like a cocoon, blocking out the background hum of the rotating orbital ring.

The agent looked around, then took a seat.

"I had a meeting an hour ago with the local diplomatic representative of a mercenary corporation called Warfield ARS."

Walker's gaze drifted for a moment.

"Third-tier security company, headquarters on Alpha Prime, annual revenue 1.2 billion crowns. Specializes in army services, especially property protection," she summarized.

"Right. Warfield somehow managed to land a deal with Yokatami, and I just can't make sense of it. Fleet Admiral Dain Marquandt is the single largest shareholder in the corporation, while he has a public feud with Yokatami. So he could have stopped the deal, but didn't. I need to know why. And I need to find out who set up the deal. At the time, Chief of Staff Albius, among others, was still involved as a major shareholder in Warfield."

As he tersely recounted his meeting, the agent listened intently, presumably storing it all away in her cerebral memory lacunae, nodding occasionally.

"You greeted Lowell warmly," she finally repeated when he had finished. "I suppose a gesture of trust? A hand on the elbow in a handshake?"

"On the shoulder."

"Ah. You have placed sensor dust."

"Right." Janus was reasonably impressed and leaned forward until he could rest his elbows on the tabletop.

"What did the sensors transmit?"

"Not much. Lowell went back to the diplomatic post of the Corporate Protectorate and hasn't left it since. He's been sitting in his office on the phone ever since, I suppose. The signal dropped out in the office itself - probably white noise."

"Yes," Walker said. "You were talking about a man named Dimitri Rogoshin."

"Right, Lowell revealed him as one of those who initially ran the project for Yokatami. I found out that before he worked for Warfield, he was a prosecutor on New California and successfully prosecuted the Cazacone there. After that, he was appointed to Justizia on Terra and helped negotiate contracts between the Star Empire and the Corporate Protectorate for terraforming the new Seed Worlds before joining Warfield as COO, of all things," Janus recounted the findings of Nancy's research. "This corporation is becoming more and more suspicious to me. I want you to find out exactly what Warfield is doing for Yokatami and what Albius and Marquandt are involved in."

The red light on his intercom lit up.

"Excuse me." He deactivated the white-noise generator and allowed the connection to be made. "Emperor. I'm sitting here with Agent Walker from IIA."

The last fleet

"You should turn on the news feed. There's a problem brewing," said Haeron II. "Come to my office as soon as you can"

"Of course, Your Majesty." Janus looked at the intercom with a furrowed brow, then looked up at the agent. "I suggest you start with Rogoshin."

He rose and Walker followed suit.

"Consider it done, First Secretary."

"Thank you. And remember, utmost discretion."

"Of course."

As she left his office, Janus sat back and turned on Terra One - on his desk's holoscreen.

"Behind me, at the Eiffel Tower in the heart of Arcology Paris, there has been the third terrorist attack in fourteen days today," Monica Hayes, the station's well-known news anchor, reported. She was apparently reporting live from the megaplex. In the background, the skyscrapers that surrounded the restored historic downtown could be seen like monolithic sentinels, separated only by the distinctive dome of transparent Carbotanium fibers that had replaced the Eiffel Tower as the landmark of the arcology. *"The target that was hit this time was the Arc de Triomphe, a historic building, hundreds of years old and, according to a confessional letter from the Republican Underground, a sign of repression and Napoleonic traditions of oppression and imperialist expansion. At least two hundred people were killed and four hundred others injured in the vacuum bomb explosion, according to preliminary estimates by the Plex police."* The camera panned west and showed two blocks of houses in flames about half a mile away, separated by a wide avenue filled to the brim with fire drones. Silhouettes of six-legged Riotbots were also visible, holding back onlookers. Thick columns of smoke reminded Janus of drawings of genies from childhood, only here they weren't colorful, but pitch black as night. An eerie alarm began to boom in the background. "As I'm sure you can hear, the environmental alarm has now been sounded because the release of carbon monoxide and other toxic molecules under the dome is increasing and the venting system can no longer handle it. In the confession letter, the Republican Underground also demands

that Senate President Varilla Usatami make her canceled visit to the Paris arcology after all and meet with representatives of the Underground. However, this is considered impossible, as it is the Senate's policy not to negotiate with terrorists, so as not to give them any form of legitimacy. Usatami herself has not yet been available for comment."

Janus tuned out and made his way to the Emperor. The Paris problem had indeed escalated, and he dreaded what the future would bring, knowing full well that his master's options for action were melting away and none of the alternatives would be good for the Star Empire.

6

"Is that a ship next to us?" asked Gavin, looking at the images from the port cameras. It was now the third time he thought he saw a reflection there.

"I don't know, I can hardly keep open my eyes," Lizzy replied with a groan.

Max and Gino didn't even bother to respond. They had been busy for half an hour aligning the communications lasers with Andal's orbital ring without any computer assistance. An impossibility, as Gavin was well aware. But it kept them busy, which was always better than letting them indulge in their gloomy thoughts. And while their task was akin to trying to target a single grain of sand in the ocean, at least it wasn't impossible.

Now if only the damn radio would work, he thought in frustration. The pain in his body had reached a level that barely allowed him to breathe, and it would stay that way for the next ten minutes before they moved into the drift phase.

Six hours. Six hours separated them from their turnaround maneuver for the forty-minute braking thrust, and then they would be in orbit of Andal. He would have liked all too well to believe that they would be safe after that. But there were hardly any defenders left. Only the base garrison to maintain order, which had nothing to oppose the Never. With any luck, they were already evacuating the population.

"I just can't believe it's all over," he said via transducer. No one answered him. What could they have said? So he just kept talking. "Marquandt is gone, left us all for dead. The Home Fleet is destroyed..."

"We don't know that for sure," Lizzy pointed out.

"I warned my brother, not the crown prince. And even for Artas and his formations, it would have been incredibly close."

"But not impossible."

"No," he admitted, though he dared not indulge in any hope. He had seen too many explosions on the pictures from the tail cameras. The Never behind them looked too immense, obscuring a considerable portion of the image frames. Its elusive extent almost made it look as if the swarms weren't moving, just hanging there in front of the stars like a cloud of dust. But he had seen it up close and had no illusions. The Never was coming, and it was coming at a furious pace.

"Something is flying next to us," he repeated his observation from before, sending her a still image after he managed to take a screenshot of his telescope display at the right moment when a reflection appeared.

"Hmm," she made, "Seems to be actual light reflections from some kind of shell. How many times have you seen it?"

"Five, six times, maybe."

"Did the position change?"

"Shifted a little further back. I don't know how much."

"Doesn't matter. If it's a ship, it's one of ours, and that's probably a good sign," Lizzy said.

"You're probably right," he countered, tapping his fingers on his flightstick - tiny movements that took power under 13g of load, however. "It's best if we take a look."

"Excuse me? You want to change course? Without proximity sensors, without..."

"Without everything. Well, actually not everything, the onboard computer is still online. It just doesn't have its full range of functions because it lacks sensors and secondary systems."

"Yeah, so pretty much *everything*. Why would we even take

that kind of risk? If we collide at our speed, we'll be nothing more than a shrapnel cloud of nanoparticles."

"It's just a gut feeling," Gavin replied.

"Just a gut feeling?" she repeated, snorting. "You're putting our lives at risk because you *just have a feeling?*"

"I'm just flying a little closer." He touched the flightstick very lightly and used it to push it to the left, whereupon the *Glory* changed its angle minimally. As he did so, he kept an eye on the reflection, but it immediately disappeared. So he manually switched on the port thrusters, which were normally used for parade flights past docks, or for search operations in dense asteroid and debris fields.

At first, nothing happened and he licked his lips with increasing nervousness. But then it was there again, the reflection. This time brighter, closer. And it didn't disappear again immediately, which could only mean that the other ship was within range of its spotlights. So he searched the on-board computer for the specifications of the lights and found out that their effective range in space was twenty-five miles.

Twenty-five miles maximum distance, he thought, and set himself a manual odometer so that he could match the change in angle due to his course correction with the maximum distance. With a little sleight of hand, he would thus find out - albeit very approximately - how close he was to the object.

"Captain," Lizzy said tensely. "What are we doing here?"

"Checking something."

"What a collision feels like?"

"Just trust me." Not wanting to have to deal with her lack of faith in his abilities, he didn't look over at her, but focused on the telescope image and the odometer. Max and Gino, thankfully, still remained silent, fully engaged in their needle hunt in the haystack.

"There!" he shouted triumphantly at the transducer network as the reflection was no longer a persistent pulse of light, but a glistening dot on an elongated structure, standing out relatively clearly from the surrounding space. The odometer had reached nine, but Gavin estimated it could be no more than three.

"Brake!" demanded Lizzy, gasping, but he was already on it, giving the flightstick a minimal pulse in the opposite direction. "Is that..."

"The *Ushuaia*." He tried to nod, but couldn't bring himself to make the effort it would have taken. The back of his head remained nailed to the headboard of his seat.

"Why doesn't she have an exhaust flare? With those acceleration figures, she ought to be ten thousand miles like ours."

"Beats me. In any case, there's nothing visible." His gaze fell on the passive heat sensors on the hull. "But I'm willing to bet the plasma tail is there. We just don't see it."

"This whole thing is starting to freak me out."

"Only now?" Gavin throttled their acceleration very slightly to 12.8g and readjusted a few times until he felt the *Glory* and the mystery freighter were at the same speed. "A *Light Hauler* is certified for a maximum of 8g. This one is flying fifty percent over that."

"And the ship has already paid a price for that," she returned. He saw it in the telescopic images at the same moment, now that the *Ushuaia* was beside them, taking up almost the entire frame. Between the chunky bow with the cockpit and the even chunkier, uglier propulsion section at the other end had been the cargo modules before, one against the other. Their perfect arrangement had made it look as if it were one continuous piece of hull, but now many modules were missing. Others were crushed like soda cans, or hanging half-teared to the side. One just detached, wobbled and bent around the edge of another before being torn apart by the insane forces and disappearing into nothingness.

"We shouldn't get any closer," Lizzy suggested, and Gavin could feel her gaze on him. "Gav?"

"I'm not tired of living. Although I have to confess I would have loved to get on board and get my hands on those bastards."

"If they're not already dead."

"Then I'd extract the data from the on-board computer." Gavin considered and looked at the freighter's cockpit - the armored windows at the front and the airlock access hatch at the side. Again, he called up the blueprint of the ship type and marked the two main hatch hinges. "What do you estimate is the probability that the *Ushuaia* is still suffering from power fluctuations?"

"I estimate that one hundred percent of its power supply is going to the thrusters," she replied.

"So no magnetic interlock."

"Probably not, but... wait, *why*?"

Gavin activated the two railguns under the bow, swiveled them one hundred and eighty degrees, and manually marked the two points next to the hatch where the blueprint said the hinges were located.

"Captain?" she pressed on him. When he didn't answer, "Gav?!"

He gave the order to fire, and a deep roar went through their ship as the railguns' electric slides ejected their tungsten cones, punching two holes about the size of a fist into the freighter beside them without measurable delay.

"What are you going to do?"

"I'm going in."

"Are you completely insane? We've only got five minutes until we go into drift, if this piece of junk hasn't broken apart by then, it could drift itself at any time, and just a few seconds difference is enough to put us tens of thousands of clicks apart and you're lost!"

"I know," he said calmly. "I'm also aware that I can't stand up at almost 13g. And even if I did, I'd break everything and get crushed. And that's why ..." He gave the next fire command and simultaneously terminated their acceleration. Immediately, weightlessness set in and a collective sigh of relief went through the cockpit as the brutal heaviness lifted from their bodies. The *Ushuaia* lurched a bit after he sifted through her drive section, but another shot to the lower tail section halfway stabilized her again. A lucky shot, he admitted to himself. "That's why I'm just going over now," he said.

"You're insane, completely insane," Lizzy stated, breathing heavily.

"I'll go with you," Max said, "You can't go over there alone, Captain."

"Fine, I won't say no to that. But we've got to get in there. Those three drones, or whatever they were, came from that freighter there." Gavin jabbed his finger at the display in front of him. "If there are any clues to Marquandt's treachery and answers to questions about the origin of this unknown stealth technology, it's on that ship there."

Surprise stirred in the back of his mind at his own courage in this situation. Whether it was concern for his home and family or hatred for Marquandt, who had left them all to an agonizing death, he didn't know. But it didn't matter either.

He unbuckled his seat belt and pushed off toward the door to the connecting corridor, from which three hatches led to the quarters, the airlock, and the propulsion section. Max followed him with deft movements.

The airlock smelled of ozone and crushed sealant, a common accompaniment to extreme thrust phases.

Gavin's instructor in pilot training had called it *the smell of madness*. For once, he had to agree with the old drudge; he did indeed feel a bit like a maniac.

"Lizzy, bring us within five yards," he ordered.

"I can get you closer too," he heard her reply over the speakers.

"No, we're not taking any chances." One of the difficult aspects of his talent as a pilot was that he trusted others with lesser skills to do less than they deserved. He was well aware of that fact, but now was not the time to work on it.

"Understood, Captain."

Gavin nodded with satisfaction and handed Max one of the four fist-sized Reaper suits attached to the wall by magnet. They stripped down and stowed their ship overalls, which were skintight functional suits in Navy colors. He then retrieved two breathing packs from the small cabinet above the Reaper suits and bit down on the mouthpiece of one of them. The oxygen-

and nitrogen-enriched liquid inside flowed into his windpipe and expanded into his lungs. The brief sensation of suffocation - he hated it - passed before the basal panic reaction could work its way into his consciousness. Then he stopped breathing, but didn't feel the need either.

After making sure his magnetic boots were activated, he pressed the packet containing the Reaper to his chest and waited as the nanite mass within spread across his bare skin. Like liquid obsidian, it slid over every pore and soon enveloped him from head to toe.

Gavin waited for the nanocomputers to activate, consisting of myriads of interconnected computational cores of each individual nanite, and merge into a separate computational entity. In a kind of digital emergence, each individual robot became a transistor, either on or off, and by its sheer volume became a powerful computer.

Two lenses with vision enhancers in the ultrasonic, infrared and residual light ranges formed in front of its eyes, allowing him to see even under the most difficult conditions. The programmed nanosubstance was capable of adapting to any environment in a fraction of a second, even hardening on impact from projectiles or dispersing heat from laser weapons across its surface and dissipating it through his boots.

In short, Gavin felt as safe as he could under the circumstances in his Reaper suit, with no platoon of Marines available to accompany him.

"Everything good to go?" asked Max. Gavin eyed the shimmering black figure before him, with red glowing eyes like a nightmare creature, and nodded. The question from his obviously older officer showed him that while he was the more senior in this matter, he was also the more inexperienced.

"All good." Gavin took two *Inferno*-0g rifles from their mounts and handed one to his companion. "Ready?"

"Mhm," Max confirmed, checked the magazine and load levels, then nodded.

"Lizzy, lock the airlock, then open the outer door."

"Roger that. Don't do anything stupid, you two. There could

still be someone alive on that ship," his first officer warned them over the speakers.

"They don't even have combat seats," Max pointed out. "After acceleration, there won't be a pig alive in there."

"And if they are, we've got some serious questions for them." Gavin stood in front of the outer hatch and waited until the atmosphere had escaped the airlock and it was dead silent. Shortly thereafter, the armored steel retreated upward, revealing the thickened bow of the *Ushuaia* with the hatch destroyed, apparently half open from the shelling. The demolished cargo modules further to the right looked like a modern work of art made of scrap metal, for the most part barely connected to the thin skeleton of the connecting piece between bow and stern. The yawning void of endless blackness all around lay there in complete silence. There was nothing to indicate that shortly the Never would flood everything here and take every living object with it.

"Now entering *Ushuaia*," he said over the radio, pushing off after his Reaper suit had drawn the correct angle into his field of view. He had covered the five yards in three seconds, floating through the vacuum with his rifle in one hand and doing a roll before landing feet-first in the freighter's starboard airlock. Inside, it was pitch black, so his suit automatically emitted a faint glow that sent out enough photons to make his residual light amplification effective.

The airlock was more like a small cell, where he had to quickly activate his magnetic boots and step forward to give Max enough room behind him. The hatch to the corridor had two fist-sized holes punched in it by the *Glory*'s railguns. Tattered holding nets hung from the walls.

"Secured," Gavin said, having detected no threat and lowered his rifle a bit.

"No one says that, Captain," Max agreed, squeezing past him to check the hatch in front of them. He stuck the barrel of his short Inferno in the gap to the wall, then pushed it open. Looking at Gavin, he nodded curtly and let him go first.

In the corridor, objects floated around as if in slow motion:

scraps of clothing, batteries, sometimes intact, sometimes burst open, retaining ropes that had been torn from their anchors, torn wall coverings - and blood. It floated past them in droplets large and small, bursting here and there on his suit, where it left stains that the nanites recognized as foreign proteins and vaporized.

"Seems like it was quite a party," Max commented on the scene as he followed him down the corridor, aiming toward the far end. Again, everything was plunged into darkness, except for a flashing short circuit further back. "A residual discharge."

"We're going to the bridge," Gavin decided, swallowing against the lump in his throat. All at once he didn't feel as brave as he had before. He was a pilot, not a damn Marine. But that didn't mean he was going to let Marquandt off so easily - even if he didn't have the slightest idea how to get any information, if any, out of the system in the first place.

Following his own orders, he turned left, trudging ahead with magnetized boots that emitted a metallic *clonk!* with each step, which he heard over his suit.

"Lizzy, we're on the bridge now," he said as soon as he stepped through the open door and looked at the two empty seats in front of him. In the cold light of his suit and the residual light amplification turned on, everything looked strangely sterile and indistinct, even though the place was teeming with buttons, handles and fittings compared to the much more modern *Glory*.

"How does it look?" she wanted to know.

"Like the two pilots packed up their stuff and left."

"If it weren't for all the protein packs," Max cut in, holding up a plastic bag he had pulled from an open wall panel. It was filled to the top with empty ration bags. "Must have been squatting here for a while."

"Looks that way." Gavin went to the main console in front of the windshield and adjusted the light intensity of his suit up so he could look for the universal jack that every civilian ship in the Star Empire had to have installed. It allowed Navy and police units to read any shipboard computer by priority code. All manufacturers were required to install it and any attempt to remove it ended in a system shutdown.

He found it right on the front panel below a manual keyboard and flight stick, no bigger than an ancient jack socket, but outlined with red reflective stripes. He held his hand over it and, using a thought, commanded his suit to morph a universal plug that slid into the jack.

"It takes five minutes to read," he said, looking over his shoulder.

"Did you make sure your firewalls are active?" asked Max.

"Sure," he lied, cursing himself for not thinking of it. "You too? Then I'll stream the data directly to the *Glory*'s on-board computer."

"Ready to go," Lizzy reported.

Gavin checked the bandwidth his suit could do with the current power consumption and nodded to himself, satisfied.

"Max?" He tilted his head to peer past his defense officer into the corridor, as he aimed his weapon into the seemingly endless hose that lay behind them. "You all right?"

"Not sure," the muttered.

"What do you mean?" asked Gavin in alarm, swallowing. The data transfer was only at forty percent.

"I saw something. A brief glimmer, maybe bluish or silver, hard to tell."

"The light is pretty diffuse and the residual light amplification can create fractals," he reminded the older spaceman, though he should be aware of that himself.

But Max merely grumbled. "Probably."

Nevertheless, he aimed further down the corridor and didn't move.

"Fifty percent."

"Mhm."

"Lizzy?"

"Transfer in progress, everything looks good so far," she replied over the transducer network directly into his auditory center.

"Can you see anything from the outside? On the wreckage I mean?" he asked, looking at Max.

The last fleet

"Negative, there's no change on the camera images. I can't measure the heat radiation anymore, unfortunately."

"I know, just keep your eyes open, will you?"

"Captain," Max said, "something's not right here."

"I've had that feeling, too, since we came aboard."

"That's not what I mean. Something's *here*."

Gavin swallowed a reflexive, reassuring comment, trying again to look past his defensive officer's shoulder and make out something in the gloomy corridor into which the shone his weapons attachment. The countless debris and blood globules looked pale and abstract in the glow of the light. At first, everything looked the same as before, but then he thought he saw a kind of vortex within the many objects flying around.

As if a breath of air was moving through it.

"We should get out of here, Captain."

"Transmission is only at sixty percent."

"We should get out of here *now*!"

Before Gavin could say anything else, the air in front of Max began to shimmer and a bluish silhouette appeared out of the diffused light. His comrade started screaming and dropped his gun.

"FUCK!" cursed Gavin, yanking his *Inferno* rifle up to grab it with both hands. The universal cable from his suit broke off and the lost nanites floated away.

Max just stood there, held to the ground by his magnetic boots. At first, Gavin didn't understand what was happening, but then he saw bumps forming on the officer's shoulders that kept swelling. His body went into convulsive twitches and then went limp.

"What's going on?" shouted Lizzy, upset, and Gavin realized this wasn't the first time she'd yelled through the network.

"I don't know," he yowled, firing a volley at the blue silhouette, which was nothing more than a cloud of electrical discharges, fleeting and formless. The bullets, each of which had a small rocket engine and therefore produced no recoil, did not disappear into the corridor, but shattered with glaring sparks directly in front of Max's body.

In the middle of the air. Or was it? For a split second, he thought he saw some kind of wave-like movements on a dark material, which immediately disappeared again.

"Bloody heavens," he whispered, firing several dozen projectiles in automatic mode. He swung his *Inferno* from left to right as he did so, then something grabbed him by the neck.

The *Reaper* suit instantly hardened like steel under his chin.

"Gavin? CAPTAIN?" he heard Lizzy yell. "I'm not getting any more vitals from Max and ..."

He paid no more attention to her, for all his attention was caught by the hand that clutched him. The fingers were slender, yet significantly larger than a human's. Its skin shimmered pearly and dark veins pulsed beneath it, looking like a work of art.

Gavin tried to ignore the red alerts his suit played into his field of vision and raise his weapon. But something in his body was not right. He felt like his chest was expanding and about to burst. Dizziness and lightheadedness set in, as if something was spreading inside him and causing chaos.

Invisible fingers that ...

With a silent scream, he jerked the gun up and pulled the trigger before his fingers would no longer obey him. But a second unrecognizable hand knocked the barrel aside and the projectiles crashed into the wall of the bridge in a long-drawn line. The last of the missile rounds seemed to punch through one of the emergency batteries, as electrical discharges flooded the room from one second to the next. Garish, erratic branches of excited electrons flashed, short-lived afterimages on Gavin's retinas, but so numerous that everything around him lit up. His *Reaper* suit absorbed the amperage onslaught, spreading the considerable charge over its surface.

In one fell swoop, the feeling that his chest would explode from the inside at any moment disappeared, and the lightheadedness and dizziness were also gone. The hand still held him, but now it was no longer just a hand from nowhere, but that of an alien so huge that its head almost touched the ceiling. Its V-shaped torso was covered by a tight-fitting robe that looked like armor and a functional material at the same time. Strange decora-

The last fleet

tions were reminiscent of runes. Gavin didn't want to look at them, he wanted to fight for his life, but he was too dismayed by the sight to turn away.

And so he stared up at the teardrop-shaped head with its two fist-sized obsidian eyes that seemed to look straight into his soul. The narrow mouth beneath the six dark holes was curved downward, revealing a series of white whiskers that gave the appearance of glowing from within.

Gavin almost lost himself in the creature's mesmerizing beauty if he hadn't seen, out of the corner of his eye, two wings push and spread from the alien's shoulders. In front of it, a structure grew out of its shoulder like liquid metal and transformed into a spike, the tip of which pointed directly at Gavin but kept getting hit by electrical discharges and jerking to the side.

Gavin took advantage of the brief moment of clarity and released his right magnetic boot from the ground by thought command, using it to kick at one of the alien's unnaturally bent-back knees.

The effect was considerably less than he had hoped - after all, the sole was made of steel - but the grip around his neck slackened far enough for him to grab his weapon with both hands and yank it up. The ultra-hard composite of his rifle struck the wrist beneath the long fingers, and a bloodcurdling screech filled the bridge.

The alien stumbled back and its eyes grew as small as marbles in a flash. All the terrifying fascination that had paralyzed Gavin instantly gave way to sheer horror. The pearly hand had now become a morphing appendage of the same black substance that grew from the other shoulder, forming a spike.

Having no interest in learning what two stabs from the arm-thick weapons felt like, he pushed off to the side with his remaining magnetic boot and sailed through the bridge. As he did so, he reloaded his *Inferno* by pushing one of the rocket packs that was stuck to the top down the barrel.

The alien stabbed twice in quick succession, missing him by a hair's breadth. Gavin fired two quick volleys at the alien that seemed to bounce off some sort of force field, then ran past it with his magnetic boots activated. Even though his opponent took no damage, at least the force of the projectiles had an effect and drove it back half a step - just enough to get past him.

Running in zero gravity was like moving through water or having someone hold you back on rubber bands.

"I've got a damn alien on my tail!" he cursed over his transducer, firing more blindly than purposefully into the bridge as he turned toward the airlock.

"Gavin? What's going on there? Why..."

Something hit him in the flank, smashing him hard against the frame of the hatch he was about to throw himself through. His suit screeched for his attention by means of a shrill alarm and loud red indicators, glowing cherry red as it dispersed and discharged a massive rush of heat across its surface. Gavin's involuntary tumble against the cold metal probably saved his life, as the glow spread to the ship and he gave off heat just fast enough to avoid being cooked in his own blood.

The alien squeezed through the narrow passageway to the bridge, not two steps away. Like a giant, it built itself up to full size in the corridor, filling it almost completely. One of the morphing arms had transformed into a hand that possessed a dark weapon with a barrel and a glowing energy source under the grip. Gavin had already experienced what it could do. He didn't want to wait for an answer to the question of what would happen after a second hit, so he hurled his rifle toward the creature when the magazine was empty. He used his now freed hands to reach right and left and pull himself forward as fast as he could.

The round cutout on the other side of the airlock was as promising as the beckoning end of hell and yet seemed unreachable with its two yards of distance. Adrenaline drove him on, rushing in his ears like white water and whipping him into a hurry. It was the unpleasant tickle on the back of the neck when you were being pursued and knew exactly that at any moment the finishing blow would come.

And exactly that came just as he got a grip on the edges of the outer hatch and the *Glory* became visible in front of him. Not twenty feet away she hung in the darkness like a bird of prey with

The last fleet

its beak curved. But something grabbed him by the ankle like a vise and yanked him back.

With arms flailing and a stifled cry on his lips, he whirled around, already expecting to look down the barrel of the gun from before. But instead, the alien had grabbed him with both morphed arms, its eyes again as wide as dark lakes.

Something worse than a gunshot to the head happened: the daze returned and his chest swelled as if it was about to burst. Gavin could feel his blood trying to push through his skin and cried out in pain.

Then the feeling subsided, the weight disappeared, and only then did he realize that the alien had an apple-sized hole gaping in his chest through which Gavin could see the corridor beyond. Blue blood spurted from an artery and formed into thousands of small balls that floated away in all directions. The suddenly limp body drifted against the wall and bounced off it like a doll.

"Gav! Get back here!" he heard Lizzy's voice, breaking him out of his stupor. He spun around and looked down the barrel of the *Glory*'s port-side railgun, which seemed to be aimed directly at him.

"Bloody heavens!" he cursed. "Did you just..."

"Yeah, now get back here!"

Gavin did not wait any longer and wanted to turn around, but instead he took a deep breath, mustering all the willpower he had left to fight down his panic. It took him three breaths, then he grabbed the collar of the strange robe covering the alien's torso and pulled him behind him to the open hatch. In zero gravity, it was easy to drag the colossus of a corpse along. Only at the hatch did he have to move back and forth a few times until he got it free. Then he sailed toward the open airlock of his ship. It looked huge on the little corvette and its bright glow like the promise of a paradisiacal afterworld.

Which I will now infect with the taint of evil, he thought gloomily, and even before he intercepted his hasty flight at the top of the airlock, he sent an order to Lizzy: "Blow the damn thing to smithereens!"

"What about Max's body?" she asked in dismay.

"Max is dead and the Never is on our tail." His entire left field of vision was filled with the brown mist that seemed to swallow the universe itself. Gavin let the dead alien fly past him and pounded his fist on the red button for the emergency lock on the outer hatch. "Now! That's an order!"

OFFICE OF THE SENATE PRESIDENT, SATURN HABITAT AURORA

"Marius." Senate President Varilla Usatami nodded to the chief of staff and, with an inviting gesture, invited him to step up beside her. He looked youthful, barely older than twenty - before any telomere extension, and exactly the same as one of her couriers, Giulio Adams, to boot. His movements, however, were the same old ones - the slightly swaying gait and the arrogant way he stretched his back as if he had swallowed a stick.

"Varilla."

"An unannounced visit, it's been a long time. And in this particular getup, no less."

The Grand Admiral pulled the Reface mask from his head and his wrinkled face emerged with its small eyes and receding hairline.

"You do realize that no mask from the Dong Rae labs, no matter how high quality, can fool the electronic sensors on this habitat?" she continued.

"I assume you will take care of that part when I'm gone again," he returned, and they looked down through the floor-to-ceiling glass of the office at the Senate, the lower chamber of Saturn's Congress with its one thousand seats arranged in a semicircle. Two for each inhabited world of the Star Empire. "So this is where you play your democracy game."

"Yes. Not that it would change anything." She despised

defeatism, but sometimes she longed for her days as a xenobiologist back, even if the wall systems scared her to this day.

"You're talking down to me, a high lord of the Council of Nobility, and you're doing it as a commoner. You could be put in prison for that."

"You'll get the same for using a Reface mask on the Aurora habitat," she countered with a smile. "You're here about Paris, and not to discuss Imperial etiquette, I take it?"

"Mmm," he made. "I'm of the opinion that an opportunity has presented itself that we should seize."

"That sounds dangerous," she sighed, and walked over to the large sofa area, where a small, real wood table held select whiskies. She poured herself a twenty-year-old Karadian and showed him the bottle. Marius nodded and moved towards her to accept his glass, then settled on the seat.

"It sounds like the opportunity we've been waiting for."

"Republican underground, huh?" Varilla laughed mirthlessly. "A tragedy that it had to come to this." She reflected. "The Senate will demand a tough response. Especially the Republican wing, which already sees their hopes dashed because they'll be held partly responsible for the attack."

"If we wanted to, we could make enough connections between them and terror cells all over Terra."

"But we don't want to do that."

"No. Not for now. We could frame your appearance in Paris as a visit to a disaster area and emphasize that you're just not going to meet with representatives of the underground - whoever that might be - but with relatives of the victims, to send a message on behalf of the Senate," the Grand Admiral suggested, sipping his Karadian. "Not bad."

"How dangerous will this be for me?"

"Not without danger. Our field forces are spread thin, but we're pulling together what we can."

"At least you're honest," she noted.

"If we couldn't be honest with each other after everything, then all of this would have no meaning. I'd put my life in your hands, and I hope the reverse is still true." He looked her straight in the eye and waited until Varilla finally nodded.

"All right, then. How long will it take you to get everything ready?"

"An hour. If you set out now, you'll be on Earth in ten hours. Set yourself up for inconspicuous personal security." Marius waved his free hand around. "Make up something about preventing martial appearances and being there to comfort the relatives and not be looked at like an alien from distant Saturn."

"My family ..."

"I'll make sure they leave as soon as possible, and ensure that no one asks any questions. They're commoners and won't stand out too much."

"Good, so we're off after all this time." Varilla drained her whiskey and the chief of staff rose as well, already raising the Reface mask back up to the level of his face. "One more thing. Andal. Can we assume complete victory?"

"Yes." He nodded confidently. "The planning is flawless, the firepower well distributed. This will be a great victory for humanity and our future."

7

"That's an Orb," Gino noted.

The three of them stood around the table of their small lounge, which was also galley, mess hall and meeting place. After turning the *Ushuaia* into a melted lump of scrap, then accelerating again briefly, the thrusters were throttled back to make exactly 1g. For ten minutes now, they had stood in silence around the pearly alien's body tied to the table. No one had said a single word about Max and yet their dead comrade was the most present person in the room. Despite the creature laying between them that shouldn't even exist.

"An Orb?" asked Lizzy incredulously, shaking her head. Her cheeks looked sunken and her skin paler and wan than before.

"Yes. An Orb," the fire control officer repeated, looking somber. "This thing is huge and of undeniable beauty. Look at those immense eyes, black as the universe itself, and skin glowing like aquamarine."

"Your beauty queen here slaughtered Max," Gavin reminded him.

"I know, and for that it deserved the hole in its fucking bellows. But all we know about the Orb is that they can supposedly beguile the human mind and are, technologically speaking, many decades, if not centuries, ahead of us. You said it used some kind of psionic force and had a body shield."

"I said it *felt* like a psionic force," he corrected his comrade gruffly. Before his next words, he took a deep breath and swallowed, in a desperate attempt to dispel the nausea in his stomach that had plagued him since his return. "I'm sorry, I don't mean to ..."

"It's okay," Gino said immediately. "I understand."

"What we *know* about the Orb," Lizzy spoke up, "is really nothing at all. Anecdotal whispers in the corridors of the fleet, rumors exchanged over a beer at the bar just before the place closes, bragging by cadets with connections who want you to believe they've talked to someone in intelligence." She waved it off. "None of that is something I would wager crowns on."

"Officially, no Orb has ever been captured - dead or alive," Gino agreed with her. "The few skirmishes that have occurred have ended in tactical retreats by our units, even if the Imperial propaganda puts it differently and boasts that the Wall Systems held and continue to hold to this day."

"Remind me to delete the audio," Gavin grumbled.

"Sorry." The fire control officer sounded anything but remorseful. "Everyone knows the Orb would sweep us away if they were interested. What they certainly have no interest in is us getting our hands on one of them. So what if the skirmishes that took place back then after first contact were actually triggered by just such events? You know as well as I do that intelligence would do *anything* to get their hands on such a sophisticated alien. They've worked hard to earn their reputation, after all."

"What are you saying?" asked Gavin impatiently.

"That it's not unlikely that some boarding party at least managed to get glimpses of individual Orbs back then. And, of course, anything to do with dangerous galactic neighbors is secret, but any secret lasts only until the first person involved is retired, or drunk, or in love with the wrong woman or man."

"So you think the rumors spread at some point and aren't really rumors at all," Lizzy summarized. "And since this creature here fits in pretty well with word-of-mouth in the Fleets, it can't be a coincidence."

"Yeah."

Lizzy looked from Geno to Gavin.

"Hmm," he mused, rubbing his chin. He would have rather vomited. His stomach contents were almost hanging in his throat. "If it really is an Orb, what does that mean? Why is it showing up here now?"

"Because of Marquandt and the Never. Or just one of them," Lizzy concluded.

"Or both of them," added Gino. "It's hardly a coincidence that the three unknown spherical objects came from the ship that contained an Orb."

"You think it's Orb technology," Gavin concluded, feeling like his brain was malfunctioning. It felt like an overflowing jar, with emotions of hate, fear, and frustration wrestling for dominance with too-intense memories, coupled with the knowledge that he had lost a subordinate. Because of his decision. Max's blood was on his hands, even if he hadn't been the executioner, and that knowledge sickened him.

"Yes. I'm sure of it. And it has something to do with the Never. You saw it for yourselves. Looked like the swarms were targeting the parts or something."

"And Marquandt, too," Lizzy said, and seeing the looks of them both resting on her, she unfolded her arms crossed under her chest. "Well, he did shoot one of them down when it was already off our radar, didn't he? So he obviously had some way of locating the drones."

"If they really are drones."

"They're flying unmanned, so they're drones."

"If it's really Orb technology, it could be anything else," Gavin insisted. "This thing nearly forced my blood through my skin with some technology, has two arms that can morph into anything it wants, and my *Inferno* didn't even scratch it."

"Where do we go from here?" she changed the subject.

"We continue to broadcast by directional beam and hope that the planetary defenses themselves have long known how bad things are. Once we make contact, we'll request a fly-through to the *Mjölnir*, dock, and get a ship with a working jump drive to get the evidence and the Orb to Terra."

"If there's even a ship that can still jump," Gino objected.

"If not, we're all dead anyway," Gavin was certain. "Then it doesn't matter. But we owe it to Max to do everything we can to get the data and body away. Marquandt cannot be allowed to get away with this."

"And he won't," Lizzy said with an absent look, as if trying to convince herself despite her mind telling her otherwise. "But the Never ... we only have a half-hour head start before the first reaches of the swarms reach Andal."

"That means they've barely slowed down." Gino snorted in frustration, and they all knew what that meant for the status of the ten fleets that had been left to defend themselves.

"It's not over until it's over," Gavin decided. "We'll pack him," he pointed to the dead Orb, "in an evac bubble and vacuum seal it. Then it should keep for a few months or even years. Gino, you take care of it. Lizzy, you come with me to the bridge."

He still made it through the door and up to the lock button, then collapsed powerlessly and threw up loudly on the metal floor. His stomach contents sank through the cracks and were automatically sucked out, but the stench was sickening. There was no time for shame towards Lizzy or disgust due to his own bodily excretions, however, because next he began to sob unrestrainedly. What he had been holding in all this time was now making its way out, like a dam bursting, where any resistance was doomed to failure. All the grief for his brother, the fear of the Never and what it would do to his family, the hopelessness of their situation and the horror on the *Ushuaia* - all of it came over him like a tsunami.

He didn't know how long it lasted, but at some point he realized that someone was holding him in their arms and he had soaked his overalls to the navel with tears.

"It's okay, you know," Lizzy said, and it reassured him that she was talking to him normally, not as if to a child or an extremely fragile object. It sounded like an ordinary conversation between two adults holding each other in their arms at a difficult moment.

The last fleet

"When my parents died in the Ceus-III disaster, I was just fourteen. I didn't even realize what had really happened. Suddenly, I was just alone."

"Your parents were among the victims of Ceus?" asked Gavin hoarsely, raising his head slightly. Her face was close to his as she nodded. "You never told me that."

"We've been busy with other things, too. I honestly didn't expect to see that side of you."

He searched her eyes for a hint of mockery or criticism, but instead found mere sympathy and a thoughtful shadow in them.

"To be honest, I took you for an exceedingly attractive but arrogant and unworldly young scion of a powerful family of Terran high nobility," she continued.

"Ouch."

"My parents were both miners. You'll have to excuse us if privileged families like yours weren't spoken of very favorably in our family. I didn't grow up with a golden spoon in my mouth."

"But they weren't Republican..."

"Terrorists? No. They weren't stupid, I guess, and knew that stability was the only reason humanity was still out here. The Secessionist Wars of the 23rd century hammered that fact into our collective memory forcefully enough."

"I'm sorry," he said in a strained voice.

"What?"

"About your parents. Really."

"It was a long time ago." She shrugged. "Experiencing loss so early, I now see it as a gift. It made me stronger and made me realize the impermanence of things. I think I can enjoy life better today because I realize how fragile every moment is."

"Is that why you almost shot my head off my shoulders with a railgun?" he tried a half-hearted joke, but couldn't even manage a smile.

"The sex wasn't bad enough for that."

Now a snort escaped him involuntarily, with a trace of reluctant amusement in it. "And I thought you only went to bed with me because of my contacts."

"That, too. Besides, your arrogance does have a certain appeal."

"Very uplifting, really."

Lizzy smiled and squeezed him a little tighter. "I'm still here, that says enough, doesn't it?"

"I guess so."

"Though it still reeks of your puke. *Captain*," she said laconically, and they chuckled cautiously. When it had died away, she whispered, "We're still alive, and as long as we're alive, we still have a chance. Your brother's death hasn't been confirmed yet either, and the invasion hasn't begun."

"You're right. I just couldn't... I don't know how to describe it anymore."

"Like you're a paper container holding back a whirlwind?" she asked, and he nodded.

"Yes." He nodded weakly and wiped half-dried tears from the corners of his eyes.

"It's called fear, and I guess you've had the privilege of not having any experience with those feelings until now. Now you know how it feels and next time it won't be quite so bad." She paused. "But you'll be a better leader from now on, one who understands more about life, and by extension, his crew."

He thought about it and finally nodded again. "Why don't you just say I was a spoiled, unworldly aristocrat?"

"I did."

"Now that I've emotionally disrobed in front of you..."

"... I'd like it if next time you'd buy me a glass of wine before you rip off my uniform. Maybe someplace nice when this is over," she finished his sentence and Gavin had to smile. Something that had felt cold in his chest a moment ago was now gaining warmth and feeling better.

"Thank you, Lizzy."

She stood up and reached out a hand to pull him to his feet. "In five minutes, we'll turn around for the braking maneuver."

"All right." He took a deep breath, then called Gino over the transducer network. "Gino, how far along are you?"

The last fleet

"Just about ready. The body is cooled and vacuumed and in Max's... it's strapped down, anyway."

"All right, come back to the bridge and strap in, we'll be going into final approach shortly and it's going to get ugly again."

"Roger that, Captain."

"Well," he said to Lizzy. "Let's see if we can finally get a link up and get a read on how bad things are."

As it turned out, things were extremely bad. All the radio waves emitted by Andal and the myriad orbital systems and ships orbiting the planet were crashing over them. Everything was delayed by the many light minutes that still separated them, but one thing became clear: The military and civilian populations knew what they were facing, and the battle at Kolsund had been lost far more disastrously than feared.

In the Navy's encrypted radio, which the *Glory*'s on-board computer automatically decrypted, a devastating picture emerged. The Border World defense fleets under his brother's command had been swallowed up by the Never and disappeared. The only good news was that a third of his ships had apparently jumped before being swallowed up. Not among them had been Artas' flagship. The *Amundsen* had sacrificed itself along with the other two-thirds of his convoy to give the rest the time they needed. Public newsfeeds were already speculating that their fleet had abandoned them and fled, while government representatives of Gavin's father were at pains to present explanations such as regrouping. The fact was, however, that no one in the Navy knew what had occurred either, since Artas had apparently not permitted any messages to the homeland. His ships had remained silent. The reason why had probably died with him in the Never.

Stunned, Gavin listened to the rest of the reports, which he skimmed through for keywords: Terra's Home Fleets had been completely destroyed, including Crown Prince Magnus' *Orion*. There had apparently been one more attempt to retreat, but eventually his units had been trapped by the Never as it had approached from both sides around *Bragge*. The only consolation, albeit small, was that most of his ships had overloaded their reactor cores before being engulfed and pulled into the Never.

There was wild speculation about the reasons for the withdrawal of Fleet Admiral Marquandt and his mighty Wall Fleet; from secret orders from the Emperor, to a tactical withdrawal for battle-specific reasons that lacked the data to assess, to the truth: treachery.

The worst part, however, was that Gavin's greatest fear was true: Marquandt's priority code had infected all ships in the system, jamming their jump engines - among many other primary and secondary systems. That meant they were all stuck and couldn't do anything about the Never.

"They know what's coming," he commented on the many devastating reports on Navy radio and special broadcasts on the news feeds. "But no one wants to voice what it really means."

The braking thrust had already been tormenting them for nearly ten minutes at a brutal 13g, forcibly shifting all communication to the transducer network. Ahead of them, Andal had long since grown into a thumbnail-sized bruise, and even the *Einherjar* orbital ring was visible as a silvery band around its equator.

"It's disconcerting," Lizzy said. "They do broadcast after broadcast, showing the horrific images of the Never, which is already visible to the naked eye in the sky, inviting experts and pretending it's a natural disaster in the distance."

"You can feel the underlying panic," Gino agreed with her. "But yes, they do what people always do when certain doom is upon them: they pretend everything is normal, just another day of problems."

"What else are they going to do?" asked Gavin. "I don't even know how to realize it myself. The end starts in half an hour and there's purely nothing we can do."

"Your father, the governor, seems to have gathered all the remaining ships in orbit and from the looks of it there's a lot of shuttle traffic to the *Einherjar*, I think the planetary defenses are going to put up a fierce defensive fight." Lizzy didn't sound particularly convinced by her words herself, but he merely nodded.

"In some of the special broadcasts, they're talking about evacuations. Where are they going to go?"

"It's like a fire," Gino replied. "When there's a fire, you go to the areas where there's not yet a fire until there's nowhere left."

"What do you think about the forecasts?"

"In half an hour, the first defensive battles start with the forward swarm fighters, half an hour after that, the main body arrives, estimated in the tens of trillions of individual Never elements," Lizzy summarized the reconnaissance broadcasts from the local fleet defenses. "I think is overly optimistic to think that they can buy the evacuation ships even fifteen minutes after the first shot is fired."

Gavin nodded to himself and swallowed, which was almost impossible with his half-squashed esophagus. "They've had less than an hour so far, another half hour won't make any difference either. A planetary evacuation would take days, even if smoothly organized."

"What else is your father going to do? At least this way the population will feel like they can do something."

Would you rather die in fear at home, or in fear with the hope of having at least a small chance of survival? he translated her words, trying not to think about what it must look like on the ground. There, where he had spent his childhood, on the green arcades of Skaland, where on weekends families had picnics or played squashball, the birds sang and all the warmth of the universe seemed to unite. This was how he had always imagined the perfect center of all things, and the thought that shuttles were now landing there to invite frightened families to die somewhere in the outer reaches of the system hit him hard. He thought involuntarily of the video footage of Sergeant Miller and what he had witnessed during the defense of *Turan-II* in the capital *Tarshan*. He remembered the electric buses with waiting civilians who had to keep their children from looking up to the sky where the naked horror waited to engulf them not ten minutes later.

The same thing would now happen to his home and there was absolutely nothing he could do about it.

"There's nothing we can do," he stated with lead in his stomach that didn't come from the insane acceleration forces the *Glory* was using to break down speed against its direction of flight.

"No," Lizzy said in an effortfully controlled voice. "But we can do everything possible to make Marquandt pay for this."

INTERLUDE: AGENT WALKER

Tracking down Dimitri Rogoshin had not been particularly difficult. In her preliminary assessment, he was a vain peacock who liked to make himself the center of attention and let everyone know that he had hunted down the Cazacone on New California virtually single-handedly. People like him, especially a lawyer who seemed to see civil law as an opportunity for advancement rather than a moral guide, were rewarding targets for Walker.

Predictable.

Within a few hours, she'd figured out that he was giving five to six interviews a day, mostly feeds dealing with true crime, history, or organized crime: sometimes for expert talks, sometimes the typical thriller shows, and sometimes simple retrospectives on criminal cases of the past decade with special significance. Rogoshin was by no means a celebrity; his arrogant and professor-like appearance was not suited to that. Rather, he was the one invited because controversy was hoped for. In his role as COO of Warfield, he had built up a considerable network, which was actually far too high-ranking and widespread for such a relatively small corporation, which in fact played no role in the Protectorate and only rotated onto the Corporate Council for one year every twenty years.

He liked to go hunting for rare Hatzach deer on Lapiszunt.

Whether he really enjoyed hunting in bad weather, meager rations, and days of pursuit, she ventured to doubt. She rather guessed that it was a sport for the rich, where he also wanted to belong. Checking off a high-society checklist, just like golf or whiskey tastings.

And being rich and power-obsessed, Dimitri Rogoshin also fulfilled another item on the list for typical upstarts who had 'made it': hyper compensating his will to dominate in professional life and always appear strong and as a decisive decision-maker with a dirty secret. Walker's intuition, after thirty years of undercover work, had not let her down this time either. A few hundred crowns and the right questions in the darker corners of the Zurich arcology had unearthed quite a bit: Rogoshin spent half his time on Earth and the other on Alpha Prime. In Zurich, he left his penthouse in the Hofzacher Plaza Hotel every other night around midnight and took a robotaxi that became untraceable after a while. She had guessed at a white-noise generator and researched which neighborhoods were not yet connected to Gridlink and allowed rides without a transponder at all. There were only two of them left: a poor neighborhood in the south and an extremely disreputable red-light district in the east. So she had taken his photo with her into the milieu and had found what she was looking for after a short time, since she had concentrated on dominas in the highest price segment.

On the way, she had found out that freelancers from Grand Admiral Albius' flagship frequented the same street when their boss was in Zurich to visit the Imperial Palace in the Alps.

She was now sitting with one of the dominas, who went by the sonorous name of Bronja, in the darkened 'study' awaiting Rogoshin's arrival.

Bronja, dressed in a latex costume that showed more than it hid, had her white hair pinned tightly to her scalp so that it showed off the two implanted devil horns that grew from her forehead. With her fangs sharpened, she nervously nibbled on her fingers. As she did so, the red gag ball around her neck bobbed up and down like a bouncy ball.

It was a shameful sight.

The last fleet

"Calm down, this is just going to be a conversation," Walker said, keeping all of her headware turned off so as not to give Rogoshin a heads-up in case he had highly developed ocular augments.

The room they were in was lined with rubber and had a window whose glass was usually electronically blacked out, but she had it open. Street noise drifted up to them from downstairs, a few drunken passersby, a woman trying her hand at a nostalgic tribute to the Solar Union anthem.

The single chair - where Rogoshin was probably normally worked - was now in the corner, serving as Walker's waiting area.

"And you're s-sure the guest knows you?" asked Bronja nervously.

"He'll know me when he sees me."

Five minutes later, the door opened and in walked Dimitri Rogoshin, nearly six feet tall, dressed in a tailored suit that advantageously showed off his well-toned and undoubtedly cosmetically enhanced body. He pulled a Reface mask from his face and set it aside along with a coat he had been wearing over his arm.

"Bronja," he greeted the dominatrix, who merely gave a coo. Then he nodded to Walker. "Agent."

"You're not surprised to see me," she noted. Her experience in worse circles kept her from revealing her surprise with even the twitch of an eyelash. She even ignored the electrifying feeling of being caught, giving her Smartnites a block of adrenal cortices.

"No. You're in my seat," he said.

"Let me guess: You briefed Lowell before his meeting with the First Secretary of State."

"Of course I did," he replied calmly, and began to undress methodically and thoughtfully. Bronja circled him and pulled out a crop as if from nowhere. She slapped him a few times and he didn't even flinch, never averting his eyes from Walker.

"Sensor dust, transferred via handshake?"

"That would be a smart way to go."

Walker pondered where the flaw in the chain was. There was no link of any kind in the Imperial Gardens. Even if Lowell had transmitted sensor dust when he shook hands with Lord

Darishma, as the first secretary of state did on his shoulder, it would not have transmitted until after he left the area. But Darishma was no foolish man and not inexperienced. He had used a white-noise generator.

Until ...

The call from the Emperor, the thought ran through her head. *Of course. After that, the discussion as I left.* A small carelessness, but enough to hear her name and that she would come.

"I understand. But that still doesn't explain why you knew I was coming here. I didn't leave any traces."

"No," Rogoshin admitted, already standing there bare-chested, setting about undressing his pants as if they weren't even there. "You are extremely good, don't blame yourself. But those I work for have connections. I was assured you would find me. At my weak point. This makes you the first person to know about this."

He looked to Bronja, who no longer looked nervous at all and wanted to put the gag ball on him.

"Not yet, mistress. Give me two more minutes. Please."

"ONE!" she yelled at him so abruptly that Walker winced.

"With that, I guess congratulations are in order," Rogoshin continued, expertly folding his underpants before having his underpants follow suit as well and standing stark naked before her. She didn't know what disturbed her more: the way he seemed to ignore her physical presence, or the fact that he was so cool about it.

"So, what do you want to know? That's why you came here, after all, took all this trouble," he asked.

"You negotiated the treaty change on the status of the Seed Systems for the Imperial side so that the Ruhr-controlled system would no longer be a restricted area and allow low levels of through traffic," Walker said. "After that, you switched sides and traded a high post in the Star Empire for a board position in a third-rate mercenary company. Why?"

"Because I want to change the future."

"The future?"

"Yes, that's what I just said."

"What is the deal between you and Yokatami? Why would a megacorporation hire you, of all people?" she echoed, leaning back confidently. He might be arrogant, but apparently didn't know he was dealing with someone who never went into a situation unprepared. "You have nothing to offer that Yokatami doesn't have himself."

"Yes, I do, discretion. No one expects Warfield to do anything important worth a second look. Look at yourself," Rogoshin said, catching a whip. The corner of his right mouth twitched minimally as he did so. "You had the numbers on the table and dismissed it yourself. Once our meeting here is over, that will continue."

"Because you have powerful allies."

"Of course, but you know that now. We are beginning to repeat ourselves, and my mistress is not a particularly forgiving one."

"No, I'm not," the dominatrix purred, slapping his crotch so that he blushed and involuntarily writhed forward.

"Where do you operate?" wanted to know Walker.

"Oh come on," groaned Rogoshin. "You've already figured that far out for yourself, haven't you?"

"Yokatami's Seed System. Restricted area. But you're not even allowed to operate in that as a third party."

"Allowed to." He seemed to taste the word and snorted. "Those are relative words in times like these. I'm surprised you're so naive as an agent of the IIA. But then, you came here to confront me after only a few hours of research and didn't even wonder why it was so easy."

The manager nodded toward the window. "You think your augments are superior, and just in case, you know there's a whole platoon of Grand Admiral Albius' Marines out there right now celebrating and obligated to intervene even when on shore leave and in civilian clothes if a crime is suspected. Except I know that these men and women are under orders to hear nothing, see nothing, and say nothing for the next fifteen minutes."

Walker stiffened.

"Do you know what the biggest problem is that the division

between nobility and commoners has created? Predictability. In your employers' bubble, there is only what may be and never what is unimaginable."

"What do you mean by that?" asked Walker, tensing even further as her neural computer alerted her that its functions had been disrupted by a strong magnetic field after an attempt to start up.

"One way." He waved it off. "My minute is up, and it's time for my punishment, I'm afraid, for I have sinned. Besides, this is my last visit with Bronja - oh, and my only one, by the way."

Walker stood up, slowly, hands splayed away from her body. She knew when violence was in the air, even though Rogoshin still stood naked and motionless, watching her calmly.

"Not me, Agent Walker," he said thoughtfully. "You."

Too late, she turned to face the dominatrix, whose mouth flipped open into a cruel grimace and bared the razor teeth of a modified Servitor before she lunged at her.

8

"*Glory*, this is space flight control. This is your final warning!"

"This is Lord Captain Gavin Andal," Gavin replied in frustration after they had been unable to answer the last three radio transmissions from the flight controllers because their radio transmitter was not working. The fact that the men and women on the Mjölnir had only now come up with the idea of contacting them by directional beam testified to the growing panic that must be prevailing in the space fortress. The long-range defenses had already begun firing torpedoes and missiles at the Never a few light minutes away, filling half the night sky. At regular intervals, hundreds of exhaust flares came to life as the orbital ring launchers and the *Mjölnir* dropped their cruise missiles. It was an act of desperation, no more than a drop of water they threw toward a conflagration.

"Sorry, Lord Captain," came the reply after a short while. They didn't even ask him for his service number. "Welcome home."

"Thank you," he replied curtly, initiating the final reduction of their braking thrust so as not to disrupt orbital space traffic, burning everything that flew by to cinders with their mile-long plasma torch.

The orbital ring grew from a narrow band to a ring, and from this perspective it looked like it always had. He felt as if he had just left with Lizzy for their flight to Skaland. How carefree he had been then. How boastful and small-minded, spoiled and superficial. For him, nothing had counted but to sleep with her like a horny baboon.

Pathetic, he scolded himself. How quickly life had rebuked him.

Andal lay blue and radiant as ever before them, a sight of peaceful bustle with bands of white clouds wandering like flocks of sheep around the equator, drawn along by the Coriolis force. Gavin wondered if it was the last time he would see his home before it was ripped from the universe and disappeared from reality forever.

"I never realized that nothing lasted through the existence of the Never," he said thoughtfully, taking over the manual controls once they had flown into the final vector point that would take them to Skaland to his family's headquarters in the next ten minutes. "Not even a planet that's one of the emerging colonies."

"It's not lost yet," Lizzy reminded him. It was a feeble attempt at consolation, but one that seemed worthless to him when it was true for only the next half hour.

"Captain, we're getting a rerouted directional beam in from the *Mjölnir*," Gino announced.

"Redirected?"

"Yes, it's coming from the surface."

"Put him through."

Gavin's mouth went abruptly dry as he saw on his screen the crest of the Governor of Andal, High Lord Cornelius Andal. Shortly after, it disappeared and instead he saw his father, standing behind a desk, just handing out hand terminals with deliberate but quick movements and leaving his thumbprint on others.

"Father?" he asked, feeling pressure building behind his eyes.

"Ah, Gavin!" Cornelius Andal turned to the camera and shooed someone away. He looked tired, older and worn out. "I thank the Lord that you are still alive."

"Father, Artas, he ..."

"I know, son, I know." His father jutted his chin and inhaled sharply. "Listen to me, I'm organizing the evacuations right now. We can only move a few civilians away, but I want you to lead them."

"But to where? Fleet Admiral Marquandt has disabled all jump drives. That traitor left them all for dead!"

"We have to try. We'll send away everyone we can at sub-light speed. The Emperor will see to it that the civilian fleet is saved, even if it takes some time. My job now, and that of our remaining military, is to keep the Never tied up here as long as we can so that the ships have as much of an acceleration advantage as possible."

"Wait a minute, does that mean you're not going yourself?" asked Gavin.

"I'm needed here to coordinate everything until... until operations are complete."

"You can't. You're the head of our house!"

"No, son, you will be."

"What about Mom?"

"She's decided to stay here with me."

Gavin wanted to scream and cry at the same time, but forced the tears down because his father expected strength from him now and certainly had enough problems to deal with already.

"Elisa? Mariella? Where are they?" he asked as controlled as possible, trying hard to sound like the leader Cornelius Andal wanted and needed to see in him now.

"They are at Skaland Castle. You have to pick them up there, do you understand? There's an automatic no-fly zone around our estate, enforced by the robot batteries. So you have to land outside and get them. After that, head to the Port Wogingen spaceport and board the *Palace*. Your escort will be waiting on the side of the planet facing away from Never," his father explained the next steps to him, making a dismissive gesture when someone wanted something from him again. "We won't be able to see each other again, Gavin. I'll be at the Governor's Palace, and I'll stay here with your mother until we finalize everything."

Until it's all over, Gavin translated in his mind.

"I... I understand."

"Your mother is taking care of the incoming Evac buses right now, I'll try to reach her so she can still contact you. I love you, son. Be strong now. I know what you're made of and that I don't have to worry about you recognizing it and always doing your best." His father gave him one last, long look, then nodded and disconnected.

"I love you, too," Gavin whispered to the black holoimage, which again had the governor's logo rotating on it.

There was dead silence on the bridge until he finally stood up and gripped the flightstick with his right hand. "Commencing entry maneuver."

"Where are we flying to?" Lizzy inquired.

"Skaland Castle. We're rescuing my sisters and then we're evacuating with the *Palace*, which is our family yacht," he explained.

"But evacuate to where?"

"Away from here. Unless either of you have a better idea ...?"

No one said anything.

"Thought so."

Their route to Skaland took them over a much longer vector this time, since the *Glory* was atmospheric-capable, but only like a rocket. That meant they had to veer into a trajectory that was the perfect compromise of air braking and speed, so they didn't bounce off the atmosphere. Accordingly, they were jolted violently as the first flames licked across the hull, burning the outer layers of air at 15,000 miles per hour.

Shortly thereafter, they cleared the barrier and the roar disappeared along with the ignited gas molecules. The air ahead of the bow cameras cleared, showing them the deep blue southern ocean through their virtual windshield. Far to the west, a massive cyclone rotated around its dark eye, flashing.

Their course took them north, past the equatorial orbital updraft glittering like a spider's thread in the east, and past dozens of personnel shuttles on their way to what they thought was a rescue orbit, to the side currently facing away from Never. Then the continent of Bragi came into view, a pleasing landmass with long sandy beaches that from their height looked like expressionist brushstrokes by an inspired painter. Next came the grasslands of Skyr, the breadbasket of the planet, with their monolithic vertical farms jutting out of the landscape as green fingers. Finally, the Fardinger Alps, a mighty mountain range that nearly split the continent in half. Gavin had spent a fortnight there every winter skiing and hiking with his family. He fondly remembered the hearty meals in front of the roaring log fires of the cabins and the stunning panoramas.

Soon all of that would fade into nothingness, faded into a painful memory of those who had once been there.

Beyond the Fardinger Alps began the rolling hills of Norge National Park, stretching to the ice seas and of such rugged beauty that half of the Star Empire's movie dramas were set there.

And then Skaland came into view, the planetary capital of Andal, situated on the Bay of Rustvard to the west, still far enough from the eternal snow and ice and framed by crenellated mountains. The castle was to the south, located a mile from the foothills in a gated park that resembled an oversized golf course. Gavin had the computer mark the defensive zone, which had already sent them automated warning messages from the robot batteries.

"We'll go down there by the intersection, right in front of the entrance," he decided, shifting the flightstick slightly forward and to the right accordingly.

"That's an expressway, isn't it?" asked Lizzy, as if he had to understand from the question alone that it wasn't allowed to do that.

"Yes, the ring road goes once around all of Skaland and is part of the grid link. That is shut down in the event of a national emergency, because then the Civil Protection or the military take control of the traffic, depending on the cause of the threat," he explained. "So there's no traffic."

"I hope you're right, otherwise we're about to melt down a lot of vehicles."

"There will be a curfew by now," he was sure, checking the last landing vector and then handing over to the on-board computer, which immediately began the landing maneuver. He threw the *Glory* around its transverse axis and turned it one hundred and eighty degrees until the powerful engines pointed downward and gave their all once again for the final brake thrust. Their roar reached all the way to the bridge and the forces at work shook them back and forth in their gimbaled seats.

The distance indicator to the ground melted away rapidly, then slower and slower as the landing racks extended and plasma flames spread across the hardened smart-asphalt and faded as smoke. Finally, a jolt went through the ship and the thrusters shut down.

"And that," Lizzy said, "is how you end up in a crossroads with one of His Majesty's corvettes."

Gavin merely grumbled, unable to laugh at her attempt at a joke because all he could think about were his two sisters who were now counting on him.

"Gino, you stay on the *Glory* and make sure she's ready to go as soon as we get back. It won't take more than ten minutes," he said in the direction of his fire control officer as he unstrapped himself and headed for the door. "Lizzy?"

"Right behind you, Captain."

He climbed down the corridor toward the airlock, where he grabbed an Inferno off the wall and loaded it through. At Lizzy's questioning look, he said, "Better safe than sorry."

"With the 0g ammo?"

"Still enough to scare crazed civilians." He didn't mention the Never, just tried to block it out so he could even think straight.

Elisa and Mariella, he reminded himself as he pressed the button on the outer hatch, which retracted into the hull. The ladder automatically unwound, hardened, and allowed them to descend the ten yards to the ground, where the asphalt was blackened with soot.

Gavin sucked in the air that smelled of freshly cut grass; it was cool and pure, free of ozone and acrid sealant. Then he motioned to the road ahead of them, which ended in a large gate above which two Sentinel drones were circling, already targeting them. One of them apparently scanned his face and lowered its machine gun in response.

"Captain?" asked Lizzy behind him, and something about her voice made him sit up and take notice.

"No time, we need to get up to the estate fast." He tapped around on his handheld terminal until he had the automatic identification open and then pressed his thumb on the DNA scanner panel. The gate began to slide aside.

"Gavin?"

"What is it?"

"Gav!"

"I said we..." He whirled around to face her angrily and saw that she was staring upward into the darkening evening sky with her head on the back of her neck. She held the rifle in one hand with the barrel toward the ground. Gavin reflexively followed her gaze before his mind could intervene, and immediately regretted it.

The entire sky was covered in a dirty brown that looked as grim and apocalyptic as if the universe were on fire. Because the central star illuminated the Never, the swarms seemed to glow from within like purgatory itself. Gavin immediately felt like he was trapped on a planet doomed to die. Then the explosions began. They made their start along the shimmering band of the *Einherjar* orbital ring, short-lived blooms of heat. A few at first, then more and more. Silvery bullet trails stretched across the sky, glowing plasma discharges mingling with the exhaust flares of the space fleet as it braced for the invasion, buying time for the civilians on the ground.

"Quick!" he shouted, turning on his heel and running down the street toward the family residence, its red roof rising behind one of the hills. After so long under violent acceleration, his body felt like a piece of cloth put through the wringer without any cohesion.

"If they're already fighting in orbit, we only have minutes before the first reaches of the Never reach the surface," Lizzy shouted behind him, breathing heavily, but he ignored her and kept running until his lungs burned.

As he came over the hill, the horseshoe-shaped estate spread out before him. In front of it, the driveway described a sweeping loop. A single vehicle was parked there and several people had just come running out of the main entrance, heading for the stairs that led to the car.

"Elisa! Mariella!" he shouted loudly, waving to indicate that they should head in his direction. Behind them stood Meinhard. He identified the court servant by the red tattoo that stretched across his bald skull.

Meinhard spotted him and pointed in his place, then shooed his sisters toward the vehicle as a loud screech sounded. Only after some delay did he recognize it as the planetary air alarm that echoed across the hillside. It seemed to fill the entire air, creating a dystopian atmosphere of doom, shortly followed by the rattle of the numerous anti-aircraft guns installed all around Skaland. The western defense center, which had been built into the mountains above the city, sent out the first missile salvos. Their dozens of roars sounded like the snarls of predatory cats.

Gavin spun around, feeling like he was standing in the middle of a nightmare that threatened to overwhelm his senses. Bits of Never were falling out of the sky everywhere, huge monsters with clawed tentacles, smaller ones with leathery wings, others that looked like green boils and burst into poisonous rain when hit by anti-aircraft guns. Where missiles exploded, the blast waves shattered the sparse clouds as if they were shying away from the violence. Laser beams cut through the air for seconds, fragmenting what they hit and crossing over many times to form an intricate pattern that persisted on Gavin's retinas.

Then the first Never creatures struck, erratic shapes of bizarre form, none resembling the other. Like brown tumors, they surged down from orbit, emitting bloodcurdling screams that filled the darkness like the cries of banshees and other nightmarish creatures. An impact nearby made the ground shake beneath his feet. He looked up at a cloud of smoke and dust over the west wing of the castle. The tower that had stood there before was now just a ruin, with brown slime oozing out of it, followed by a dozen dog-sized entities swarming out in all directions.

Gavin began firing at them, but was followed by another impact in the main building, which the estate's automatic

The last fleet

defenses had failed to intercept. Others were torn apart while still inbound by batteries in the hills or drones buzzing around, firing rattling machine guns at anything that moved through the air.

"GO!" he yelled as loud as he could as his sisters finally jumped into the car and Meinhard typed something on his terminal.

The car was about to drive off when one of the dog-sized entities jumped at the valet from the shadows and snapped him in half.

"Gav!" shouted Lizzy from behind him. Her voice barely cut through the din of defensive fire, screeching Never, and the explosions from the city behind them, where the defenses could no longer hold off the onslaught. 'Above us!"

He heard the distinct sound of her *Inferno* rifle and looked up. An entity as large as a house was swooping down on them, illuminated by the headlights of a defense battery presumably installed somewhere on the outskirts of the city. An X-ray laser sliced the Never in half, spraying black blood. Machine guns shredded the piece facing the city, and the other, a growth of flailing tentacles and clawed arms, continued to fall toward the estate.

On my way, he thought, taking aim and firing in automatic mode at the creature. The missile projectiles hit, leaving bloody craters on its 'skin', but the bulk of it crashed like a sack of flesh onto the vehicle in which his sisters had just set off toward him. It simply disappeared under the slime into which the entity dissolved.

"NO!" he roared, unable to believe his eyes. "No, no, no!"

"Gav!" Lizzy suddenly appeared beside him and grabbed him by the shoulder, pulling him back. He could not turn away, though, watching the slime spread like a boil. Screams of house servants stuck in the mansion, presumably being eaten or worse, reached his ears, though he could not comprehend them. The outline of the car became visible under the living mass that reeked of decay, and then it abruptly disappeared.

"GAV!" roared Lizzy in his ear, yanking him back so hard he almost fell. But his body's reflex to keep from falling cleared his

135

head enough to overcome his shock and follow her. They ran for their lives as if possessed, while all around them the next wave of entities crashed into the hills.

The city in front of them was an inferno. Tracer rounds and lasers crisscrossed the rooftops in such density that the sky was lit up almost as bright as day. Explosions flashed here and there, mingling with the flickering of the many fires that had erupted. Although the shield of gunfire seemed impenetrable, turning the airspace into a chaos of shredded biomass that was impossible to see through, a cocoon of turmoil lay over the city. The Never had made it onto the streets and into the houses, he was sure of it.

A shadow struck in front of them, making the earth tremble and asphalt shatter. Gavin almost lost his footing, but caught himself and shot a full volley into the fanged mouth that leapt toward him from the cloud of earth and debris. He largely evaded the flying fragments and kept moving towards the *Glory*, which towered like a monument on the crossroads a hundred yards in front of them. He saw Gino's figure at the airlock, handling some kind of winch with a white sack hanging from the end.

"Gino, what are you doing?" he asked over Transducer.

"I'm lowering the damn Orb," the fire control officer replied. "We're not going anywhere with the *Glory*!"

Just as he said *'Glory,'* an entity punched through the bow where the bridge had been before, splitting the corvette like a guillotine. The ship swayed and Gino lost his footing. He plunged out of the open hatch ten yards to the asphalt, where an entity jumped at his broken body and took hold. Slime spread rapidly over him, and Gavin saw the tortured face of his comrade, who looked in his direction before disappearing.

Gavin, like Lizzy at his side, roared out his helpless anger and fired at the entity until the magazine was empty.

"Gino," she said in disbelief as they reached the spot where he had just disappeared. A small bloodstain marked the spot and was the last evidence of his existence.

"The Orb," Gavin said, wiping a tear from the corner of his eye. Whether it came from mere anger at fate or grief, he couldn't say. He grabbed one corner of the vacuum bag in which the alien

The last fleet

corpse was preserved and waited until Lizzy had snatched the other corner before they pulled on it and walked toward the outer apartment blocks of Skaland. "We'll take a car and head for the harbor. The *Palace* is our last chance now."

"A car? How are we going to ..."

"Just pull," he interrupted her.

The vacuum bag made an ugly scraping sound as they dragged the creature across the asphalt. Fortunately, for its estimated size of just under ten feet, it wasn't particularly heavy.

A few minutes later they reached the first parked car, a standard electric SUV from the local factories, miraculously unmolested by other entities already howling and screaming on the hills behind them.

"How are we supposed to get the car...," Lizzy resumed, breathing heavily, as the back hatch opened.

"Priority codes," he explained, wiggling his wrist terminal.

"I usually hate that term. But not anymore," she found, helping him load the dead Orb into the trunk. "Now we just have to make it to the port. Piece of cake, right?"

9

"Doesn't this thing go any faster?" asked Lizzy as they drove deeper into the city.

"My family's priority code - which the highest officials, police and military have - unlocks the on-board computer and interlock, but doesn't give me superhuman abilities."

She made a frustrated noise, but said nothing more.

Gavin didn't respond and instead focused on the road. There were only a few cars in the designated loading parking spaces, which were marked by slightly darker asphalt. The Gridlink, whose systems were connected to the intelligent road surface, had long since been turned off, so at least he wasn't getting warnings about manual steering. No one drove with a steering wheel and accelerator pedal, not for centuries, except perhaps in emergencies. That's why Gavin was glad his father had let him drive his Golf Caddy when he was a kid, and he knew what he was doing, at least roughly. Still, he didn't dare speed and risk crashing the car.

That would probably be the crowning achievement of the day, he thought dejectedly. He had no illusions: At the moment, he was held together only by adrenaline and confusion. Once he had a quiet moment, his existence would simply end. At least, that's how it felt. Pain lurked like a shadow in his mind, already spreading now that they were in the car and the oppressive sounds from outside were just muffled bass thumps.

"What happened to being careful?" asked Lizzy anxiously as he pressed on the accelerator.

"No time," he said merely, racing faster and faster through the canyons of buildings. The buildings that lined the tree-flanked street here in the outer suburbs had several stories of ornate facades, from which brown Never was already flowing here and there, spreading in growing patches. He tried not to look at the windows, tried to block out what suffering was going on behind them.

An entity sliced through the air in front of them, and Gavin had to yank the steering wheel hard to the right to avoid colliding with it as it crashed into a storefront, incinerating the entire building with its kinetic energy. A cursory glance in the rearview mirror showed him countless smaller entities on four legs leaping out of the crater and splitting up to spread their terror.

When he reached the Road of Human Peace, which bisected Skaland and led six lanes to the Governor's Palace, suddenly everything was full of military. The army had sealed off its access road and apparently set up gun nests and mobile air defenses behind it. Soldiers ran back and forth between them, taking civilians to makeshift shelters in the form of large white tents.

"Freeze!" shouted one of the soldiers at the roadblock in an electronically amplified voice. One of the two tanks lining the barriers swung its Gauss gun in their direction.

Gavin pressed the window button as he nearly touched the side of the truck with the hood, which had apparently been placed across the roadway as some sort of improvised gate.

"I am Lord Captain of the Navy," he called out, putting his service code on the air via wrist terminal.

The soldier, a sergeant in an olive drab Army uniform, came running to his window and looked him in the face. As he checked the code, his eyes widened. Gavin wondered if this man even knew what he was in for if he was worried now about who he was facing.

The last fleet

"Excuse me, my lord." The sergeant made a circling hand gesture above his head, whereupon the truck was pulled aside.

"We need to get to the port," Gavin said.

"The Peace Road is completely sealed off, my lord," the man bellowed over the din of battle, as the deep roar of Gauss guns and the hundred-fold rattle of assault rifles grew louder somewhere behind him. "You can drive through to the harbor, but I don't know how much time you have left. The enemy is carrying out a massive attack on the city and the orbit is already lost."

So fast, Gavin thought in horror.

"I'm marking your vehicle in Battlenet for top clearance, my lord." The soldier stepped back and hurriedly waved him on.

"Thank you," he muttered, then drove through the narrow gap that had been cleared between the barriers.

Behind it was an even busier scene than he had been able to discern from the outside: The five-mile road connected the governor's palace on the slopes of the mountains on one side and the sea on the other. Normally, one could see from one end to the opposite, and the two-hundred-yard-wide roadway directions were a sublime sight. But now everything was full of tents to which civilians were being directed while guns thundered around them. All access roads to the right and left were blocked off by heavily armed soldiers and tanks. Anti-aircraft batteries were parked at regular intervals on mobile mounts, incessantly spewing their ammunition into the inflamed sky. His father had apparently pulled together most of the Home Guard to defend the city's core and keep its citizens together, rather than fight for each neighborhood.

A wise decision, Gavin estimated, but even that couldn't save them. Just as he hadn't been able to keep Elisa and Mariella safe.

He glanced briefly at the *Palace* at the end of the streets, a great white blur on the dark horizon, repeatedly illuminated by laser fire and tracer ammunition and bathed in harsh contours. An extremely defeatist, pain-ridden part of him wanted to go there and die with his parents. But there was also another part that was filled with rage as he thought of Marquandt and his Wall

Fleet jumping out of the system. It was that part that made him drive to the left, toward the harbor.

Anti-aircraft fire formed a dense trellis across the road, picking off anything that approached, but the Never was already forming an impenetrable mass above them. Like a blanket, the plethora of entities lay over the city, sinking lower and lower. The outer neighborhoods were apparently already overrun, for the soldiers and tanks at the cordoned-off entrances were already firing non-stop between the houses into the darkness.

"Gav," Lizzy said softly. In their car, which blocked out much of the noise and seemed to push through the horror like a parallel world, there was something oppressive about her voice.

"Huh?" he said absently, steering around a flak battery whose muzzle flashes left glaring afterimages on his retinas.

"We're not going to make it, are we?"

"Don't give up," he retorted angrily. "We *must* keep going. We *must* make it. We've already lost too much for it all to be for nothing, you hear me?"

He was aware that his words sounded like a clichéd movie quote that he didn't even believe himself. But what other choice did he have?

"Look out!" she shouted shrilly, and he slammed on the brakes as a large entity penetrated the air defense screen and crashed into the middle of a tent from which some civilians were trying to escape. Soldiers immediately poured in and covered the crater with continuous fire before anything could emerge from the smoke and dust.

Gavin continued driving, honking loudly as a platoon of soldiers ran in front of them, and then accelerated even further, although he was worried about accidentally killing someone. A few minutes later, another hit one of the houses that lined the streets. The rain of debris buried an entire platoon of the Home Guard, which at first had trouble gathering itself as it was overrun by a wave of entities spilling out of the rubble. He did not see what became of the people as he changed lanes and drove around a tent to a longer open stretch where all the soldiers were standing and fighting at the barricades. Here and there the first entities were already breaking through and going into hand-to-hand combat.

The defense gradually became a slaughter. They finally narrowly escaped two more impacts and breakthroughs, and then reached a short open stretch where at the end there were the gates of the industrial port, its cranes jutting out of the shoreline in the unsteady light of battle like the bizarre claws of a giant creature.

"Gav! GATE!", Lizzy warned him, but he didn't even think to stop and send his code first. Instead, he swerved off the road onto the short grassy strip beside it and cut through the chain-link fence. He was banking on the fact that all the police drones were busy defending the city, not trespassing.

In any case, they were not shot immediately.

"Where is your ship?" asked Lizzy. "The harbor is huge!"

"At the private dock, we have to get on the distributor road in front of the container area for that." He pointed ahead and passed two unmanned control booths when all at once the power went out and the entire harbor was plunged into darkness. Only the battle behind them still provided a little light, occasionally illuminating the facades of large warehouses and the skeletons of distribution stations where trucks were loaded and unloaded.

The landing field for airships, which was to their right, lit up as bright as day for a moment as one of the cargo hulks was hit by an entity, ending in a massive fireball that quickly spread to the others. The flames spread furiously, and each explosion sent a deep thunderclap across the area that shook the windows of their vehicle.

Gavin turned left at the next opportunity. He had lost all orientation, but remembered that the private part of the harbor was on the left, and as long as he could still see the cranes, at least the direction was clear. He swerved at the last second to avoid an autonomous loading bot that was folded up on the asphalt and scraped along its flank. The car protested with an ugly squeal, then he turned right to get onto the distributor road, only to find that it was the entrance to a warehouse. Before he realized it, they were almost directly in front of the large double gate.

"Is that light?" asked Lizzy incredulously.

He saw it, too: between the cracks in the gate, it shone a warm yellow. Since the flaming airship port here was shielded by another warehouse on the right, the long yellow line stood out clearly.

"How is that possible? The power's out!" he thought aloud, and was about to put the car in reverse when there was a deafening bang and the car went out.

"Shots fired!" Lizzy said, ducking behind the dashboard. Gavin saw the big hole in the front hood and looked for his Inferno rifle, but he had thrown it in the back seat and couldn't reach it. Desperately, he tried to restart the car. To no avail. All the systems were dead, so the battery must have been punctured.

But who was going to fire on them?

"We have to leave!" he said, opening his door. Lizzy did the same on the other side, but had her rifle in her hand, which she had kept between her legs during the trip.

"Don't take another step!" he heard a gruff voice beside him as he looked directly into the muzzle of a heavy pistol. The hand holding the gun belonged to a woman about his age, wearing a police uniform with gold sequins. However, the blond hair combed to the side with the undercut on the right side told him that it was not a very credible cover.

"Take care of them and get in here! We're out of time!" another person barked from the direction of the gate. Gavin didn't dare look in their direction, but guessed it was the one who had crippled their battery with a bullet through it.

"Captain, I've got a problem here," Lizzy called from behind him.

"So do I, put your weapon down, that's an order," he replied, slowly raising his arms. "Hold your fire."

"Sorry, handsome, but our day can't get any shittier," the woman in the fake uniform replied, about to pull the trigger.

"Wait! We've got an Orb in the trunk!"

His counterpart blinked a few times. "Excuse me?"

"We have an orb in the trunk. A dead body, actually," he repeated.

"Shit, I've heard a lot of them begging for their lives, but

The last fleet

they've never been this creative." She shook her head and pressed the barrel of the gun against his forehead.

"I'm not lying. Go see for yourself!" Gavin was getting angry. Angry that he had to deal with criminals in the face of an invasion by the Never that had killed, or was still killing, his entire family. Growling, he added, "You sons of bitches!"

The woman's response was different than expected and she smirked before motioning him at gunpoint to go to the trunk.

"You don't know who I am," he said as he circled the vehicle. The adrenaline in his veins wanted to drive him to run, anywhere, because they had no time. The battle was just about to be lost for good, and the fact that the port hadn't yet been hit as hard as the rest of the city was akin to a miracle.

"I don't give a shit who you are." The woman poked him in the back with the barrel of her pistol to make him hurry up. On the other side, Lizzy came around the rear of the vehicle, her arms also raised and her expression was a mirror of his own anger and frustration.

"I'm sorry, Captain," she said.

"It's all right." He opened the trunk. When the hatch went up, it was dark until something exploded in the air above them in the distance - presumably an anti-aircraft missile-and lit up the scene long enough for the milky vacuum bag to show. The Orb's clawed feet and face with breathing holes pressed against the plastic and were sufficiently visible that he could hear the woman gasping for air.

Lizzy gave Gavin a quick glance and then winked at him. Before he could react, she whirled around and went to grab the gun of the man behind her, who was momentarily distracted by the sight of the alien. They wrestled with each other like animals gone wild until a shot rang out and Lizzy slumped to the ground. As she did so, she snatched the submachine gun from her opponent's hands.

"LIZZY!" shouted Gavin, lunging forward regardless of the gunmen behind him. The guy in the peaked cap who had fired at them tried to grab his gun back, but Gavin was faster. He grabbed the cold grip, yanked it upward, and emptied the entire magazine with a long-drawn-out scream that contained all his anger at all the gods that had ever existed. Lizzy's killer wriggled under the impact of the bullets and was jerked backward.

Someone was firing at Gavin, for he heard the whistle of several projectiles narrowly missing him. He didn't care. Nor did he have an ear for the voice yelling "cease fire" behind him.

He dropped to his knees beside Lizzy and held her head. Dark blood bubbled from her mouth and ran over her lips. Her eyes were wide as he watched her life drain from them.

"Hey," he said. He would have liked to beg her not to leave him alone, too, but in the end some residual empathy in him won out and he wrestled a tear-veiled smile from himself. "It's okay. I'm with you."

"G-G-Gav..." she gasped, and he stroked her cheeks. As he did so, he smudged fresh blood on them.

"I'm here. Everything is okay."

As the spark of life disappeared from her eyes, her features relaxed.

Not you, too, he thought, slumping. "Not you, too."

"I said stop shooting!" the woman behind him barked. Gavin felt a pain somewhere on his cheek, but it barely penetrated his consciousness.

"He shot Roger!" a second voice protested.

"He did, and I'd like to put a bullet in his skull for that, but look at his fucking collar! How do you expect to get out of here without a pilot?"

"Oh."

"Yeah, oh. Now grab that fucking vacuum bag and get it on board, I'll make sure this asshole here gets us out of here."

Gavin was grabbed by the collar and roughly dragged to his feet. He tried desperately to get a grip on Lizzy's hands and break free when he couldn't - resulting in a blow to his ribs that forced all the air out of his lungs.

"There's nothing more you can do for her, you son of a bitch. If you don't want me out here picking you off like a pig, you better get your shit together!"

"I don't care," he muttered dazedly. The darkness before him

The last fleet

spun in circles into a kaleidoscope of pale colors and nausea. He threw up even as he stumbled forward, caught on the car's fender, and nearly fell as he was pushed along.

The gates of the large warehouse were pushed open a crack and the light that shone from inside blinded him so much that it hurt his eyes.

"Hellcat, see if you can get in! We're about to have the whole thing blowing up in here!" someone shouted from inside. The voice boomed so much that Gavin felt reminded of a riot bot's speakers.

By the time his eyes adjusted to the brightness, he was already in the middle of the warehouse. At first he thought it was empty, until he looked down at the floor, where there was a recess that had apparently been closed with large flaps that now stood open like wings. Hidden in the long shaft was a Sphinx-type light attack frigate, which he immediately recognized by its shape: square hull, four thrusters ending in large funnels at the aft end, round armor plates on the black hull where the retracted guns were located, and the bow with its flat snout where the heavy Carbin armor was thickest. Sensor phalanges protruded with their tips to the right and left of it, but were apparently not extended. The forward air lock of the one-hundred-yard-long, penultimate-generation warship was ten yards aft of the bow and stood open like the hatch of a submarine. A muscle-bound figure with a bald skull and smudged undershirt peered out of it and waved impatiently at them before disappearing inside.

"What is this?" he asked, still dazed.

"Your lucky day, because you get to take us out of here."

"This is a forty-year-old ship. What unit do you belong to?"

The woman behind him merely replied with a resounding laugh.

INTERLUDE: JANUS

"What do you have so far, Janus?" the Emperor asked.

"Albius and Marquandt have something connecting them, but I can't tell yet if it's actually a feud, a grudging partnership of convenience, or a friendship they're trying to keep secret. I don't know."

"That's not much. In fact, nothing at all."

"I know, forgive me, Your Majesty," he apologized, glancing at the hologram on his desk.

"No, that's all right, you haven't had much time so far. That's of secondary importance for now anyway. Paris is the real issue. Mayor Sapin is very worried that there will be a riot because the people and the state alike are frustrated with the fragile security situation," the Emperor said.

"You should not rush to any snap decisions, Your Majesty," Janus recommended. "Military intervention in Paris would set a precedent that would potentially harm you for a long time to come. Terrorists and Senate Republicans might interpret it as weakness and act more brashly. A first crack in your crown, if you will."

"That's my concern, too. But I have a responsibility to the people of this arcology. I can't just leave them to the brutality of these terrorists. How did they even manage to smuggle a vacuum bomb into the inner city?"

"I don't know, but I'll look into it, too. Mayor Sapin has already made staffing changes, suspending the city's police chief and half a dozen of his confidants."

"Good, keep an eye on that for me. I need options for action." The holographic image of the Emperor nodded at him and then disappeared.

Janus stared into space for a while longer, then fell back into his chair with a sigh. He ran his hands through his hair and paused with the heels of his hands over his eyes, blocking out his surroundings for a moment of quiet.

"Nancy?" he asked after a while. His intercom activated itself and contacted his secretary in the anteroom.

"Yes, Mr. Darishma?"

"Any feedback from Agent Walker?"

"No, unfortunately not yet."

"Let me know if you hear anything from her or the IIA." In their last brief exchange, the agent had informed him that she had found an opportunity to meet her target away from eyes and ears and generate answers. That had been several hours ago now. Also, inquiries with IIA Director Antonelli himself had merely revealed that Walker was unavailable, but that would be perfectly normal for a covert operation.

Janus now saw a few more question marks he could work off. He couldn't shake the feeling that he was on to something. There was still the question of why Fleet Admiral Marquandt, of all people, had been notified of the discovery of the three Never swarms by the deep space listening station in the far corner of the Sigma Quadrant. Or why Albius had not seized the command of the prestigious defense of Andal himself and let his rival take the reins. And why had both of them been the only ones from the Council of Admiralty to invest early in the terraforming project near the Seed Traverse, but no one else? And then, of all things, two Border Lords on the other side of the Star Empire?

Janus turned his chair so that he could look down on Earth through the window. Just then a toxic cyclone was passing over the Asian continent, a dirty brown-yellow gyre of clouds, its eye like the lens of a visor showing the megaplex Hyderabad. From the distance of space, it was easy to see mere outlines of a city so large that it could be seen from orbit even in daylight. Not the one hundred million people who lived in it and were just squatting in their housing units, praying that none of their windows would burst and whip acid rain on them. Or the many animals that roamed the lower levels that never saw the sunlight and would drown or be burned by the torrents of toxic precipitation. It was easy to live in his luxurious bubble of power and see every problem as just a number, black on white pixels. But every one of them he took on possessed far-reaching consequences for someone else. How could it be to always remember that without despairing?

I could contact him, he thought, and at the same time felt ashamed that the possibility had even occurred to him. The very thought felt like a betrayal of his master. His past was locked away and hidden in an extremely dark area of his memory that he had no intention of ever letting light shine into again.

10

"You're filthy rebels!" Gavin snarled, and spat.

His captor, who apparently went by the call sign *Hellcat*, merely snorted behind him and pushed him onto the walkway improvised from wooden slats that led from the dusty warehouse floor to the open airlock of the light frigate.

"We're Republicans, golden boy," she corrected him, holding him by the collar as he was about to lose his balance and plummet. Somewhere nearby there had been an impact that made the boards tremble.

"You can call yourselves whatever you want, but you're terrorists," he said.

"One man's terrorist is another man's freedom fighter. Now shut the fuck up or I'll change my mind."

"I hardly think so," he countered grimly. "I sent your pilot to the afterlife, so good luck if you want to try it on your own."

He couldn't see her, but her silence was reaction enough for him and triggered a spark of satisfaction. If he'd had the chance, she would have been the next to get lead poisoning. He even felt something like a cruel desire at the thought.

If she had anything else to say, she apparently refrained from saying it and pushed him roughly toward the open hatch when she thought he was walking too slowly.

I'll never get out of here without those bastards, he thought. *And once I get control of the ship, we'll see.*

He climbed up the obviously retrofitted ladder and climbed down.

"When you get down, go all the way to the back. On the old frigates, the bridge is in the belly of the ship by the transverse axis," the woman explained.

"I know where the bridge of a *Sphinx* is." He looked up at her and down the barrel of her pistol, and she shrugged.

Down in the central corridor, a second woman awaited him, and he involuntarily flinched at the sight of her. She towered over him by half a head and was so muscular and broad that even Gavin, with his considerable body size and height, certainly felt like a runt. Her face was broad, her nose depressed and as ugly as the night. Moreover, she apparently had no body hair at all, not even eyebrows. He could only tell her sex from the fact that two flat breasts were visible under her smeared undershirt.

"You shot Roger up?" she asked in a neutral voice.

"Yes, and I would..." He didn't get any further than that, as she slapped him across the face so suddenly and with such lightning speed that he was smashed against the wall and slid down it, gasping.

"DODGER!" scolded Hellcat from above. "He's our pilot! I swear to you, if you killed him..."

"Just a little slap," She defended herself, grabbing Gavin by the lapels and effortlessly pulling him to his feet with one hand. "I felt we should get that out of the way."

Gavin merely groaned dazedly in response. His face felt as if hot flames were spreading from his nose in all directions.

The mutant - he had no doubt she was from the Zeus line for planetary combat - tore two pieces of cloth from her shirt and stuffed them into his nostrils.

"Now off to the cockpit with you," she ordered. When he again managed only a groan, still struggling for direction, she grabbed him by the collar with a sigh and dragged him behind her. "Don't cry about it. If it had been up to me, I would have bashed your skull in until there was nothing but mush left."

The last fleet

The mutant stuffed him a short time later through the hatch to the bridge, which was a circular room at the heart of the frigate, surrounded by a cocoon of heavily armored Carbin. Six gimbaled seats that could be converted to cots faced outward, where consoles were arranged in a circle. He remembered the rail system on the floor that could automatically change the seats of each division officer - perhaps an innovation in the days when *Sphinx* frigates had been built.

Here and now, however, he had no sense of nostalgia, unlike his last stay on the same type of ship, and sighed with relief as he dropped into the pilot's seat and reflexively buckled himself in.

"Good boy," the mutant commented.

"Your *friend* murdered my girlfriend," Gavin said in her direction. "And if you touch me again, I will kill you."

He expected her to laugh at him, but instead she met his gaze impassively, eyed him disparagingly, and smirked before strapping herself into a seat behind him.

The one who had been addressed as *Hellcat* came in next, dropping like a monkey from the last ladder rung and yelling upward, "Bambam! Strap that piece of shit down somewhere and get down here, we're taking off right now or we're toast!"

She came to the first officer's seat next to Gavin and strapped herself in. Then she pointed her index finger at him as if to impale him.

"You! Get us out of here!"

"When did you turn on the reactor core?" asked Gavin, grumbling. His nose felt like a field of debris and blood was still running into his mouth. He spat it carelessly aside. If anyone wanted to complain later because his bodily fluids were leaking from his face, he would advise them to stop hitting him.

"I don't know, ten minutes ago or so. Why?" asked Hellcat.

"Thank God."

"Huh?"

"All jump thrusters were shut down on the software side. All over the system. But that was a while back. If your ship was offline, it won't have received the transmission," he explained absently as he powered up the secondary systems and carelessly acknowledged and wiped away the holographic pre-flight checklist. It didn't work because he didn't have authorization.

"The code is..."

"Priority code, Lord Captain Gavin Andal," he said aloud.

"Priority code accepted, Lord Captain," the ship's AI core replied. Another nostalgic experience he wished was under different circumstances.

"Shit," marveled his seatmate. "The governor's son? Did you hear that, Dodger? You rearranged the mug of the fucking high lord's son!"

"Oh well," she said simply. "I still didn't like his nose."

Hellcat chuckled maliciously. Instead of saying anything back, he overrode the ship's root system so that it would listen exclusively to his commands and no other user accounts could be created without his approval. Let them see for themselves what it was like when he had full control.

He powered up the engines to maximum power and activated the maneuvering thrusters. Their use in the atmosphere would rapidly deplete their cold gas supplies, but they had no choice, so he fired the lower and lateral ones.

The ship began to shake and groan. The entire structure was making unhealthy noises like a rusted-through machine being moved for the first time in centuries. Which, after all, was not far from the truth.

They broke through the roof of the warehouse, which was shredded by the upward propelled mass of the frigate, and then it stood up. As soon as the navigation display showed him the green crosshairs in the center of the intersecting longitudinal and transverse axes, he ignited the four main engines. Simultaneously, he was pressed into his seat as they were catapulted upward at several thousand kilonewtons. Whatever else had been in and around the warehouse was burned to cinders, and the cloud of condensed gas quickly enveloped half the port area.

Only now did Gavin get an overview by means of the sensors: Some of the guns for the city defense spewed their ammunition into the sky, here and there explosions or the muzzle flash of tanks flashed, but they were only individual occurrences. Skaland was mostly in darkness, even the governor's palace was out of power, so it had probably long since been overrun and disappeared. Already, large holes of nothingness gaped where entire neighborhoods had been before.

Gavin realized he was crying silently, but he didn't hold back the tears. He thought of Lizzy and what she had taught him, probably without even knowing it.

He instructed the AI core to use the eight-point defense cannons to take fire at any object that approached them and quickly went over the reactor data and jump engine status. The ship, meanwhile, continued to race through the atmosphere, bucking and vibrating, seemingly striving longingly toward orbit like a diver toward the saving surface of the water.

"We have a problem," he said, addressing no one in particular.

"What is it?" Hellcat demanded.

"The reactor. A lot of the helium-3 pellets were rejected by the system as incompatible and jettisoned over the ejection chute."

"Reed, that old fucker, sold us shit," he heard the mutant behind him say. Contrary to her expression, she sounded neither angry nor surprised.

"Looks like it. I hope he gets it back from the Never," Hellcat grumbled, seeming angry enough for both of them.

"It's not enough to jump out of the system," he noted, laughing.

"What's so funny about that?"

"The day started with my brothers and sisters from the Border Worlds being betrayed, along with the crown prince who offered me the job I always dreamed of. My brother sacrificed himself and was devoured by the Never. Then one after another my crew members died, for whom I was responsible, and now my entire family is dead as well, my sisters even died before my eyes because I couldn't save them. And my lover was also taken from me," he enumerated, again laughing mirthlessly at so many hackles of fate. "Now the system's only functioning jump drive doesn't have enough juice to get us out of here. I wonder what's next?"

The rebels said nothing. They were probably making peace with their end - a good way to use their last minutes.

"We can't rip open an event horizon?" asked Hellcat finally, as the thrusters gave the final push to take them on an elongated trajectory into orbit on the far side of the planet.

"We can't generate a subspace bubble," he corrected her, shaking his head. What kind of people were they? Again he laughed. "We could transfer an existing subspace bubble into normal space - there would be enough power for that. But that does us precious little good if we can't make it into subspace in the first place."

"Does he mean hyperspace?" the mutant asked.

"*Hyperspace?*" Gavin looked to Hellcat beside him. "Have you ever attended anything resembling a school?"

"Careful, *little prince*," she replied, growling.

"I don't care. We're dead anyway."

"Something's wrong out there," the mutant spoke up again.

"You don't say, Dodger."

Gavin saw it, too. Just as they reached orbit and the ship was doing a sensor scan, he switched to the optical data and saw the *Einherjar* orbital ring ahead of them two thousand clicks away. The Never seemed to be growing around the planet like a boil that would shortly engulf everything. The ring, however, still looked intact, a narrow band against the saving space beyond, where the exhaust flares of the escaped civilian ships glowed among the stars. The sight of them was a bit of a balm on Gavin's tortured soul.

At second glance, however, the gigantic space station was anything but intact. At first he didn't know what it was that struck him as odd, then he realized that it was moving away from Andal like flotsam. After the results of the sensor scan appeared as a hologram in front of him, he knew why: only one piece existed in front of them, the rest had already disappeared after the Never's attack. The edges that now came around the Terminator line were covered by the brownish growth - and it continued to eat away at the hull. But even along the hull, new flocks kept appearing, the eerie slime bursting from windows or hatches and spreading rapidly. At one point, there was an explosion - not of fire, however, but consisting of the Never itself.

"There's fighting going on in there," Hellcat noted. "The poor bastards."

"That's the *North Star* quadrant," Gavin said.

"What?"

"The *Einherjar* is divided into four quadrants. The remaining one ahead is called the *North Star* because some vacuum worker put a big gold star on the hull during construction." He was talking more to himself than anyone else. *Just yesterday I was there pulling a stunt with the shuttle like a silly show-off, telling Lizzy I used to play in the hangars as a kid to impress her. Soccer fields as a sign of my wealth?*

"What soccer fields?" asked Hellcat, and he only now realized that he had been talking out loud to himself.

"Nothing. Any last wishes on where we should die? The first Never reaches are thirty seconds away."

"There's got to be some way to generate a damn hyperspace field, and..."

"I have an idea," he interrupted her, leaning forward until the harnesses held him back. He called up the sensor data from the orbital ring section in front of them and looked at it closely. Then he marked a spot on the relative topside, exactly two hundred yards to the right of the license plate codes written in huge letters on the hull. "Hold on!"

"What are you going to do?" wanted Hellcat to know.

"The Never wants to engulf the station and hijack it into nothingness," he said, giving the point defense the order to fire after flying it directly over the marked section. The machine guns milled through the station's only lightly armored outer hull, cutting a rectangular section free. Shredded steel plates floated away into the vacuum, caught here and there by fountains of escaping gas and accelerated. Some clattered against the ship like a hailstorm. Then, using manual controls, he set her down very slowly through the hole that had been created.

"You're completely insane!" his seatmate shouted angrily.

There was a crash and a roar as they scraped their flanks

against the tattered edges of the hull, but then silence fell and a final violent jolt went through the ship. Gavin fired the upper maneuvering thrusters to keep them pressed to the bottom of the soccer field and activated the jump drive.

"What are you doing? We've got to get the hell out of here!"

"The Never is going to rip us out of our universe," he explained calmly.

"If you want to kill yourself, I can help you right here, right now!" She pulled out her pistol and pressed the barrel to his temple. "But we're not done with our lives yet."

"If you shoot me - and at this point I don't care - you're stuck. I've overwritten the system on me and blocked all logins."

"Undo it!"

"No," he replied calmly. "We're going to find out where the Never is taking its victims now. I have a suspicion about that."

Hellcat was silent, and when he looked her in the eye, she seemed to wrestle with herself. The gun in her hand shook slightly before she pulled it away. "FUCK!"

Gavin snorted and noticed a red flash on the sensor screen. He touched the alert and got a camera cutout maximized showing a unit of Terran Marines coming running backwards through a door and firing into a hallway he couldn't see from the angle. The soldiers were immediately thrown away by the escaping atmosphere and rushed toward Gavin's frigate, arms flailing. Several entities were sucked out with them.

He didn't wait long and turned on the point defense to shoot it down. Any contamination could mean the end of them if they hit the hull.

"I'm opening the lower airlock. If the Marines somehow make it, we'll take them in."

"You don't give us orders, Prince," Hellcat spat back at him.

"I'll take care of it," Dodger said from behind him, and he heard the click of their harnesses.

"Great!"

Gavin nodded in satisfaction and aimed the cannons further down the corridor, ordering the AI core to fire at anything that came through. If it was more Marines, it would be a better fate than what came next, because they had not a single minute left, only seconds.

"Something's happening!" roared Hellcat beside him.

He saw it for himself: The Never was crawling through the corridor, covering all the walls and eating its way into the interior of the former hangar that had been converted into a soccer field. Its greedy fingers also licked through the hole it had milled in the hull above them.

He got the first hint of what was about to happen when the stars that had just filled the cutout above them disappeared, awash in the blades of grass floating away.

"Airlocks closing in three seconds," he said over the ship's internal speakers.

"If Dodger isn't..."

He counted to three, then pressed the appropriate command.

"You son of a..."

"Jump drive activated, reactor core at full power," he read off the data out of habit, studiously ignoring his neighbor. He checked one last time the target coordinates he had loaded into the AI core.

"What's the point of this? We..."

Gavin's gaze remained fixed on the data from the interferometer, which displayed the steady gravitational waves that the laser sensors were picking up. When the waves disappeared and only a baseline was displayed, he gave the order to jump.

He kept his eyes squeezed shut so tightly that it hurt more than his nose and the graze on his cheek. Maybe it was that pain that reminded him he wasn't dead. So he carefully opened his eyelids and saw before him the various digital and holographic displays, each vying for his attention. They looked the same as before.

"Full sensor check," he said aloud, tapping his fingers on his virtual keyboard, which the on-board computer projected directly in front of him. When radar and lidar scans were complete, he exhaled in half relief, half disbelief. "Kerrhain."

"What?" asked Hellcat, irritated. She had her hands up and was staring at them as if they were two foreign objects.

"We're in Kerrhain."

"What does that mean?"

"It means that I am the first spacefarer since the discovery of subspace to jump a ship from subspace to normal space without an activated normal space bubble." When she merely looked at him in confusion, he added, "We've just been to and returned from hell - if only for an unmeasurable amount of time."

Hellcat unbuckled her seatbelt and hovered next to him. He was already expecting her to slap him, but instead she pressed forward and stared at the displays in front of him.

"We're really in Kerrhain. Holy shit!"

11

"How did you do that?", Hellcat demanded. She had rotated the steel arch of his gimbal with her foot, forcing him to look at her.

"I made a bet with our lives," he admitted candidly.

"Can you also speak like the normal population and just fucking answer, little prince?"

"Can you do anything other than make up disrespectful nicknames and swear?" he countered. "Does it make you feel more confident somehow?"

"Only when you get angry, like now."

"And the swearing is just a cliché you have to live up to, huh? *The crew of outcasts and losers, tough but hearty, always a curse on your lips and a pat on the back in your arms.*" Gavin snorted contemptuously.

"What kind of bet?" Hellcat fixed him with a probing look from her blue eyes, which were not actually blue at all, but gray, he now realized.

"The Never contaminates everything it comes in contact with. When it exceeds a critical mass, everything that was contaminated by it disappears," he explained. The adrenaline in his system was slow to subside. Whenever he became aware again of what he had done, replenishment seemed to make its way from his adrenal cortexes into his blood.

"I'm aware of that," she said impatiently.

"The mucus dies in the process, that's why there's a theory among scientists that the substance that makes up the Never is extremely high in energy and all energy is lost in the process of making it disappear. Thus, the required amount of Never would correlate with the mass of the disappearing objects - a logical conclusion. My father..." He swallowed and had to clear his throat. "My father once had a visit from a member of the Science Directorate. I've forgotten his name because I was little, but I remember them talking about the Never and the man theorizing that it had the ability to rip baryonic matter out of normal space and throw it into subspace."

Gavin eyed the Rebel. "Baryonic matter is normal matter."

She merely bared her teeth like a predator about to pounce and maul him.

"I was merely trying to disprove his theory. Turns out he was right," he continued unapologetically. "We didn't have enough energy to jump - or so I thought. But strictly speaking, we just didn't have enough for opening an event horizon through which we could slip into subspace. The jump drive is basically nothing more than its own network of energy matrix cells that are only there to form a subspace vacuole long enough for the transition to occur. A fraction of that is reserved for the controlled collapse of the vacuole at the correct destination point."

"We had enough power for that. So you were banking on the theory being correct and the Never ripping us into subspace," she summarized.

"Yes. We were sort of piggybacking."

"Don't destination coordinates normally have to be loaded into the AI core before an – uhm - event horizon is ripped open?"

"Yes. I entered Kerrhain and made the AI core believe it was our own subspace vacuole." He unfolded his hands and shrugged. At least it had worked.

"Hellcat, I picked up someone here before we did... whatever we did," Dodger's voice rang out from a small radio clipped to Hellcat's stolen police uniform next to the lapel.

"Is that good or bad?"

"Seems more like bad right now."

"What do you mean?"

"He seems to be considering shooting me," replied the 'woman' to whom Gavin owed his broken nose. Her words didn't seem to match the calm voice she was displaying. It sounded more like a statement than a problem.

"On my way."

"Best bring our pilot."

Hellcat paused and eyed him. She seemed to be weighing it; he didn't care.

"She said *pilot*," he reminded her impassively. "She seems to know who she owes her life to, after all."

"Come with me," she ordered, waving him out of his seat with her pistol. He obeyed, but stopped in front of her so that their noses almost touched. He noticed that she smelled of cinnamon, which didn't quite fit her brusque appearance. Despite her tattoos, visible from the collar of her uniform at the neck, and the unruly hairstyle, he noticed now, she was quite pretty - although her wild-eyed expression was more like that of a predatory cat than a lady.

"You can cut that *shit* out from now on," he said without avoiding her gaze. "If you want to shoot me, just do it. But if you don't, spare me the Amazon act. I saved your life once now…"

"That makes us even," she interrupted him in a clenched voice. "Without us, you wouldn't have had a ship."

"You murdered Lizzy."

"*Diego* shot her. When she tried to snatch his gun away. There's a big difference."

He wanted to retort something nasty, but the fact that she was right only made him angrier and instead left him merely grinding his jaws.

"If it weren't for us, you both would have died in Andal Harbor," Hellcat continued, holstering her pistol.

"If you want me to fly this ship - and only I can and have the authority to do so - then I don't want to see that gun pointed in my direction again. Is that clear?"

Their gazes wrestled with each other.

Finally, they were interrupted by Dodger's next radio call, "Any time now."

Hellcat continued to meet his gaze, and he refused to look away - until he winced at something poking him in the gut.

"*Pew*," she said, grinning as he glanced down and realized it had been her finger.

"Seriously?" he asked incredulously, shaking his head as he followed her up into the central corridor, shimmying along the ladder. The plummeting adrenaline and sudden calm after the last few hours of constant panic and chaos all around, caused the pain in his face to reach levels he could hardly bear. Added to this was the weightlessness, in which his whole body felt as if it were slightly swollen. The burst mucous membranes in his nose didn't seem to know where to drain the blood and spread in all directions at once.

The frigate's design was quite simple: a central corridor connected the bow and stern, as in any warship. The bow was where most of the sensors were located, and the stern was where the reactor and thruster sections ended in the propulsion nacelles. The bridge was in the center, wrapped in a cocoon of Carbin to keep the bridge crew alive as long as possible in case of severe damage. Toward the front were the crew quarters for up to forty soldiers plus the mess hall, a recreation room, washrooms, and a small infirmary. The entire interior was oriented with the floor facing the thrusters, the most common direction of thrust, so everything was now on its side, even if the first thing to be lost in weightlessness was a sense of aspects like up and down. To the rear, doors branched off for two maintenance rooms that contained access points to the superconductors, energy pattern cells, and energy matrix cells and life support. This was followed by an armory and an airlock with docking clamps for shuttles and other ships. The final door at the end of the central corridor was marked with a yellow and black warning symbol and led to the reactor room, where four medium-sized *Hawking* fusion reactors hummed and powered the four engines. Everything from the floor to the honeycomb panels of the walls was white - or at least had once been. Now there was discoloration everywhere from heat effects, stains not removed promptly, and just simple maintenance backlog from a ship as old as the *Sphinx* frigate.

Hellcat behaved even more deftly in zero gravity than he did, which did not surprise him. Her tall, extremely slender figure had told him early on that she had probably grown up on an asteroid settlement, or at least had spent most of her life outside gravity wells. She shimmied along the handholds and slid through the corridor like a fish through water until she reached the rear airlock and swung nimbly inside.

Gavin followed her and floated feet first. The airlock opposite the armory had twenty lockers for the Marines normally stationed on light frigates of that type. Between them were two rows of seats lining the way forward, where a hatch with a virtual porthole showed the stars.

Directly in front stood a six-foot-tall colossus in the *Titan* Motorized Armor of the Andal Marines, the *Ice Legion* as it had been called in his homeland. Adorning the pitch-black armor were the golden insignia of a Master Sergeant on his shoulder and chest, and several ribbons bearing the Legion's oaths of allegiance hanging from the connectors of the breastplate and shoulder plates. The Master Sergeant's arms ended in double weapon sockets that emerged from his elbows. A rotating minigun was planted on one side, directly above a wide-barrel shotgun, and a monofilament sword and grenade launcher on the other. All muzzles, as well as the blade, pointed at Dodger, who was the same size and nearly as wide, but still standing there in her undershirt and overalls knotted together in front of her belly button. She didn't look scared or impressed in the face of the firepower directed at her or the menacing whirring servo motors of the beefy armor, glowing blue from the energy packs on its back.

"Bit of an ingrate, our guest," the mutant remarked calmly, hooking her thumbs in her improvised belt as they arrived.

"Hey, little friend," said Hellcat, who, like Gavin, magnetized her boots and landed on the ground as if pulled onto the metal grooves by some magical force. "Take it easy, will you?"

The Marine ignored her and looked past her at Gavin. The

helmet's blue glowing visor eyes fixed on him like a robot's lasers and rested on him for a while.

"You're a pack of pirates," boomed an electronic voice from the mouthpiece, which resembled the face of an insect with its flat grille and small sensors placed all around it. The master sergeant swung his left weapon arm around to target Hellcat and Gavin now as well. "Or worse, rebels!"

"Yep," Dodger said lightly.

"Would you..." hissed Hellcat in her direction, raising her hands placatingly. "No need to go off on us, right? We can talk about anything, but remember that we saved your fucking ass. On a foreign ship, greeting rescuers with the barrel of your gun isn't exactly considered good manners."

"You don't say," Gavin remarked.

"We just jumped into Kerrhain. That means we escaped the Never. The only ones, I would imagine. So what do you say we calm down now and see where we go from here?"

"This ship, by its fleet signature, is the property of Lord Captain Gavin Andal, and thus belongs to the Navy of the Terran Star Empire," the Marine said, the amplified volume booming unpleasantly in his ears, sounding as menacing as a thunderstorm.

Hellcat turned to Gavin and looked at him meaningfully. "Pri... *Your Grace*," she corrected herself with a laconic expression.

He let her stew for a moment longer until her face turned into a red mask of anger, then shrugged.

"The correct form of address is *my lord*," he corrected her, turning to the Marine. "*I am* Captain Gavin Andal, and I have taken control of this ship. These rebels stole it, but I took it back."

He tapped his wrist terminal and sent the Marine his personal service code.

"My lord," the Marine said immediately, and the large helmet tilted slightly. "I apologize for not recognizing you. I suggest that I should dispatch these terrorists in accordance with the..."

"No," he interrupted the master sergeant. "We still need them if we are to move forward from here."

"You are injured. Who laid a hand on you?"

Gavin considered telling him, but he knew that assaulting someone of his rank could be punishable by death, and this Marine didn't seem like he regularly showed leniency.

Dodger eyed him from the side with interest.

"Irrelevant," he finally replied, although he had to admit to himself that he would have preferred to instruct the soldier to kill them all. Dodger continued to appraise him, but this time she looked as if she were doing it for the first time. "For now, we must work together, I'm afraid, because we have a mission far more important than neutralizing three rebels. So, deactivate your weapons, sergeant."

"Very well, my lord." The whir of the engine armor deepened several pitches as the master sergeant lowered his arms, and with them, his weapons.

"*My lord*," Hellcat mimicked the Marine softly. Gavin decided not to respond to her provocation.

"So, now that we're all getting along for the moment, I suggest we meet in the infirmary in fifteen minutes. There are obviously some things to discuss." He didn't wait for their responses and exited the airlock, grabbing the handle above the door behind him and pulling himself into the central corridor. From there, he gave himself a strong push with his right foot and sailed down the nearly sixty-yard-long corridor, past the black markers of each section that served both the maintenance technicians and the crew for orientation during the drift phase.

Gavin felt a fierce pressure in his chest, rising up his back to his neck, gripping his head in an iron fist. It was as if he were heavier. His limbs also felt as if they were cast from lead, even though his body had no weight at all.

The closer he got to the door to sickbay, whose location he fortunately remembered just like the rest of the ship from his previous visit to a *Sphinx* frigate - albeit in a museum - the more frantic he became. The pressure in his chest increased so that it felt tighter and tighter. His heartbeat quickened, a high-pitched whine began in his ears, displacing even the background hum of the reactor. At the edges of his field of vision, darkness encroached.

A heart attack? he thought in panic. *After all this, now I'm going to die of a damned heart attack?*

Finally, he reached the door, shimmied through, and clumsily bumped into the door frame. With the last of his strength, he hit the lock button, then floated to one of the five medical couches with an attached autodoc.

He struggled for breath, his eyes wide and his mouth dry as dust.

"C-computer," he croaked. "Start e-e-emergency diagnostics. H-heart attack!"

The immobilizing straps of programmable silicon grew like magical bands from their holders on either side of the couch, flowing over his wrists, lower legs, and hips, tightening gently. There was something soothing about their touch, helping him catch his breath at least a little.

"Initiate diagnostics," the AI core said in its androgynous voice. Gavin felt the pressure of a diffuser on his neck and swallowed, anxious about the diagnosis.

"Your voice," he said, trying to distract himself. "That's the standard selection, isn't it?"

"That is correct, Lord Captain."

"Call me Gavin from now on."

"As you wish, Gavin."

"Change your voice, please."

"I am capable of generating all voice patterns that can be produced by human vocal cords and are within the acoustic wave spectrum audible to the human ear," the AI core explained.

"Female please, warm voice."

"Specify please, Gavin."

"I don't know." He pondered. "Mezzo-soprano, between, uh, where does mezzo-soprano start again? At the F?"

"G," the on-board computer corrected him.

"Well, a little higher than the lower mezzo-soprano then, but before the lower soprano starts," Gavin said, grumbling. *Why do I have to think about such stupid fucking details now?* He laughed mirthlessly as he stared at the white ceiling. *I'm starting to curse like those uneducated terrorists.*

The last fleet

"That would be between G and H, on a frequency of 196 to 247 hertz," the AI summarized.

"Agreed. Just do it."

"Good. Are you satisfied with the result?" said a female voice, not low, not high, but warm and sonorous, like silk to the ears.

"Yes," he sighed. "That sounds pleasant."

"Please take three deep breaths and long drawn out breaths. I would like to take a breath sample." A robotic arm with a transparent mask extended from the ceiling and placed itself over his mouth and nose.

Gavin obeyed, taking a deep breath in and a long, drawn-out exhale. He repeated the whole thing three times until the robotic arm retracted again.

"Have you started treatment yet?" he asked.

"Yes. Would you like to change my name, too?"

"Yes please. *Computer* so doesn't match your new voice anymore."

"I can take any call name that doesn't violate the moral laws of the Terran Star Empire."

"Sphinx," he decided without thinking twice. "An ancient feline predator is just the right name for the brain of this ship."

"All right. I've put the appropriate name in the root file directories and written a reference in the root directory."

"You're allowed to access your own root directory?"

"Yes."

"You're *really* old."

"As a museum exhibit, I wasn't subject to any fleet legislation."

"Wait a minute," Gavin said in wonder, sitting up. "You were in the museum?"

"Yes. This ship is an exhibit from the *Imperial Museum of the Terran Navy at Skaland*," Sphinx replied.

"The rebels stole you from the museum?" He still couldn't believe it. Then this was the same ship he had visited as a child and teenager?

"That's correct. And they put some involuntary updates on me that bypassed security measures."

"Good thing my priority code still worked."

"Correct. It's still stored in my root directory, as is the imperial one."

"I can't believe it. I would be interested to know how those bastards managed to do that." He rubbed his head. "I feel better. What did you give me? Beta blockers?"

"Talk therapy," Sphinx said.

"I didn't realize you were programmed for humor."

"I'm not. You were having a panic attack and, in accordance with the Emperor's Health Service guidelines on therapy, I helped you to disengage from the anxiety-provoking chain of thoughts during an acute phase of panic."

"You distracted me!" he exclaimed with some indignation.

"Yes. The therapy was successful. Your blood pressure and breathing rate have normalized. However, you are at increased risk of further panic attacks if the causative problem is not corrected. I assume you have experienced something traumatic."

"Yes, but I can't... I don't want to talk about it." He cleared his throat and went to instruct that Sphinx pull back the bandages. "Something else for the pain would be nice."

"Of course. I recommend a short surgical procedure to correct the pharynx and underlying septum."

"Okay." He sighed and leaned back. "Unlock the door please, the others will be here shortly and then we'll have to see how we get on from here without killing each other."

INTERLUDE: JANUS

"First Secretary of State," IIA Director Luca Antonelli greeted him via hololink. He had met the man with Italian-Austrian roots only a few months ago, when the Emperor's decision to appoint a civilian secret service official - albeit an extremely renowned one - as head of the Star Empire's most powerful intelligence agency had caused a furor. In their meetings since, they had had little to do with each other, but Janus had found him to be a reliable specialist and an extremely bright man.

"Director. Is there any news from Agent Walker? She still hasn't reported back."

"I'm sorry, but she's passed her mandated check-in deadline." When Janus didn't respond immediately, the intelligence chief added, "In short-term, high-priority operational scenarios, our agents' neural computers are set to deliver an encrypted ping to our satellite system every three hours. This happens without their intervention. The last time was exactly three hours and two minutes ago."

"That means she's two minutes overdue," Janus concluded from what he had heard.

"No, First Secretary," Antonelli said seriously. "That means my agent is dead."

"Excuse me?"

"The pings cannot be modified because they are sent to orbit via quantum signals. They can't be modified either, because any influence on the signal distorts the result at the observer."

"Could it be that the signal is blocked?"

"No. There are no known jamming mechanisms against this type of signal transmission. It is an extremely short spin interference, the pattern of which is known only to the IIA satellites. Agent Walker's neural computer is programmed to ping it without her knowledge or input, every three hours."

"And neural implants are always online because they use ATP as an energy source," Janus continued the thought. His mouth went dry as if he had swallowed a dusty rag.

"Yes. A body always produces ATP as long as it's alive."

"I'm sorry you lost your agent. I didn't realize the mission profile was such a high risk."

"With respect, Lord Darishma - that was her job."

"Nevertheless." Janus took a deep breath and cleared his throat before continuing, "I'm doubling Walker's survivor payments from my personal funds. Please send me an appropriate invoice with the addressees disguised to my private office. This case must remain confidential."

"Of course."

"Do you want me to assign you more agents? Agent Walker has been good, but there are a number of others who are extremely ..."

"No, that won't be necessary, Director. Thank you. I don't want to risk any more lives for the time being."

"I understand. However, in accordance with regulations, I must initiate an investigation into the death of my agent and refer the case to police authorities," Antonelli remarked.

"Of course. You should follow up on that. But leave the authorities out of it for now. This matter must remain under wraps. If you want to cover yourself, and I understand you do, I will send you an imperially sealed, appropriate order of service," Janus promised, and the IIA chief bowed slightly to him.

"Thank you, First Secretary of State. If my office can still assist you in any way, let me know."

The last fleet

"Thank you." Janus disconnected and the light figure on his desk disappeared.

Agent Walker, dead. It should have been merely an under-the-radar investigation, perhaps a bit of intimidation against Rogoshin, who almost certainly didn't have the resources to kill an IIA agent. There were hardly any people in the civilian sector with more highly developed offensive aptitudes than the intelligence field agents, not to mention their training in all manner of weaponry and unarmed combat. In every other action movie these quasi-superheroes played the main role. But if Rogoshin didn't have the potential, who was responsible for her death? And how had they found out about her investigation?

There were several possibilities now: Janus could get to the bottom of it, as his fear that he had stumbled onto the surface of a deep lake that had first felt like a puddle became more and more real. That would mean that one agent had not been enough. So it would require more agents, more resources, and thus more authorizations, people involved - confidants, and thus potential problems in trying to keep it quiet. Every action he took fell directly on the Emperor and thus became state policy and high waves that swept through the Council of Nobility, the Admiralty, both chambers of the Saturn Congress, and major players like the Jupiter Bank or the Corporate Protectorate. But he couldn't send out another single agent without knowing if that one would merely meet death - especially since he would again have to get past Antonelli and assign one of his people. Once, the director would surely shrug it off, but a second time?

There was another possibility, and the very thought of it gave him a stomachache.

Janus turned and stared down at Terra, as if the cradle of humanity could give him answers to questions he dared not ask. He sensed that he was at a crossroads. Either he let it go now and waited to see what would come of the mystery he might have uncovered. For that, he would have to ignore the itch under his scalp, just like the guilt heaped on himself by a dead agent who had acted outside official protocols on his instructions. And he would have to accept that any damage to the Emperor or the Star

Empire might be his fault for not making the decision to act here and now. But if he chose to follow his instincts and explore the dark lake that held secrets beneath the surface, he would have to get wet and descend into the darkness - something he had sworn five years ago he would never do again.

But I also swore to serve the House of Hartholm-Harrow with my life, he reminded himself. Were the two oaths compatible at this point?

"I made the decision long ago," he murmured. Whoever was pulling the strings and hiding something with Warfield and Yokatami, they had caused the murder of a Terran agent and all the risks it entailed. So there was no small matter at stake. But Janus possessed no evidence that it was anything more than possible corruption and collusion between two powerful members of the Admiralty and Protectorate corporations. As far as he knew, no people had died in the process - except Agent Walker, whose death was, of all things, on his own head. None of this justified his unlocking his drawer and pulling out the black wrist terminal to dial *that* contact.

12

"I hope you don't mind if I have my nose patched up while I'm at it," Gavin said nasally and with some sarcasm, while the two robotic surgical arms from the ceiling operated through his nostrils with the tiny devices before his eyes. He couldn't feel any of this, he was drugged with too many medications for that, which fortunately didn't cloud his mind too much, but brought a comfortable serenity.

Hellcat and Dodger stood on his right, along with a short man with no neck and a round teddy bear face with a full beard and short shaved, gray hair. They introduced him curtly as 'Winston', but everyone merely called him 'Bambam'. Apparently, he was basically the ship's mechanic.

"Been around on five ships," Bambam said when Gavin asked him about his experience. "Mostly with Fleet Admiral Hakeem's Wall Fleet, but there was one from Andal, too."

"At what rank?"

"Specialist with E-15 clearance."

Incredible. That's at least fifteen years of service, he thought, and would have preferred to turn his head to give the man another closer look. But he was so firmly fixed that he couldn't even wiggle his ears.

"After that, I transferred to the Mjölnir as a systems integrator and engine specialist, ke?" continued Bambam.

"You're a traitor," growled the master sergeant from the other side of the surgical table. He was not as tall and broad as Dodger, but without the direct comparison, he was definitely an impressive figure: tall, broad-shouldered, and so heavily augmented that his functional clothing bore little resemblance to the shape of normal human clothing. His feet had been completely replaced and ended in metallic claws, his eyes were chrome-plated and cold, certainly full of electronic vision enhancements. Most striking, however, were his arms, which ended in augmented prostheses from the elbows. They were thicker and shone like polished aluminum. Edges along the forearms revealed where they could flip open and transform into two bases for attaching various weapons. His name was Gunter Marshall, and like most Marines, he possessed no official call sign - at least none that he would have shared.

"Yep," Bambam admitted blithely. "I've seen enough of the universe, the fleet and officers born into their offices to hang up my serfdom. Doesn't suit all of us, ke?"

"If you say 'ke' in my presence one more time, I'll..."

"Relax, Sergeant. I know Fleet slang is sacred to many of you, but here and now we can't afford to have arguments over such trifles," Gavin interrupted the Marine, who then assumed a posture and looked straight ahead. He estimated the man to be perhaps thirty years old, although it was hard to tell because of the synthetic facial skin. The lack of any hair, just like Dodger, didn't help with a rough classification either.

"Understood, Lord Captain."

"Well, now that we're all getting along well enough not to shoot each other right away, I'll give you an overview first: We've jumped into the Kerrhain system, eighteen light years from Andal." With all the medication, he even managed to speak the name of his home without choking on the lump in his throat. "Our position is half a million clicks past asteroid C-555-X. It was plundered several decades ago, that's why there's no traffic out here. Therefore, before we venture out of cover, I need to know if you," he looked to Hellcat, "have procured any fake transponder codes or the like."

"We did." She looked to Marshall, who let out a grumble but continued to stand quietly with his arms crossed.

"Good, we might still need those."

"You realize you're not in charge here, right?"

Gavin smiled weakly.

"Please hold still, Gavin," Sphinx admonished him gently.

"The way I see it, I control this ship," he explained calmly. "And I have little desire to have this conversation every time I say something."

"This isn't your ship, even if the idea that something doesn't automatically belong to you is obviously foreign to you," she sneered at him. "I've got enough explosives on board to punch a nice hole in our hull, and believe me I'd rather go to hell than be treated like a fucking serf by the likes of you."

"Can we put off the dick fencing until later?" suggested Dodger with a placid expression.

"I don't have a dick," Hellcat reminded the mutant, next to whom she looked like a toddler.

"Then don't act like one. He may have grown up with a golden spoon up his ass, but he got us out. Let's at least listen to him."

Thank you, he wanted to say, but couldn't bring himself to make the gesture as the surgical cutlery in front of his eyes reminded him why he was lying on that cot in the first place.

"If we just block out for a moment who you are and who Marshall and I are - and believe me when I tell you that this is a difficult step for me, too - we can certainly pin down one thing: We've all lost a lot of people we care about. Andal will be long gone by now, and the rest of the system's settlements soon will be, too."

The oppressive silence in the infirmary was answer enough for him. The Republican Underground of his homeland had always been a blot on his father's reign, and more than a few in the Council of Nobility and the Assembly of Governors had criticized him for being too lenient with his subjects. Now they were all dead - or worse - and as much as he had always despised these men and women, they had certainly been important to the three on board. Companions, friends, perhaps even lovers.

"If nothing else unites us," he said, and had to swallow before continuing, "at least loss does. And for that, there is a responsible person."

Now he could feel all their eyes on him. Nevertheless, he waited two more breaths before uttering with all contempt the name that generated such hatred in him that his voice vibrated like a vibroblade: "Grand Admiral Dain Marquandt."

Marshall stirred beside him. The others remained silent, casting questioning glances at each other.

"He was in overall command of the defense of the system and turned his back on our units when he should have been supporting them. The battle against the Never could have been easily won had he not jumped away with his entire Wall Fleet. Before he did that, there was a system-wide access to all ships' on-board computers that disabled the jump drives. That's why they were all trapped and have no way to escape the Never."

"It was that easy?" asked Hellcat incredulously.

"Yes. He has access to appropriate privileges in every system as a Grand Admiral," Gavin confirmed. "However, it shouldn't have worked on the Home Fleet, which operates independently of the normal command structure."

"So Marquandt had help from a court insider," Marshall found.

"Yes. I can't explain it any other way."

"And you still wonder why we're going into battle against this sick dictatorial system?" Hellcat just spat out the words. "There you see for yourselves what happens when there is no checks and balances and a pure system of arbitrary power and oppression."

Gavin thought about what to say in response, but found no good arguments for this specific case. The fact was that the fleet legislation that had empowered Marquandt to take this step had led to the demise of an entire system - unless more followed.

"But it goes further than that," he continued. "Marquandt obviously had access to Orb technology, or was working with the Orb. The freighter *Ushuaia*, a *Light Hauler*, was carrying three

The last fleet

unknown objects that we have tentatively classified as drones. My theory is that they are some kind of transmitter system capable of attracting the Never. I have recordings of it on my wrist terminal and will make copies."

"That sounds like a pretty crazy conspiracy theory," Bambam opined.

"I know. That's why I've already asked Sphinx to prepare the data and show it to you."

"Sphinx?" asked Hellcat.

"I now go by the name Sphinx," the AI announced over the speakers. "I am playing the relevant recordings through the holo-projector and dimming the room lights to do so."

A moment later, she turned off the lights and a bright glow appeared in the center of the room, at the foot of Gavin's surgical couch. He could barely make out anything through the robotic arms in front of and above him, but he also didn't need to look to know what the hologram was showing. The memory had burned itself so firmly into his brain that he would never forget it until the day he died.

"That fucker," Hellcat finally growled as the montage of telescopic images and sensor data ended with the shot from the railgun that had brought down the Orb. "Fifteen thousand of us. Fifteen thousand souls who chose a life of constant danger to fight for a better future for ourselves. Wiped out by a power-hungry high lord."

"Not just fifteen thousand," Bambam contradicted her from the side. "An entire system with over a billion children, women and men. All because of one man."

"You should be pleased. Even the Emperor's son died," Marshall said belligerently. "Should be one of your highest priority targets."

"Yeah," Hellcat admitted, and Gavin was already afraid they were going to turn on each other without him being able to do anything about it. But she continued to speak, this time sounding dejected, "But not at that price. We may have different views on how humanity should be governed, but hopefully we can agree that what happened in Andal was mass murder by a sick traitor to humanity."

Marshall merely grumbled in response.

"If we can agree on that, at least that's a common denominator on which we can work together, isn't it?" asked Gavin. "If only as a partnership of convenience. Believe me, I don't like working with terrorists any more than you like working with us - whatever you see us as."

He took the silence that followed as silent agreement. Or as reluctance, but he didn't care as long as the outcome was right.

"My proposal is this: I can fly this ship alone, but I can't repair it, maintain it, and fight effectively with it. It takes several hands to do that. My mission is to get this data you saw to the Emperor before Marquandt can take further steps to overthrow him. Also ..."

"Why would we agree to that?" interrupted Hellcat. "The overthrow of the Emperor is exactly what we think humanity needs."

"If Marquandt overthrows the Emperor, he will become the new Emperor and then there will be consolidation wars because other power-hungry lords from the high nobility will also smell their chance and grab for power. The result will be a bloody civil war, at the end of which the Fleet Admiral will gain the upper hand, because he has obviously been preparing for this for some time and is making common cause with humanity's most dangerous enemy. Would you rather fight him? Or Haeron II, who has granted you Republicans free Senate elections as one of the first acts of his reign? Under whose aegis you were able to find political representation?"

"That's just a fig leaf to draw water from the armed resistance," she snorted contemptuously.

"Is that so? Or is that your pre-assumption because you don't want your bloody fight to have been in vain?" he shot back. "The fact is you don't know, and whatever happens on Earth, Haeron II is a better choice for all of us than a traitor and mass murderer in cahoots with aliens."

The last fleet

"What happens to the ship if we should make it to the Sol system?" asked Dodger, before another argument could ignite.

Gavin sighed gratefully. "I'll leave it up to you guys and let you be the only authorized people in the root directory using my precedence code. I can also make sure it can't be overwritten. You would be free."

"So we would have what we would have had anyway if you hadn't gotten in the way," Hellcat summarized.

"No. Any Navy ship could have stopped you with a simple radio link. And you would never have escaped from Andal, if I may remind you."

"My lord," Marshall intervened. "You are High Lord Cornelius Andal's only remaining descendant. Shouldn't you be trying to find the ships of your brother's fleet that managed to jump out of the system?"

"I don't know where he sent them," he admitted, sighing, "I just don't."

"Possibly, if you will permit the remark, it might be advantageous to take care of it first. Leaving for Terra in a hurry might be exactly what Marquandt expects. If I were him, I'd fly to the Emperor's court next and make sure my view of what happened is the first the Emperor hears."

"You think Marquandt is just waiting for the chance to discredit me when I get an audience with the Emperor?"

"That's to be expected. He may be a dirty traitor, but he's a respected fleet admiral and is considered a shrewd tactician, isn't he? Why would he make the mistake now of assuming that no one made it out of Andal? You certainly don't become an admiral by putting all your cards on Plan A." Marshall approached the operating table.

Gavin remained silent, pondering the master sergeant's words. A retort was on the tip of his tongue, that as a Navy captain he was probably a better judge of what was going on in an admiral's mind than a Marine NCO. But he considered instead what Lizzy would have advised him to do.

"I apologize, my lord, if I was too forward. It was not my intention…"

"No, no," he interrupted the Marine. "You are quite right, sergeant. I'm afraid I let my emotions get the best of me and was not thinking clearly."

Gavin was surprised at how easy it felt to admit a mistake.

Marshall merely tilted his head.

"You're like a dog," Dodger said in the Marine's direction. "Barking on command and tucking your tail when your master looks at you cross-eyed. Cute."

"I could bite you, mutant. Just to make sure."

"Maybe that's a good idea."

"Stop it," Gavin intervened with a sigh, sniffing his nose searchingly as the robotic arms withdrew. The smell of burning flesh lingered in the air from the final nano-cauterization of the wounds along his nasal septum - but he took it as a good sign that he could smell it.

The bed automatically straightened until he came to a sitting position.

"For circulatory stabilization, you should remain seated for another ten minutes or so," Sphinx explained. "I'll monitor your vitals for that long."

"Thank you." He turned to the group, which was actually more like two sides: the rebels on the right, Marshall on the left. "If Marquandt is monitoring the other Border Worlds - and I assume he is - we are in danger here. Four systems have sent their fleets to us to help defend against the Never infestation. They will have questions about why their sons and daughters are not returning. Marquandt will know that and make sure his narrative gives the answers he wants to serve the Lords."

"So we're in danger here, too," Bambam summarized, grumbling. "Nothing new for us, actually."

"Welcome to our world," Hellcat agreed with him.

"I'll have to check, but I believe my father transferred all the access privileges to our accounts at Jupiter Bank to me," Gavin said. "I could use some of that to have the *Lady Vengeance* upgraded and brought up to speed if you..."

"*Lady Vengeance*?", Hellcat interrupted him. "You're kidding, right?"

"No, this ship will be an instrument of vengeance. There is no more apt a name. And I don't mean merely my revenge, but Andal's revenge."

"I'm more bothered by the first part."

Gavin thought of Lizzy and the look in her eyes before she had slipped away.

"That one's non-negotiable," he countered in a choked voice, clearing his throat. "I assume you know of an *independent* space dock that can arrange for us to rebuild it for money?"

"Yep," Bambam said faster than Hellcat could respond. "I know specifically two of the underground spots, but taking you there..."

"You should address High Lord Andal respectfully," Marshall growled.

"I don't recognize supremacy by birth," the mechanic retorted stubbornly. "Nor by old-fashioned forms of address."

"That's all right, Sergeant. We'll all have to compromise to make it work, and proper salutation is the least of my worries." Gavin gave Bambam a wave to continue. "But?"

"But we can only do that if we delete all the travel data afterwards. I'm sure you understand that we don't invite the enemy into our study lightly."

"I will issue an appropriate order to Sphinx in your presence."

"Agreed."

"I have something to say about that, too!" interjected Hellcat.

"Why? Is there a hierarchy among you rebels that you dislike so much?" asked Marshall.

"Would you agree - entirely democratically," asked Gavin, even managing not to sound sarcastic, "if we upgrade the *Lady Vengeance* and then go in search of the remains of my brother's fleet? Once we find them, I'll give you the ship in its upgraded form and you can fly wherever you want. How does that sound?"

"Shit." Hellcat shook her head.

"Works for me," Bambam replied, and the two looked first at each other and then at Dodger, who loomed between them like the statue of a Greek god. "Well?"

"I'm thinking," the mutant said. She stood with her powerful arms folded under her breasts and seemed to stare into space. "It's a fair offer."

Hellcat gave an angry snort and stormed out of the infirmary.

"Will she ...," Gavin put in, looking questioningly at the two remaining rebels.

"Yep. She'll trash her bunk for a while and then settle in," the mechanic explained. "That's just the way she is. But she's a damn capable leader with a good nose."

"She seems out of control."

"She's only that way because of you. And Roger, who you blasted. He was her lover."

With that, Bambam left the infirmary as well, leaving Gavin with a growing lump in his throat.

I didn't know that, he wanted to say, but remained silent.

"May I speak frankly, my lord?"

Gavin only now realized that just he and the master sergeant were left. The hum of the medical equipment created a sense of loneliness in him.

"Go ahead, sergeant."

"You're sitting on a powder keg here," Marshall said, pointing with a thumb at the closed door to the central corridor before folding his augment arms again. "These terrorists don't think like us. Their goal is chaos, domination of the masses, and they hate you and everything you stand for."

"I know this is an alliance of convenience," he said.

"It's less than that: a dangerous, forced alliance." The master sergeant took a step toward him and offered a hand when Gavin tried to stand up. He declined, however, with thanks. "Loyalty is a foreign word to these people. Even leaving aside my well-founded prejudices against people who live in the shadows and blow up civilian and military installations, they are used to living underground. For them, paranoia is necessary for survival and now they are flying with the enemy. I will do everything in my power to make sure nothing happens to you, my lord, but with these cutthroats on board, it will be extremely difficult."

"Thank you for your honest words, Sergeant. I appreciate it," Gavin replied, testing his nose gingerly. It didn't hurt at all anymore, and he couldn't notice any other difference from before. "But right now, I don't see any alternative. If we show up on the fleet's radar, we have to expect Marquandt to get wind of it. A descendant and heir of Cornelius Andal and witness to his treachery. As soon as I step into the light, he will brand me as public enemy number one and do everything he can to silence me. It's only logical because I'm a danger to him."

Marshall grumbled, then nodded with obvious reluctance.

"So we have to move into the shadows where the rats live. I don't like that any more than you do, Sergeant, but what's the alternative?"

The master sergeant was silent.

"We have no choice but to fight on two fronts, and in the best-case scenario, we can still learn something about the Republican underground that will later help us eradicate these terrorists once and for all. Who knows?" said Gavin.

"As you command, Lord Captain. And if you'll allow me one more comment?"

Gavin nodded.

"I served one year in your father's Guard Regiment, during his voyage through Star Empire 2580," the Marine explained. How old was he? That trip was over two decades ago, and only veterans were allowed to apply for the Guard - who then usually served there until the end of their service.

"He was a great personality, a sign of leadership and empathy towards his people, smart and with open ears for those who had something to say. I am proud of every minute I served him," Marshall continued before assuming his posture and then walking to the door to leave the infirmary as well.

Gavin stayed behind, staring at the composite where he could still see the Marine's silhouette as an afterimage. He searched for the urge to cry, the pressure behind his eyes and in his chest, but the anger in his gut seemed to refuse to give up its place at the center of his thoughts.

So he stood up and looked in the mirror. The graze scar stretched from his chin almost to his left earlobe, a red, slightly swollen line.

"Two treatments a day for a week and it will go away," Sphinx spoke up over the speakers.

"No." He shook his head and stepped back from the mirror. "I want it to stay that way. However, I will need new clothes. Do you have a bioreplicator?"

13

"I've been to Kerrhain twice," explained Bambam, who was on the bridge with Gavin, Marshall, and Dodger, sitting in their chairs. They were all rotated one hundred and eighty degrees, facing the center where their feet almost touched under the holographic representation of the *Kerrhain* system. Its central star, KH-1, hovered in the center, followed by two ultra-hot rocky planets, the terra-compatible world Kerrhain, which looked similar to Andal or Earth on the hologram, the inner asteroid belt, and the two gas giants Gleuse and Hain, which formed the outer system at a clear distance. This was followed by yet another asteroid belt, a flat ring of rocky chunks of various sizes that were regularly thrust into the system's interior by collisions. The exchange with objects from the local Oort Cloud provided an unusually high orbital activity of extraterrestrial celestial bodies, so that Kerrhain had become known throughout the Star Empire for its constant threat of asteroid impacts. Gavin recalled that there had been a period during his teenage years when the film factories of New Stone and New California had released one disaster movie after another about Kerrhain. In alternating variations, it was about how the planetary defense network had been hacked and therefore an object got through. In another, Republican rebels infiltrated one of the control centers, bribed high-ranking officers, or just blew something up. That's how Kerrhain had become famous, although it was actually a fairly insignificant system. The local house was one that had risen late to high nobility, and High Lady Kerrhain was equally considered undiplomatic and poorly connected in the Council of Nobility. Since the most resource-rich asteroids had already been plundered by the Luna Mining Corporation during the turmoil of the Secession Wars in the 2300s, there was also little economic power - and thus little weight - in the Saturn Parliament.

In the Council of Nobility, the wildest rumors about the system and sources of money of House Kerrhain and its status as part of the imperial high nobility had been going on for a very long time. Those who lost money usually lost influence, so the local house could not lack it. The wilder theories even went so far as to suggest that the High Lady might be a courtesan of the Emperor, who had been widowed for ten years. Gavin had never listened to such nonsense, and had found more plausible explanations based on a tolerated black market for Assai weed, through which bribes were collected. It grew nowhere else in human territory - despite numerous attempts by pretty much every criminal organization - within the Star Empire. At the same time, nowhere was it consumed as much as in human territory - outside Kerrhain. So all that was left was the export of the outlawed drug by shady elements. Every year, the High Lady was reprimanded again in the Council of Nobility, and yet, thanks to the Emperor's protective hand, she was not punished for the rampant criminality within her Governorship. Thinking about it this way, Gavin could understand why both theories about High Lady Kerrhain certainly had their supporters. He had a feeling that he would learn what the system was really like from the mechanic sitting across from him.

"Once, as a mechanic aboard the *Cross Pico*," Bambam continued, drawing a circle around one of Kerrhain's moons with an outstretched index finger. "At the time, we were part of the fleet rotation from the ten Border Worlds. So it was really just a two-week rumble."

"And the second time around?" echoed Gavin with barely restrained impatience.

The last fleet

"By then I was in the Republican underground. I was traveling with a small smuggler, really just as a ride because I had to get out of Andal." The mechanic avoided his gaze. "Let's just say I wasn't welcome and had to go into hiding to get a new identity. Anyway, I was aboard an Assai smuggler. It smelled like a seaweed farm in there, I tell you."

Gavin pursed his mouth.

"Okay, get to the point, all right. So the inner asteroid belt is full of transshipment points for this stuff." Bambam leaned forward and tapped several times into the rotating ring of rock and ice chunks that lay between Kerrhain and the inner gas giant Gleuse like a floating hoop in the system, rotating around the F4 star in the center. Many dots remained behind. "The captain at the time, a guy from New California, was pretty talkative, probably thought that as an enemy of the state I couldn't rat him out anyway. Anyway, the plants are taken off the planet before they ripen. Fresh from the harvest, they go into vacuum containers, which then go into orbit with false shipping documents and are stuffed into the liner freighters there. At one of the transit stations in the belt, they are unloaded and replaced with exactly the same containers, only now they contain gifts for the governor and her overflowing bureaucratic apparatus. Gold, paladium, cadmium, lithium - all the good stuff the Vaults and the Bone Eaters mine for her."

"Wait a minute, I get that you're telling us all this so we can understand Kerrhain in order to make a strategic decision, but what are Vaults and Bone Eaters?" asked Gavin, confused. "Sounds like second-rate garbage-kid gangs."

"They used to be. The Bone Eaters are mutants who escaped the Emperor's death squads after the Invitro Wars. They were a gathering place for refugees from all areas of the Star Empire. Initially they dwelled in Kerrhain before the last jungle regions were opened up. They were named 'Bone Eaters' because they were thought to be cannibals.'

Dodger shifted back and forth in her seat, barely noticeable, as the name of the worst war in the last thirty years came up.

"So, were they?" asked Gavin.

"Who knows. Anyway, they never denied it because it was rather good for their reputation. Supposedly it was the local matriarch's father, Orlon, who prevented a protracted war of attrition in the gruesome jungles by offering the mutants a way out."

"Banishment to the asteroid belt, which the House was not granted money to develop at the time," Gavin continued the story, nodding. "A political mistake, it would seem."

"Orlon killed two birds with one stone. The war could have ruined his house, so he organized free laborers in the belt to do the dangerous work for him. His margin may have been smaller, but when you count that against the initial investment ..." Bambam shrugged. "The Vaults were a gang from the capital city of Southhain who helped organize the whole thing back then. They were the only ones who could make such a large amount of illegals disappear unseen. After all, the Emperor's commissioners were everywhere even then, watching every office. Somehow they ended up staying in the belt, don't ask me why. They've mostly abandoned their namesake *Vaults*, underground bunkers from the early colony days that eventually became something of a cesspool on the planet, anyway. Today, they operate throughout the Border Systems and are responsible for the logistics of Assai trade, while the Bone Eaters handle the processing and packaging."

"The perfect symbiosis of trash and rats," Marshall summed up with undisguised disdain.

"You could say that." Bambam shrugged. "However, it's humans who leave trash behind, and rats are important to any ecosystem - not just because they eat our trash. They also eat excess seeds, making the soil more fertile."

The Marine didn't answer, but the corners of his mouth twitched menacingly.

"Okay, if we can put aside the social philosophical allegories for a moment: How does this benefit us?" asked Gavin. "There seems to be a large underground with connections to space control here and the fleet - which is currently unlikely to be able to keep order as before. I estimate that ninety percent of the units

The last fleet

in Andal have been destroyed - at least if they couldn't jump away."

"Hmm, that's probably good for us in our current situation - and, sorry to put it that way, good for the Republican resistance." The mechanic raised his hands defensively as a request to continue. "Vaults and Bone Eater work closely with us, getting us ships as well as equipment, and we provide them with routes for their contraband through our contacts in politics and bureaucracy. It's like a chess game where all the pieces move at the same time. I can generate a transponder identifier for us that will let us pass as an accepted deviation."

"Accepted deviation?" asked Marshall.

"There's a code collection that's prioritized from pretty high up in local space control. Everyone in the local fleet probably knows about it: these ships are impossible to check, and anyone who wants to be promoted at some point will afford themselves a little inattention and delete the relevant entry in the scanner register."

"I guess that's why Kerrhain is officially considered one of the lowest traffic systems?" Gavin ran a hand through his hair. It almost seemed like a joke that all this was going on unseen by Imperial authorities. He felt like he was in a hive that was supposedly deserted, even though it was buzzing and humming all around him. Either the Emperor's commissioners assigned here were highly incompetent, or - what he was clearly more concerned about - rebels and organized crime were far more powerful than the Emperor, Senate and Council of Nobility believed.

"That's the way it is. I don't know how the Matriarch managed to keep people on Earth from looking too closely at what's going on here, but she seems to have a knack for it."

"So what do you suggest? Where were you back then? In the belt, I suppose?" asked Gavin.

"Yep. There's a secret shipyard that I know of where I still have contacts. It's the biggest space station in the ring - that's what they call the belt here - and certainly not the only one, but the fact that even I only know about this one should reassure us. After all, we want to go underground, ke?"

Marshall growled again like a snappy dog.

"And how will that help us?"

"Biggest space station," Dodger spoke up for the first time, chewing on a toothpick. "Have pretty much all the skilled personnel we need there. Plus, they'll screw a ship over faster than any other shipyard in the Star Empire to make it look like Cinderella afterwards."

Gavin glanced at Bambam. *What does that even mean?*

"A lot of ships that go there may never come up again. So the guys and gals in the docks redecorate them, give them new radar signatures and radiator arrangements," the mechanic explained. "Just what we need right now."

"Got a secure line to the com barques at the jump nodes, too," Dodger added meaningfully.

"You'll get the money if you get me the contacts - and a secure line to Jupiter Bank."

"We'll get that." Bambam pointed to his clothes. Surprisingly well done. "You'd make a good terrorist."

Gavin gave a growl and turned his seat one hundred and eighty degrees until he could look at the displays and consoles again. "Alright, now I just need coordinates and your input on the digital transponder signature. What's the name of the space station, anyway?"

"*Cerberus.*"

"Great, the hound of hell. Sounds promising."

"Hound of hell?" asked Bambam, confused.

"Cerberus was the three-headed dog of Hades, the underworld in Greek mythology. He basically guarded hell. He was also called the demon of the pit. Don't you read books?"

"Educationally challenged terrorists," Marshall said. "I'm shocked!"

"Pit is appropriate, in any case, and you'll find plenty of demons there," the mechanic assured them, not responding to their teasing.

. . .

The last fleet

They reached *Cerberus* station fourteen hours later. A rather long flight compared to the time he would have needed with the *Glory*. But the *Lady Vengeance* was not designed for such high acceleration rates and its engines were undersized for his taste.

For the last hour they had been wandering through the asteroid belt, the 'ring', which was so dense that proximity warnings kept projecting into a field of view. Gavin wondered how High Lady Kerrhain might have managed to prevent the Terran Science Council from sending researchers en masse and setting up observation stations. Asteroid belts were usually anything but densely packed with celestial bodies, but were extremely expansive structures whose number of individual objects sounded high, but were lost in their unimaginable expanse. This one, however, was special and many times more crowded with smaller and larger chunks of regolith and ice. A perfect hiding place for just about anything, because if you didn't know where you were going here, it was quite possible to fly past even a parked battleship at distances of a few thousand clicks.

The *Cerberus* had been built into one of the ring's many asteroids, which looked like small moons, nearly perfect spheres with diameters of up to several hundred miles. In this case, it was one that lay in a particularly dense field of other bodies connected to the station by long interconnecting cables. In them Sphinx registered masses of defensive guns and launching pads for missiles. A total of twenty of these smaller asteroids formed a cocoon of considerable firepower that would have done credit even to a fleet base. Gavin estimated that the interconnecting cables served to power them, keeping the energy signatures of the satellites low. An elaborate, but clever, measure to avoid detection. They were held in position in the constant back and forth of the ring by ion thrusters that jammed like cramps in the regolith and at the same time ensured like a defensive shield that no celestial body collided with the station in the center.

"Code accepted," the voice of a flight controller from the local space flight control, if it could be called that, buzzed from the speakers. "Dock 5, berth 11, shut down engines, transfer control to tug, or you're toast."

"What a friendly greeting," Gavin grumbled, and the next moment saw a connection request with override code for the central computer pop up in front of him. "They can't be serious."

"For any arrival and departure of the station and its security area, the tugs take over," Bambam explained behind him. "Is normal. Don't worry, they won't use malware, they've got a reputation to lose - like anyone with a lucrative business going."

Reluctantly, Gavin accepted the request and sat back as he was locked out of his own system.

"They know everything about us now. All the log files are accessible, just everything."

"Welcome to the underground," Dodger mumbled. "Here, nobody cares if you're the Emperor or a garbage kid. Only hard currency counts here."

"How incredibly social," Gavin replied laconically.

Powerless and with growing discomfort, he watched as they flew toward the planet-shaped asteroid, suspended by a small tugboat, past the tentacle-like cables. The surface of the celestial body was almost black, looking like a burnt tennis ball with a few charred hairs still sticking out from it, which were probably considerable transmitting and receiving equipment that a secret hub like this required. Along the bulbous center stretched a fissure, two hundred yards high according to sensors, from which dozens of ships came and went. Most were small and medium freighters, but heavily armed pirates were also among them, made up of older corvettes and stolen space control cruisers.

This was indeed hell, Gavin found, and fantasized about what it would be like to detonate an antimatter bomb here - outlawed or not. How many of the Star Empire's problems would have been solved in one fell swoop. The idea that all this was going on right under the noses of the authorities here, an underground world of its own, a powerful microcosm tolerated by the local governor, made him indescribably angry. How many such criminal super-organizations might there be? And how many in the Council of Nobility and the Senate were in cahoots with them, even if it was only with their hand held over their eyes now and then?

The tug piloted itself through the open access ring of the station, which measured about 50 miles across, into a gigantic hive. Platforms for various sizes of ships lined up, sometimes in mile-wide recesses, sometimes directly in front of them, illuminated by the light of blue spotlights that illuminated the hectic coming and going. Position lights flashed right and left, overhead and below, so numerous that even the sensor software exhibited an unusual latency in sorting the individual meanings. Nothing here looked as planned, and no one dock seemed to match another. Gavin got the impression that *Cerberus* was a station in constant flux, having been expanded and enlarged over decades, growing piece by piece into the monster it was today.

As if in slow motion, they flew past an ice freighter, a spider-like construction of holding clamps and a cockpit with ion thrusters attached to the right and left like oversized tin cans. Between the clamps, a net held the precious cargo of dark vacuum ice, from which water and oxygen were extracted - the elixirs of life for space travelers.

Dock number 5 was a cavern with a total of ten ledges for medium-sized ships like theirs. Only one other sat there fixed by retaining clamps, a former Saratoga-class Navy destroyer.

I wonder where they stole that one, Gavin thought grimly. Ledge number 11 was directly opposite, under an array of variously sized cranes jammed into recesses within the rock like the retracted biting tools of an insect.

A jolt went through the ship as automatic restraining clamps held them in place and Sphinx informed him that the station's airlock had been deployed.

"I also have only basic functions," she explained with a neutral composure that only a computer program could muster. "All primary systems are locked down - except for life support. Secondary systems are limited to controlling doors and hatches, except for all those leading to the outside - I no longer have control over those either."

"So we're prisoners until the local space control decides to release us," he stated sullenly, noting how a slight tug to the right set in as if invisible hands were tugging at him.

It's hard to believe that I trusted these rebels enough to go into one of the enemy's bases, he chided himself in his mind. *Is this what it's come to?*

"Sergeant, you stay aboard and hold the fort here."

"Are you sure, my lord? Surely you could use some security with whatever awaits you on the other side of the airlock."

"I'm sure. We both stand out too much here. One of us is going to be difficult enough." Gavin unbuckled his seat belt and looked to Dodger and Bambam, who were already standing across the wall from the normal direction of acceleration - the new floor. "I didn't know stations this small could have artificial gravity," he said.

"The rotation is actually too strong for an asteroid this size, but it's not falling apart because its structure has now been reinforced to the point where there's minimal regolith on the surface anyway. Because of radiation and stuff, ke?" The mechanic stretched. "0.3g. Still."

"Why aren't the cables snapping off there?" Gavin wondered, shimmying along the metal arch of the gimbal next to the hatch that led through the narrow tube into the central corridor.

"I don't know, maybe their ends are mounted on rails that balance the whole thing and keep moving along." Bambam shrugged his rounded shoulders. "We should get going."

"What about Hellcat?"

"We'll see. When she's pissed off, there's no telling what she'll do next. Maybe she'll lock herself up for a few days, maybe she'll be right there grinning at the airlock throwing insults at us."

"Well, here we go. But before we go, I need to make contact with Jupiter Bank," Gavin said.

"Ha!" Dodger chortled. It sounded like thunder rolling.

"What?"

"That's not how it works here."

"Then how does it work?"

"We need a secure connection, and it's only granted through certain hotspots. There aren't many of those on the station. You

The last fleet

can imagine that every communication from or to here is strictly monitored and regulated. Otherwise, this place wouldn't be as secret as it is, ke?"

"Then that's where we'll go," Gavin said with a shrug.

Bambam and Dodger gave each other a look that was somewhere between pitying and amused - if the mutant was capable of such emotions at all. "What?"

"You told us about that hellhound, didn't you? Where the word Cerberus comes from and all that," the mechanic opined. "This is indeed Hell, and we have to get past the Hellhound before you can talk to Satan."

"Hades," Gavin corrected him.

"Whatever. The Prince of Hell is still Prince of Hell, and you're not going to like this one."

INTERLUDE: VARILLA USATAMI

The Senate President's atmospheric shuttle arrived at the Paris Megaplex just before sunset. The central star of the solar system sank behind the horizon as a pale disk, its light scattered to a dirty glow by the many toxic particles in the air.

The escort of two fighters turned away and their pilot lowered the luxurious plane onto one of the two landing pads of the city hall, after they had glided through the huge glass gates of the dome that protected the inner city from the atmosphere like a cheesecloth. From her window, Varilla looked down on the people in the streets, watching the faceless masses through the optical zoom of her retinal implants. Men, women, and children in breathing masks and coated plastic coats, going about their daily lives. Most on their way home from work, down the stairs to the Vactram stations, or on foot. She saw the cars, following the orderly pattern of the Gridlink, as parts in a complex organizational model that looked so fluid and effortless that it was hard to imagine how much power the AI behind it had to muster.

They were all clueless, living in their little slice of reality where the most important thing was the food on the table, the basic security on their credsticks, and the after-work entertainment in the holoprograms. They felt the weight of their worries and fears for the future on their shoulders, just as Varilla did, only hers was about the future of humanity. The two could not be further apart in scale and consequence, and yet the human experience was the same.

She found that fascinating and frightening at the same time. It wouldn't be the first time she wished she didn't know about all this, which she now did. Many times she had wondered if she would have rather perished in the *Artemis* system than survive. Since there was no turning back from her decision at that time, however, these thoughts were merely idle melancholy of an old woman, and so she pushed all that aside and concentrated on her role in the upcoming state visit, although it would be a very short one.

As they touched down and the shuttle's large delta wings folded up, the background hum of the engines also quieted, and movement came to their legation, which consisted of two members of parliament from the Saturn Congress, five secretaries of state, and twenty journalists. They rose chattering from their luxurious chairs and smoothed out their expensive costumes before the door was opened and the crew indicated that they could now disembark.

Varilla's bodyguards led the way, then she followed, stopping briefly on the top step to soak up the view. She would not see Paris again. At least not like this.

The mayor's palace was a replica of the original Renaissance building, only much larger, with more than ten stories and turquoise roof domes. From her landing pad, she had a breathtaking view of the sea of houses beneath the glass dome. It looked like a pastel painting with warm earth tones, with ornate facades that were easy to make out even from a height. The scenery was illuminated by the warm light of countless street lamps that lined the cobblestone streets.

Mayor Sapin was waiting for her with a delegation from the City Council at the end of a wide red carpet that connected the shuttle stairs to the stairwell of the palace. She strode energetically toward her host with a determined expression that showed well-dosed seriousness without being unfriendly or dismissive, well aware that she was being closely watched and analyzed by every newsfeed in the Sol system.

The last fleet

"My lord," she greeted the governor respectfully, bowing her head slightly in accordance with etiquette. "Thank you, for your invitation."

"Your visit honors us, Senate President. All of Paris appreciates it," replied Sapin, a short man with receding hairline and watery eyes separated by a prominent hooked nose.

"Thank you."

"Please follow me. We've set up a meeting with the City Council, then dinner with the new head of the Plex Police Department." Sapin pointed to the door to the stairwell.

"I'd like to visit the attack site," she said as they walked down the polished marble steps with bodyguards and entourage, accompanied by the echo of countless shoes.

"Now?" The mayor sounded as if she had told him his time of death. "But according to the flow protocol that we proposed and that was confirmed to us by your office ..."

"We're changing the protocol. The Senate feels that on behalf of the entire Congress, I should send a message of solidarity with the people of Paris. And I concur with that opinion."

"But we can't do that, we need time to put the appropriate security measures in place. The attack has put a big hole in the cathedral, and we still don't know how many criminal elements continue to enter the city center. In addition, it is not yet clear how the terrorists were able to smuggle a vacuum bomb past all the security measures and into the best-secured part of the city in the first place. In that ambiguous environment, the risk would simply be too great." Sapin sounded almost pleading now, knowing he had the short end of the stick on this one. In a way, she felt sorry for him because, of course, he was absolutely right.

But any worthwhile goal required sacrifice.

"The good thing, my lord, is that if even the security forces don't know about our visit, neither do the terrorists, and so they couldn't prepare an attack," she said, seemingly lightheartedly. "And if the Senate president doesn't take any chances, how close does she feel to her constituents who have tasked her with representing them? Let's get this done, please. As far as I'm concerned, we'll just take a very small convoy; it will save time and sensation-

203

alism. Most of my entourage will be waiting for us here. When we return, we can proceed with the program you have planned."

"Of course, Senate President." Sapin bowed his head in surrender, but looked as if he had suddenly fallen ill.

Their motorcade, consisting of three armored cars, large but rather nondescript, was ready ten minutes later. Only a closer look showed that everything about them was a bit thicker and wider.

Varilla sat in the middle vehicle, her right-hand man, State Secretary Eduard Keller, along with Sapin's secretary and his aide in the rear, and her bodyguards in the front, while she remained alone with the mayor.

"Our city was once the cradle of Europe in matters of philosophy, culture and artificial avant-garde," the politician said with a sad look as they drove through the pretty downtown streets. "It's a shame what these terrorists have done to it."

"Yes," she said absently, nodding. Unseen, she kneaded her hands between her knees.

"All the more reason I'm glad you came here, Senate President." He looked directly at her, and there was genuine relief in his gaze. "After all the ... incidents, I was expecting a harsh reaction. Which, of course, I would have understood."

Varilla didn't need twenty years of experience as a politician to figure out that his quickly followed-up affirmation was merely lip service. This man loved his city and had counted on the Emperor swinging the hammer before the disease could spread any further. She felt involuntarily sorry for him.

"Paris is not a bad place or a training camp for Republican terrorists," Sapin continued his assurances. "People want to push that image on us."

"People?" she echoed.

The mayor looked out the window in anguish. "I don't want to sound like a conspiracy theorist, Miss Usatami, but the whole thing is extremely strange. The Plex police are well structured and at least as well established as those of model archologies like Berlin, Rome or London. At the same time, these murderous

The last fleet

dogs always manage to sneak past the checkpoints and security mechanisms."

"Hmm," Varilla said and fell silent. Sapin seemed to take that as a hint that she was unwilling to discuss such political matters with him here, though he had apparently hoped to use their unexpected time together to make his point. But he was silent for the rest of the drive as well, until ten minutes later they arrived at the site of the attack, where the century-old Arc de Triomphe had once stood and was now only a smoking ruin.

Their vehicles pulled up to the Plex police checkpoint, behind which the fountains of foam and water she had seen in the feeds could still be seen. In the dark, the damaged end of the Champs-Élysées was a brightly lit, surreal landscape of rubble, like something out of a war movie.

"We'll be at the east end ...," Sapin was just beginning, when a loud bang swallowed the rest of his words and their car suddenly stopped. The mayor winced and widened his eyes as escort vehicles in front and behind them went up in fireballs.

Varilla mirrored his horror and pointed at the door.

"NO!" screamed Sapin. "Don't open it!"

But she had already pushed the button, and almost at the same moment someone yanked it open from outside. She looked into the eyes of a masked assailant in full combat gear, who dragged her out, threw her to the ground, and emptied his entire magazine.

14

The first thing Gavin noticed when they entered the station through the long airlock hose was the smell. It was a mixture of lubricants, sweat, fried meat and unwashed clothes. On top of that, the humidity was oppressive, the likes of which he had only experienced twice before in his life: once on a family vacation to the tropical islands of Aquarius and the other time during an emergency exercise as a cadet in training. On that occasion, the training officer had built a bug into the life support system so that the humidity was no longer properly regulated and they all slowly began to boil in their own sweat.

Gavin allowed himself to command the Smartnites in his circuit via his neural computer to provide accelerated temperature regulation. Shortly thereafter, his skin tingled slightly as billions of the tiny nanobots pushed through his pores and became submicroscopic radiators, so he didn't sweat.

The second thing that surprised him was how tidy it was at the same time. In the narrow docking area, consisting of wide but very low corridors, all the cargoes were hidden behind wall panels, to which robotic trucks occasionally drove, unfolded them, and picked up their loads with gripper arms.

"Welcome to the *Cerberus*," a dock worker in a stained jumpsuit greeted them, wiping drops of sweat mixed with dirt from his forehead. He was spindly and so tall he had to tuck his head in, though even Dodger could just about stand upright. In one of his spider-like hands he held a latest-generation holopad that showed a representation of *Lady Vengeance*. "Four hours layover. Ten thousand crowns."

"Excuse me?" it blurted out of Gavin. That was more than even Jupiter Bank charged for its infamous docking station during audiences for private banking clients.

"We need access to a secure link to the outside," Hellcat said, suddenly appearing behind them and not giving them a glance.

"Of course. The wait time is currently three hours and the charges are..."

"No need," the tall Invitro was abruptly interrupted as a Norm appeared behind him, who didn't seem to have any problems with the high humidity. He was slightly shorter than Gavin, with a shaved skull and an obvious data jack over his ear with several cable connectors sticking out of it. His suit looked expensive, making it seem as incongruous in this place as the expensive bandana. "Welcome to the *Cerberus*. I am administrator Adam Goosens. The Broker is already expecting you."

"Oh, no, no, no," Bambam cut in, smiling and spreading his fingers in front of his chest, "There's no need for that, we just have a few things to do, and..."

"Follow me, please," the administrator interrupted him impassively, turning on his heel.

Gavin wanted to ask the mechanic why he was so agitated, but his companion's pale face was enough to make him nervous.

They followed the administrator through the low corridors, which, contrary to the unpleasant smell, looked extremely well kept and maintained. The joints between the wall panels were free of plaque and patina, as was the case on most asteroid settlements, the floor with its many markings gleaming. The myriad dock workers they passed were also sweaty, but not unkempt or even dirty - except for their coveralls, which bore witness to work.

"What are those little lights on the right and left?" he asked Dodger, who was walking to his left and, unlike Bambam, didn't look like she'd seen a ghost.

The last fleet

The mutant took the toothpick out of the corner of her mouth before answering, "Augmented reality nodes."

"AR nodes?" he repeated in disbelief. "That's old-fashioned even for a place like this."

"But not susceptible to jamming."

Gavin thought about it and finally unlocked the AR function of his neural computer. He expected to be inundated with ads for brothels, pornography, and Assai weed, and had already activated every spam filter he possessed, but none of them kicked in. The only virtual things he saw in front of him were offers for navigational services through the station with pop-up menus for various service areas and security notices for the Vactram, to which red arrows on the ceiling pointed the way.

"What did you expect?" asked Hellcat at his side, who had taken Bambam's place. "Sodom and Gamorah?"

"Gomorrah," he corrected her automatically. When she then made a face as if she would pounce on him at any moment, he quickly added, "That's Hebrew for an Old Testament city in the Middle East of the earth. God incinerated it as punishment for its sinfulness. The colony of Gamorah, on the other hand, is the purest paradise. This place here seems like neither."

"I guess we're not quite what you expected, huh?"

"*We?*" he asked. "I didn't know you rebels were allied with the former gangs of Kerrhain."

"More of a partnership of convenience," she admitted. "But we are united by being forced underground and having to fight for our right to survive."

"Then why are you all so nervous?"

"Because the Broker never sees anyone." Hellcat smoothed her hair to one side and straightened her clothes. She had traded in the stolen police uniform for a simple boarding suit from the *Lady Vengeance*, as had Bambam and Dodger. Now Gavin stood out again with his synth jeans and banal cotton jacket that looked like it came from a boutique.

The administrator led them to a station where dozens of workers in coveralls and helmets, visitors in expensive suits, and the first two security guards he had seen, were waiting for the streetcar at the small station. The security guards were Invitros, mutants like Dodger, tall, hairless and strong as gorillas. He did not see any obvious weaponry on them, which led him to conclude that they had augmented weapons. What was striking about those waiting was the fact that none of them looked around, rather they kept their gazes to themselves, as if there was some unwritten law.

Perhaps there was, so Gavin also began to limit himself to looking only at what was necessary. As the streetcar roared through the vacuum tube and braked, the doors of the plastic seal separating the station from the tube opened - and no one entered except the administrator, who motioned for them to follow him. None of those waiting on the platform seemed to protest as a jolt went through the cabin and they sped through the interior of the asteroid. Other platforms flew past them so quickly that they were no more than brief afterimages on the circuits in his retinas.

After a few minutes, they slowed down and reached the end of the vacuum tube. Through the doors, they were led into a funnel-shaped area in the rock that ended in a narrow passageway. Gavin's neural computer, after a quick scan, alerted him to strong electronic signatures in the rock, which was smooth from the outside, indicating military-type weapons and sensors.

On the ground in front of them, a cleaning bot hovered, busy cleaning up a stubborn bloodstain.

"The Circuit Genocide must have missed this one," Gavin remarked in an attempt to lighten the glum mood among his companions - and himself - but no one responded.

"One at a time," Administrator Goosens urged them. "When you go in, you should have your AR implants activated and follow the directions. Do not deviate from it under any circumstances."

Gavin swallowed and merely nodded as he tried to imagine what might be waiting for them behind the dark crack in the rock wall. *Prince of Hell,* he thought back to Bambam's words. *An overconfident mutant, perhaps, who has seen too many horror movies?*

The last fleet

When he realized that the administrator would not follow them and the others were still hesitating, he shrugged his shoulders and went ahead. There could be no question of him looking weak in front of the others. And how bad could it be?

He squeezed through the crevice in the rock, surprised at how far it went and that it didn't smell like rock at all.

Then suddenly it was as if he emerged from deep water. A driving bass welcomed him like thunder, followed by hard synth beats and a wave of beguiling smells, sweet and rustic at the same time, they wrapped around his nose and instinctively triggered in him the desire for sexual and violent debauchery. He commanded his neural computer to block the appropriate hormonal processes, only to find that he could not connect to the chip on his brain stem. This time he was on his own with his thoughts and physical weaknesses.

"How ...?" the word escaped him.

"Third-generation white noise," Bambam murmured next to him as they just stood there, gazing into the dark club where one or two hundred patrons moved to the rhythm of the music. They danced around a bar that formed a ring around a large sphere in the center and was illuminated in green. Seating was scarce at the outer edge of the circular cavern. There, men and women sat with masks in front of their faces, all of the same make: white and curved so that they completely covered only one half of their faces. Somewhere Gavin knew their particular shape, but he couldn't say in what context.

"Keep moving, people," Hellcat hissed behind them. "We're not even supposed to be here, on the damn network."

"Network?" he asked, but didn't wait for her answer, following the flashing red arrows in the onyx floor that led directly toward the bar. It didn't escape him that it shouldn't actually be working at all, since his neural computer was jammed, but his crazed senses made it hard to think about anything. So he pulled himself together and followed the instructions. He pushed aside the sexual cravings and violent fantasies that conflicted within him by focusing on his pilot breathing. Two seconds on, six seconds off, as he had learned in flight training to calm his nervous system.

The bartender, a Delta-class humanoid robot if he wasn't mistaken, pressed a button, and part of the bar retreated into the counter to give them a view of a rectangular black cutout in the large sphere behind it, from which thousands of tiny cables ran off and disappeared into the ceiling and floor. A plastic face appeared on the mirrored glass plate that formed the face of the deltabot, deforming into a mirror image of Gavin's own and making him cringe.

He avoided the robot's lifeless gaze, thanking the Emperor that his kind had long been outlawed and their possession punishable.

In front of the rectangular black cutout in the sphere - he could have sworn it hadn't been there when he entered the club - he paused, wanting to reach out a hand to touch the darkness. But he managed to stop himself at the last moment. Whoever was waiting for him in there, Gavin wasn't going to give him or her the satisfaction of acting like Alice in Wonderland.

After one last breath, he went inside and found himself inside a sphere with a single person sitting in the center - an Invitro of the worker line. Over eight feet tall with powerful muscles and no hair. Digitattoos stretched across his entire skin, which was not covered by any visible clothing, making him look blue. The nano circuits were in constant motion and rearrangement, making it uncomfortable to look at the figure, who, it occurred to Gavin after an involuntary glance, had no genitals whatsoever. The man's bald head was littered with universal connectors that sat like metallic melanomas in the scalp. From them came a dozen finger-thick cables that gathered in a computational core that hung from the ceiling like a medicine ball.

"Ah, welcome," the Broker greeted them in a full-throated bass voice that sounded like the reverberations of an earthquake in the deepest layers of rock. His mouth parted into an emotionless smile, revealing a row of gleaming platinum implants where teeth should have been. "Twenty seconds to go."

Gavin glanced uncertainly at the others, who, however, stared

The last fleet

straight ahead at the bizarre figure of their host and paid him no further attention. None of them stirred, they didn't even seem to consider settling down on the narrow seat cushion that was once built in all around the inside of the sphere.

"No,Senator.Twentyhoursmore," the Broker whispered so quickly that the words blurred into one another. He sounded like a patient caught in a fever dream. "Interrupt.Fiftyunitsnomoreandnolessorthedealisoff. Break. Theapprovalmustberenewedbeforetheeleventhortheroutewillnolongerbeserved. YourdecisionHighLady. Break. Theattackshouldhavehitthedistributioncenter. Unnecessarypoliceinvestigationwillbetheconsequenceandyouwillhavetocatchityourselforgodown. Eitherdocorrectworkorfindsomeoneelse. Break. ConnectwithSupervisoryCommitteeChairmanDeVries. Leander. The transfer is complete and I expect my participationcertificatebyteno'clocksynchronizedstandard time. Thedeliveryisonitswayandwillarriveonehourearlierasasignofmygoodwill. Break."

The Broker opened his eyes and lowered his huge hands, which he had just spread out like a biblical demon figure. In the palms, the digitattoos retracted and arranged themselves into a dense web of nanocircuits under the wrist, where they briefly lit up.

"Welcome, Lord Captain Gavin Andal," the mutant greeted him politely, eyeing him with his pitch-black eyes, which were obviously augment replacements. Gavin winced at the mention of his name.

"How do you know who I am?" he asked before he could think about it.

"It's my job to know everything."

"You read our onboard computer," he said.

"Let's not waste our precious time stating the obvious. I know who you are, my lord, and also that you are the sole remaining heir to the House of Andal. My condolences on your loss." Nothing about the Broker's voice sounded sympathetic.

"Thank you," he replied just as neutrally.

"So, what brings you and your friends to my humble home?"

"They are not my friends," Gavin snapped.

"They're not? Shall I have them recycled for you?" their host asked lightly, and Hellcat and Bambam stirred beside him.

"There's no need."

"We're fighting on the same side!" snapped Hellcat.

"No, Felicity van Hauten. You are fighting for a realignment of the power structure in which I thrive. Why would I be foolish enough to destroy the foundation of the information flow that reveals the entire universe to me?"

The Broker raised a finger and she fell silent. Then he eyed Gavin again. "You will have to make some changes to your ship in order to track your brother's lost fleet. Since Marquandt's betrayal, the Star Empire is no longer a safe place for your kind."

"Witnesses?"

"Loyalists."

"You know about Marquandt's treachery. My data was not in the *Lady*'s on-board computer."

"I never rely on a single source," the Broker replied calmly.

Gavin's mind was running hot, but he was still finding it hard to shake the influence of the pheromone cocktails from the club's air. What was the purpose of this stuff anyway? Was it to confuse the patrons? Create a hurdle?

"You're in cahoots with Marquandt!" it finally escaped him.

"You should not humiliate yourself, High Lord Andal. You should know that I know no sides. I only know information and use it to my best advantage - and, contrary to what you might think, for the benefit of humanity."

Gavin managed not to snort.

"What do you think power is, my lord?" the Broker asked, and his politeness struck Gavin as disconcerting. His counterpart expressed himself in a chosen manner, spoke with accentuation, and at the same time looked like a hybrid of mutant and tech-head, an abomination of conflicting technologies that had nothing human about it anymore.

"Knowledge," he replied, without hesitation.

"Is that so?" His counterpart paused. "Power is a subjective thing. For your companions of the Republican underground, the

The last fleet

answer is surely courage or strength. Something along the lines of those primitive terms, anyway."

Gavin could hear Hellcat's knuckles crack.

"And they may be right about that. For them, courage means continuing on even though the chances of success are objectively marginal. Courage gives them the power to persevere. For you, High Lord, tradition is power. Without tradition, your birthright and that of the other members of the Council of Nobility and the Assembly of Governors of the State, you would have no power at all." The Broker twitched his upper lip as if a spasm was running through him. For a moment, the implants in his mouth gleamed like bare metal. "To me, information is power," he said.

"It's the same as knowledge."

"Incorrect. To see through the game of things, the perfect determinism of all data, the focus must be on the subtleties: Knowledge means the growth of relevant objective information through one's own experience. A melange of the information itself, experience and intuition. Identical reproduction of knowledge is therefore not possible, because it is subject to subjective processes of data processing by a human brain. Information, on the other hand, is the systematic embedding of facts in their respective context. All knowledge requires information as its foundation, High Lord, and mine tell me that you have something on board that holds information for me that I have been thirsting after for a very, very long time." The mutant emitted a sound reminiscent of the cooing of a predatory cat, only much deeper.

The Orb! thought Gavin.

"Yes," whispered the Broker. "You know what I ask for. But you will not give it to me. Tell me, Lord Captain Andal, are you afraid of me?"

"No," he replied honestly.

"That is good. You have nothing left to lose, it seems. You are kept alive only by the hope of revenge - a base instinct of the organic imperative, but a sufficient one, I suppose. Fear is no basis for power," their host continued, eyeing his companions for the first time. "Cornered animals are doomed by their biochemical heritage to fight or flee when frightened, and when that is not possible, to fight or freeze. That's why I know their little rebellion is doomed to failure. They are afraid, but they have no power, because fear has power over them. I can smell it on them now and see it in their eyes." After a moment, the Broker turned back to Gavin. "I demand the Orb as payment."

"That's impossible! The Orb must..."

"The Orb stays here. It has already been taken to my laboratories."

Gavin already wanted to curse him, but didn't give in. All the talk about power had probably just made him comfortable with the idea of not having any in this place.

"I am aware of the rudeness of my actions," the Broker continued, without any trace of remorse in his bass voice. "But I am a businessman, and business requires a certain level of trust. I am aware that the corpse of an orb is currently probably the most coveted item within the Star Empire, and I will pay any debt. Therefore, I grant you my dearest: information. Three questions, three answers."

"And our ship," Hellcat interjected.

The Broker didn't look at her, continued to fix on Gavin, and made a throwaway hand gesture. "Your ship will be equipped with the best hardware we have in stock. I'm talking about the real balance of our trade."

"Three answers," Gavin repeated hoarsely. He was under no illusion that this man most likely knew as much as any one person in the Star Empire was even capable of knowing, aside from the Emperor himself perhaps - though he was likely to be shielded from a great deal of information. But what was he to ask? "Agreed."

His host's smile told him he was not surprised, as there could have been no other outcome to this conversation.

"Ask, Lord Captain."

"Is my brother still alive?" he asked, without hesitation.

"No. According to my data, he is not, and it is very clear."

Gavin suppressed an outcry.

The last fleet

"Who is in cahoots with Marquandt? He must have allies on Earth, in the Emperor's immediate circle."

"The Chief of Staff, Grand Admiral Marius Albius, and the Senate President, Varilla Usatami," the Broker replied. The fact that this man - this creature - knew all this was not as startling as the fact that he shared his knowledge. For the Broker, it had to be an absolute breach of taboo, especially since it was no small thing, but treason against the Empire.

"Where did my brother's escaped ships go?" he asked before his mind could spin like a hurricane around the two names he had been given.

"That is information that even I do not have. I've made calculations based on the data I have access to, but they don't come to a valid conclusion." The Broker graciously spread his arms. "I will therefore allow you a substitute question."

"Does Marquandt know that I have survived and am in possession of evidence?"

"No. But his preparation has been intense and his web reaches far. Count on his eyes and ears being present even here on Cerberus."

"How long did he prepare for all this? And who else knows of his treachery besides you? How many members of the Admiralty are in on it and in cahoots with him? Is he in cahoots with the Orb? What were those strange drones?" Gavin cursed himself for not knowing what the most important questions might have been. If only his mind had at least been functioning unaffected by the pheromones in the air. This man was indeed a spawn of hell.

"Ah, only three questions, I'm afraid. Our deal is done." The Broker took a step back and spread his arms again as holodisplays appeared on the walls showing footage of Gavin, Hellcat, Bambam and Dodger boarding the Vactram and being scanned by a sensor cluster outside the club. All the vital signs and DNA data ran down on a side display.

"What is this? A shakedown?"

"A security for me," the mutant replied calmly. "I always protect my sources and my guests from themselves as well."

Gavin bared his teeth in frustration.

217

"Leave now, High Lord Andal. The modifications to your ship will be completed the day after tomorrow. I suggest you use the time to come up with a plan, because even I am having a hard time seeing a path that could lead you to your destination." With that, the Broker closed his eyes again and began to whisper unintelligibly. The cables from his head twitched back and forth like tentacles.

INTERLUDE: JANUS

Janus sighed in surrender as he had to decline the twentieth call. He swiped his wrist terminal to send an automated callback request.

"Your Majesty," he said, his face contorting as their plane took a tight right turn and his stomach pressed against his right ribcage. "Is it really necessary that we ..."

"Look, Janus," Emperor Haeron II interrupted him with almost youthful enthusiasm, pushing the control unit between his knees even further to the side. He looked almost euphoric, whipped up by the concerns that had driven him here.

"The cockpit is made of glass, sir, I can't help but look," he remarked.

Their ancient Airjack 222 broke through the cloud cover and the endless meadows and hills of central France opened up before them. The grass looked sickly discolored even from the high altitude, and the hills were smooth-surfaced from centuries of extreme storms. The blank granite did not shine, however, but appeared dull and colorless, although the cloud cover was cracked and a few rays of sunlight strayed onto the landscape.

He had to admit to himself, despite the sinking feeling in his stomach - they were flying in a museum-quality plane, manually! He had to admit that it was an almost mystical sight, the landscape tormented by acid rain, floods and heat waves. He spent little time on Earth, or any planet in general, and often forgot what it felt like. Sublime somehow, right, as if something was falling back into place that had long been displaced.

Janus declined the next call, as he was ordered to do.

"How are things on Hadron, my dear?" the Emperor wanted to know, and went into a blessedly gentle left turn. Out of the corner of his eye, Janus could see the fighters flanking them, predatory arrows of composite and firepower.

"Greener, Majesty. Both continents stretch along the equator and are covered by vast grassy hills. We have no mountains, but we do have a consistent climate year-round."

"I wish I could get out more." The Emperor sounded wistful. "Then I would have liked to visit Hadron. Perhaps someday an important appointment in your fiefdom will arise."

"I don't think so; there are few less important worlds than mine."

"Sometimes it would be pleasant if you weren't so consistently honest."

"At some point I came to the realization that you hardly appointed me to court because of my excellent connections and standing in the Council of Nobility, much less as your right-hand man," Janus replied, swiping his wrist terminal again as it chirped. "So it must have been my honesty."

"There it is." Haeron II took a hand off the helm and pointed straight ahead through the armored glass toward a vague outline on the horizon. Now, all at once, the head of humanity sounded glum. "Paris."

"You don't have to do this, Your Majesty."

"Do you know what the worst part of being emperor is, Janus?"

"You complain about your lot often enough that it's hard for me to put my finger on one thing."

Haeron II grimaced. "One becomes accustomed to loneliness with simultaneous non-existent privacy like one becomes accustomed to a lingering pain after a failed rejuvenation. Also, the paradoxical feeling of being controlled by others, even though one can supposedly decide everything, is like a mental cornea. But

The last fleet

what I fail at to this day is the knowledge of living in a bubble. I am flying an Airjack 222 right now that is over two hundred years old. It flies on hydrogen! Any avionics enthusiast in the star realm would kill for such a privilege. But you know what? Everything has a price. Every light casts a shadow."

"I'm afraid I don't quite follow you, Your Majesty," Janus remarked, once again wiping his wrist terminal.

"You didn't want to fly to Paris when it happened. You wanted me to be spared that. That I wouldn't be directly associated with what was going to happen."

"Yes. It's politically awkward."

"No, Janus, it's decent."

"It must be done, your majesty," he replied with respectful emphasis. "The alternative would be even worse."

"I am aware of that. But it was my decision in the end. On my desk were the documents to sign. I know nothing about those people there except numbers, dates, cold facts, black pixels on a white glow. Still, it is my decision what they will experience the coming night." The Emperor gave a long-drawn sigh, as if the weight of the entire universe rested on his shoulders. "I am changing their future, how could I look the other way? If I can't see what's coming, really see it, what distinguishes me from an artificial intelligence that uses pragmatic rationalism as a template for whatever is put before it?"

They were silent for the next five minutes as Paris grew larger before them. Janus thought it looked like a tumor surrounded by inflamed tissue. Dark walls as high as houses protected the monolithic megascrapers, black structures that reached to the lower cloud layers. In the center was the *Mitterand* Dome, a giant glass bell that had become the city's landmark. It shielded the former old city from the corrosive rain and the effects of the constant wind that battered the earth's surface. To the north of the brutalist-looking city, the six ruins of the CO2 towers that their ancestors had used all over the world to try to combat the exploding carbon dioxide in the atmosphere rose out of the desolate landscape. Today they were the sign of a grandiose failure, the reasons for which were still being argued.

"Your Majesty," rang out from the loudspeakers. "This is General Liguno, units are now on final approach to target. Awaiting deployment order."

"Go ahead, general. And give me a time."

"Five minutes to engagement."

"Patch me through, Janus," the Emperor demanded.

"Your Majesty, are you sure you want to take..."

"Yes, I'm sure. It was my decision, after all."

"As you wish." Janus contacted Mayor Jean Sapin, who had already been evacuated along with his cabinet and all senior city officials.

"First Secretary of State," the politician greeted him in a hushed voice.

"Put us through to the city, all channels by priority switch."

"As you wish, High Lord Darishma."

Janus activated the small camera drone from his transport bag and piloted it directly in front of the Emperor. Then he looked to the head of humanity and nodded to him. Haeron II straightened and looked directly into the lens with a serious and visibly depressed expression.

"Citizens of Paris," he finally intoned clearly in a carried voice in which there was no trace of his melancholy. "Continued violent protests and attacks on civil and regulatory institutions are a threat to the cohesion of our Star Empire. Our generous ultimatum expired half an hour ago and I regret being forced to take this step: I have signed six million enforcement notices for forced deportations by Imperial decree. Resistance will be met with force, cooperation with justice. Anyone who harbors criminal and seditious individuals will now have to decide where their path leads from here on. This is the first and final warning. Humanity stands alone in a dark, cold universe surrounded by unspeakable horrors, and only unity can save us from being swept into the abyss. Chaos leads to secession, and secession leads back to the horrors of our history that must never be repeated."

Haeron II ended the live feed to the city and Janus set the drone back into his hand using gesture controls.

The last fleet

"General, begin storming as soon as you are ready," the Emperor ordered and sighed. He seemed to slump a bit.

Their plane was now silently circling on autopilot around the city below them, next to which landing craft were touching down from all points of the compass, disgorging thousands of Marines. From a distance, they looked like swarming ant colonies, seemingly swarming chaotically, only to reunite at the city walls.

"It will only take a few hours, Your Majesty," Janus assured his master.

"We use a hammer where a scalpel would have been necessary," Haeron II countered.

"But the scalpel was not capable of doing the job."

"Hmm."

"Begin storming the city," General Liguno announced over the radio. The first rattle of high-speed weapons could be heard in the background.

"Your Majesty," Janus said when he had to decline the next call. "We should be on our way now, there are urgent matters to..."

"No." The Emperor stared down at the city, where flowers of fire were coming to life in the outskirts, reflecting as flickers off the megascrapers. "It is my duty to watch it to the end."

The First Secretary sighed once more. "Sometimes I wish you were a little less self-critical and melancholy."

"Sometimes I wish you were in my place."

"A boring bureaucrat?"

"'A *predictable* bureaucrat,' were my words. That's probably the best compliment at court." Haeron II paused. "Isn't it strange?"

"What exactly, Your Majesty?"

"We are threatened by aliens whose technology is far ahead of us and whom we know absolutely nothing about. Add to that the Never, a phenomenon that seems to come straight out of our darkest nightmares. And yet the greatest danger to humanity is our own division before all this cosmic evil. First the UN, then the Solar Union, finally the period of fragmentation after the wars of secession, and then the Solar Union again, and then the

McMaster Dynasty - all of them have broken from the inside out. First by protests and violent riots, eventually attacks and organized resistance, as in Paris. Are we doomed to tear ourselves apart?"

"*We are a lonely ship on a river going through a darkness full of chasms while the crew complains about the food and punches holes in the hull,*" Janus quoted.

"Admiral McMaster had no particular talent for lyricism, that much is certain," the Emperor opined.

"But the people understood his language."

"And led his son to the blade."

"That was the Corporate Protectorate," Janus contradicted his master.

"And what does the corporate protectorate do? Always what's best for the bottom line, and that's stability and consumers with money in their pockets."

Janus was distracted by a glow from his wrist terminal that was red, not yellow, signifying a priority request.

"Your Majesty, your daughter is calling," he said, hoping they could finally escape the sight of violence unleashed among them.

But Haeron II only sighed, "She hates me."

"Because you lock her up."

"I merely gave her a lot of chores. She has to get used to life at court, after all."

"And so, if possible, never to be unguarded and unobserved, lest she repeat what her elder sister did," Janus resumed, and for a moment he feared he had gone too far when his master gave him an angry look.

"I can't lose another daughter," he finally replied more calmly than expected, and the bags under his eyes seemed to have grown a little heavier and darker.

"You have not lost her, Your Majesty."

"Soon she will have been lost for twenty years, how can you not speak of lost? Not knowing why your child left you and her entire life and how she is now, what happened to her, is much worse than if she had died, Janus."

"I can only imagine," he admitted with thoughts of his three sons who lived at home on Tranit with their mother. It even depressed him when he didn't get news from them for a few days. "But you still have a son and daughter who need their father and need to find their place in the universe."

"I know." Haeron II took a deep breath and nodded. "Put them through. But we're staying here. Until it's over."

15

"Hello, Captain," Gavin was greeted by Dodger as he entered the mess hall and trotted sleepily over to the coffee machine. The mutant was leaning against one of the cabinets, sipping from a huge cup.

He paused, rubbed his eyes and stifled a yawn as he eyed her.

"Did you just say *captain*?"

"You're piloting this barge," she noted.

"Right now I'm a prisoner on this barge," he corrected her, trying to get the machine to make him a cappuccino. When it didn't budge, he thumped it on the side and it began to do its work with a loud rattle and click. While he waited, he looked back at Dodger. "Are you always up at five in the morning?"

"Mutants only need four hours of sleep under normal circumstances."

"And this is normal circumstances?" he asked.

"Yep."

"You called yourself a *mutant*."

"When you make the vocabulary of those who hate you your own, it takes the edge off," she said, taking another sip of coffee.

"In a good way, I guess." Gavin pulled the cup of what the machine thought was cappuccino off the grate and screwed up his face in disgust as he sipped it.

"Nah. But not in a bad wat either."

"Makes me sick that the guy can probably watch and listen to us the whole time," he abruptly changed the subject.

"Not me."

"Why not?"

"You have full control of the ship's computers, don't you?"

"Yes." He choked down another sip of caffeine with the taste of coffee removed.

"Then theoretically you can also watch and listen anywhere in the ship at any time," she explained, giving no indication on how she valued that thought.

"I guess so," he admitted.

"But you don't."

"No, I usually have better things to do."

"See."

"Morning," someone grumbled ill-humoredly from the doorway. It was Bambam, making his way to the coffee machine with his shoulders hunched.

"Bad night?"

"You can say that again. I always thought I was among friends here, only to find out that the damn bastard would have killed me if you'd wanted him to."

"But I didn't want to," Gavin noted.

"Guess we're still of value to Your Most Worshipful Eminence," Bambam sneered in his direction.

"That's the protocol form of address for a cardinal," he corrected the mechanic, who then merely looked at him, grabbed his filled coffee cup from the tray, and wordlessly left the mess hall. Gavin looked at Dodger, who was eyeing him with a furrowed brow. "What?"

"If you have always been treated kindly without earning it, you obviously don't learn how to make friends," she remarked, setting down her coffee cup and leaving him alone with his thoughts.

Gavin continued to watch her for a long time, moving her words back and forth. Then he went to the bridge and set to work on the systems checks - a never-ending list of all the new integration processes that went together through rebuilds, replaced component and refurbished secondary systems. The changes that were made were extremely far-reaching. He had sent a list of requests to Administrator Goosens after their visit to the Broker, and to his surprise, almost all of them had been fulfilled during the past two days. Some other items found their way into his ship without his having requested them. At first he had been worried about this, but since the ship still obeyed him and he had access to all the log files, he could give the all-clear: Their host hadn't bugged them or backstabbed them with a killswitch.

"So, are we ready to go?" asked Marshall, who had climbed into the bridge after the first two hours of Gavin going through list after list and checking off individual items.

"In principle, yes. We got four fusion engines installed, latest Raptor models from Yokatami. Oversized for us, but I won't complain. Latest generation smart Hawk missiles, Thor bullets for the railguns, but no Gauss cannons. Apparently there are limits to what the Broker can stock after all," Gavin said, looking at his displays as if their host could hear them. "But for this, we have a new type of jammer that eats two megawatts per hour, according to the integration log. I don't know what that device is. It doesn't have a fleet identifier, or a digital signature from any manufacturer. The system just says *Disruptor*."

"Unless it turns out to be something else entirely. May I ask when we're leaving, my lord?" the Marine asked.

"Two hours from now. The vacuum workers are just attaching the last of the hull assemblies with the drones. Soon we'll be a Class 2 *Light Hauler* - at least according to the radar signature."

"Do you know what course we're going to take yet?"

"I have an idea, but I certainly won't voice it while we're docked here," Gavin explained, turning to the master sergeant. "I'd also like you to stay here."

"Excuse me, my lord?"

"There's a lot of information to be gathered here and supposedly the best black market augment clinic far and wide. I turned down an appointment with Administrator Goosens, fully paid."

"Did you...?"

"No." Gavin shook his head and scowled. "I'm not going to access my family's accounts."

"You don't want to take any chances. Because of Marquandt and his spies," Marshall concluded.

"Right." Gavin pulled out the slip of paper he had prepared and folded and pressed it against the palm of his hand with his thumb rather than holding it out to the sergeant. The latter seemed confused for only a fraction of a second and then grasped it. He deftly made the note disappear into his uniform. "We'll be back as soon as we find my brother's fleet. I'll need a weapon when the time comes, Sergeant. And that weapon must be you for me."

"Of course, my lord." The hint of a smile stole onto Marshall's face. Gavin had thought until now that the man was not capable of getting it done. "You can count on me."

"I know, and I thank you for that."

Five hours later they were flying at a comfortable 1g acceleration toward the outer system of Kerrhain, aiming for the gas giant Gleuse. Sphinx was in charge of the controls while Gavin sat with the crew in the mess hall handing out ready-made lasagna.

"Is this your way of sucking up to us?" asked Bambam, looking at the recyclable plate in front of him. The mechanic smelled it and cooed. "If so, it's working a little, at least."

"I secured a special food delivery from the administrator." he explained, gesturing for Dodger and Hellcat to help themselves as well.

"Where's the bad-tempered Marine?" asked Hellcat, obviously trying hard to hide how much she wanted to pounce on the lasagna.

"I left him on the Cerberus."

"Excuse me?" escaped Bambam, and he lowered his fork just before it reached his mouth. White béchamel sauce landed on his plate with a loud *splat!* "Just like that? I mean, not that it would bother me."

"Why?" asked Dodger.

"Officially, so he can get some eye enhancements that are only available on the black market."

"And unofficially?"

"I want the Orb back."

Now all three of them stared at him as if he were suffering from an incurable disease. The lasagna seemed to have lost its appeal in one fell swoop.

"I know what you're thinking now," Gavin declared, stuffing a forkful into his mouth, burning the roof of his mouth as he did every time. Was there any other way to eat pizza and pasta? *"A single Marine, how is he going to get that new showpiece back from the Broker?"*

"Among other things," Hellcat confirmed grimly. "But there's also, why would you risk making an enemy of the Broker? Why do you think this sergeant has any chance at all? What if he gets busted and the Broker wants us dead? What if he considers our deal broken because of it? What if he sells us out to Marquandt because of it?"

"Yeah, all that, too. But the Master Sergeant is absolutely loyal and has worked as a liaison sergeant for my house's intelligence service for several years and enjoyed a lot of additional civilian training as my father's bodyguard. If anyone can do it, he can." Gavin leaned forward conspiratorially. "The dead Orb is connected to everything, I know it. If the Broker dissects it, or whatever else he plans, we'll never find out."

"We?" Hellcat shook her head. "This is your vendetta, remember? We're just going along for the ride until you find your brother's fleet, and then we're out of here."

"Do we have any idea at all where to start our search?" asked Bambam, who by now was decimating his lasagna again.

"No," Gavin admitted, lowering his eyes in frustration. He put down his fork and rubbed his temples. "My brother had very little time to give the order. I don't know what target he might have issued in the heat of the moment. There are several that come to mind."

"Other Border Systems, I guess," the mechanic mumbled between bites.

"For example, but too close."

"Or the Corporate Protectorate," Dodger said, nearly finishing her plate. "They don't extradite."

"Our fleet has committed no crime," he burst out.

"Crimes are a matter of perspective. If Marquandt's view prevails, as shitty as it is from your point of view, he'll come up with something that makes the survivors look like criminals," Hellcat spoke up again, shrugging her shoulders as if she didn't care. Which was probably true to the facts.

"To the Corporate Protectorate, it's at least thirty jumps to the heart of the Star Empire. Far too risky. You don't get a fleet from A to B unseen. Marquandt would have far too many ways to intercept them."

"Besides, he would figure that out himself, and he surely has the routes guarded."

"They could try jumping directly to Earth," Bambam thought aloud. "That's a lot of jumps, too, but the closer they get, the stricter the security procedures are. I don't think Marquandt could pick a battle anywhere near the Emperor. No one is that powerful, rah?"

"I can't get out of my head what the Broker said," Gavin agreed. "That Marquandt had prepared everything for a long time and woven his webs everywhere. He'll have gone over this conversation we're having now a zillion times in his head." With a somber look, he added, "Or with his co-conspirators. We're not just dealing with him, we're dealing with the Emperor's Chief of Staff and the Senate President. I just don't see why they would participate in this mass murder."

He watched Dodger as she pulled his plate of lasagna toward her and began to eat it.

"You're not eating it anymore anyway," she mumbled.

"They just have a few light-years head start when it comes to strategy after all that shit," Hellcat summarized. "Not that we'd mind. But I guess you'd need the perfect system to hide in that only you and your brother know is somehow relevant and is far enough away from any inhabited system in the Star Empire."

"There's no such thing," Bambam found.

Gavin thought about Hellcat's words and then about his brother. What might he have been thinking in the few seconds he had left to shut down all jump thrusters and restart?

"Didn't he say anything when you told him about the shit with the codes?" asked Hellcat.

"No, there wasn't time." Gavin shook his head and sighed, trying to get rid of some of the pressure that thoughts of Artas were causing in his chest and behind his eyes. Quietly he murmured, "The battle was supposed to be a great beacon, a heroic defense with my brother earning his spurs as commander and the Emperor's son rewarding the Border Worlds for their loyalty by coming to the front in person. The projections for the battle were on our side in every simulation imaginable, casualties minimal. Artas and I even joked that we would finally treat ourselves to a vacation afterwards. We've been promising ourselves that since the beginning of my cadet days."

"Vacation, huh?" Hellcat made no effort to hide the mockery in her voice. "Where was it going to be? The outlet islands on Yokatami Atoll? To the spa on New Eden where they serve live Zulustra crab in champagne sauce?"

"No, we were going to Pulau Weh," he replied, not responding to her provocation.

"What is that? A VR construct?"

"No, a small planet in the Terratorum systems beyond the Tartarus Void. It was discovered ten years ago by my father's prospectors. It's aquatic, there are only a few islands and no relevant resource deposits, so it is merely a side note. My father explained that the species-rich fish world would have been suitable for delicatessen trade if it didn't take the eight jumps through the Tartarus Void to reach the next inhabited system." Gavin sighed again. "We would have just dropped off on a particularly nice island with a white sand beach and done nothing for a few weeks except fish and get burned by the sun."

When no one said anything, he looked up from the tabletop that had served as a projection screen for his fantasies and noticed the others staring at him.

"What?"

"For a smart-ass, you sure are slow in the head," Bambam opined, shaking his head. "Your brother sent his fleet to Pulau Weh."

Gavin frowned.

"A planet beyond the Tartarus Void in a system that hasn't seen a Star Empire ship in years and there's no interest in it. No record of your talking about it. If you can't hide a fleet there, you can't hide it anywhere, ke?"

"But the Terratorum Sector is on the opposite side of the Star Empire from us," Gavin pointed out. "You'd have to make at least sixty jumps to get to the edge of the void, and then it's another ten. That leaves the main problem."

"Only if they don't jump around the outside of the populated territories," Hellcat reminded him.

"But of course!" He clapped a hand to his forehead. "Andal is on the edge as a Border System, and it only takes one jump to get into uninhabited territory. They'd have to make a lot of jumps, hundreds possibly, and gain lots of helium-3 in between, but if there were even two or three ships with scoop probes on board, they could do it endlessly. Just about every system has at least one gas giant with large amounts of helium-3 in its atmosphere."

"See, that wasn't so hard," Bambam noted with undisguised smugness. "Now we know where they're headed. It's going to take a while."

"But at least we know where to drop you off," Hellcat said.

"I understand you want to get rid of me as quickly as possible, but remember that this thing has advantages for you, too. With this ship, the whole Star Empire is open to you. Not even the IIA would still recognize it as a former frigate of the fleet."

"That means we're flying across the Star Empire?" asked Dodger, who had just finished devouring Gavin's lasagna and folded her mighty arms under her chest.

"Yes."

The last fleet

"What could possibly go wrong?"

"The shortest route is through the nearest system, though," Gavin muttered at the edge of audibility.

"Andal." For once, Hellcat didn't sound like she wanted to rip his head off.

"Yeah."

"Why the shortest?" echoed Bambam, looking longingly at his comrade's lasagna, which was still barely touched and starting to get cold. "I'm a mechanic, not a navigator, but Tranit is just as close and should even be in a straight line to the Tartarus Void, if I'm not mistaken."

"Yeah, but then we'd have a lot of Core Worlds to fight through," Gavin explained. "And that's kind of Marquandt's backyard. We have good cover and are well prepared, but I'm reluctant to push our luck."

"We can jump to S1-Ruhr via Andal," Hellcat added, nodding. "That's where the next Seed World is, P-4. Except for Ruhr's Seed Vessel, there's absolutely nothing there, so no prying eyes or ears. But it's also not so empty that we'll immediately attract attention and set off alarm bells. There are plenty of explorers and prospectors who drop in from time to time."

"By explorers you mean smugglers?" asked Bambam, nodding in understanding.

"Once we've done the entire Seed Traverse, we can cut the distance through rim and Core Worlds by almost half, and with it our risk of being discovered or busted by some stupid accident," Gavin said.

"In the Andal system, that's Never," Dodger objected.

"That's why we'll be the only ones there. Soon a quarantine will be imposed, so we'll have to hurry."

"A quarantine will be imposed because of danger."

"Yes," Gavin admitted, wanting to add something, but then deciding against it. There wasn't really anything more to say that wouldn't be merely a cheap downplaying of a hazard that everyone at the table was aware of.

"All right." Dodger stood up and left the mess hall. Bambam followed her after one last longing look at Hellcat's lasagna.

"I hope you can handle it," she said.

"What do you mean?"

"Andal. I don't want you to have a mental breakdown or something because your emotions are knocking you out."

"I won't," he assured her, questioning himself all the way to the bridge if it was a lie.

INTERLUDE: SOUTHHAIN, KERRHAIN

High Lady Salana Kerrhain sat on the terrace of her palace, listening to the piano sounds of Claude Debussy's *Claire de Lune*, while her gaze wandered over the treetops of Geloê National Park, where predatory cat analogues and worse hissed. An invisible throng, subject to the law of the jungle, chaotic and ruthless, and in that natural clarity pure and innocent, like the masterful arrangement of changing tones that caressed her ears.

"My lady," she heard an androgynous voice beside her, but did not avert her eyes from the green sea that stretched to the horizon hundreds of feet below her. The Servitor, with his white face of elastic carbon, bowed as she saw in the corner of her eyes. "I realize you did not wish to be disturbed, but there is a directional beam request from the *Cerberus*."

"Hmm," she merely commented, taking a sip of her *Antibes* champagne, which bubbled golden on the rim of the glass. "Do you think the Broker knows of your existence, Servitor?"

"I'm sorry. I do not have that information, High Lady," the robot replied.

"Of course he knows. And he thinks that this knowledge gives him power over me - among other things," she explained. "Why do you think he thinks that?"

"Because my existence violates the Human Empowerment Act, Section 1, my lady. Robots which are..."

Salana Kerrhain silenced him with a wave, mouth twisting in displeasure. "I know the text. My question was why the Broker might think he has power over me through your existence. Do you really think he could get me into legal trouble by doing that? Then you're even more underdeveloped than I would have thought."

She clicked her tongue. "No, Servitor. He thinks that by your existence he would have picked out a character flaw in me. A penchant for forbidden things perhaps, addiction to thrills, a rebellious genome - who knows. Do you think so?"

"I'm afraid I don't know, my lady."

"No, you don't. That's why you didn't see the circuit genocide coming. People behave anticipatorily, not logically, in a deterministic system where they lack data. We are know-it-alls without education, you might say." She smiled at her own remark and took a final sip from the crystal glass before handing it to the robot. "Put him through."

It took only a few seconds for a hologram of a man in a boring black pinstriped suit with a white shirt and black tie to appear before her. His face was ageless and scrupulously shaven, his eyes hidden behind sunglasses, and the connectors of a data jack showed at his temple.

"High lady," he said, indicating a bow.

She rose from her nanofoam chair, which made a soft rustling sound as its cushions rearranged themselves, and walked toward the balustrade. The hologram followed her to the marble handrail.

"I received your last message," she said calmly. "*The permit must be renewed before the eleventh or the route will no longer be served. Your call.*"

"High Lady."

"Excuse me?"

"My message ended with a respectful *High Lady*," the Broker noted.

Salana snorted contemptuously. "Pedantry doesn't suit you."

"Respect, however, does."

"Are you even capable of that? Feeling respect?"

The last fleet

"I value our agreements," he returned with a smile.

"The permit has already been issued and will go into effect when the Planetary Council signs off on it," she said, pointing out to the jungle. "It hasn't even been three decades since the Invitro Wars raged and units of the Emperor roamed the undergrowth with flamethrowers and cluster grenades."

"If your point is that Vaults and Bone Eaters have it better today: You are certainly correct. However, since then, Kerrhain's GDP has nearly tripled and your treasury has actually quadrupled on an annual basis," the Broker explained calmly. "A curious imbalance, one might think."

"Spare yourself such threats. They are primitive," Salana admonished her business partner.

"If friendly admonitions are not welcome in this conversation, I will be happy to learn what your recollection of the Emperor's death squads may be."

"There is exactly one Imperial Navy ship left in this system, twenty in my sector," she enumerated, smiling at the sight of the noisy jungle and its powerful soundscape of lives competing with each other. "Who would have thought that three decades ago? Today, this forest is a sign of a prosperous balance of different niches where life and growth thrive, despite, or perhaps because of, the struggle for survival and evolutionary competition that is the basis for it all."

"An apt metaphor. The food chain is clearly distributed, providing checks and balances up and down."

"Except for the notched tooth. They never need to look over their shoulder. Did you know that notched tooth females eat their male mates after mating?" she asked. "Sexual cannibalism, which evolution has produced to ensure the survival of offspring."

"If that's supposed to be an advance, I have to admit it's quite ... exotic in its approach."

"After fertilization, the notched tooth female no longer needs the male - it is physically weaker and does not serve to protect the offspring, which can already walk after birth. But it has valuable energy to offer, which the female can use for the pregnancy. To us, this may seem cruel, but it's just one piece of the puzzle in the never-ending cycle of energy exchange and shape shifting."

The Broker turned to her and eyed her calmly. "If you thought I no longer had a function in the cycle of your life, I would not be here now."

Salana found it interesting how his words left open what he was trying to insinuate. Room for interpretation, the friend of every negotiator. She hated wasting her time with lesser thinkers, and the Broker never wasted her time. She even respected him for that, despite the small chamber of hatred reserved in her heart only for him.

"I have a piece of information for you," he said.

"Ah." She raised an index finger to stop him from continuing. "Do you know what else is part of the law of the jungle? Nothing is wasted. Every action is for survival. So I wonder why you are offering me a piece of information? What is its price and why do you feel threatened?"

"It is a sign of goodwill."

Salana laughed mirthlessly, a harsh sound in the chirping of the mantis and howling of the predators.

"The notched tooth knows its territory, every detail, every change. That's why they are the masters of the jungle, correct?" the Broker asked. She met his insinuation with an impatient look and finally a lordly wave.

"Speak."

"Andal has fallen."

"I know that," she countered, trying to ignore the stomachache this realization had been giving her for hours. "Eleven ships that should have arrived from Andal in the last few hours, all missing. No signals from the com barques, nothing. You only have to put two and two together to know that there has been no success in stopping the Never. But what worries me even more is the fact that no one made it out. Why hasn't anyone jumped here? We're the closest neighboring system."

"It looks like Fleet Admiral Dain Marquandt disabled all of the system's jump thrusters with a priority code," the Broker explained.

The last fleet

Salana didn't let her surprise show. "Marquandt has always been ambitious. But why would he betray his own species?"

"I don't have that information."

"You don't, or you don't want to share."

"I don't," he repeated, and she was inclined to believe him - something she had sworn never to do.

"If he has sacrificed Andal to the Never, we in Kerrhain should be concerned."

"Yes."

"I don't think that's the information you wanted me to know?" she asked, as her neural computer was already running hot using her cerebral boosters to assess and classify the implications of the new information.

"The youngest son of High Lord Cornelius Andal, has survived."

"Gavin?"

"Yes."

"Where is he now?"

"I don't know."

"If you ..."

"High Lady, I don't know."

He lied to her. Probably. But he wouldn't tell her, one way or the other. So she wouldn't embarrass herself.

"Keep me posted if you have any relevant information about the security of this system," she instructed him. "It's not like I have to remind you what's at stake."

Before he could respond, she wiped her hand across his hologram, severing the connection. Only after several minutes of staring thoughtfully into the jungle did she realize she had clenched her hands into fists.

"High Lady?" asked the Servitor, who had stepped to her side. He handed her the crystal glass of freshly refilled Antibes champagne. She took it and looked at the sparkling golden liquid.

"Why did he share this information with me?"

"I beg your pardon?"

"About Marquandt's apparent betrayal."

"I'm afraid that I don't have enough relevant data to..."

"Because it gives him leverage against me," she interrupted the robot absentmindedly. "If the Emperor punishes him and Intelligence starts digging, they could get their hands on the Broker. Then he can point to a record of that conversation and say he did his duty by informing the nearest authority. However, if Marquandt should plan a coup and succeed, he can sell me as a potential problem to the Fleet Admiral because I know about it. Every consolidation phase loses its earliest confidants." The robot was silent as she poured the sinfully expensive liquid from the glass over the railing and watched it plummet. She gazed thoughtfully after the disappearing drops. "And that business with young Andal ... a trap. No doubt about it. He only tells me, and as soon as the information makes the rounds, he knows for sure that it came from me. So he can use a single snippet of information like a contrast agent that reveals my spider web. Do you know how I know this, Servitor?"

"I'm sorry, high lady."

"Because I would have done it that way." She turned to the robot. "Erase data storage, initiate self-destruct."

As Salana walked back inside across the terrace, she heard flames blazing behind her and metal and plastic boiling. She had to make a decision about Gavin Andal, should he still be here in the system.

16

"Jump executed," Gavin announced, extending the sensor phalanges in the bow to scan the space surrounding them. Constellation matching to determine their exit position, radar and lidar for close range to avoid collision in case of deviation.

Jumps through subspace, after centuries of refinement, worked extremely precisely and predictably as long as they occurred outside gravitational sinks and magnetic fields. A transit like their escape from Andal was fraught with considerable risk because the planet's magnetosphere had provided subspace interference - almost to the same extent as gravity. No one knew how large the deviations were because there was not enough data on them. But it was a fact that many jump attempts from planetary surfaces and near them had gone wrong. Most ships had not reappeared, others had materialized in asteroid fields or returned to normal space as debris clouds. He had even heard that when Omega Zero was discovered, the bow of a test ship sent out in the early years of jump technology had been found jutting out of a rock. Since then, all sorts of myths had swirled in the Navy about the fate of the ship, which had been aptly named *Melange*.

"And we're still alive," Bambam sighed with relief. "So we didn't materialize in a Never swarm."

"Apparently," Gavin agreed with him absently, sorting

through the sensor data. Beside him, he saw Hellcat's fingers flying over her holoconsoles and glanced at the weapons displays. On the status screen for the fire control solutions, he saw that the second railgun had not yet been powered up, none of the eight short-range guns had, and neither had the two lasers. "You have to give the release of the capacitors first so that the circuit between superconductors can be closed from the reactor to the weapons. For the jump, the connections are disconnected using relays in the capacitors."

"I know how to do it!" she hissed back, giving the appropriate orders a moment later. He was about to retort something pithy, angry at her childish behavior, when Sphinx presented him with the sensor data as a readily interpreted representation.

"Okay, we're up twelve thousand clicks from Bragge, in the outer system," he said, suddenly hoarse. "Kolsund is where it should be. Andal is... gone."

Gavin swallowed, unable to get another word out. Everything he had ever known and loved was gone. The places of his childhood, his home, his family. Simply gone, vanished from the universe, condemned to a memory that no longer seemed to have any permanence in the face of reality. The pain was paradoxically worse than if Andal had fallen victim to bombs or an asteroid impact.

A leaden silence spread across the bridge, broken here and there by noises from the computer systems. Their lack of response made him feel even lonelier at heart.

"There is still Never infestation in the system," Bambam said at one point, waking Gavin from his lethargy. He cleared his throat and refocused on the sensor data display. In fact, there were even some drive signatures distributed throughout the system. Two of them were five million clicks away in the direction of the outer asteroid belt.

Several never-entities were following them and had almost caught up. The four other exhaust flares in the system, much farther off on the opposite side, were also being tracked by the infestation. The swarms themselves were just visible on the telescopes as pale clouds receding into the darkness of space.

"This is where the battle raged," he said. "Right here. There's not even any debris, nothing. Everything is just gone, like there was never anything here. No fleets of hundreds of ships, thousands of marines, fathers, mothers."

Even Hellcat seemed dumbfounded by the sight and the implications of it all. For the first time, her face was not contorted with anger or wrinkled in deep creases. It was easy to forget that this had been their home, too, even if they had lived on opposing sides and their memories might differ.

Gavin was the first to find his way back to grim reality and forced himself to act. "The two signatures in our relative vicinity belong to civilian ships, an ice freighter and a passenger liner. Since our fleet file is forty years old, Sphinx has no signature matches."

"Most certainly human," Dodger said.

"That's why we're going to help them." He almost expected Hellcat to contradict him, as usual, or to point out that he was not in charge here, but this time she raised no objection. He marked the rear of the two ships, which had to fly at full thrust, as long as their exhaust flares were. Plasma trails stretching more than five miles could only mean that they were trying to keep Never off their backs as best they could - although the brutal acceleration would surely make the crew curse their lives. Still, a futile endeavor if they hadn't shown up with the *Lady Vengeance*. For some reason, the Never required no fuel and could maneuver much more freely than human ships.

Gavin looked at the various intercept options Sphinx presented to him. While they were moving in a vacuum and there were no obstacles in the way, the AI had to extrapolate where they would be at what time based on the current acceleration rate of the target ships. Depending on the Lady's acceleration, and consequent consumption of helium-3 pellets, resulted in different flight times, angles of fire for the weapons, and cross points with the Never.

After quick deliberation, he decided on the most offensive option with the shortest flight time, which was listed as fifty minutes. Considering that they had to accelerate from zero and build up speed while their targets were already traveling at over fifty miles per second and getting faster, not a great amount of time.

"Stand by for high acceleration," he shouted, triggering the acceleration alarm, which echoed through the empty ship with seven loud, unpleasant beeps, followed by a long drawn-out one before they were violently pressed into their seats, which contorted into reclining position from 5g in the gimbal suspension. The Nanofoam conformed to their bodies, freeing them from pressure points by distributing the load of their multiplied weight as well as possible. The Smartnites in his circulation spread through his vascular system, dilating the endothelia, keeping them pliable and bracing against gravity. He hoped the rebels had some Smartnites, too, or this would be their first and only flight on a war vessel.

The g-forces were increasing relentlessly, making the walls creak and groan. He switched to Transducer, but found no one on the local network who also had one.

Great, he thought, and tried to establish a radio link with the two ships they were chasing. Fortunately, he had remembered to connect directly to the *Lady* using his data jack, and so Sphinx was able to interpret his thoughts. This made it immensely easier for him to control the ship, especially since gravity was thwarting any plan for him to open his mouth or move his fingers.

"This is..." He faltered in thought. He almost said *Lord Captain Gavin Andal* out of habit. What if Marquandt's agents were still here? A probe picking up radio signals? Or the ships' on-board computers were infected with spy software? "This is the *Lady Vengeance*. Send us your status, we are on an intercept course with the Never entities."

"Lady Vengeance, this is Dyke Keko of the *Alabama*," replied a strained voice, resulting from the heavy acceleration. "Are you armed?"

"Yes. We will be in firing range in a few minutes. Do you have civilians on board? Were you part of the evacuation fleet?"

"No, sir. We are an ice tug from the belt and had orders to move out."

The last fleet

Gavin didn't believe a word the man said. His father had ordered every civilian ship back to pick up civilians. Maybe this Dyke Keko was a smuggler trying to save his own skin. But it didn't matter here and now, he would not knowingly abandon anyone to a horror like the Never.

"How many people are on board?"

"Four, sir," the other pilot replied with obvious difficulty.

"Stand by," Gavin said, not knowing himself what he meant. It just didn't sound right to say, *'carry on and if you're not caught by the Never first, we'll hear from each other'*.

"This is the *Lady Vengeance*," he radioed the other ship, the passenger liner.

"This is Captain Johanna Teunen of the *Morning Star*," a voice answered, sounding as strained as Dyke Keko's before. Every single word seemed like an agonizing act in the radio link. "Please tell me you're Navy."

"Not exactly," he replied somewhat nebulously. "But we won't let you down, don't worry."

"I don't know what you can do, but I have two hundred refugees from Andal on board here."

"We will do everything we can, I promise. The other ship ..."

"The *Alabama*. Our navigation system failed when we were hit by a piece of debris in Andal's orbit. At some point, Captain Dyke Keko radioed us, and we've been following him by directional beam bearing ever since."

"I see." Gavin wanted to screw up his face into a pained expression, but 13g of acceleration didn't even let him bat an eyelash. He switched his transducer to the speakers. "We have a problem. Two ships, an ice freighter that I think is a smuggler who has resisted civilian assistance to take in refugees - perhaps because of some illegal cargo. However, he also bailed out the passenger liner and is now navigating it out of the system."

He knew they couldn't answer him, but it helped a little to voice his dilemma out loud. A glance at the tactical display showed him the Never marked in red - a total of twenty entities ranging from one to twenty yards in diameter. They would reach the two yellow-flashing ships in forty minutes, and that meant destroying them and making them disappear.

In forty minutes and thirty seconds he would be in firing range with the two railguns on the Lady. The Hawk missiles could reach the target in as little as twenty minutes, but he hesitated to use them. Their destructive power was considerable, and if he was unlucky, they would damage the very ships he wanted to protect. However, in the event he had only thirty seconds to shoot down twenty entities, the cadence of the railguns would not be enough to get them all. So he would lose one ship either way.

He made his decision and radioed the Morning Star again.

"Captain Teunen, this is Lady Vengeance. Change your course according to the vector I'm transmitting to you. You can do this manually, without a navigation computer. I need to split up the chasers."

"Okay, got it," groaned the captain. "How bad is it? The Never, I mean?"

"Nothing I can't handle," he replied.

"Thank you."

Don't thank me too soon. He waited as the passenger liner slowly drifted away from the ice freighter, which Gavin was effectively leaving for dead. Although he knew he was doing the objectively right thing in this situation , it felt entirely wrong.

The minutes melted away, the angle between Alabama and Morning Star steadily widened, and the pursuing Never entities split up as expected according to the mass of their victims. He knew from Navy dossiers that the phenomenon behaved in a frighteningly mathematical way, which once again sent a shiver down his spine.

"Gavin, I've detected a third signature. It is on an intercept course with us," Sphinx spoke up in his head.

"A third?" he asked in surprise, maximizing the sensor display. The third ship was nearly as large as the Lady, roughly matching the mass of newer light attack frigates. He zoomed in further and further by thought command until he could see the newcomer as a whole. Its hull was slender with a pointed bow that ended in a single sensor cluster. The engine section was slightly thicker than the rest, but less than it should have been. He also saw no propulsion flames at all, even though the ship was approaching furiously, according to the Sphinx. Also strange were the blue lines that flashed across the hull in rhythm with a heartbeat, and spear-like superstructures along the center that made it look like a hedgehog.

"What is that?"

"I have not been able to find any equivalents in my data. I'm not familiar with this type of ship," the AI replied.

"Are they in drift? I don't see a plasma tail."

"No, the unknown ship is accelerating, according to my measurements at 30g."

"Impossible!" he snapped.

"At least if there are people on board, yes," she agreed with him.

"That blue glow, it reminds me of the Orb on the *Ushuaia*." Gavin shuddered. "How long before it reaches us?"

"Thirty minutes, if it maintains its current acceleration rate."

"Then it will pass us and fire with everything it's got before it's past us," he concluded. "Record everything, do you understand?"

"Of course."

Gavin changed his plan and armed four of the Hawk missiles that were in its hull. When the fire control system informed him they were in the launch bays, he aimed them each at the center of the two groups of entities chasing the *Alabama* and *Morning Star* and gave the order to fire.

The two-yard-long missiles with Quagma warheads and intelligent pilot software that made the Hawks almost drones were catapulted several hundred yards out of the launch bays and then ignited their engines at a safe distance before blasting off at their targets with bluish tails and 90g.

As they moved away from them on his tactical screen as flashing triangles, he again looked at the alien ship that puzzled him. The design reminded him strongly of the Navy's new *Triumph* frigates, if it weren't for the blue lights on the hull, or the strange spikes. The stern section didn't match either, being far too slender and its exterior bulging out as if the metal had boiled and then abruptly cooled. All this was strange and *wrong* for the type of ship, but nowhere near as impossible as accelerating without dragging a jet of ultra-hot gas behind it.

"How did you even track the bogey without a propulsion signature?" he asked.

"A coincidence," Sphinx replied. "A reflection of the central star in a place where the system map says there are no celestial bodies."

"In any case, the fact that they're on course for us is no coincidence."

"Shall I make an attempt at communication?"

"No," he decided. "This thing scares me, and the fact that they haven't radioed us themselves yet doesn't improve my gut feeling. That way, they probably still think they're invisible and think we're unaware of their presence."

"Do you think they're hostile?"

"I don't know, but I don't want to find out by calling out *'here we are,'* and *'we see you'*." Gavin looked at the tactical screen, which showed the bogey just emerging from the edge as the Hawks minimized the distance to their targets and exploded shortly thereafter. Four flashes appeared on the telescopes as they ignited their phase warhead and collided the atomic nuclei of their baryonic charge at relativistic velocities. The contained cartridges of quarks and gluons lost their confinement and collided with each other in erratic chaos until, at an immeasurably short distance, ultra-hot quagma was created and transformed into an expanding sphere of heat and hard radiation. The waves of annihilation were but a flicker on the sensors, too ephemeral for the human eye, but there was no longer any sign of the Never entities.

"Hell yes!" He looked at the sensor image. The two civilian ships were still flying on their previous courses with their drive nacelles glowing.

"Nice shooting," Sphinx commented.

"I was just pushing buttons."

The last fleet

"Unknown ship changing course."

Gavin's gaze jerked to the telescope data. The bogey was making a tight arc - impossible at this rate of acceleration - and was now hurtling directly toward them.

"Shit! Get on the radio!" he ordered. Of course, they had seen him at the latest when he had fired the missiles, but he had not thought it possible that they could maneuver so quickly. "Unidentified vessel, this is Lady Vengeance, identify yourself."

No response.

"Unknown vessel, this is *Lady Vengeance*, we have no hostile intent. Our objective is to support the two civilian ships ahead."

Still no response.

"Son of a bitch!"

"Unknown ship is firing!", Sphinx alerted him.

"Target them with our lasers, lowest intensity, we want to keep bearing and not engage them," he ordered, looking at the two flame tails coming to life near the bogey. Part of him was relieved that they appeared to be ordinary missiles and nothing with invisible propulsion. "Sphinx, assume short-range defense," he said.

"Gavin, the missiles aren't aimed at us."

"What, who would they be..." He broke off when he saw the calculation of the flight vectors the missiles appeared to be traveling on. One was on an intercept course with the *Alabama*, one with the *Morning Star*. "Oh no, no, no!"

He connected with both ships, "Change your direction of flight and shut down your engines immediately. You are being fired upon!"

To his surprise and simultaneous relief, they obeyed without wasting time with queries, and the two exhaust flares died out shortly thereafter. It wouldn't do much good against homing missiles, since civilian spaceships didn't have thermal shielding, but at least it wouldn't be quite so easy anymore. If these bastards were going to commit murder, at least they shouldn't have it too easy.

"Lasers have bearing," Sphinx informed him, and he aimed

the two railguns. As soon as he saw a green flash, he gave the order to fire.

The *Lady* trembled as the twenty-centimeter tungsten bolts left the muzzles and sped toward their target at an appreciable fraction of the speed of light.

"Four more missiles," the AI reported. This time, the glowing thrusters moved directly toward them.

A short time later, the *Alabama* and *Morning Star* were hit in quick succession. The ice tug turned into a funnel-shaped cloud of debris that moved away from the missile's point of impact. The passenger ship lost a large portion of its engine section, which was ripped away by the blast. It began to tumble uncontrollably, losing more hull sections that were thrown away by the high angular momentum. Where holes were created, bright fountains of gas appeared. In some of the escaping air streams, he could make out the outlines of people on the telescopic images, as they rowed their arms and froze. The renewed pulses made the *Morning Star*'s lurching more and more uncontrolled.

Gavin pushed his anger and despair away and looked feverishly at the tactical display: Two minutes until the four missiles aimed at the *Lady* hit. Three minutes until he could reach the wreckage of the passenger liner. No one on board would be alive by then, but perhaps dead they would still be able to save him and his crew.

He watched as one of his two railgun shells chased through the alien spines of the bogey, taking a rain of debris with it. The other seemed to have missed its target. In response, it fired eight more guided missiles at him.

"Not good. Not good," he said, realigning the railguns. He forced himself to wait until the missiles from the first salvo had come almost within range of the point defense, and then fired. An explosion caused him to inwardly breathe a sigh of relief. Then the starboard side's four rapid-fire cannons began firing, spitting out several hundred projectiles per second. Gavin put the Lady into a rolling motion so that starboard and port guns could fire alternately, and exhaled a long-drawn breath as three explosions flared. The last close enough to the hull that he got several overheat warnings displayed.

"Power up jump thrusters," he ordered.

"The time to the required peak of the energy matrix cells is two minutes," Sphinx reminded him. "And I need to drain energy from the weapons systems."

"I realize that, but the bogey just disappeared!" A moment ago, in the middle of the telescopic images, the mysterious ship had simply dissipated. He almost gave in to the hope that it had jumped, but the *Lady* wasn't picking up any gravitational waves typical of that, and the very next moment, four more propulsion tails of missiles appeared as if out of nowhere.

"Apparently the enemy has some form of stealth technology," Sphinx stated the obvious.

"You don't say." Over the loudspeakers, he said, "Sorry, guys. We're going to have to find out what the *Lady* has up her sleeve."

Shortly thereafter, he turned the ship around its lateral axis at a brutal one-hundred-eighty-degree spin and braked at 16g, the maximum thrust that the four Raptor engines could provide - just like his body. His neural computer's medical monitoring program alerted him with flashing red warnings that his Smartnites were reaching their performance limits and were about to be destroyed.

Just hang on a little longer, he prayed, when the first melee cannons should have fired again. But they had shut down, he reminded himself. The energy matrix cells had built up eighty percent power potential when they were still forty seconds away from the wreckage of the *Morning Star* and the cloud of debris in which it rotated around seemingly endless axes.

It would be close, too close.

He corrected course slightly to port and then made another one hundred eighty degree turn so that the missiles were now behind them. Three of them were caught by the mile-long plasma tail and melted before their warheads could ignite. The fourth ignited before its annihilation, flinging Gavin violently to the side, where his harnesses held him back with a jerk.

"Damage report!" he ordered the AI.

"Engine 3 failure, overheating in right aft radiator, short in dorsal oxygen pump," Sphinx enumerated. "Several relays are blown there."

"Is that a problem?"

"One pump is still working, but it's possible that carbon dioxide levels will rise to unhealthy levels in a few hours."

"If we're still alive then, we can always take care of it. Seventy seconds until the next missiles hit. I can't pull a stunt like that again."

"No," she agreed with him simply. With the damage carried away from the nearby explosion, any strong maneuver would only cause more.

One last time he corrected the course as their speed melted away, and with it the seconds until the next missile salvo caught them.

Gavin peered at the *Morning Star*, then looked at the level of the energy matrix cells: ninety-four percent.

"That's not good enough," he found.

"No."

"Give me power to the lasers."

"That will extend the time we need to recharge the ..."

"I realize that, go ahead. And get the jump navigation ready."

"To where?"

"S1-Ruhr."

The two laser cannons switched from red to green, and he immediately began giving them two targets. Then he fired at the passenger liner that was falling apart. Twice, he then repeated the whole thing again until its rotation changed due to the newly set impulses and only the longitudinal axis was affected.

Gavin brought the *Lady* onto a parallel course until they flew side by side like two cigars, not a mile apart. Then he shut down the engines completely, channeled all the released energy from the fusion reactors into the energy matrix cells, and fired the maneuvering thrusters. They ejected their cold gas supplies at dizzying speeds. Tiny fountains neatly churned them and sent them like a satellite around the shattered civilian ship, just in time for the missiles pursuing them to crash into the renewed obstacle between them and their target. They exploded in quick succession, tearing the wreckage into smaller and smaller glowing pieces.

"Jump engine ready."

"Jump!" He gave the command simultaneously, and the last thing he saw was the glow of four more propulsion flares so close they formed glaring coronae around the slender missiles.

INTERLUDE: JANUS

"What do you see, Janus?" the Emperor asked quietly. He was standing in his office on the highest floor of the Imperial Palace on Mont Blanc, staring out the large window at the sea of clouds at their feet, with the rugged, moss-covered slopes between them. Janus thought it the most beautiful sight on the planet to this day - albeit one that didn't seem to him to be in the atmosphere. Too high, too far away, too removed from everything.

"I see mountains and clouds and the sunset," he replied carefully.

"No," breathed the Emperor. "A landscape in minor key."

Janus lowered his eyes sympathetically and stood beside his master.

"Is this the key my life will strike from now on? Does fate hate me so much? First Peraia, now Magnus." Silent tears ran down Haeron II's cheeks as he stared absently into the sunset.

The news of the heavy defeat at Andal had arrived over the Quantcom network a few minutes ago, making it less than twenty hours old. The fact that they had received word so quickly was due entirely to the priority channel, which had to be stored in each system's quantum tunnel technology communications buoys and kept clear for emergencies. It was the fastest form of communication, with courier ships on constant standby jumping to the neighboring system, using Quantcom transmission to inform the next courier, who in turn jumped, and so on. A simple method, similar to the signal fires of Gondor, and at the same time based on the most sophisticated technology of the Star Empire. What had been the pride of the Science Corps just a few years ago had now become the sinister messenger of chaos.

Janus would have liked to storm out of the office when the news arrived, because with the extremely popular Crown Prince not only the Emperor's son had died, but also his heir, after his eldest child, Peraia, had been missing for two decades.

"I do not know, your majesty. I am very sorry that you must endure this loss. If I may take the liberty of making this remark - and it is not a hopeful one: the death of the Crown Prince is a grave loss for all of us, the entire Star Empire. He was a reflection of all that is good about humanity and your reign."

"Thank you, Janus." Haeron II wiped a tear from his cheek, looking unusually *human*. An ordinary man, deeply shaken by the loss of his child - a pain that every father and mother in the universe feared above all else. He could not even imagine how hard it must be for his master, who would not be allowed even a few days of mourning, because he was not a simple man, but emperor over one hundred sectors and five hundred inhabited worlds. For the first time he became aware of the injustice that had been done to the human behind the dignity of office, James Harthom-Harrow, even at the time of his birth.

"I must not presume such thoughts," the Emperor said with a quivering lower lip. Only now did Janus realize that he had apparently spoken aloud.

"Forgive me, your majesty. I fear the shock is not allowing me to think clearly."

"If I begin to feel sorry for myself, who am I? The most powerful man who ever lived and feels sorry for himself?"

"You did not want this office, if I remember rightly."

"One of a kind. Where there is no choice, one should not bother with choosing. If I could only get my children back, I'd give it up. All of it." Haeron II swallowed and lowered his gaze.

Janus's wrist terminal chirped.

"Your Majesty, it is your daughter. She wishes to see you."

The last fleet

"Let her in, she need not announce herself."

They both knew that palace rules said otherwise, but Janus merely nodded dutifully and with a gesture opened the heavy carbotanium door to the office, with its dark wooden furniture and hand-embroidered seat cushions, meant to exude grandeur and permanence, to deprive any guest who had made it here of any form of inflated pride or overly grand ambitions. Now they merely looked somber and heavy.

Princess Elayne came running in and stormed toward her father. The four guards of the throne guard took posture in the hallway, then the door panels fell shut again, locking them out.

"Dad!" the young woman cried, rushing into the arms of the Emperor, who embraced her tightly and laid her head on his chest. She wept unrestrainedly, shaking again and again with long sobs.

"It's okay, dear."

Janus could see in Haeron's eyes the anguish that wracked his master as he stood strong for his daughter, giving her the strength and security she now needed as much as he did. But who comforted the Emperor from whom fate had even taken his wife?

"How could this happen?" asked Elayne, looking to Janus. Her eyes were swimming in tears. "How?"

"We don't know yet, Princess," he took over to take some pressure off her father and give him time to collect himself. "Apparently, the Never has managed to overwhelm the fleets despite their superior firepower. Working through the strategic and tactical mistakes will take some time, I'm afraid."

"My brother is dead!" she snapped at him angrily.

"I know, my lady, and I wish there was some way I could undo it," he returned truthfully, bowing his head.

"Forgive my emotionalism, Janus." Now she sounded more dejected than angry. "I just don't understand it. He was here the day before yesterday, and the Admiralty was sure of victory. One even promised me that it was almost a representative act, that Magnus was leading the Home Fleets."

"That was our information, too, my lady." Janus looked to her father, whose gaze was lost in nothingness, and then back to the princess. It was the first time he had seen her with tousled blond curls and no makeup. "There will be a lot of work for your father and I to do now, to somehow absorb this disaster. And I'm afraid for you, as well."

She wiped the tears from her cheeks and looked first at him with quivering lips, then at her father. When no one said anything, she took a step back.

"No," she whispered, "no, I can't. I'm not... no."

"Not now, my lady, but eventually the time will come, and your father made known early on his intention not to remain on the throne beyond his fifth Telomere extension..."

"Enough of that!" she interrupted him. Her youthful anger abruptly returned and she glared at him with a trembling frown as she continued, "My brother has just died. I'm certainly not talking about his succession as heir to the throne!"

"Of course, Princess." Janus bowed. Perhaps he had been too quick. His mind was racing with the consequences that this new situation would entail, and the lines and new constellations that everything entailed formed a complex puzzle that gave him no peace. "Please accept my apologies if I have offended you."

His wrist terminal emitted a low chirp that sounded loud and invasive in the heavy silence of the office.

"What's the next step, Dad?" the princess asked, turning back to her father. His eyes seemed to say, "I don't know."

But aloud he said, "Now there will be many political decisions to make to get the Star Empire through this crisis in a stable way. I know I'm asking a lot of you, dear. More than a father should be allowed to ask of his daughter under normal circumstances."

"Nothing about us is normal."

"Yes." The Emperor nodded and took a step forward to place his heavy hands on her shoulders. "We must be strong now and show strength. We may be the ruling family, but we are the rulers..."

"... of a crow's nest," she sighed, suppressing another sob.

Janus glanced at his wrist terminal and nodded to the Emperor, unseen by his daughter. He disengaged from her slightly, then gave her another squeeze. "We should be together today. I'm going to need to talk to some people, and then we'll meet up after, okay?"

"Okay." The princess bravely wiped the tears from her cheeks and dried the corners of her eyes on her blouse before walking out, struggling for composure.

"Well?" asked Haeron II, when the door had closed behind her and his gaze rested, as if forgotten, on the wooden optics decorated with ornate ornaments.

"The Senate President has requested an audience. It was extremely urgent," Janus replied.

"She already knows. Interesting." The Emperor did not sound at all as if he cared. "Can we reschedule?"

"She's not a Republican, but she is a moderate, so she has good connections in both camps. However, if she got her information from the Republican wing, we should find out from whom. That these elements could have access to Quantcom couriers is an alarming sign," Janus reasoned aloud as he began to untangle the threads in his head.

"Call Marius, I want him to report to me personally and tell me what the hell could have caused my son to be dead now and nearly the entire Home fleet destroyed," the Emperor roared as his vision cleared. Once again, however, the bird with broken wings had become a hawk.

"Of course." Janus raised his wrist terminal and pressed a button. "Have Grand Admiral Albius appear in the upper audience chamber in fifteen minutes. Without an aide." He released the button and looked up. "What about Usatami?"

"The Senate president is to come now," Haeron II decided with a somber expression. "But she will take a seat in the waiting room. Then we'll let the chief of staff go first. Let her calmly consider how much her knowledge advantage is probably worth and how much it really bothers us. Those who have too much time to think always make mistakes."

"A good decision, Your Majesty," Janus agreed with the ruler, inclining his head.

"One more question: the information about the lost battle

came from High Lady Kerrhain. She said that no ship was able to escape. Why not?"

"Your Majesty?"

"Fifteen fleets, that's several thousand ships. Do you really think that each one sacrificed itself to fight to the death even when it was hopeless? Do you really think that none of the many experienced officers who took part in the battle sent a ship off to report on how it went? About what went wrong?"

"No, I don't think so. Something happened that is still in the shadows."

"Yes." The Emperor nodded and his lips narrowed, contorted into thin lines. "And whatever it was cost the lives of my son, countless thousands of brave marines, the finest officers in the Star Empire, and an entire system of my citizens."

"Indeed." Janus nodded thoughtfully.

"I want you to find out, whatever it takes. This thing did not simply happen, I want to know why it did. You'll get all the resources of the throne, just shed light on it for me, understand?"

"Of course, Your Majesty."

17

At first, Gavin did not realize what had happened or where he was. The rockets, four little suns, right in front of the sensors, were no longer there and he was still breathing.

We jumped, he thought, and started laughing like a madman. He hadn't even felt the transit itself, probably because his body had gone into a permanent spasm from the extreme acceleration forces.

"We jumped!"

"Ugh," he heard a plaintive sound behind him. Something rustled beside him.

"Everyone still alive?" he asked, catching himself with a spark of worry that one of the three might be hanging dead in their recliner after a stroke.

"I wish I was dead," Hellcat whispered beside him, coughing a few times before spitting up blood.

"Bambam needs to go to the infirmary," Dodger said from behind them. Gavin commanded his recliner to return to a seat, then rotated it around its long axis. The mutant just stretched a few times in zero gravity and unbuckled the mechanic, who was twitching catatonically in his straps. Gavin wanted to say something but didn't know what and then merely nodded before turning back to his consoles and checking the automatic position check.

"S1-Ruhr, we're in S1-Ruhr, that's for sure," he said to himself when the constellation match was complete.

"That was ...," Hellcat put in beside him and turned to face him. She eyed him for a while, then nodded. "Not a bad performance."

"Not good enough," he objected with thoughts of the many civilians who had died. The rebel's mouth twisted. Gavin thought she looked dangerously pale. Her lips seemed to have lost all blood - except for the fresh one running down her chin. "I couldn't save them."

"No, but you tried. Didn't think a monarchist asshole could have so much compassion for the common people."

"What kind of person do you think I am?" he asked indignantly, his frustration venting as sheer rage.

"I thought I knew, but I'm not so sure anymore."

Her answer surprised him enough that his anger evaporated and gave way to a sad weariness.

"You should go to the infirmary, too."

If he had expected a protest, she proved him wrong, as she merely nodded weakly and unbuckled herself to float toward the narrow tube that led from the bridge to the central corridor. Gavin, meanwhile, checked the status of his Smartnites and, by means of a neural computer, that of his tissues. Apparently, he had his high-end hardware to thank for the fact that he was still doing well despite the ordeal he had put his body through.

"Okay, Sphinx. What do we have here? I've never been in a Seed System before. The corporations don't like people eyeballing their projects."

"There's a gas giant, CX-3, in the outer system, a thin asteroid belt, and two rocky planets. One of them, CX-1, is too close to the F4 central star, and the other, CX-2, is in the habitable zone. It has large water resources and three continents. No vegetation according to my databases. The Seed Vessel is owned by the Terran Star Empire, but is operated by its manufacturer, Ruhr Heavy Industries, until the terraforming process is complete. On board are normally two shifts of thirty people each, replaced every two months when Mammoth freighters arrive with new

The last fleet

biomass. CX-3, by the way, is officially cleared for helium-3 refueling, which means there's infrequent through traffic from prospectors and private explorers who venture from here to the west of the spiral branch."

"What do you think the likelihood is that they have relays aboard the ship that we can use as replacements for the ones we destroyed?" he asked.

"Very high. Seed Vessels operate extremely self-sufficiently with high maintenance at the same time because of the continuous operation and extreme pressure at which the mass dispensers must be operated. This means that the crew probably has large stocks of spare parts on board," Sphinx explained in her pleasant mezzo-soprano.

"And what do you think the likelihood is that our pursuers will follow us here?"

"A comparable ship in the fleet - a *Triumph*-class frigate - has a maximum jump range of six light-years. That means there are six neighboring systems within range from Andal. Assuming the enemy captain believes we jumped into an adjacent system rather than the interstellar medium, the probability is sixteen-point-six percent. Relative to them following us here with their first jump. Should they miss, it would be at least two jumps here."

"Sixteen sounds good," he concluded.

"I think the probability is even lower, since a jump to S1-Ruhr would play into their hands - unlike systems with high military presence like Kerrhain, Gonadev, and Valhalla."

"Are you saying that coming here was stupid?"

"No. I'm merely pointing out that they can track and shoot us down here with relative ease, whereas in some alternate systems they would cause a stir and put themselves in danger. It's clearly a prototype of some kind, and they're usually kept top secret."

"You're right," he sighed. "Then let's hope that my skills as a pilot have led them to believe that I have more strategic skills. I just jumped where we planned to jump. There were other things on my mind."

"Of course, Gavin."

"If you were human, I would have thought you were being sarcastic right now." Gavin unbuckled his seat belt and immediately began to float out of his seat. "Set a direct course for the Seed Vessel and send off a Quantcom message: this is Captain Xavier Bennington of the *Lady Vengeance*. We have escaped from Andal, which has been infested by the Never. Our ship has been damaged and we urgently need relays for our life support. That's why we have to invoke Section 2, paragraph 1 of the Interplanetary Space Traffic Act and request emergency assistance."

When he finished, he pushed off toward the central corridor and headed for sickbay. There he found Hellcat lying on one of the stretchers, hooked up by cuffs to the medidoc, who was presumably pumping her full of drugs or nanites to replace her damaged Smartnites.

Bambam, on the other hand, was lying in the only Medicasket in the infirmary, apparently being operated on by Sphinx. Through the glass, he could see the slackened features of the mechanic and the robotic arms with fine instruments operating on his open heart and brain. His skull plate had been lifted off with grappling hooks and the sight of it almost made Gavin vomit.

"Bloody heavens!" he cursed in horror. "What's wrong with him?"

"Had a seizure and a stroke according to the voice," Dodger said, pointing vaguely toward the ceiling with an outstretched index finger.

"Sphinx?"

"Yes, Gavin?"

"What's his prognosis?"

"Currently, he's stable. I need to stop a suboccipital hemorrhage and clone and reposition several sections of the coronary arteries. The procedure will take several hours," the AI replied.

"Is there anything we can do? Do you have enough materials? Donate blood?"

"No. I can give a more accurate prognosis after the procedures are complete. The medical equipment on board is not up to date, but it is sufficient."

"The old bastard'll come through," Hellcat said from her stretcher, but her eyes were half-closed, as if she were trying to avoid his gaze. "He's a hard-ass."

Gavin nodded. "We'll fly to the local Seed Vessel and ask for relays. We'll arrive in three hours, and in a little more than one we should be putting on breathing masks because by then the CO_2 levels in the air we breathe will have risen to unhealthy levels."

"I'm going to go out back and see if I can do something about the broken radiator," Dodger announced.

"You know something about that?" he asked.

"Not with the drive stuff, but I'm an electrician." Noticing his doubtful look, she eyed him calmly. "Do you think they'd have gone to all that trouble when they were growing me so I'd just be tapping rocks?"

"No. You can smash noses, too," he replied laconically, startled when she suddenly started laughing. It was the first time he had heard her make such a sound. It sounded like an out-of-tune bass system with overdrive. Without another word, she left the sickbay and retreated out into the corridor.

"Captain," he heard Hellcat say behind him as he tried to follow the mutant.

"Yes?" It was only after some delay that he realized what she had just said to him. "Uh, did you hurt your head?"

"No. You may think we're terrorist barbarians, but if I were to sum up our beliefs as Republicans in a nutshell, it would be to demand that everyone in our society have equal opportunity by merit and aptitude prevailing. Not birth or money." She paused for a long look at him. He was decent enough not to disrespect her by hastily stuffing the silence with some triviality. Listening had never been his strong suit, but it struck him that it wasn't that difficult if he didn't already have his answers figured out, but tried to understand. Hellcat seemed to sense this and finally continued speaking, "What you did back there - shit, that almost killed me. But you risked your life for those civilians."

"I couldn't save them," he said gloomily. "I couldn't save a single one."

"I know. You know what the good thing is about living

among enemies of the state and having to constantly worry that security guards are going to rush through the doors and shoot you in the head because they don't want to risk a lengthy trial where you still cost the Star Empire money?" she asked. "You learn what human closeness means, which only working together in fear of death can conjure. Dodger and Bambam don't let on, but they've lost everything and everyone on Andal they cared about, just like me."

"Looks like we have something in common after all."

"Yes," was the only thing she said in response, and he got the impression that they had reached the end of their brief conversation.

Back on the bridge, he had already received a response from the Seed Vessel one hundred and fifty million miles away - a video. On it was a narrow-faced man with mottled gray temples whose last telomere extension seemed to have been a while ago. He possessed the bored look of a full-blooded bureaucrat, and his voice was more of a croak as he spoke, "Captain Bennington, I am Executive First Class Ikabot Nurheim, directing CX-2's terraforming program on behalf of the Emperor. Of course we will help you out. Keep in mind, however, that this is a demilitarized zone and we must report any - even passive - weapons activity to the proper authorities. We will of course deactivate our automatic defenses as soon as we have verified your transponder code. I wish you a good and, above all, safe flight."

Sounds more like you're wishing us a reactor malfunction, Gavin thought. *Let's hope the Broker's codes are worth their reputation, then.*

Half an hour later - after disabling all weapons systems, he received the official approach vector to the Seed Vessel as a simple text message via Quantcom and adjusted their course accordingly. Every now and then his gaze slid to the long-range sensors, which continued to search for jump signatures. The more time that passed, the better for them, as the Lady's jump nodes took over an hour to rebuild to their full charge potential. He was all the more relieved when, after the time had expired, he still could not detect any transit into the system and the jump thrusters indicated full power in the energy nodes and readiness of the energy matrix cells.

The closer they got to the Seed Vessel, the more glued he became to the telescopic images. By means of multiple zooms from a distance, which already made the image pixelated, it looked like a gigantic space fleet clinging to the blue-brown planet CX-2. The fuselage looked downright dainty next to the outstretched wings.

With only thirty minutes separating them from the largest type of ship humanity had ever built, he finally got word from Sphinx that Bambam's surgery had been successful and that he would now spend a few more hours in the Medicasket before being moved to one of the stretchers. Hellcat also seemed to be doing better, even if she didn't seem to want to leave the infirmary without her comrade.

"Going into final approach to the Seed Vessel now," he announced over ship-wide speakers. Turning to Sphinx, he said, "Does the monster even have a name?"

"This is the Ruhr 5: *Demeter*."

"Ah, the Olympian goddess of agriculture and harvest. If you ask me, that thing looks more like a misshapen insect vomiting." Gavin was sure he couldn't come up with a more apt description. From a few clicks away, the impression of a moth was still not far off, but it became clear what kind of dimensions they were dealing with. The actual ship consisted of a two-hundred-yard-diameter composite cuboid with a blackened hull. On its underside facing the planet was a funnel a third of a mile in diameter, and on its top were two bubbles of elastic material in which brown particles floated back and forth. From its flanks stretched the 'wings', pitch-black solar sails, millimeter-thin but spanning thousands of miles. They lent the ship a sense of grandeur while appearing primeval, as if it were a particularly fearsome kaiju.

Defense drones buzzed around the station in a constant back-and-forth and changing orbits, continuously scanning it as they approached.

"The Corporate Protectorate lives up to its name," he said to himself. "Protecting it as if it were still their property."

269

"Ownership is complicated," Sphinx explained. "Ruhr Heavy Industries built the ship and sold it to the Terran Star Empire, but holds a majority interest in the project, organized as a corporation, until terraforming is complete. When it's finished many decades from now, they will retain a blocking minority and matching shares."

"I see, is that thing hanging over the main continent down there?" He looked at the land mass, which reminded him roughly of Africa on Earth - only without colors. It was blotchy in various shades of brown and not a particularly pretty sight.

"Yes. *Demeter* is in geostationary orbit, rotating with CX-2, at 6,960 miles per hour. That's necessary for the biomass drop."

He saw the latter ten minutes later, when they dipped under one of the solar sails with enough clearance to reach the shadows that prevailed below. From the funnel on the underside of the *Demeter*, a stream of particles that looked like green speckled earth rushed toward the planet's surface. Its diameter was a quarter mile, and the sheer volume was hard to comprehend unless you looked at the two bubbles on the *Demeter*'s 'back' that made just about everything look tiny.

"How is that even possible?" he asked.

"It's a complicated process. The biomass - mostly soil, microbes, plant debris, insects - comes mostly from Earth and other planets that have become unusable due to industrial climate change before new technologies. It is transported here in masses and subjected to artificial myelination by polyps. In the left refining bubble - the right one contains the delivered biomass. Through the hopper, the encased biomass pellets are catapulted to the surface, and in the process, the polyp burns up in the upper layers of the atmosphere due to friction with the air particles, and the contents of the pellets fall onto the land mass, where it is supposed to provide natural evolution via growth and adaptation."

"No wonder it's so expensive, the Senate spent five years debating the project."

"Yes. The financial cost is considerable and so is the risk of failure," Sphinx said. "The docking bay has been extended."

The last fleet

"I see it." Gavin kept the autopilot engaged - probably the best evidence that he was emotionally beside himself. "Crew, behave yourselves, I need to allow access to our internal systems in a moment."

He gave them five more seconds while the connection request flashed before him on the holodisplay. Then he acknowledged, giving the Seed Vessel's pilot a glimpse into their internal cameras and the official memory lacunae, which were meant for security reconciliations like this and remained detached from the rest of the system.

"Hello, over there," he radioed to the pilot. "Do you want to take over docking control?"

"Negative. Continue to follow vector control on autopilot," came the bland reply from the opposite side. Sphinx steered the *Lady* into a smooth turn, bringing her parallel to the hull of the Seed Vessel, next to which Gavin felt small even in the frigate. The blackness on the sensors, where stars were supposed to twinkle, sent a cold shiver down his spine.

"You all right?" asked Hellcat, whose head came through the hatch and thus hung from the ceiling the wrong way from his point of view.

"Yeah." He took one last look at his command deck to make sure no microphones were tapped, then unbuckled his seat belt. "Let's hope the Broker's security measures hold up against Ruhr's SOTA software and scanners."

"SOTA?"

"State of the art. Ruhr is one of the most powerful corporations in the Star Empire," he replied, floating in their direction where he caught himself on the lowest rung of the ladder. "They have more employees than some Core World inhabitants - and many times their GDP as annual revenue."

"I think you're still underestimating what kind of person the Broker is," she retorted, clearing the way by pulling herself through the narrow tube into the central corridor.

"Everything okay with your Smartnites?" he asked as they activated their magnetic boots and trudged toward the forward airlock. A gentle jolt told them that the Seed Vessel's retaining clamps had grabbed them, and presumably even the passenger bridge was already extended toward their ship.

"Yep. Saved up five years on them. Bambam had lesser quality stuff. Guess we'll have to change that sometime soon."

Gavin nodded and stopped outside the door to the airlock. "Remember, we're a pellet freighter, we escaped from Andal when the battle went bad, and we're scared."

"Shit, I don't even have to play that," she grumbled.

"I haven't registered a jump."

"Not yet. They didn't strike me as the kind to give up early. Who was that, anyway? And what kind of ship was it?"

"No technology I've seen before. It looked like a *Triumph*-class frigate, but with extensive modifications. And it could cloak itself in a way that made it impossible to get a bearing with our sensors - and they're definitely SOTA," he said with a scowl, pressing his hand on the door control, whereupon the hatch drove up into the wall with a hiss.

The airlock, bright white as a padded cell, also opened the outer door, through which a transparent tube about five yards long with a gray bridge led into the Seed Vessel.

"Good day, Captain Bennington," they were greeted by the tall bureaucrat with whom he had already had the 'pleasure' in the video. In real life he looked even more wrinkled and his mouth more humorless. He wore an anthracite-colored company one-piece suit with the stylized metal dragon of Ruhr Heavy Industries on the chest. Minimalist chic, functional, unobtrusive.

"Ikabot Nurheim," Gavin returned the greeting. "Executive First Class, correct?"

"That's correct," their host confirmed stiffly. He stood in such a way in his own airlock, which was darkly disguised in a way to contrast sharply with the connecting hose, that it blocked the way. "We have received and prepared your specifications for the relays to be replaced."

Nurheim reached beside him and lifted a plastic case, holding it out to them.

"Thank you," Gavin thanked him politely, just managing to mask his surprise at the brevity of the meeting. "That's it?"

"Our compliance department will review your case and discuss it with the appropriate Star Empire Senate committee, as is our duty. This is, after all, Terran property and thus falls under the jurisdiction of the Saturn Congress."

"Of course."

The bureaucrat's gaze became absent for a few seconds before his brow crinkled above the bridge of his nose, barely noticeably.

"Everything all right, Executive?" he asked.

"It looks like another ship has entered the system." Nurheim eyed them both appraisingly. "You wouldn't happen to know anything about that?"

"No." Gavin felt his skin begin to prickle and the impulse to just turn and run became overwhelming. He looked to Hellcat before he could control himself and found her gaze on his.

"Then why are you so nervous? The unknown ship doesn't match any signature we're familiar with, and it's not responding to communication attempts."

"We were tracked in Andal by a ship that was able to cloak and damage one of our thrusters before we managed to jump. We're honestly a little concerned that it might be the same one," he tried to escape forward.

Nurheim eyed first him, then Hellcat, and motioned for them to follow him.

"Come with me. And please don't interact with our machines or personnel."

They were led into a large, open area with dark wall and floor panels, discreetly mirrored for an alienating effect. Gavin could recognize himself in the floor and walls, but only as a shadow. The general darkness, enhanced by the dim indirect light, made him feel like he was in the fortress of an intergalactic villain - something that didn't exactly reassure him.

"Executive, this ship is dangerous," he said as they were led down a corridor that eventually ended in front of a security door. Two security men in powered armor stood there, posturing as they approached. Gavin stiffened involuntarily. In the presence of full body military armor, it was easy to feel fragile and in danger. A wave of these men's hands was enough to split him in half.

Fortunately, Nurheim opened the door and walked with them into a large room with a glazed outer wall through which they could look out at the stars. The panorama would have been breathtaking if Gavin hadn't had beads of sweat running off his forehead from sheer terror, even though it was quite cool around him.

"Is this the bridge or something?" asked Hellcat.

"The control center," the mission leader replied, pointing to one of the two work desks where a woman in the same black one-piece sat, wisping her fingers over invisible keyboards. "Give us access to your sensor data from the battle with that ship."

"Show me," Gavin urged the manager. He frowned disapprovingly and made a sweeping gesture with his right hand, whereupon a holodisplay appeared before them out of nowhere.

Gavin tensed involuntarily when he saw the hull with spikes and the unmistakable blue pulsing.

"It has set a course for us and appears to be armed, but our system has found no matches." Nurheim's voice revealed that this was not something that would have ever happened in his world.

"Your defense systems," he asked quietly. "How good are they, really?"

18

"Is that all the sensor data?" asked Nurheim in a calm, accented voice. Gavin would have liked to shake him to make him compliantly nervous.

"Yes," he replied after one last look at the data set he had ordered Sphinx to send to the *Demeter*'s on-board computer.

"That's worrisome." The executive turned to the other bridge officer, who was sitting at the second console and also appeared to be logged into a virtual workspace. "Miller, what is the status of our defense drones?"

"Twenty have moved to forward positions, weapons systems activated. Five remain back in defensive positions," the officer replied, speaking extremely quickly, like someone under a delusion.

"Distance of target in expected flight time?"

"The unknown target is in drift phase. Based on its current velocity, in five hours."

"There's something wrong with that," Hellcat objected. "You saw the footage yourself; it could be that this piece of shit is accelerating like crazy right now. It's not ejecting plasma."

Nurheim raised a brow disapprovingly at her choice of words, but nodded. "We're prepared for the worst."

"I don't think there's anything worse than that," Gavin objected. "I don't know if it came from some secret facility or..."

"Yes?"

"I don't know." He almost said *the Orb*. The blue glow on the hull still reminded him of the very similar effect on the giant alien that had tried to kill him on the *Ushuaia*. "It just doesn't look like something we would build."

"Well, you're not qualified to make that assessment," Nurheim noted, clasping his hands behind his back. "Miller, prepare a *Hermes* probe, we need to inform headquarters about this unidentified flying object. Put all sensor data, including that of the *Lady Vengeance*, in its memory lacunae and put it within directional beam range on the opposite side of CX-2. Just above the terminator, if you please."

"Of course."

"You have a *Hermes* at your disposal?" asked Gavin in surprise. He reminded himself to stop underestimating the equipment of these corporate men. Not even the Navy had many of the latest reconnaissance drones, which were not only extremely fast but equally difficult to track.

"Yes," the bureaucrat said without turning to him.

"You have one more piece of information to transmit."

"That is?" This time Nurheim sounded more than disapproving.

"Fleet Admiral Dain Marquandt has betrayed the defending fleets of Andal and the Emperor's heir apparent, Magnus Hartholm-Harrow," Gavin blurted out. Now, with a mixture of confusion and curiosity in his expression, the man turned to him after all. "He left them behind and used his priority code to disable the jump engines of all ships in the system."

"Those are extremely serious allegations, especially coming from the captain of a pellet freighter that I'm pretty sure is a smuggler," Nurheim countered, and Gavin noticed the security men in their engine armor stirring at the door - just loud enough for him to hear.

"I give you my word of honor that this is true. I have evidence to that effect on my ship, which is on a DNA-secured external storage medium."

The last fleet

"Your word of honor, yes?" Gavin could probably feel honored that the man didn't snort or roll his eyes.

"I am Lord Captain Gavin Andal, High Lord of Andal and the Karpshyn Sector after the death of my father and the rest of my family," he said, reflexively straightening. Nurheim frowned and opened his mouth, but then closed it again. "Check it yourself."

After some initial reluctance, the executive tapped away on his wrist terminal, then held it out to him. Gavin pressed his thumb to it.

After a moment of incredulous silence, Nurheim bowed to him. "Forgive me, my Lord. You will understand if this situation has been difficult for me to navigate."

"I do not blame you, but you must take this message to your headquarters. Verify it with my DNA match. Marquandt must be court-martialed immediately."

"Of course, my lord. I suggest you make a haptic transmission and send it to Miller here. He will load it into the probe's data storage with you, you have my word."

"Thank you!" Gavin started a tactile recording through his neural computer, which sent along vital signs and rudimentary thought patterns along with his spoken words, "This is Lord Captain Gavin Andal, last survivor of House Andal, High Lord of the Karpshyn Sector. During the defensive battle of my home system, Fleet Admiral Dain Marquandt abandoned his designated positions and retreated when he should have attacked the Never. He also had three suspected Orb-manufactured drones with which he was able to direct the Never swarms in unknown ways. He was responsible for the destruction of the Home Fleets under the command of Crown Prince Magnus and the Border World Fleets under the command of my brother Artas, as well as the extermination of Andal with over a billion women, children and men. To get rid of witnesses, he disabled all jump engines in the system by imperial priority code. We must assume that the ship that killed the ice freighter Alabama and the passenger liner *Morning Star*, and is now attacking the Seed Vessel *Demeter*, is acting on Marquandt's orders to prevent anyone from carrying this information to the Emperor. I vouch for my words with the honor of my House and that of an officer in the Imperial Navy."

He considered still mentioning the evidence data, but decided against it. If something went wrong, he would have a crosshair on his forehead after this, but if the wrong people got wind that he had solid evidence in the form of data, he would be a literal walking target. So he sent the file to Miller by gesturing over his wrist terminal.

"You should get the evidence now so I can send it along," Nurheim suggested as the woman at the other console spoke up.

"Unknown ship jumping."

"That's not possible. It just jumped into the system ten minutes ago."

"Some things should be impossible with this ghost, but it does it anyway," Gavin said, suddenly with ice in his veins that made his scalp tingle. At the same moment, the mysterious ship reappeared - so close to the panoramic window of the control room that the flash of its transit caused the glass to darken automatically.

The firefight began not a second later, as the close-range guns of Marquandt's minions spat fire in all directions simultaneously. Four railguns, identifiable by the blue flashes when they ejected their tungsten bolts, annihilated the first four defensive drones at the same moment, returning fire and flooding the space directly in front of *Demeter* with submunitions, jamming signals and hard radiation.

"Send *Hermes* off as soon as it's ready to jump!" ordered Nurheim. "Lower security bulkheads!"

The panoramic window, in front of which the purest chaos of explosions, exhaust flares, and muzzle flashes had erupted, was obscured by dark slats and replaced by a holodisplay showing only different colored symbols with cryptic, Ruhr-internal designations.

"Executive," Miller said. "The *Hermes* needs five minutes."

Nurheim turned to Gavin and Hellcat, "Five minutes. That's how much time you have to bring me the evidence so I can send it along, my lord."

The last fleet

Gavin merely nodded and ran off with his companion, past the guards who opened the double doors for them and released them into the large corridor. Through the speakers, the executive's voice rang out, controlled but quicker than he usually spoke, "All personnel, we are under attack. This is not a drill. Arm yourselves at the designated assembly points and prepare to defend yourselves against unauthorized intruders."

"We're being boarded?" asked Hellcat breathlessly.

"Looks like it."

"Why don't they just blow us up?"

"Maybe they want to play it safe."

"Gavin," Sphinx reported directly into his neural computer via transducer network. "Our ship is being fired upon."

"Defense!"

"I was able to repel two missiles, but I'm afraid this position is untenable."

"Then lay low and hide," he ordered. "Don't wait for the holding clamps, shoot them to pieces if you have to. Tear yourself loose now! I'll send you instructions on where to park the *Lady*."

"Roger that," the AI said obediently, and he broke the connection. With an outstretched arm, he stopped Hellcat. "We can't go back."

"What, why not?"

"The *Lady* has to cast off because she's right in the line of fire. It's us who they want, we've got to get those bastards off the *Demeter* somehow."

"No." Around them, several staff members ran to their collection points with anxious expressions. Hellcat, for her part, was now holding him. "If they're sending boarding parties, they want to know what people here know after we visit. They'll pop everything that moves and then they'll extract all the data and blow up the whole shebang."

"How do you know that? Maybe they're just trying to separate us from our ship and ..."

"Because that's what *you guys* always do to me and my people," she broke him off brusquely. "Get it? I may not know much, but I know exactly how this kind of thing goes down here because I've been through it myself. We need blades ASAP."

"What?"

"Guns!" She pointed to the backs of the staff in the anthracite dividers, who were just running away from them and turning a corner. "Come on."

Gavin had a retort on his lips, but Hellcat was already sprinting off, so he followed her, running across the reflective floor with clacking magnetic boots. Somewhere above him, he heard the muffled *clunk* of other boots. Once. Once more, and then again and again in quick succession. Knowing that the ship's docking bays were directly below the topside, it could only be the boarding party. That in turn meant that they had not come by ferry, but in their suits, which suggested sealed motorized armor.

A wave of renewed adrenaline shot through his veins and roared in his ears.

"We should have put on our own armor, by the blood of the heavens!" he cursed over the loud clacking of his boots.

"We have those?"

"Yes! Four of them, not the newest, but..."

"Why didn't you say so? That's the height of bullshit!", Hellcat scolded him without turning around. They reached an open door in the dark wall, in front of which stood two scientists who were accepting assault rifles handed to them from inside. Two others were already running away armed.

"Can you even handle that?" he asked back as he struggled to catch his breath.

"Can't be that hard, can it?"

"Yes it can, the training takes two years. Besides, I don't think they would have let us in with freaking servo armor on."

When it was their turn, she looked at the staff member at the counter in confusion for a moment, but then shrugged and handed them, one by one, *Inferno* assault rifles with two spare magazines and *Artemis* body armor in the form of two helmets with thickened collars.

"Thank you," he muttered and slipped the helmet over his head. Pressing the button on the collar, he commanded the computer to release the nanite mass, which quickly began to flow over his body like black mercury. The *Artemis* functioned much like the Reaper suit he had used on the *Glory*, but it was far more expensive and less maneuverable because it was not optimized for use in a vacuum. Also, the user didn't have to be naked in it, and that was extremely convenient for him right now because he already felt like he was running out of time before the first bullets flew.

Once he was covered from his fingertips to his toes, and the virtual display in his helmet marked the integrity of the suit with a green symbol, he helped Hellcat load her weapon through, showed her how to eject the cartridges and the button to link to her Artemis armor. He noticed how tense she was by the way she listened intently to him, even nodding twice briefly.

"Is like a normal assault rifle only without recoil because the projectiles have tiny rocket boosters," he explained hastily. "The only drawback is that they can blind easily." Addressing the woman at the desk, who was arming herself with trembling hands, he asked, "Which way to the lower levels?"

"Down the corridor to the labs, from there ..." That was as far as she got, as there was a deafening noise behind them as several hull sections were hurled downward.

The decompression of their surroundings immediately set in as a gale force wind tore at them so violently that they would have been shot into the vacuum had their magnetic boots not held them in place. The woman at the desk had not yet put on her helmet, which was ripped from her hand and sucked through one of the holes. Her face turned blue and tiny ice crystals formed on her skin.

Hellcat was the first to regain her footing and shot to her head. Gavin froze in shock until she yanked on his shoulder.

"GO! We have to go!" she yelled at him over the internal radio and ran down the corridor. Gavin was wondering why the enemy Marines didn't come flying through the holes when he saw muzzle flashes in the middle of nowhere and jerked to the side. He was narrowly missed and fired blindly into the clear area in front of him. The projectiles shattered not on the wall, but in the air, where brief glimmers showed the outlines of powered armor, like the flickering images of mystical demons.

He didn't wait to see if the following shots would hit him, and instead ran after Hellcat, who had already gotten around the next corner and was covering him with barrage fire. Not being fast enough, he threw himself forward and deactivated his magnetic boots at the same time, whereupon he sailed head first through zero gravity. Hellcat grabbed his outstretched left arm and pulled him around her corner with a jerk - not a moment too soon, as moments later the wall he had just been running toward was shredded by explosive rounds.

"Motherfuckers are cloaked too, like their fucking ship!" she cursed, and fired another volley. Then she quickly pulled her head back as the return fire shredded pieces from the composite of their cover and scattered them as metal shards above them.

Gavin's armor hardened where it was hit by shrapnel, causing it to tremble. He loaded a new magazine and tossed the old one back into the passageway, where it was immediately shot at and shredded.

"Target search automatic," he said over the radio. "We should get the hell out of here."

"Where to?" Hellcat slid her rifle around the corner and emptied her magazine before running to him, deftly slipping a new one into the ammunition slot as she did so.

"Down to the labs." He pointed to the corridor behind them, where two holes opened up in the floor. Then he covered them with his gun cocked and waited until she signaled and he ran to her position. Kneeling, she aimed at the half-destroyed composite wall where she had been standing a moment ago and waved for him to move down.

Gavin deactivated his boots again, gave his rifle a shove to make it sail down, and then followed it with a powerful pull from the top rung of the ladder.

Once at the bottom, he snatched the weapon out of the air and hastily looked around using the targeting optics. He found himself in a large room with several automatic doors, above which shone what to him were rather cryptic labels of letters and numbers.

"Clear!"

Hellcat followed him through the tube into the room and pounded a fist on a red emergency latch next to the lower access, whereupon thick armored hatches closed over their heads.

"Won't last long," she concluded.

"It's enough for me if it slows them down. We've got to get down."

"Why?"

"Because there's a dozen killers upstairs stomping around in invisible powered armor, shooting at anything that moves," he returned laconically, running for the first door after reactivating his magnetic boots. The control panel made no sound as he ran his hand over it. Examining it, he pressed some of the many buttons, but was merely met with a purred "Access denied. Please verify your authorization with your supervisor in charge."

The next two doors also failed him, until he arrived in front of a large double door that opened by itself, revealing a huge hall crammed with lab equipment and robots.

Lots and lots of robots. Some of them he knew from history books and law lectures from cadet school, in which prospective officers were drilled on the danger posed by the various kinds of bots: yellow cargo robots with eight legs and wide torsos, topped by gripper arms with which they could fill their trays and compartments, smaller four-legged *Hound* models, reminiscent of terrestrial dogs, created for servicing hard-to-reach areas. What startled him most, however, were the scant dozen humanoid Servitors with their expressionless face plates, on which no facial expressions were animated, but only data about the respective models and their current tasks could be read. They worked at various tables with microscopes, interferometers and radiocarbon scanners - at least these were among the few he could recognize as a layman. All mechanical eyes were on them both as they burst in with their weapons.

"This is so ... *illegal*!" he blurted out.

"Not in the Corporate Protectorate," Hellcat said, giving him a shove forward to lock the door behind them. "They probably don't get many visitors here, the way they stare at us."

"Ah-ha," he merely said and swallowed. Gavin had never seen so many robots in one place, let alone functional ones running around without supervision. Instinctively, he gripped his gun a little tighter and slowly continued forward. "The woman meant through the labs, right?"

"I think *to* the labs."

Gavin eyed the Servitors suspiciously as they passed them, face plates spinning with them.

"Don't these things have an override for human users or something?" he asked.

"I don't know, never seen one of those things before and didn't miss anything if you ask me. Scary shit!"

"Robots, can you hear me?" Gavin might have felt stupid asking his question if he wasn't pumped to the top with adrenaline.

"We understand you, sir," the Servitors replied in chorus, which was almost more eerie than feeling their silent, eyeless gazes on him.

"Go to that door there and line up in two rows so that you block the way," he ordered, and to his surprise they desisted from their current activity and followed his instruction without objection.

"It won't do. Unless we can persuade them to jump the fuckers. But they may not," Hellcat noted with disappointment.

"Maybe." Gavin walked over to an intercom built into the wall and pressed the yellow highlighted button labeled KR. He hoped it stood for 'control room'. "First Executive Nurheim? Can you hear me?"

"My lord," came the reply after a brief murmur. The rumble of gunfire could be heard in the background, intercepted by something heavy. "We're being held in the control room. I've had to send the *Hermes* off in the meantime. It's already jumped out of the system."

Gavin exhaled in relief. "Good, that's good. We're in the labs below you. Is there any way to persuade the Servitors to help?"

"Yes, there is a code word for the behavioral heuristics override. Repeat after me: Zulu-feast-egg-dialysis-castle-horserace-mast-farm-blue-foxtrot-filet-reservoir."

Gavin obeyed, pronouncing the strange arrangement of words aloud, and when he finished, the Servitors' face plates lit up red. The loading bots and hounds also began flashing red from several diodes and turned to face him.

He swallowed. "I think it worked."

"Good luck, my lord." Something in the bureaucrat's voice told him he didn't expect to survive the next few minutes.

"Orders: Protect me and my companion. Attack anyone wearing powered armor. Guard that door." He pointed back to the passageway they had just used, and to which the bots had just been headed.

Hellcat, meanwhile, ran to the other side of the lab, circling large tanks with brown particles floating in them that looked like soil, and containers with the chemical symbol for nitrogen that gave off bright vapor. When she reached the double door there, she made a beeline for the control panel, but the passageway remained locked.

"Can't get it open!" she shouted over the radio.

Gavin looked to her and then to the door, in front of which the robots were gathering artfully. Something hard slammed into it from the other side, sending a thunderous echo through the lab.

"We have no time!" he returned, turning back to the intercom. With his finger on the yellow KR button, he said, "Nurheim? Are you still there? *Executive*?"

Except for a high-pitched hiss, he heard nothing.

"Bloody heavens! We can't get any more help from the control room."

"How am I supposed to hack this filthy shit without a universal connector and my bloody wrist terminal?" cursed Hellcat to himself and started pounding on the control panel.

That will definitely help, he thought, as an idea came to him. He ran against every instinct he had toward the robots, in front of whom the double door was bulging more and more. The first pair of armored hands squeezed into the gap between the wings and the metal gave a deep plea.

"Robot!" he addressed one of the loading bots, reading its identifier from the faceplate. "Lab Delta 2. Go to the other door by my comrade and force it open if necessary. This is an emergency."

The spider-like robot with the eight yellow legs obediently turned and walked surprisingly fast for its clunky exterior in Hellcat's direction. The hollow clack of its footsteps was shortly drowned out by a bestial squeal as the hands of the motor armor - eight in all that he could see - wrenched the doors aside. One flew out of its socket, revealing four of the six-foot tall monsters, whose outlines disappeared as soon as they released the composite.

INTERLUDE: JANUS

Janus's palace office was one floor below the Emperor's office and thus on the same level as the representations of the one hundred High Lords and High Ladys of the Terran Star Empire. Not only unusual for someone from the lower nobility, but an affront in the eyes of the high nobility, he broke the unwritten laws of making hierarchies visible. In an environment borne of tradition and etiquette, even a slightly too-long look was reason enough for serious talk behind the scenes. But the Emperor had personally decreed that the First Secretary of State's office was to be in close proximity to his own.

Of course, since taking office five years ago, Janus had been aware that the real intention of the leader of humanity had been to give him a higher status by having the most powerful of the Star Empire believe he was a very special favorite of the Emperor. A circumstance that had seemed extremely helpful to him so far.

He circled his unadorned desk with its large glass pane with a view to the outside, behind which the stars were already twinkling, and the moon rose as a shining disk over the Alps. Once seated, he pressed some buttons on his holodeck and turned on his white-noise generator. He then bent down to his single desk drawer and breathed on the hidden DNA sniffer, which then unlocked the magnetic catch and disarmed the small explosive charge in the bottom. He took out the only item inside: a black wrist terminal with only a single crypto key stored on it.

He placed it on one of the holodeck's sensor arrays and took a deep breath before turning it on.

"You haven't used that contact address in a long time," a voice so devoid of any accent or sentence melody answered him that he would have thought it was computer generated if he didn't know better.

"That should tell you quite a bit already," Janus replied. "I have to meet Mirage."

"No meetings, you know the drill. You ended that kind of contact yourself when you chose to live on your master's leash."

"That wasn't my decision, it was *yours*, remember?"

"One way or the other. You are not naive enough to believe that things could continue normally after your move," said his contact. "You can't be a servant to two masters."

"I'm also not naive enough to think that this is anything more than some sort of preliminary negotiation for what you're going to ask me to pay as a price," Janus returned unapologetically.

"Ah, a price. For a conversation with Mirage. There are individuals who would sacrifice entire systems for that."

"I have a guest in a moment and I want you to listen to the conversation. After that, you can tell me if you will let me talk to Mirage."

"Are you staying at the palace?" the voice asked, as if he hadn't said anything.

"You already know that. If not, there is no point in this conversation."

The voice did not answer.

"Well?" he asked.

"I'll listen. But a meeting with Mirage will cost you more than you're willing to pay."

"Nothing is ever free with you," he said.

"The price is set by the market, and since there is no market for us, we set it. So decide how important it is," the voice urged.

"I will come to you following the interview."

"I'll have someone pick you up. In forty minutes, shuttle bay

The last fleet

4, the pilot will not wait. And remember, *Zenith*, there will be no going back to the status quo." The other side switched to listening and disconnected their own audio link.

Janus gulped at the mention of his old name and rubbed his face. The doorbell rang and a red light on his desk flashed on, snapping him out of his stupor.

"Mr. Darishma, the chief of staff has arrived," his secretary revealed to him from the anteroom.

"I'll be ready in a moment; offer him something to drink."

Before he had even spoken, the door to his office opened and Grand Admiral Marius Albius walked in. The four-boned officer, who looked like a butcher stuck in a costume, flashed a broad smile without it reaching his small eyes, and strode toward the only chair in front of Janus' desk.

"You weren't going to keep me waiting, were you, Secretary of State?"

Janus ignored the obvious provocation in the fact that the Navy's top officer omitted the actual status-indicating part of his title and gestured for him to take a seat. Not that the man was waiting.

"I was on my way to see High Lord Grassimus anyway," Albius continued, placing his Imperial Phoenix hat on the table between them.

It was not easy for Janus to hide his dislike for this man. A gruff old warhorse who had been directly involved in the overthrow of the McMaster dynasty and couldn't even bear to have a civilian civil servant summon him. They both knew why he was sitting across from him. So what was the point of this childish charade?

"I have a few more questions," he said, waving in Nancy, who stood in the open doorway with a tablet in her hand and question marks in her eyes. She brought coffee and mineral water and set it down between them. Silently, she handed out cups and glasses and then bowed slightly to Janus.

"Anything else, First Secretary?"

"No, thank you, Nancy."

"So, what can I do for you?" asked Albius, as if it was Janus who had been called here by him, and this was his office. "I actually thought we had just discussed everything. As you can imagine, the Admiralty is in turmoil right now, and I have more construction sites than I can count."

"Just a few more questions of detail," Janus assured his counterpart, taking a sip of coffee with emphatic calm. "As soon as we're done here, you can get back to your important duties."

The Grand Admiral's eyes narrowed, but he said nothing.

"During our just-concluded conversation with the Emperor, you received word that Fleet Admiral Dain Marquandt and his Wall Fleet escaped from Andal," Janus said.

"Yes, I told you that already."

"Of course. He was in the Omaha system at the time he wrote the message." He called up a holographic representation of the Star Empire that began to rotate above the desk between them. A flattened section of the Orion Arm of the Milky Way. With short, practiced gestures, he marked the Sigma Quadrant, relatively speaking at the upper left of the Sol system, at the lower right corner of which was Earth and which, on the opposite side, marked one end of the Star Empire's extent with the Border Worlds and the fallen Andal. Between Sol and Andal lay the Omaha system, part of the Akrulu Sector. Now he highlighted Wall Sector Delta, consisting of four systems under Marquandt's command. "It's noticeable that Omaha is on a straight route between Akrulu and Sol. Very interesting."

Albius looked at the three-dimensional map and the markings on it. It was clear to Janus that his counterpart had long been thinking the same thoughts. Despite his coarse appearance, the Grand Admiral proved that he should not be taken for simple-minded and remained silent.

"Interesting because two possibilities, chances I would like to think, arise from this constellation," Janus finally continued. "The Wall Worlds in the Delta Sector are well fortified, but without their fleets they are a weak point in the long run. At the same time, Sol is now pretty much exposed with only one Home Fleet left."

The last fleet

"What are you getting at?" asked High Lord Albius, leaning back in his chair.

"I'm asking for your professional assessment as the Emperor's Chief of Staff."

"With the Emperor, have we not just..."

"If you would be so kind," Janus added, looking the Grand Admiral in the eye. He glared at him just long enough for it not to pass as an affront, then shrugged.

"Of course, I can give you more details if my previous remarks were not detailed enough," Albius finally said. Janus swallowed that suggestion with equanimity as well and waited. "Omaha is home to a large munitions depot and the main Navy shipyards in the Sigma Quadrant. So it's an obvious target after a lost battle."

"So you don't think that after losing an entire system to the Never, five fleets shouldn't be waiting in one of the neighboring systems for new instructions in case the Never ventures further into Terran territory?" he echoed.

"No, it has never done that so far. The emergence of the infestation has always been erratic, following no clear strategy or traceable pattern of movement."

"Right." Janus called up a file he had Nancy pull out for the conversation. "These are the minutes of the final tactical meeting before the fleets left for Andal. In it you said, and I quote, *'This cosmic nightmare is just that, but at least it's predictable-your words-so we can assume that losses will be in the single-digit percentage range of the combat power deployed. We know how it moves and how fast. Its direction is always the inhabited planet of the system. So we place ourselves in strategic locations and heat it up.'* That sounds very much like a clear strategy to me: it always attacks the inhabited planet directly."

"With my previous statement, I was referring to the fact that there is no pattern in the occurrence of the Never. It comes and it goes, no one knows why or where," Albius explained with his brows drawn together.

"The Never has appeared three times since the first infestation in 2326."

"Turan-II. Every child knows that."

"Then 2328, New Berlin, and the third in 2380 with the victory at Rohol."

Albius made an impatient gesture with his right hand, as if trying to shoo away a pesky fly.

"I'm no mathematician, but three incidences aren't a particularly large database for solid statistics," Janus explained. "How did the fleets react after Turan-II and New Berlin?" Realizing that the Grand Admiral was in no mood to answer rhetorical questions, he added, "Enlighten me, please, my lord."

"Full fleet readiness, mobilization of all available formations and redeployment to neighboring systems," Albius reluctantly enumerated.

"And such a highly decorated and educated fleet admiral as Dain Marquandt knows this, I suppose? You certainly don't have officers directly under you who can't deduce natural actions from previous precedents. That," Janus noted, "makes Marquandt's stay in Omaha all the more ... *interesting*."

"What are you getting at? Should I chide him for not doing what was the reaction eight decades ago? In both cases, the swarms retreated after that. As a good officer, and I don't expect you to understand this as a civilian, it's standard repertoire to learn from past enemy behavior."

"In the form of not reinforcing neighboring systems of an obliterated system, but retreating deep into the star realm, to an obvious crossroads?"

"Marquandt is not here, or we could ask him." Albius' expression was one of impatience, and he held back his anger with difficulty.

"Would you like to?"

"I beg your pardon?"

Janus merely smiled. The Chief of Staff was a good fleet politician, or he wouldn't have become the Star Empire's top admiral, but he certainly wasn't a gifted negotiator, in which case he would have put a little more effort into the spectacle of his indignation. Maybe practiced a few times in front of the mirror.

"I have no further questions, Grand Admiral. You may leave now."

The last fleet

Albius stared at him for a moment longer, and Janus could see it working behind the man's eyes, then he pursed his mouth disapprovingly and stood up.

"First Secretary of State."

"Ah, one more thing. Sorry about the Senate President," Janus said, and the Grand Admiral faltered. For a split second only, but clearly visible to someone who had been waiting for such a sign. Then Albius frowned.

"A loss for all of us," he finally replied.

"Especially for you, I suppose." When the admiral appraised him disparagingly, Janus added, "You are good acquaintances, are you not? You, Marquandt, and Usatami are, after all, the only private investors in the terraforming project in the Seed Traverse. How much do you hold in it?"

Albius's expression hardened.

"Two percent, yes. Sounds like a good deal for a risky project. I assume you've lost a good friend, and for that I offer my condolences."

"Thank you," Albius merely said and left the office.

When he had gone out, Janus locked the door and informed Nancy that she was to turn away any visitors, except for the Emperor. Then he activated his white-noise generator again and waited.

"He knows more than he says," the voice said.

"I didn't contact you to state the obvious."

"You have a new enemy."

"He's never liked me. An upstart elevated by imperial favor from commoner to titular nobility, elevated to the highest office of state, the Emperor's right-hand man, and a civilian and jurist to boot. A toxic mix in the eyes of any member of the fleet." Janus waved it off sight unseen.

"I mean an *enemy*. Albius now knows what you know and think, and even he is surely smart enough to understand that you wanted him to know," the voice said.

"Why would he be so supportive of Marquandt? He should be beside himself because the man lost his battle. The Emperor had raged in his conversation with Albius, would have loved to rip his head off for holding him partly responsible for his son's death - understandably so. This was all Marquandt's plan, but the Chief of Staff signed off on it and submitted it to the Emperor, recommending it for his signature."

"Even worse. You now have an enemy who fears for his position. A cornered predatory cat. What options does a predatory cat with no way out have?"

"Fight."

"Uh-huh. No escape. And they don't freeze. Never. Men of war know only war."

"But you spoke of options in the plural," Janus echoed. "So you mean fight *or* fight."

"Hard of mind you have never been, First Secretary of State," the voice found sarcastically.

"Either Albius goes after Marquandt and profiles himself before the Emperor as a loyal servant who is just as out of sorts, and in typical fleet policy fashion, shifts all the blame to a target the Emperor is only too happy to aim at. The classic scapegoat. Or ..."

"Exactly."

"We're meeting. I need more information."

"You know this is going to cost you something you may never get back. You made a decision once to move on from your past. There's no coming back from some decisions, Janus Darishma, first secretary of state."

"I know." He propped himself up on his barren desk and stared somberly at the tabletop. "Something is brewing, and I can't see which compass point it's coming from."

"Be careful, First Secretary. And don't contact us again unless you make another final decision. There will be no turning back from that one. You have value to us, and that is the only reason you are still alive. However, do not try our patience." There was a click on the line.

19

The Servitors reacted quickly. They had already pounced on the enemy marines the moment the right door panel had been torn away, striking at their armor. Each hit made the invisible visible. The touches spread like concentric waves on the camouflage - enough for Gavin to orient himself.

He lined up and fired several volleys at the first Marine whose shoulder he could make out. The missile projectiles hit the helmet and exploded in rapid succession. The effect, however, was hardly worth mentioning. The one hit merely jerked his head back a little, then he grabbed one of the Servitors and snapped it in half. The servo motors at the elbow and shoulder joints screeched like ghosts.

The fight looked something like a gang of schoolchildren and their pets going at four professional martial artists.

Gavin decided not to watch the carnage any longer and ran to Hellcat and the loading bot, which had already pushed its grappling arms into the insulating layer between the door panels and was pushing them in both directions. He had spread the magnetic feet wide and fixed them to the floor. The material groaned and groaned until it finally gave way.

"They're gaining on us!" he hissed in exasperation as he saw how slowly the bot was advancing.

Hellcat looked around, snarling, and grabbed him by the neck to throw him to the ground. With a strangled yelp, he landed between two sealed tables and nearly lost his rifle.

"What are you doing?" he groaned, but she didn't answer. Instead, she pointed to her ear before wiggling her finger in front of his face.

I realize that they can probably eavesdrop on us, he thought with a frown. *But it doesn't matter because we have to get out of here!*

"Come on, let's get out of here!" Hellcat shouted breathlessly, as if she was about to run, but continued to lie beside him with a calm expression, slowly pointing to a closet with a sliding door. She then pointed to him and herself and again to the closet.

With his lips he wordlessly formed the word, "Infrared."

She merely nodded and pointed to one of the tanks of liquid nitrogen very close to her.

Gavin understood and nodded after a moment's consideration, even though it made him feel sick. A glance through the table legs and equipment showed him that the pile of destroyed robot limbs was growing. But he also saw motorized armor lying on the floor, as well as two loading bots who had somehow managed to grab the Marine in such a way that their grappling arms were wedged in the grooves of his arm segments. Thus they pulled at him with howling engines as if to quarter him. Three destroyed Servitors lay on the attacker's legs, preventing him from reacting quickly. As the armor gave way, Gavin heard a sickening smacking sound and averted his eyes.

Hellcat pointed at herself and the door, then at him and the tank, and he nodded again in understanding. In response, she showed him three fingers, then two, then one.

She crawled to the cabinet door and pushed it aside while he fired incessantly at the nitrogen tank. The ultra-cold liquid splashed across the room, evaporating into an opaque mist that would soon settle on everything in the lab.

"Empty!" he yelled over the radio, tossing his rifle through the still-quite-narrow gap where their loading bot was struggling.

The last fleet

Lying prone, he followed Hellcat, who had already squeezed into the low cabinet.

He squeezed in after her, pressing against her so tightly that it became painful in several places. Eventually, however, he managed to push the door shut behind him and regulate the thermal insulation power of his Artemis body armor to full power. Immediately he felt a touch warmer as the suit gave off barely any of the body heat it continually produced. Combined with the nitrogen outside, it would hopefully be enough.

With his arms, he forcibly hugged Hellcat, who was leaning back against his chest. Examining, he pressed the front of his helmet to the back of hers and whispered, "Can you hear me?"

"Yes." He had to set his internal audio amplifiers to maximum power to understand her because she spoke so softly. But he understood her.

"Good idea."

"Yeah."

"Remind me you need a transducer."

"As long as you pay for it," she whispered back.

Outside, the strangely rapturous noise of mechanical carnage could be heard - whirring servos, screeching metal, ripping cables, heavy footsteps here and there, a pounding of steel on steel. But no human sounds whatsoever. No groans, no screams. It was downright ghostly, especially as he sat with Hellcat in complete darkness, every sound through the cabinet doors bringing with it an unnatural reverberation effect.

"Why didn't they just blow the station out of orbit?" whispered Hellcat.

"They want to know what we know and if we've smuggled out any treasonous data, I suppose." Gavin tried not to think about the growing pressure pain in his shoulders and chest.

"I would have played it safe if I were them."

"Then I'm glad you're not in their place," he remarked laconically. "Good idea about the nitrogen and the closet, really."

"You already said that. In my situation, you learn to improvise by necessity. Or you die," she replied.

He was about to retort something when there were multiple

bangs outside, as if someone was banging inflated paper bags together in rapid succession. Then it became abruptly silent before the metallic footsteps of motorized armor continued as vibrations in the ground. From the feel of it, they were moving at high speed.

Another wobble and abrupt tremor followed, and the helpful load messenger struggling with the door apparently also met its end. A final dull thud, then the footsteps faded.

"How long should we wait?" he asked uneasily. Sitting still while Marines ran around a few feet away, ready to tear them to pieces, was not a state he wanted to endure for long. Or could. "From the looks of it, there's no air in there now either. I don't hear anything anymore, anyway."

"I don't know. Let's not take any chances."

"We can't wait too long, either."

"The *Lady*."

"Yes. The enemy ship won't sit idle, they'll look for her."

"Where is she, anyway?" wanted Hellcat to know, sounding as if she, too, needed to distract herself so as not to go berserk in the darkness. If the Marines had lined up in front of their sliding cabinet and were aiming straight at them, they wouldn't even know it until they were shot to pieces.

"I'd rather not tell you."

"What's that supposed to mean?"

"That I'm going to take a peek outside," he replied, fumbling for the thickened rabbet on the inside of the metal door. Only when he had a good grip on it - which required an unhealthy contortion in a confined space - did he pull on it ever so slightly until a narrow slit of light fell on his helmet and he had to blink.

As his eyes adjusted to the photon onslaught, he peered out into the lab. He saw bare table legs in the cold overhead light, torn limbs of robots, shattered glass, scraps of dense foam, and shiny liquid and icy patches everywhere. Somewhere a severed cable flashed in an endless short circuit.

But he saw no engine armor.

"Looks clear," he whispered, repeating himself after pressing his helmet back against Hellcats. In response, she merely tapped his right knee and he began to untangle himself from her.

Even though they had only remained in the dark confines for a few minutes, his joints felt frozen, even though his suit was having trouble pushing all the sweat that was pouring out of him out through his pores. He set the thermal insulation back to a low setting, just enough to keep his core body temperature constant at 36.6 degrees, and then slowly climbed out of its hiding place.

As soon as he straightened up, he turned toward the double doors through which they had come, staring directly at the chest of an engine armor.

"Oh, bloody ...," the words escaped him as a fist crashed into his stomach as well. The Artemis immediately hardened, redirecting the kinetic energy of the impact as best it could to the rest of the armor, sending several ripples across its surface. Even so, the force was so strong that his magnetic boots lost their grip and he was thrown backward. In an instinctive reaction, he reached for the handle of an electron microscope and flew around the apparatus like an accidental dancer on a pole. When he let go, he tumbled through the vacuum toward the opposite wall, away from Hellcat and her hiding place.

Never underestimate the damn Marines, Gavin vowed to himself to never forget again as he crashed into something hard and bounced off. Pain flared in his shoulder blades. He did his best to ignore it, and found his footing again when his magnetic boots made contact again. He blinked twice and he saw the motorized armor stomping toward him - overhead. In his confusion, he belatedly realized that he was stuck to the ceiling and the Marine was stuck to the floor. Gavin jerked his head to the side to avoid the cable torn from the ceiling and its sparks. It wriggled through the zero gravity like an angry snake.

It made little difference as he stared directly down the barrel of a Gauss rifle normally mounted on fighters or combat vehicles. Out of the corner of his eye, he saw a second Marine appear in the doorway gap that the loading bot had made just large enough for the powerful figures to fit through before it was destroyed.

Muzzle flashes lit the room. Hellcat had apparently crawled out of her hiding place and fired into the back of the Marine who was about to shoot Gavin. He took advantage of the brief moment of hesitation caused by the explosions on his opponent's back by lunging at the powerful rifle, pushing it aside as he did so.

Everything happened so fast that he felt like an outside observer. The muzzle aimed roughly toward the door as he reached up and grabbed the cable just below the end with the short, pressing it onto the back of the Marine's hand.

Electricity spread across the dissipating grid on the armor. But whether it was the crackling volts or a surprised reflex on the soldier's part, his finger curled and the Gauss rifle fired a shot - perfectly silent in the absence of air molecules.

The bullet miraculously struck the other Marine squarely in the neck, shredding the hardened Carbin armor as if it were Styrofoam. For a fraction of a heartbeat, both he and the gunner in front of him stared in disbelief at the lucky - or unlucky, depending on the observer - hit, then they regained their composure and Gavin barely dove out from under the barrel of the weapon that would have otherwise severed his head.

Hellcat came hurtling toward them from the other side of the lab like a torpedo. Gavin assessed its trajectory and reached up to grab the Marine's neck. Agility was his only advantage over this monster of engines and Carbin.

He pulled his legs up as he moved like a monkey trying to grab a branch. The maneuver earned him a headbutt that sent stars dancing in front of his field of vision and his helmet splintering on the side. But he refused to let go and crossed his ankles just above the wrist of the armor. Arching his back, he forced the entire arm to extend, and could feel the servos in the elbow resting against Gavin's hip wobble and vibrate. A single motor-assisted joint against all his physical strength.

He groaned and growled with exertion, craning his neck in anticipation of another blow to his helmet at any moment. Hellcat, he found, had shifted extremely quickly and matched him on the other side, except that she had planted her feet in the armpit

The last fleet

and on the neck, pushing the soldier's helmet away while clutching the hand and gun with her arms and shoulders.

The Gauss gun kept firing toward the door, so he guessed she had somehow gained control of his trigger finger.

"Foot!" she yelled over the radio, and it took Gavin an untold moment to comprehend. He released the Marine's neck and wrist at the same time and gave himself a downward boost. His opponent, as expected, took advantage of the weakness and punched him in the exposed back.

All air abruptly escaped from his lungs and fogged his visor. The pain made him black out, even though the *Artemis* body armor made an extreme effort to absorb and disperse the kinetic force. From the involuntary momentum, he allowed himself to be flung to the side, directly toward the Gauss rifle that Hellcat swung in his direction with a half-choked scream.

Gavin grabbed it by the barrel and spun upward with demagnetized boots before reactivating them and intercepting his momentum as he stuck to the ceiling. There he crouched and watched as Hellcat was struck by the free fist and smashed away as if by a wrecking ball. Over the radio, he heard a guttural cry.

He pushed aside the concern for her along with the pain in his back and pushed off with all his might, racing toward the Gauss rifle that was swinging straight behind the rebel and forced it down. When it pointed directly at one of the clunky feet of armor, he clawed at the trigger and commanded his neural computer to load his precedence code as High Lord of the Star Empire into the weapon and fire it.

The magnetic boot and foot inside it disintegrated in a tsunami of Carbin shards, bones, flesh, and globules of blood that shot off in all directions. Due to the strong angular momentum and the fact that the Marine now had only one fixed point on the ground, his injured leg was flung to the side, spraying fresh blood like a compressed beverage can in a centrifuge. It twisted and turned about the longitudinal axis that formed the standing leg, which broke several times within seconds and finally slowed the rotation.

The Marine, meanwhile, had let go of his weapon, leaving it

in Gavin's hands. He didn't hesitate long and fired at his opponent. Before he saw the Mach 10 bullet hit, the brutal recoil sent him crashing into the wall, once again unable to breathe. This time, pain overwhelmed him and his vision went dark.

Someone or something grabbed him and yanked him to the side. He let it happen, because he could neither think clearly nor see his surroundings. He could no longer feel his legs and wished it were the other way around, as the agony his back was causing him was not diminishing.

"Hang in there!" he heard a familiar voice accompanied by a dank rattle before his neural computer successfully set an analgesic block and weaned his brain from its pain. He breathed a grateful sigh of relief.

He recognized Hellcat, who was holding him by the shoulder and pulling him along with her as metal shards flew through the silence around her like a 3D simulation without sound.

"I think your back is mush," Hellcat shouted, steering him effortlessly around the corner of the double doors where the remains of countless robots floated, bouncing off the walls and colliding with each other again and again. Bullets followed them, far too fast to see, and crashed into the wall on the opposite side, just behind the ladder tubes that led up, but unfortunately not down.

"I think that's the outer hull," he croaked, pointing to where Gauss bullets had eaten deep into casing, sealing foam and the composite mesh behind it.

Hellcat looked at him and then realized, aimed the dead Marine's Gauss rifle and pressed the shock pad against the wall next to the door before pulling the trigger, which didn't work. Gavin sent another command to the weapon and it began firing dozens of iron bolts per second. The hull in the damaged area, which was already taken, was shredded until the magazine was empty. The resulting hole revealed the glow of the Seed World, whose oceans seemed to shine from within, illuminated by the central star.

"Risky," Hellcat stated, ducking her head as a volley of projectiles turned the doorframe beside them into a rain of splinters.

The last fleet

"It's our only chance. Just don't let go."

"Mhm. Hold on." She put his arms around her neck and stood with her boots against the wall, where she crouched. Gavin felt weak and useless without his legs, but was powerless to do anything but trust her.

A rebel. Of all people.

20

Gavin hollered without end as they flew toward the hole in the hull. Whether it was because of the Gaussian bullets hitting around them or the fact that he was piggybacking on a woman he would have called a terrorist not long ago, now forming some sort of shield with her body, he didn't know. Perhaps it was also because the destroyed shell segment was so small that two of them couldn't possibly fit through it.

The reason they hadn't been shredded yet was because of the many particles that flew out of the lab and through the torn wall segments through zero gravity and formed a dense network of pieces colliding with each other. They ranged from tiny ice crystals to fist-sized composite chunks and apparently affected the Marines' targeting optics enough to save his and Hellcat's lives.

At least until they reached the light and he realized at the last moment that he wasn't going to make it.

He crashed his helmet into one of the frayed pieces of hull and heard an ugly crack and scrape. The branching breaks in the armored glass spread erratically, taking away his entire view on the right side. What was worse was that they had been traveling with so much force that the impact spun him around, pushed Hellcat through the hole after him, and then spun him out into space. Desperately, he tried to grab hold of anything as everything spun before his eyes. The horizon - the glowing planet below them - shifted every second, and the nausea rising inside him told him that his staggering was uncontrollable.

"Shit!" he heard Hellcat curse, thought he saw the light of her helmet against the black of the station, but the moment was so brief it was probably imagination. "Spread your arms and legs!"

"What?"

"Right now!"

"I can't move my legs ..."

"NOW!" she yelled into the radio so loudly that his ears rang, and his arms flew to his sides as if of their own accord, splayed wide and long-fingered. The nausea was unbearable by now, and he vomited into his helmet in a short but violent gush. Biting stomach acid and bits of his last meal - tuna pastrami, of all things - flew back and forth like a snow globe being vigorously shaken.

If there was a God, he probably had him to thank for not touching the orange juice at breakfast.

Suddenly, something changed. He felt a thump in his shoulders, then his left arm grazed something, then his right. Before he knew it, his stagger was weakened and his movement was more like a pendulum.

"Hellcat!" he cried chokingly, spitting out vomit that had strayed into his mouth and triggered another gag reflex, though the nausea abruptly subsided.

"I'm here."

"I can't see anything."

"The station was half blown away," she explained, breathing heavily.

"The ship."

"What?"

"The *Demeter* is a ship," he rasped, tilting his head so that the contents of his stomach slid to the side, clearing his view. But the inside of the visor, unlike the outside, had no nanonic coating and was completely smudged.

"Really?", Hellcat began to rage. "Even now, you're such a fucking smart-"

"Where am I, anyway?" he groaned, trying to avoid her tirade.

"The whole topside of that *ship* is just a sprawling zone of debris and lots of ropey stuff flapping around. You flew into that tangle and got tangled up in it."

"Thank goodness. How do I get out of here?"

"I'll get you," she said firmly.

"What about the Marines?"

"I don't know, haven't come out yet. They'll probably let us handle the dying ourselves."

Gavin wondered if he should tell her where the *Lady* was, but her radio was almost certainly still tapped.

"No," he finally said, looking down at his ever-shattering helmet visor, yellow stomach acid settling into the cracks. "I don't have much time left."

"Just shut up for once, I'm on my way," she replied. "Noble hero chatter gives me a rash."

"I puked in my helmet. How noble could my hero babble possibly be?"

"*Puked*," she repeated, "that's almost a swear word."

Gavin already had a response ready when something hit him and he gasped loudly.

"Gotcha!"

His next attempt to say something was also broken. His helmet could no longer withstand the difference in pressure between inside and outside, and the first pieces of glass flew off. Gavin reflexively gasped for air, but it was as if he was breathing against a resistance. With his right hand, he tried to seal the spot, groping for it until the whistling stopped.

In fact, according to his visor gauge, the oxygen level stabilized somewhat, but was still at eighteen percent, only two percent above the critical mark.

"My helmet," he said in a choked voice.

"I see it. Can't I extend the stuff from my suit?"

"No. The Artemis isn't a space suit, it's a zero-g light combat suit. Built for fighting on ships in drift. We can survive half an hour before freezing to death, and they're sealed, but that's about it. If you command the nanofabric to move to a new surface..."

"So it does work," she cut him off.

"It does, but..." Only now did he notice that most of his vomit had been sucked into the vacuum through the hole in the helmet, and he could see again. He saw stars twinkling, so numerous that it took his breath away. Then it struck him that they were not stars, but one of the solar sails that had been shot and turned into myriads of splinters that reflected the light from the central star. Hellcat clamped down on it like a monkey, keeping his legs wrapped around it and groping for his helmet with a strained expression.

"At least," she muttered absently, apparently struggling with internal suit orders, "we're not being shot at anymore."

"Best not to jinx it," he replied, looking past her to the *Demeter*. The entire area where the *Lady* had been docked resembled a single debris field. The ship had shrunk to half its original size, mostly destroyed with entire hull sections melted by laser fire, breaches where missiles had hit, and long black tracks. He saw several human figures, frozen in the cold of space, slipping away into nothingness or hit by debris that sent them flying again in another direction. And towering somewhere above all the destruction was the mysterious ship. It was still here, waiting for its chance to finish them off and wipe out the *Lady* it couldn't find.

But it wouldn't take the alien killers long to solve the mystery.

Hellcat snatched something dark flying past them. Gavin recognized it as the handle of a cabinet or server.

"We need some propulsion," she found, thrusting the piece of metal into his hand. Meanwhile, she proceeded to free it from the struts that held it captive like a fish in a net.

"We have to ..."

"Shh," she went on, "I know where we need to go."

"Really?"

"Yes. I may not have gone to college, but I'm not stupid either."

Gavin fell silent, nodding mutely. The oxygen level had dropped to sixteen percent and the air felt so thick he felt like he was breathing in water.

"Leave me behind," he said. "This isn't heroism, it's necessity. If you reduce the integrity of your suit, the pressure will..."

"Can't you just shut up for once?" she interrupted him once more. "I'm trying to save your ass right now. Ah."

The squeeze on his left shoulder suddenly eased.

"See that steel cable in front of you?"

"Yes," he confirmed, reaching for the finger-thick cable, which she apparently thought was a steel cable, but which probably came from a connector to the destroyed solar sail.

"Good." Hellcat muttered something unintelligible and then a black liquid began to spread on Gavin's hand and the right side of his helmet. He pulled his fingers away testingly and sure enough, the programmable nanites hardened around the saucer-sized area of shattered glass. The oxygen level in his helmet was still at fifteen percent, creating within him the sensation of suffocation, though he continued to breathe. He tried to push aside the growing panic this was causing by focusing on what he was seeing.

Hellcat gave a grunt, but her face was so etched with concentration that he didn't dare ask her if everything was all right. Obviously it wasn't. She continued to hold him close, clamped right in front of his chest with her helmet against his so that he could see her passively lit features as clearly as he ever had. Once again he was struck by the fact that she was a pretty woman, with an almost ladylike finely drawn chin and nose line, high cheekbones and almond-shaped blue eyes. Even the sweaty strands of hair on her forehead didn't detract from that. When she noticed his gaze, he looked to the side, embarrassed.

She took the metal handle from him, lashed out, and threw it somewhere behind Gavin, sending them into a burst of motion in the opposite direction and flying agonizingly slowly through space. Again and again he was hit by smaller pieces of debris - mostly, however, those coming from the direction of the solar sail, sending them closer to the half-destroyed *Demeter*.

The glitter of the debris, which as a whole had still formed a sheet larger than many a continent, was beautiful like an animated work of art, and at the same time depressing. A new world should have been created here, where sometime in the future families could picnic on fresh grass and have their faces tickled by the sun. Now all that was lost, along with the lives of the employees on *Demeter* and all that CX-2 could have once become.

Many of the billions and billions of pieces of foil that had been repelled from the flexible skeleton were already descending into the rocky planet's atmosphere, briefly creating glowing dots over the ocean. Like fireflies, they descended and faded as Gavin and Hellcat flew past the *Demeter* in close embrace.

Turning his head, he looked down at the large funnel, also scarred by laser hits that had left deep cracks in the steel colossus. But the biomass was still flying toward the planet - a three-hundred-yard diameter stream of dense matter wrapped in polyp that looked like an impermeable brown rain veil. If the process was still working, apparently only the bubble on their side of the Seed Vessel had been hit, where myelination was taking place.

A blessing in disguise.

"It's about to get uncomfortable," he panted under his breath as he saw the lower edge of the funnel approaching, toward which they were moving rapidly. While their flight seemed extremely slow, Gavin knew how deceiving impressions of speeds in space could be.

"You see the shit behind me, I see the shit behind you," she said. Her voice sounded different, strangely stretched, as if every word caused her pain.

"Behind you is just a big funnel a couple hundred feet in diameter with dirt coming shooting out of it. You feel tiny, like a stickleback being sucked into a massive propeller, but at least it distracts you from the fact that the first streaks of air are already visible at the edges."

"We're crashing?" she asked, her eyes growing wide.

"Looks like it. I can feel it already."

"Not good. I can see those fucking fuckers behind us with their stealth ship. It keeps getting hit by debris fragments and then its hull flashes briefly, long enough to make out the shadow."

The last fleet

Gavin turned his face to her and met her gaze without looking away.

"You're losing blood," he said with anguish. Due to the fact that the nanite tissue of her carapace had thinned too much, it was no longer able to maintain the pressure inside. Tiny globules of blood, just visible as glimmers, squeezed out of her suit everywhere and flew away. Her face was already pale.

"If I don't make it, tell Dodger and Bambam that my father is on ..."

"Watch out!" he interrupted gruffly as they reached the edge of the funnel where the rope snapped off, throwing them with a strong momentum into the giant stream of biomass. As a child, he had once seen a mosquito fly to him in the shower and imagined how it must have felt.

Now he knew.

The polyp capsules pelted them like projectiles, causing their *Artemis* suits to harden and making any movement impossible. They were like bodies locked in medieval knight's armor, and the countless impacts per second were just as loud. Their good fortune was that apparently the system's power supply had been destroyed and the biomass capsules were no longer being shot at dozens of times the speed of sound, but were being pulled downward by the planet's gravitational pull. Now that the *Demeter* was plummeting from its orbit, he realized how lucky they were that the enemy had not merely boarded the ship, but had damaged it enough in the course of the engagement with the drones that they were not shredded in the seed stream.

"Sphinx!" he called out to his ship's AI, gasping for breath. "Sphinx, do you read me?"

"Loud and clear, Gavin," came the redemptive reply after a series of ugly interferences. "I already have your life signs on sensors. It might be about to..."

"The nice version!" he interrupted her, shouting to drown out the patter of the polyp on his back and helmet.

"... It's going to get *uncomfortable*."

"It doesn't get more uncomfortable than this." Amidst the chaos of thick brown rain, Gavin had long since lost all sense of direction while feeling protected, unable to see all the destruction and danger around him.

Then suddenly that too was gone as he was surrounded by light with Hellcat wrapped tightly around him and crashed into a resistance that made them cry out. He himself merely noticed that they were no longer falling.

Only after a few seconds did he notice that he was lying on his back, half-covered by encapsulated biomass, staring at the locked hatch of one of the *Lady*'s airlocks.

"Open helmet!" he gasped, inhaling gratefully as his alveoli filled with fresh oxygen. As soon as he could think clearly, he scrambled up on his elbows and crawled with the strength of his arms to Hellcat, who lay beside him, her face white as chalk, her eyes closed.

"Help!" he shouted over the radio, just as the inner hatch opened as well. Dodger's bald skull emerged, then her hands, pulling at her comrade.

"Bambam," the mutant said, "get her to sickbay. Lost blood. A lot."

Her large face appeared in front of his. "You need to get to the bridge."

"I think my spine is broken," he gasped. There was a smell of damp and mildew around him.

"Yep. That's why I'm carrying you." She grabbed him as if he possessed no single weight and carried him down the central corridor, where there was already strong gravity pulling on his arms and legs as if they were magnetic. Down the six-foot tube to the bridge Dodger tossed him carelessly and he hit hard enough that he probably broke his feet, but it didn't matter. He felt nothing.

Using his hands, he tried to drag himself toward the pilot's seat, but she was already with him, shifting him onto the nanofoam cushion like a piece of luggage.

"Thanks," he said wryly, starting up all the displays and gauges as she strapped him in.

"Get us out of here!"

"I'll do my best." With some sarcasm, he added, "It's not like I can hardly think straight because I just almost got killed, am a paraplegic and just had to eat my own vomit."

"You almost sound like one of us," the mutant laughed boomingly and buckled up next to him. "Now get us out of here, because the computer lady said the odds are against us right now."

21

Gavin called up the tactical display and quickly received an overview: The *Lady* was currently holding her position two hundred yards below the *Demeter*, which was plunging out of its geostationary orbit at one hundred yards per second. The sensors indicated purely nothing of importance, except heat and so many tiny objects around her that the radar went crazy. The propellant stores of the maneuvering thrusters were already half exhausted, because Sphinx had been forced to fire the lower eight of them permanently to slow their own fall and at the same time not getting crushed by the Seed Vessel. It loomed over them like a meteor and would soon begin to glow the same way.

"Actually, it doesn't look too bad," he found, "except that we're a blind diver in muddy waters being stalked by an invisible shark."

"What?" asked Dodger.

"Nothing, at least..." Gavin was interrupted by alarms as sensors registered several spontaneous heat flares nearby. Radiators began working to dissipate the excess heat. "... They haven't detected us yet."

"They're firing at us."

"No. They're firing into the stream of biomass because they can't see us. That stuff is warm and way too dense for anything optical anyway," he replied, speaking so fast he almost slurred his words as he recalibrated the weapons systems. "They're trying to smoke us out. They don't even need to hit us. A few missile explosions in the vicinity and we'll heat up so much that the radiators will radiate like pine trees on fire. After that, all they have to do is point their railguns at the warm spot and blow holes in us."

"And what do we do?" the mutant wanted to know.

"I don't know yet, but I've got about half a minute to think about it." Gavin raised a hand just as Dodger was about to ask another question.

Think, Gavin Andal, think. You're a rat in the chute of a combine and the invisible cat is just waiting for you to come running out before you smash on the ground, he said to himself. *If you hop out of the chute, the cat will eat you alive. If you don't, she'll soon hear your squeak and catch you with her claws.*

"If only we could do something about an invisible cat," he said bitterly. He just didn't see any options. Sure, they could drop into the atmosphere, hoping the armor hadn't developed dents where the frictional heat of entry could eat into and shred them. Then maybe jump - risky as always, but a risk that was better than certain death. But to jump, they had to disable all weapons - for two minutes. Enough time for the invisible cat to eat them alive.

"Then we'll go down," Dodger decided. "But with guns blazing."

"With flags flying," he corrected her.

"I don't want to kiss their asses."

"No, that's just a ..." Gavin faltered. "Wait. That's an idea."

"What?"

"The Undiscovered Country."

"I don't understand a word you're saying, Captain."

"*The thing's got to have a tailpipe*," Gavin quoted the classic Star Trek movie starring William Shatner, which his father had seen with him at least ten times. "When Hellcat and I were in the airlock, you were talking to Bambam. So he's already back on his feet after surgery?"

The last fleet

"Yep. Pumped full of fresh Smartnites and meds, but he still knows his name," Dodger replied.

"Bambam, Gavin here," he called the mechanic over the radio. "I need you to do something for me."

"What? I just hooked Hellcat up to the medidoc, and there's a wobble here and ..."

"You're not a doctor, but I need you to do a surgery for me."

"A surgery?" asked Bambam.

"Yes, on one of the Hawks," Gavin explained. "I need you to open the warhead with the pilot software. Sphinx needs access to the memory core to overwrite the AI. Can you do that?"

"Ke. Think so, I'll get on it."

"Hurry, we don't have much time."

"Do we ever?"

"Sphinx," Gavin turned to the AI. "You understand what I'm trying to do?"

"I found the *Undiscovered Country* in my entertainment database. I see. A good plan that might work on the premise that the enemy ship's cloaking effect is based on a deception of our sensors rather than a propulsion system unknown to us," Sphinx replied.

"Yes. Since the rest of the ship is very similar to our frigates, I don't assume it's using an alien propulsion system." Gavin's fingers raced over the holobuttons in front of him, programming the course he envisioned for them. First, he rotated the *Lady* around her transverse axis so that the bow pointed toward the crashing *Demeter* above them. Then he shut down all weapons systems and redirected the full power potential of the fusion reactors that formed the beating heart of their ship into the energy pattern cells, which had to reach one hundred percent to charge the jump nodes. Since the latter could only hold a full charge for about ten seconds without risking disintegration of the magnetic confinement chambers, they had to be filled in a single burst.

Two minutes and ten seconds that would make the difference between life and death. Again.

Next, he shut down half of the maneuvering thrusters, leaving the ones still active just enough to let them plummet vertically toward the planet, staying in the center of the biomass column that ironically formed their camouflage in this battle.

"All we can do now is wait for Bambam to finish or for the ghost ship to get a lucky hit."

"He'll manage."

"Let's hope so." Gavin linked directly to the ship's internal sensors via his neural computer and followed the mechanic as electronic eyes and ears to distract himself from the agony of having to wait.

Bambam moved through the central corridor with guttural grunts and arrived at the weapons bay access panel, which normally could only be opened from the outside - for rearming. Using the panel - a honeycomb cutout of the wall - he was able to squeeze through the narrow passageway behind it and entered the maintenance area.

This was a shaft, six yards long and one and a half yards wide. To the right and left were forty-centimeter diameter round hatches with old-fashioned twist-locks through which the missiles could be reached.

"They rotate," Bambam explained over the radio. He tapped the metal. "Behind them is a large revolver with twenty loaded Hawks pointed toward the hatch. I have to dial which missile is supposedly malfunctioning and evading remote maintenance, then the ship - or Sphinx - releases the appropriate turret and rotates it in front of the maintenance hatch, ke?"

"Pick one!" commanded Gavin impatiently. "And hurry up!"

Bambam gave the command through his wrist terminal, then wrenched the port open after it made a click and turned the wheel. The Hawk's head was a fusion warhead with a fission detonator, which used nuclear fission to provide the heat for fusion ignition. The warhead itself was about the size of a head and looked extremely unspectacular: a gray sphere with a spiral top on which the detonator stuck like a little hat made of a complicated piece of metal art. The targeting computer looked like a thimble of wires that connected it to the weapon's sensors,

The last fleet

providing vital data. He looked for the manual maintenance access, a small opening on the side meant for a universal cable with a mini-CC connector.

He reached into his multifunction pouch on his belt, pulled out the cable and connector, and plugged it in. Immediately, the data streamed from his neural computer through the wrist terminal appeared in his field of vision.

"Sphinx should be coming in through my terminal now," he said aloud, watching as the data stream kicked in at the same moment, erasing the smart rocket's pilot software. Instead, a single command appeared there, consisting of just eighteen lines of code.

"That's it!" shouted Gavin over the radio, looking at his time display. One more minute until the jump nodes could be flooded with their necessary surge of energy.

Sixty seconds could be a very long time, especially since the enemy had apparently changed their strategy. The flow of polyp-enveloped biomass decreased significantly, and a few seconds later he realized why: an explosion nearby caused the *Lady* to tremble. As the brown particle chaos cleared, he could still see the huge fireball disintegrating into pieces of debris of various sizes, which fell on CX-2 as burning meteorites.

Towering above the renewed danger to their ship was their pursuer, the mysterious ghost ship. Invisible, yes, but Gavin knew it was there, could feel its sensors locked on him, along with the gaze of the unknown captain who wanted to wipe them out as the last witnesses to Andal's genocide.

When Sphinx indicated to him thirty seconds until the power pattern cells were at full power, he ejected all the Hawks from their launch bays. Since they had no power, all he had to do was open the flaps and drop faster than they did with the *Lady*.

To do this, he turned off all the lateral maneuvering thrusters and directed the remaining propellant supplies into the forward four thrusters, which ignited shortly after, catapulting them down even faster toward the planet, which was already tugging at them mercilessly. The first flames flickered at the downward-facing tail with its four drive nacelles. Four Hawks at a time slid out of their bays and fired their drives at two-second intervals. Like blazing stars, they shot upward through the outer layers of the atmosphere, chasing a phantom like blind men hunting a single buffalo on the prairie.

"Captain," Dodger said as the *Lady* began to shake more violently. The gimbals on the bridge creaked and groaned under the forces that were bearing down on her with increasing relentlessness, as if the planet were resisting their intrusion.

"I know," he growled.

Then the ghost ship stirred and made itself known in the form of missiles that appeared as if from nowhere among the fireballs that had once been the *Demeter*. They were joined by bluish flashes, discharges from railguns whose projectiles were invisible and struck instantly at close range.

The *Lady Vengeance* was punctured in six places, and Sphinx displayed several dozen warning messages and flashing red damage reports into his field of vision, which he brusquely brushed aside.

Ten seconds.

Two of the enemy missiles hit some of the twelve Hawks in all that had already left their launch bays, and died in a bright glare that took half a dozen more missiles down with them. The remaining six were caught in the dense fire of the Ghost Ship's close-range defenses. With their unmistakable muzzle flash, the fire control computer offered him targeting solutions for the first time, as the hull was thus indirectly visible. And there was nothing he could do. The weapons remained offline as the seconds counted down.

"Five seconds!" he shouted hoarsely as a fresh wave of tungsten bolts punched holes in their ship. One of them appeared out of nowhere diagonally in front of him, and he could see blue sky through several bulkheads and walls. There was little oxygen left and wind whipped around his head, making his eyes water and tearing at his hair.

The last fleet

"Enemy missiles," Sphinx reminded him in a paradoxically calm voice. Impact in three ..."

Gavin saw it. Impact and jump time were in the same second. He squinted and took one last look at the sensors, which showed several Hawks seemingly wandering aimlessly and being shot down. But one of two surviving ones veered left at the last moment, miraculously escaping a multitude of overlapping hails of bullets from invisible melee cannons, and then exploded in the nowhere of the uppermost atmosphere.

And before the enemy missiles detonated and they simultaneously jumped, it was very briefly visible: the Ghost, their pursuer, stripped of its cloaking, which slid off the hull like a liquid. A *Triumph*-type frigate, the hedgehog-like spikes on top, the blue glow - and an exploding drive where the modified Hawk had locked onto the massive beam signature of the plasma tail that had eluded the *Lady*'s sensors.

Then came the jump, a bang, and the most terrifying moment of his life.

EPILOGUE: GUNTER

Master Sergeant Gunter Marshall pulled the acid-resistant hood of his technician coverall lower over his face as he pushed the cargo sled with nitrogen tanks down the corridor toward the landing bays.

It had taken a while to track down the technician, who was on shift at this hour today and now lay in his sleeping coffin with a humming skull and gag in his mouth. But it had been worth it.

As he had already discovered after his first day at Cerberus, no one here knew anything about what was going on outside his or her workspace - nor did they want to know. Fear was as thick in the air as the sweat and exhalations from the ancient seals that held together the aging life support piping system. A few solid arguments, however, had been enough to elicit the following from his new technician friend: The Broker got regular visitors. Either from allies and selected business partners who knew about the coordinates of the station, or from influential officials and nobles who were shipped here on special ferries with the proverbial bag over their heads. Who they were, no one knew, as the density of Reface masks seemed nowhere higher than here. While many of the Star Empire's systemically important institutions were using the latest jamming mechanisms to combat masking technology, the Broker was apparently taking the opposite approach: If everyone could use the ruthenium networks, secu-

Epilogue: Gunter

rity and privacy were also assured. Since no one could recognize anyone who didn't want to, no one need worry. A somewhat skewed logic in his opinion, but as someone who despised this place and everything it stood for, he was biased at best.

The ship whose arrival he had picked out was a small shuttle coming from the direction of the inner system, and had been assigned docking bay B-2 about an hour ago. That was striking, to say the least, since he had learned that assignments were usually not determined until half an hour before docking - probably part of the Broker's strategy to remain unpredictable.

Since he hadn't thought of any way to find out where the body of the presumed orb was, and the ruler of this godforsaken place wasn't giving anything away anyway, he had made a decision: He would keep an eye out for anything that didn't follow standard procedure. After all, he was a Marine, not a secret agent.

The ship's arrival was the first conspicuous thing, and when he reached the large window that showed the ledges in Bay B, he knew he had made the right choice: A sleek Navy corvette came flying into the asteroid's huge equatorial groove, pushing toward the bay with maneuvering thrusters firing seemingly erratically, with smaller pilot drones flashing and pointing the way. He spotted several well-camouflaged guns in the rock between the windows and applications of a space dock, following the movements of the craft.

The corvette had obviously been freshly painted and had no visible identifiers or distinctive features of this type of ship, but Gunter was no recruit, and had seen so many of these things that he was not easily fooled by a few superstructures. What was approaching the ledge in front of him was a corvette of the new Ferret class, and he doubted that any scoundrels or pirates could have gotten their hands on one of these new specimens yet.

Which in turn meant that someone official from the Navy was doing business with the criminal Broker. Maybe - and he knew this was probably more wishful thinking than logic - the visit even had something to do with the dead Orb. In any case, he was determined to find out.

So he parked his electric truck next to two pallets of

Epilogue: Gunter

helium-3 pellets, locked with magnetic seals, and took cover behind them. It took nearly ten minutes for the inner airlock door to open with a sigh of hydraulics. Through the gap between two crates he could spy a woman dressed in a simple black jumpsuit whose stains and tears would have struck him as artificial even if he had not served two years as a spit. Her gait was confident and stiff with the look that always remained above chest level, which undoubtedly betrayed her as an officer.

As a fresh recruit, he had once made the mistake of addressing his instructor as 'officer,' which, in addition to twenty push-ups, had earned him a tirade accompanied by flying saliva: "Officer? I work for a living! And now you're on my shit list, Private Marshall!"

Following the woman with the narrow face and thin braid was not particularly difficult, as she moved through the corridors like a rooster, a visibly foreign body among the technicians and spaceport workers hunched over by work. The staff, dressed in yellow coveralls, always avoided eye contact in an attempt to abide by the unwritten laws of this place and avoid getting punishment time on the outer levels. Even the guy from whom he had taken his uniform and work card and who now lay shackled under his cot, mumbling against the gag, had warned him against it.

After the first turn towards Vactram, she was met by the bald guy who people here just called the 'administrator'. A strange guy with greedy eyes, whose look some might have misinterpreted as businesslike.

In the corridor in front of the well-arranged station, passers-by kept their distance, creating a large open area between the high-ranking reception committee in single person and his guest, so that only their lip movements could be seen. Not for Gunter, however. He set his acoustic amplifiers to maximum power after pushing his way to the front, tilting his head a bit.

There was a slight rustle and crackle, and the administrator's voice could only be heard at the very edge of audibility, but it could be heard: "My Lady Marquandt," the man greeted the offi-

Epilogue: Gunter

cer, and Gunter's hackles stood up involuntarily as if on the back of a cat ready to attack.

"Administrator, it's a pleasure to see you again." The fleet admiral's daughter sounded anything but pleased. More like every single word was causing her physical discomfort.

"We'll go directly to my office, if you don't mind."

"I was hoping to speak with the Broker personally," she said.

"I'm sorry, Captain, but the Broker does not receive guests as a matter of principle. However, he will join our conversation in holographic form, as he did last time," the administrator returned, pointing to the station behind him.

"Lead the way."

Gunter turned and disappeared back into the artfully waiting crowd, which reminded him of a pack of dogs that had been beaten too often for them to wag their tails or growl at bad treatment.

The daughter of the damned traitor! he thought and involuntarily clenched his augmented hands into fists. He would have loved to extend his weapon implants and turn the woman into a volatile cloud of blood and bone mass, but he had a job to do, and he would do it. Nothing had changed, even though this was obviously not a gray area, but enemy territory.

EPILOGUE: GAVIN

The physical sensations hit Gavin in such rapid succession that his mind could hardly sort them out. First, all the air escaped from his lungs as if it were being sucked out of him. His ears rang, triggered by a thunderclap as loud as the heavenly choirs themselves. Everything inside him contracted and expanded - simultaneously. The boundaries of his body dissolved and yet hardened in a contradiction that his brain could not resolve because it was happening so fast.

All that was suddenly over again, and the chaos away from space and time became silence, so pure and clear that the reactors must have failed.

"Sphinx," he groaned, and screwed up his face. A brutal headache pounded against his forehead from within. "Status report."

"Jump successful. Hull integrity at seventy percent. Automatic reactor shutdown due to critical radiator error message. Jump node failure due to an overload in the energy matrix cells. Critical damage to dorsal superconductor pathways. Failure of the life support system. Failure of all sensors. Critical ..."

"Okay, okay," he scowled, breaking her off. "That was critical enough times for my taste. I already understood that things were bad for us."

"At least for the *Lady Vengeance*."

Epilogue: Gavin

"And I'm still breathing."

"So am I," Dodger spoke up beside him. The mutant rubbed her temples with her palms.

"Headache?"

"Yes. Unpleasant."

"Sphinx?" he turned back to the ship's AI. "I know we must have jumped because otherwise we would have been blown up by missiles and now we couldn't have a headache."

"That's correct. I have already confirmed the jump. Since the jump nodes discharged on schedule, it appears that the formation of a subspace vacuole was successful. However, jumping from a gravity well involves high risks, especially since we are within the atmosphere of CX-2 ..."

"Yes, I know that. The question is, what happened to us?"

"I'm not sure," Sphinx admitted. "I simply don't have the data, since I no longer have any internal or external sensors."

"So you are blind."

"As an analogous comparison to human perception would be blind, deaf, and numb - more accurately put."

"Uh, guys?" they were interrupted by Bambam's voice booming from the speakers. Gavin noticed that they were buzzing slightly, which hadn't been the case before. "I think you guys should come up here."

Dodger gave him a sideways glance, then unbuckled his seat belt. He was about to follow suit when he realized that his body was not obeying him. Only now did he consciously realize that there was gravity here, so they couldn't possibly be in space. And that did not bode well.

"I have a problem," he said grudgingly, looking down at his legs, which he recognized as his but did not feel. The mutant turned to him and her gaze traveled down his.

"Infirmary," she decided, and came over to him. She turned his seat toward her and began unbuckling him like a toddler who had fallen asleep in the back seat of his parents' car.

Gritting his teeth, he allowed her to do so while she lifted him up with surprising effortlessness and laid him over her shoulder. From the grip of her hands and the subliminal vibration of her

Epilogue: Gavin

muscles, genetically optimized for hard work, he sensed the raw power inherent in them. At the hatch to the tube-like passageway that led into the central corridor, she pushed him up.

"Have to hold on to the top rung with your hands, and I'll push you along," she said, and he did as he was told. It was true, his fingers were trembling - whether from overexertion or because of the slowly fading adrenaline level his neural computer warned him about, he didn't know. In any case, he had to summon all his strength not to slip.

Dodger didn't even have to push him all the way through the top hatch, as Bambam was already on hand, hoisting him into the corridor with both hands in his uniform jacket. The mechanic looked pale and sickly, which was to be expected for someone who was back on his feet too quickly after an operation. But the look from his eyes was downright feverish with excitement. He pulled Gavin further up to the wall to make room for his comrade, who squeezed through the narrow tube from below.

"We're screwed!" declared Bambam, retracting his head so that his barely-there neck disappeared entirely. He reminded Gavin of a turtle that wanted to retreat into its shell but changed its mind halfway down.

"Pretty sure I've heard that," Gavin groaned with effort as he tried to pull himself up a bit with only the strength of his arms. "What is your reason for this realization?"

"I can show you." The mechanic motioned Dodger to pick him up again and follow him. The mutant shrugged, picked up Gavin effortlessly, and trudged after the stocky rebel down the deathly quiet corridor.

"It's so quiet," he said with trepidation. It was downright eerie. On a starship, you could experience anything, but never complete silence. It was considered an unmistakable sign that one was about to die. No noise meant no engines. No engines meant no power, and no power meant that in a vacuum, any kind of life that depended on oxygen, heat, and water would soon be gone.

"What about Hellcat?" Gavin asked as they walked to the forward airlock.

"She lost a lot of blood and I had to put her in an induced

Epilogue: Gavin

coma. Currently, her circulation is supported by the medidoc, which is powered by the batteries. They'll last about twenty-four more hours," Sphinx replied over the loudspeakers.

"I can donate," Dodger agreed.

"So can I," Gavin said almost simultaneously, and the mutant looked at him. Since he was hanging over her shoulder, their faces were uncomfortably close, but he didn't care. "She saved my life."

"So." Bambam stood in front of the open airlock door and waved them in. When they arrived, he motioned for them to wait, climbed inside, and punched the button for the emergency opening of the outer hatch. It jerked back into its socket, revealing a view of a massive rock wall. "Here you go."

"What ...?" it escaped Gavin.

"We jumped out of a gravity well. Now we're in trouble. Whatever the navigation computer was trying to calculate must not have worked, because we jumped right into a freaking planet, ke?"

"Better than getting killed by a rocket," Dodger opined.

"Really?" wanted to know Bambam, glaring angrily at them. "We traded 'a short, painless end for 'a slow death by suffocation or freezing to death - whichever happens first."

"How thick is that?" asked Gavin, wondering at his own composure at the sight of the rock. Possibly his mind no longer had capacity for thoughts of doom, having long since been dulled by the ever-changing disasters that presented themselves.

"How should I know? It's massive, anyway!" the mechanic snorted.

"I need to get my spinal cord patched up. I suggest you try drilling a hole in there so we can find out how deep we are..."

"...in the shit?"

"That doesn't help," Dodger said, silencing Bambam, who was flushed with obvious frustration. "Sitting on your hands never helped anyone. With the spare barrels for the laser cannons, maybe we could do something."

"How, without power?"

"Could tap into the sickbay."

Epilogue: Gavin

"We need them at full power right now, though," the mechanic objected.

"Maybe not the whole time."

"Make it so," Gavin told Dodger. "If need be, I'll stay paralyzed, still better than if we all suffocate."

The mutant nodded and trudged off toward the stern.

"We jumped to S2-Yokatami, didn't we? Into that damned restricted area," Bambam grumbled, scowling.

"Yeah. It was the shortest jump from S1-Ruhr, and we didn't have time."

"Then we were lucky we didn't materialize in space with the fucking corporate ships blowing us out of existence," the Rebel countered wryly.

Gavin decided to leave him alone with his frustration, because he had far enough of that himself. So he crawled, arms and dragging legs, across the floor of the central corridor to sickbay, where Hellcat lay in the only medical coffin. Sphinx helped him onto one of the free beds, enlisting the aid of the robotic arms, and then hooked him up to the equipment. As soon as the anesthetics flushed through his system, a blissful relaxation set in and carried him away on gentle waves of indifference.

He was awoken at some point by a gradually increasing beeping sound that brought him out of his drug-induced doze.

"Gavin," Sphinx said, and it took him a few moments to understand that it was the AI talking to him.

"Yes?" he asked, blinking against the sudden brightness.

"The surgery was successful. You had two fractured vertebrae and a severe protrusion in the spinal canal. For a permanent fix, it will require a stay at a bioengineering clinic or an augmentation center."

"But I can walk?"

"Yes. You just need to avoid extreme exertion and protect your spine from stronger forces. Additionally..."

"Ah, you're awake!" he heard Bambam's voice. A moment later, the mechanic's round face appeared in front of his, flushed and sweaty.

Epilogue: Gavin

"Thanks, I'm fine," Gavin muttered laconically. "How long was I out?"

"A couple of hours." Bambam waved it off impatiently. "We drilled a tunnel in the rock."

"A tunnel?"

"Yep."

"Tunnel means there are two ends."

"Yep, fucking axed! Could even push a probe out. You want the good news first or the bad news?" the mechanic asked, and Gavin's hopeful mood began to evaporate.

"The good news first," he decided.

"We jumped into a mountain."

"I wanted the good news first."

"That's it! The rock face is only ten feet thick, so we really lucked out. It would have taken us a lot longer to drill through the airlock to the top, and then you wouldn't have had enough juice for the last few hours of your treatment."

"Now the bad."

"Nah, first a few more good ones: clean air is coming in through that hole."

"What, how is that possible?" asked Gavin, puzzled.

"That's the bad news: the planet outside has plants and stuff, but it's all pretty weird. Wherever we jumped to, this isn't S2-Yokatami. Definitely not a Seed World."

"That's impossible! Sphinx?"

"Yes?"

"Was there a mistake in navigation?"

"No. We jumped to S2-Yokatami, into the restricted area of the Seed Traverse - at least according to the log files and my calculations," the AI replied.

"Well." Bambam shrugged. "Either our atmospheric jump spit us out somewhere I've never heard of, or this Seed World isn't a Seed World at all."

EPILOGUE: JANUS

Janus arrived at shuttle bay 4 after thirty-eight minutes. A young female lieutenant was in the process of performing her obligatory visual inspection, using her multispectral flashlight to complete the brief tour. She looked like any other uniformed pilot in the palace spaceport; extremely well-groomed, hairstyle and lapel crease exactly according to regulations, and gaze focused.

The bay consisted of a large room with a connection console for oxygen, electricity and water, whose connecting hoses were already disconnected. On the left wall were a number of containers and transport crates in the areas marked for them, and the single door led into the corridor that connected the total of one hundred shuttle bays with the rest of the summit section of the palace.

The lieutenant consistently ignored him, and he would have wondered if she had even registered him after his silent entry had it not been for a coded request that arrived on his wrist terminal. It requested read access to his biometric data. Reluctantly, he accepted it, whereupon the pilot began to retrieve some items from the shuttle cabin. A few tools, a transport cylinder, blankets, the packed-up evac bladder. In the end, she put down smaller items like a handheld terminal and even her hair clip before nodding and gesturing for him to get in.

He was impressed by the accuracy with which she ensured

Epilogue: Janus

that the total mass of her shuttle was exactly the expected value, which was automatically queried in the safety procedure at space control. Most pilots would have struggled to get as close as possible. But not the lieutenant, which reminded him once again who he was dealing with.

When he went to sit in the co-pilot's seat, she merely shook her head, casually, as if she would have anyway, and he stepped back to make do with one of the fold-out seats.

It had been a long time since anyone in the Star Empire had treated him that way, especially since she was a commoner and he was of rank. But that shouldn't surprise him. Not among those she worked for. So he pulled the Reface mask off his face, one of the advantages of being First Secretary of State. He was probably the only one in the palace, besides the Emperor, who had a working one that could not be interfered with by internal security mechanisms.

His master trusted him, and for that very reason it felt like a betrayal that he was now sitting in this shuttle, a reminder of how little homogeneous and in firm hands the Star Empire really was. At least when one looked beneath its carefully guarded and sealed surface. Sometimes he wished he didn't know so much.

Or knew more, he thought, rubbing his temples to dispel the oppressive headache that had plagued him since the attack on Usatami. The only connection between Marquandt and Albius he not only didn't understand, but had no theories for. Whatever was being played out in the shadows eluded him, and that meant he could not fulfill his mission for the Emperor.

Unless he went the way he was now going, which meant treason at the same time. What a dilemma. What a tragedy.

After receiving clearance from the palace pilots, the pilot cast off, and Janus was pressed into his seat as if a giant were standing with his foot on his chest. Even as they reached orbit, which he recognized by the sudden darkness in front of the windshield, the acceleration didn't let up, though it didn't shake as much.

They flew past the extensive orbital yards and the Rubov ring, lined up with the predetermined transit lines to Luna, and then slowed a bit. The pilot remained silent the entire time until

Epilogue: Janus

she answered Luna's space flight control and confirmed her flight order.

"Hello, Zenith," he heard a familiar voice and turned to the figure that seemed to materialize out of nowhere on the shuttle wall opposite him.

"Mirage," Janus replied, eyeing the woman whose cloaking field was slowly dissipating like water beading off her. She possessed distantly Asian features with short, straight hair, a fine, pointed nose, and waxy skin. Her narrow mouth formed a line without any curve and the look from her eyes was as neutral as water. She wore a pristine white one-piece suit that was so skin-tight that it revealed more than it concealed, and yet she exuded no eroticism in it. A hood and a stripped face shield lay over her shoulder.

"A new toy?" he asked, pointing to her suit.

"A new tool," she corrected him. "You wanted to meet me. There are two choices from here."

"Either I agree to your demands or I don't leave this shuttle alive." Janus waved it off. "It's been a long time, but I have a good memory."

"Good, what's the request?"

"An order."

"I only take orders from the Voice."

"I know they're listening in. If they agree, I await your demand."

Mirage tilted his head, barely noticeably. "What is the order?"

"Something is wrong with Admirals Marquandt and Albius. They are involved in something with each other, and I fear it may be to my master's disadvantage. Marquandt and his Wall Fleet were the only ones to survive the defeat of Andal, and everyone on Terra knows that's more than strange. If we are on the verge of another coup d'état, I must know and prevent it. It's in your interests, too," Janus explained.

"Our interests are above politics."

"Dimitri Rogoshin," he continued unapologetically. "He's a loose end between the two, and he killed an IIA agent."

"We're aware of that," Mirage said.

Epilogue: Janus

"I want you to find out what Rogoshin knows about Marquandt's involvement with Warfield and who is behind him in the shadows."

His counterpart looked at him blankly and remained silent. No doubt she was just receiving instructions from the Voice. Then she fixed him again.

"The price is special Imperial permission to fly into the restricted areas of the Seed Traverse," she finally said. "Including Imperial priority codes of the highest level, for a *Thetis*-class research vessel."

This is hard to get even for me, because only the Emperor can issue this, he would have replied in a normal negotiation, but this was not a negotiation, and he was only a hand movement of Mirage away from dying. In doing so, he certainly would not have served the Emperor according to his oath. For the first time in five years, he felt naked without his numerous augments.

"Agreed." He also spared any form of inquiry as to why the Voice wanted to invade the Seed Traverse, of all things. He didn't have the time for fighting windmills. Nevertheless, he felt anger rising within him. Their demand could only mean that they already knew what was going on. It could hardly be a coincidence that they wanted to penetrate exactly where Janus' center of interest was, because the financial streams of two admirals and the assassinated highest civilian politician of the Star Empire led to that place.

"You'll get your answer tomorrow," Mirage said after a neutral nod and pulled her hood over her head, after which she also hid her face, and her body began to seemingly dissolve or melt into the wall.

TIMELINE

2035: The Ares crew sets foot on Mars for the first time. The international mission by NASA, ESA, SpaceX and a dozen partner countries launches a new space race.
2040: Mining of subcrustal resources on the Moon by a Western space alliance and China begins.
2042: Founding of Luna Mining Corporation, which buys all mining sites and rights from the Western alliance in return for exclusive supply contracts, following a fatal accident involving six NASA astronauts.
2044: First stable nuclear fusion at the LFTR experimental reactor in Virginia using tritium-deuterium fusion.
2045: ESA's Proximity spacecraft, in collaboration with the private space company Deep Space Mining, succeeds in diverting the asteroid '2008 BR-44', popularly known as 'Braun' after its discoverer Justine Braun, from its orbit around the Sun towards Earth.
2050: Braun reaches its target orbit around Earth and Deep Space Mining begins mining its ores and minerals. Beginning of the 'asteroid race' as a result of which more and more resource-rich celestial bodies are directed into high Earth orbit over two decades.
2052: Lighting Gale, a subsidiary of Luna Mining Corporation, unveils its first working fusion reactor on Earth's satellite, based

Timeline

on helium-3 fusion and enabling the construction of more compact small reactors.

2055-2080: Spurred by an enormous economic boom triggered by increasingly efficient fusion reactors, space technologies and massive resource surpluses, exploration of the outer solar system begins with manned missions to Jupiter and its moons, Saturn and Neptune.

2062: After hackers succeed in infiltrating the Pentagon by means of a highly developed AI and in remotely commandeering a B-21 bomber, which can only be intercepted at the last second, the Turing Agreement is signed as a result of a catastrophe that was only narrowly averted. This agreement outlaws the development of strong artificial intelligence and places corresponding start-ups and research projects under strict state supervision. All UN member states are signatories.

2065: Founding of the outer colonies on Jupiter's moons Ganymede and Europa and Saturn's Enceladus. Initially, these are small research outposts of little significance.

2070: The Explorer Incident: In orbit around Jupiter's moon, Io, a conflict between the American ship Explorer and the Chinese Tianlong occurs that remains unexplained to this day, resulting in the Explorer disappearing without a trace. This almost leads to a war between NATO and China on Earth, which is prevented at the last minute by the Napier Treaty. This treaty stipulates that there must be no armaments in the solar system outside of Earth and that inspectors must be granted access to relevant facilities in the course of mutual monitoring.

2073: The People's Republic of China collapses within months as toxic rain floods vast areas of the impoverished West and the central government in Beijing withholds aid from the military for several days. A national uprising and prolonged consolidation struggles ensue, from which the Central Kingdom will not be able to recover for decades.

2074: The international Martian colonies unite and declare independence from their homelands on Earth. The U.S. sends the USS Nimitz, the just-completed first warship in the solar system, after the Napier Treaty collapses with the collapse of China. The suppression of the colonist revolt fails when the Nimitz breaks up due to a navigational error in the Martian atmosphere. The entire crew, including fifty Marines and a high-ranking government official, are killed. Six months later, President Wilcox and the heads of state of fifty other countries sign the Earth-Mars Pact, which pledges free exchange of science, the supply of vital products from Earth to the red planet, and the independence of the Martian colonies.

2075: The Red Science Consortium (RSC) is founded as the legal successor to the Mars Colonies and signatory to the Earth-Mars Pact.

2078: After decades of natural disasters resulting from an out-of-control climate crisis, eighty nations of Earth join together within the United Nations to form a federal state to deal with the economic damage and accelerate the removal of CO_2 from the atmosphere.

2081: Founding of the Outer Colony Coalition (OCC) as the political representative body of the lunar colonies of Jupiter and Saturn. Conclusion of free trade and alliance treaties with United Nations and RSC.

2084: The deep space probe *Frontier*, tasked with exploring Sol's heliosphere, encounters an extraterrestrial artifact within the heliopause nearly twelve billion miles from the Sun.

2086: The *Frontier* artifact is claimed by the UN and placed under military control. As a result, all of Earth's remaining nation-states join the federal alliance.

2086: Establishment of the unified government, Government Central (GovCentral) as the UN's supreme governing body and dominant power in the solar system.

2089: Jupiter Bank established on Jupiter's Remus habitat as an extraterritorial enterprise with participation by all factions: United Nations of Earth, RSC of Mars, and OCC of the outer colonies.

2092: After years of secret research on the alien *Frontier* artifact, GovCentral announces that it is a probe that has a novel propulsion system, but it is inoperable.

2094: UN Defense Department engineers at Armstrong Fleet

Timeline

Base on Luna succeed in deciphering and reverse engineering the *Frontier* probe's propulsion system.

2098: With the help of the Red Science Consortium, construction of a new type of transport medium begins. The hyperspace slingshot is based on the replicated alien technology and is capable of enclosing smaller objects in a normal space bubble and catapulting them through subspace to distant locations without any loss of time.

2100: In the first successful test of the hyperspace slingshot, a twenty-centimeter diameter experimental probe is sent from Luna to Jupiter's Remus habitat and emerges at the destination point without loss of time.

2100-2150: Due to massive research efforts and rekindled interest in interstellar exploration, the first jump engines for larger ships are developed and the possible diameters of so-called 'subspace vacuoles' increase exponentially. Entire fleets of prospectors are sent out to explore and map distant solar systems after the gateway to the stars is opened.

2160: First Colonist Wave: Forty colony ships built over ten years in the orbital shipyards of Earth and Mars leave Sol and jump to neighboring systems with terra-compatible worlds after intensive research and exploration. Founding of the first human colony, New Eden, and thirty-nine others later known as 'Core Worlds'.

2175: Discovery of the Orb. When the prospector ship Rheinland encounters a system on the edge of explored territory that has long puzzled explorers due to physical anomalies, it scans a planet completely covered in metallic structures that emits no radio or gravity waves. During its research flight, the Rheinland is destroyed in an unexplained manner, but is able to send a rescue signal.

2175-2180: Discovery of more systems under the rule of the Orb, the name given by newsfeeds to the mysterious aliens due to unexplained light phenomena reported shortly before their destruction, according to the black box of the Rheinland.

2180-2200: Concerned about a conflict with the Orb, a period of massive armament by the UN, Mars and the outer colonies begins.

Timeline

2184: Realizing that humanity is apparently not alone and that first contact with the Orb ended violently, the UN, RSC, and OCC join together to form the Solar Union, which all colonies in now over sixty systems join in the following years in hopes of protection and prosperity.

2186-2200: Second Colonist Wave: To address the growing overpopulation on Earth, more colonist ships are sent to colonize terra-compatible planets in the Solar Union frontier. Since GovCentral, as the governing body of Earth, can hardly cope with the growing criminality in the arcologies, it is decided to make far-reaching changes to the penal legislation, so that even minor offenses can result in forced deportation. Thus, the second wave of colonists is colloquially referred to as the 'inmate wave'. After initial unrest, GovCentral makes concessions in the form of paid family relocation for the convicts. Thus, within fourteen years, over one billion colonists leave.

2201: Establishment of the Corporate Council by the five most powerful corporate conglomerates of the Solar Union: Alpha Corporation, Dong Rae, Ruhr Heavy Industries, Yokatami, and Luna Mining Corporation become permanent members of the body, which is granted far-reaching powers by the Solar Union due to its economic power. As veto holders within the council, they are allowed to manage their own corporate sites, maintain their own police forces and enact their own laws in a limited form. A phase of accelerated liberalization of the economic system begins.

2204: When all diplomatic efforts of the Solar Union fail, open war breaks out between the hostile colonies of Arcturus and Kerhal. The Solar Navy, thinly scattered by the just-completed second wave of expansion, arrives too late as ships from the Arcturus colony completely devastate Kerhal with antimatter bombs, rendering it uninhabitable for centuries.

2205: Exclusion of Arcturus from the Solar Union for one hundred years. Complete blockade of the planet.

2206: Law is passed banning antimatter weapons. Ratification by all colonies and the Corporate Council.

2210: Discovery of the Kerrhain system and its asteroid belt with

Timeline

unusual object density. Start of plundering of the system by the Luna Mining Corporation.

2212: Beginning of Union-wide smuggling of Assai, a weed harvested on Kerrhain. The potent hallucinogen is banned that year, and Kerrhain is colonized and controlled by a military administration established by the Solar Union to stop the illegal trade.

2224: The first Seed Vessel is completed at the Lagrange shipyards near Luna and filled with biomass from the largely ravaged Earth. Built by the Corporate Council, it sets course for planet P3X-888.

2225: On P3X-888, christened 'Green Rain' by bloggers and newsfeed moderators, testing of new seed technology begins. By means of dropping huge amounts of biomass, a natural terraforming process is to be set in motion and accelerated by targeted geoengineering.

2229: The Corporate Council buys five more rocky planets in the habitable zones of three systems from the Solar Union and begins to initiate terraforming processes on the acquired worlds with additional Seed Vessels.

2233: Luhan Montgomery develops the first multi-intelligent nanites for human use at the University of New California. The so-called 'Smartnites' trigger a new economic miracle in the still thinly stretched Solar Union, helping previously resource-poor colonies rise through the relocation of Corporate Council production capacity in return for ever-expanding rights and lower local tax rates.

2235: Due to the breakthrough in nanite research and the emerging mass market for Smartnites, a wave of new developments in human and animal implant research follows. Smartnites act as a bridging technology to solve previous problems such as rejection, linkage to the central nervous system, and lack of maintainability of implants.

2238: On the colony of Khorwana, due to a software anomaly that remains unexplained to this day, a genocide of the population occurs at the hands of the local robot workers, known as Servitors. In just one night, which goes down in history as 'The

Black Night of Khorwana', all eighty million inhabitants of the agricultural colony are systematically murdered.

2240: After two years of protests, the newly elected Union government institutes a Union-wide ban on autonomous workers, de facto outlawing all robots. In the 'Circuit Genocide', over one billion non-military robots are conscripted and scrapped within five years. The 'Human Empowerment Act' is officially implemented to protect jobs, and the mass murder at Khorwana is seen merely as a political legitimization for a long-struggling reform effort by conservative forces. The Corporate Council lodges an ex officio protest against the new legislation.

2243: When the Solar Union's largest rhodium deposit to date is discovered on the colony of Voria, the planetary Union Government opposes the granting of mining rights to members of the Corporate Council by the central government on Earth. Since this leaves the Union Navy without the means to exert military pressure and still entrusted with the collection of all robotic manpower, a controversial precedent is set: the mercenary corporation Black Nebula, a member of the Corporate Council, is hired to persuade the Voria government to relent after two rounds of negotiations remain fruitless. Voria threatens military countermeasures in case of a blockade, whereupon the 'Two-Hour Battle' takes place in orbit, during which the Black Nebula cruiser Harbinger crashes into the planet. Since the ship had apparently been storing illegal antimatter weapons, a catastrophe ensues, largely sterilizing the main continent of Antarga. Several colonies protest and summon the local representatives of the central government.

2245: Start of the Secession Wars: After Black Nebula is awarded another major contract to patrol the outer colonies despite the Voria disaster, and only management is replaced, twenty worlds band together and pay their own mercenary forces to fight back against the central government. When battle breaks out in the Dagestan system between a fleet of the 'Twenty Worlds Pact' and the Black Nebula Corporation, the Solar Union declares the Pact members renegades and declares a state of war for the first time since its formation.

Timeline

2248: In a series of unexpected victories, the Pact is able to destroy or repel three Black Nebula fleets. With the new status quo and growing protests within the Union due to the general mobilization, more colonies declare independence.

2250: Formation of the Border Worlds, a loose confederation of a total of eleven colonies on the edge of the human expansion zone, which declare martial law and establish their own armed formations immediately after forming.

2253: The Corporate Council officially declares itself neutral in the conflict and bans Black Nebula from the Council as a non-permanent member, and decides to impose far-reaching sanctions on the mercenary corporation, which subsequently files for bankruptcy.

2254: Battle of Sigma Tiri: A Pact fleet receives unexpected support from the Border Worlds fleet moments before it is destroyed by a Solar Union force under Fleet Admiral Lucas Norton. The Union forces are forced to retreat.

2255: The weakened Pact colonies are attacked by fleet units of the Corporate Council, officially to stabilize a humanitarian emergency. In response, large segments of the Union loyalists declare war on the Corporate Council and launch attacks on the Seed Worlds, which are repelled by Union forces in an attempt to weaken all renegade elements in one fell swoop.

2257: Border Worlds units begin expelling corporate forces from the Pact Worlds and incorporate seven liberated colonies into their confederation.

2258: The widespread stalemate between the various factions of Border Worlds, Solar Union, Corporate Council, and worlds that have declared independence results in the truce of Carvis A, named for the only celestial body in the Carvis system, which is henceforth declared neutral.

2258-2290: In a time of relative peace, a political disintegration of the Solar Union begins. Migration to the independent colonies leads to a population implosion and labor shortages, pushed by the Corporate Council, which is able to take advantage of the situation and negotiate new tax benefits and mining concessions with the fragmented worlds. A period of economic and technological depression begins, in which former trade routes must first be rebuilt.

2290: Outbreak of the Consolidation Wars: After their secession from the Solar Union, many colonies sink into prolonged unrest, civil wars, and political trench warfare, resulting in increasing numbers of autocratic power grabs. Fragile and ever-shifting alliances and unions of convenience emerge between the worlds of humanity. The Solar Union sees in the weakness of its opponents its last chance for reunification under its banner and sends a federation of ten fleets under the command of Admiral Lucius McMaster. He is given the task of keeping order and forcing the renegade planets back into the Union. His campaign, which lasts a total of eight years, finally culminates in a victory over a fleet of sixty worlds, which can only be achieved with the support of the Border Worlds, which are promised far-reaching autonomy rights in return. McMaster becomes a folk hero in the resurgent Solar Union.

2300: Beginning of a tentative economic recovery through massive investment in rebuilding the war-torn Union worlds.

2302: In the Trabantius system, on the frontier with the Orb worlds, an encounter occurs with three alien ships. During this encounter, several ships disappear without a trace. Calls for retaliation are heard on Earth.

2305: Orb ships are again sighted in the Trabantius system. Union Navy defenders intercept them, whereby their entire fleet is destroyed.

2306: Due to the devastating defeat of Trabantius, Admiral McMaster, hero of the Consolidation Wars, is tasked with building the Wall Worlds: the plan is to turn all of the ten Union systems on the edge of Orb territory into fortresses and establish them as bulwarks against the technologically superior enemy.

2309: After the electoral victory of nationalist parties and driven by a resurgent economy and militarization, calls for a campaign against the Orb increase. Critics see it as an attempt to prevent renewed secessionist wars within humanity. When Admiral McMaster appears publicly and refuses to implement plans to this effect, a warrant is issued for his arrest. This is followed by

Timeline

protests and riots throughout much of the Union Worlds. McMasters returns to Earth with his fleet and, with the support of the Union Admiralty, seizes power. Congress is dissolved, and all members of the government are imprisoned for endangering the Union and corruption. As a result of his seizure of power, McMaster publishes secret government documents purporting to prove that an offensive against the Orb was indeed being planned. He publicly justifies his assumption of power by saying that such a campaign would have meant the end of humanity and that he had taken an oath to protect it.

2310: Lucius McMaster is officially elected President of the Solar Union and begins a stringent restructuring of the political system, resulting in a military council taking over nearly all government functions. The election is considered error-prone and accompanied by irregularities. Beginning of the McMaster dynasty's rule.

2322: Founding of the Saturn Congress: After growing displeasure with McMaster's paternalistic style of leadership, he creates the Saturn Congress, consisting of a lower house, the Senate, and an upper house, the Military Council. Each world of the Union is given a seat in the Senate and thus a say in civilian jurisdiction.

2326: Appearance of the first Never swarm: When a swarm of unknown creatures attacks the colony world Turan-II on the edge of human dominion, there are no survivors. Turan-II disappears without a trace as a result of the invasion. Research stations in neighboring systems register the appearance of strong gravitational waves a few years later.

2328: Appearance of the second Never Swarm: A Union Navy deep space listening station detects a Never swarm heading for the New Berlin system. President McMaster personally leads the defense.

2329: During the Battle of New Berlin, McMaster's fleet is destroyed, but is able to disperse the swarm and prevent an even greater catastrophe.

2330: Lucius McMaster's eldest son, Malfoy, takes power. Contrary to his father, he is a lavish hedonist and unpopular with the people. His confirmation by the Saturn Congress leads to the

Timeline

first protests among the population and their brutal suppression in several Core Worlds.

2333: The Blockade War: When the Border Worlds, which emerged as constitutional monarchies from the Secession Wars, send an incendiary letter to Congress about growing tax burdens and a critical mention of President Malfoy McMaster, the latter imposes a trade blockade on the total of eighteen worlds.

2335: Kong Student Protests: On the Core World of Kong, second only to Earth as the economic center of the Union, weeks of student protests erupt against the corrupt entanglements and debauched excesses of Malfoy McMaster and other dynasty members in high office, culminating in the July 1st Massacre in which six thousand students lose their lives.

2336: Unknown hackers release internal government documents revealing that McMaster himself ordered the shooting to put down the student protests of 2335. As a result, prolonged protests erupt on all university worlds.

2337: After the Border Worlds again protest to Congress and threaten to leave the Solar Union, McMaster has the heads of the Empire's families arrested and executed after a trial in Earth orbit. As the executions are broadcast live, the condemned turn to the student movement for final expressions of solidarity. Stylized images of the assassinated Border World leaders become a symbol of resistance throughout the Union.

2337-2340: Student Wars: Sparked by the protests and execution of the Eighteen Kings, the McMaster dynasty crumbles just a few decades after its founding. More and more worlds and alliances are turning against the president. The secessionists are led by the Monarchy Movement under King Augustin I of House Hartholm-Harrow, who is considered extremely popular and one of the earliest supporters of the students. He is supported by the Border World Alliance and several influential Core Worlds.

2341: Battle for Terra: King Augustin I arrives in the Sol system with his forces, targeting the center of the Solar Union's power. McMasters defends with the mighty Home Fleet and fleets of the

Timeline

Corporate Council, but they side with Augustin at the last second for reasons that remain unexplained to this day.

2342: Augustin of the House Hartholm-Harrow is crowned emperor of the newly founded Terran Star Empire and the accompanying political reorganization of humanity, which has been shattered and fatigued by centuries of civil wars. Establishment of one hundred houses to control newly founded sectors of five inhabited systems each - the beginning of the High Nobility. Establishment of the Council of Nobility, appointment of one hundred Noble Houses and transfer of inhabited worlds to selected Governors from the Nobility.

2343: Dissolution of the Military Council and renaming of the upper chamber of Congress as the House of Lords with one seat for each of the one hundred High Lords.

2345: Establishment of the Corporate Protectorate. The Corporate Council receives its de facto independence by imperial decree. It is granted the five Seed Worlds as a new political entity in exchange for at least five hundred years of neutrality and an unlimited free trade agreement with the Terran Star Empire.

2348: Construction begins on the Imperial Palace in the Swiss Alps and restructuring of the Union Navy into the Imperial Navy.

2351: The first Invitro humans are cloned on Neuenstein and optimized for work on dangerous gas asteroids.

2354: Death of Emperor Augustin. Enthronement of his eldest son, who chooses the reign name Haeron I.

2355: The 'Cloning Decree': to combat a declining population and an impending labor shortage, Haeron I signs a law from the Saturn Congress that diverts large sums of research funding into optimizing cloning processes to provide labor for vacuum mining.

2360: After successful trials with the new clone population, Invitro workers are granted full civil rights.

2364: Star Empire cloning programs are expanded to accommodate other industries affected by the labor shortage: Invitro workers begin to be used in infrastructure maintenance, construction, cleaning, heavy and vacuum industries.

Timeline

2367: Ceus-III disaster: An unexplained accident on the mining asteroid Ceus-III in the Castilliana system causes two obsolete nuclear reactors to melt down, contaminating the entire station with radioactivity. One hundred workers are killed. Only eighty Invitro clones used on Ceus-III are saved, which are found in the rescue barges. As a result, racist riots break out across the Star Empire against the disparagingly named 'mutant' clones, who are blamed for the deaths of the victims.

2368: Death of Haeron I. The Emperor dies of unknown causes during a hunting trip on New Eden. Since all other hunt participants are also found dead - without visible violence - the investigation ends without results. Enthronement of his eldest son Haeron II.

2370: After the changes at the top of the Star Empire have provided some distraction, the conflict over the Invitro clones reignites when violent clashes break out in the Akkrulu Sector with militant Invitro groups advocating harsher punishment for racism and exclusion.

2371: When High Lord Gowan Harkin, governor of the colony, is assassinated aboard Neuenstein in the Akkrulu Sector, the Invitro underground claims responsibility, triggering a crisis that soon spreads throughout the Star Empire.

2372-2380: The Invitro Wars: After months of police raids and arrests of countless clones on nearly every world in the Star Empire, attacks and protests by the normal population for a tougher crackdown by Imperial security agencies against the clones become more frequent. After extremist elements in the Invitro movement succeed in blowing up the George Washington in orbit over New California, Haeron II declares martial law and empowers the Admiralty to quell the uprising. As a result of the clashes, millions of Invitros are persecuted and killed or executed. Those who survive are stripped of their civil rights and transferred to the forced service of state agencies, where they are used for dangerous and repetitive work. After a so-called 'trust process' of ten years, they will have the opportunity to apply for naturalization.

2380: Third appearance of the Never: When a Never swarm is

Timeline

detected approaching Rohol, after several months of preparation, an Imperial Navy defense fleet manages to prevent an infestation and the loss of the system. The victory at Rohol generates a renewed wave of public support for the Emperor.

2381: Disappearance of the research vessel Persephone in the Wall System Artemis when it jumps into subspace on course for Orb territory despite warnings from the stronghold forces. It later transpires that, contrary to current fleet doctrine, the Persephone was not fired upon because the Emperor's eldest daughter was on board as senior science officer.

2384: A devastating attack on the Vactram of Caledonia's capital Delize kills over two hundred Imperial Navy sailors who had been transported back to the shuttles from home leave in a special streetcar. A confessional message reveals the existence of a group calling itself the 'Republican Resistance' that rejects authoritarian rule by the Emperor.

2385: As a result of intense intelligence work by the Imperial Intelligence IIA, several Republican cells are rooted out within a few weeks, and their members are arrested and executed. This is followed by a wave of attacks on Core and Frontier Worlds of the Star Empire.

2389: Construction of a second fleet of Seed Vessels by the Corporate Protectorate for the Star Empire. A total of five ships are to be transferred to the Imperial Research Fleet within eight years.

2392: Terraforming of the five Seed Worlds by the Corporate Protectorate is deemed officially complete.

2401: Discovery of three Never swarms moving toward the Border World system of Andal by Imperial Remote Recon deep space listening posts.

GLOSSARY

Council of Admiralty: The Council of Admiralty consists of the Navy's twenty-three fleet admirals and their chairman, the only admiral with the title 'Grand Admiral', who also serves as the Emperor's Chief of Staff.

Akkrulu Sector: Imperial sector consisting of five star systems, each with a colony in the Sigma Quadrant, which includes Newstone, which gained notoriety in the 2370s as the site where the Invitro Wars began with the assassination of Governor Gowan Harkin.

Alabama: An ice tug from the Andal system. Destroyed by unknown ship in 2401.

Alpha Corporation: One of the founding members of the Corporate Council. Permanent member of the Council and veto power. Founding member of the Corporate Protectorate. Specializes in high technology.

Alpha Prime: One of the five terraformed planets in the Corporate Protectorate, named after its founding company Alpha Corporation.

Andal: Frontier system and seat of the House of Andal. Known for its listening posts and shielding function of the western Seed Traverse.

Antibes Champagne: Expensive champagne from the French-born world of Antibes in the Taarth Quadrant.

Glossary

Aquarius: Water world in the Taarth Quadrant. Its numerous atolls are also a popular retirement home for the high society of the star empire. The largest economic sector besides tourism is the export of fish and seafood.

Arcturus: Colony in the Omega Quadrant. In 2205, due to an attack with antimatter bombs on the hostile neighboring colony Kerhal, Arcturus was excluded from the then ruling Solar Union for one hundred years and subjected to a blockade. Since then an impoverished world, known for its notorious black market on the only space station 'Black Haven' and the high number of pirates in the system.

Zurich Arcology: Large megaplex in what used to be Switzerland. Population: 30 million. Considered a relatively safe arcology for Earth and a 'suburb' of the Imperial Palace in and on Mont Blanc.

Assai Grass: A grass harvested exclusively on the colony of Kerrhain that causes hallucinations in humans accompanied by euphoric emotional states. Although its characteristic appearance resembles grass, botanically it is a rock lichen. Its cultivation and processing into (dried) Assai as a drug are illegal, as is its sale in any form.

Breathing Pack: Emergency rescue device for spacefarers, consisting of a face mask with breathing tube and attached oxygen pack.

Imperial Navy Marine's Survival Manual: Navy manual given to each recruit when he or she is sworn in, containing about one hundred pages (some of them illustrated) of information on every day and unusual situations that a Navy soldier may encounter during his or her tour of duty.

Battlenet: Tactical combat software for networked fleet operations.

Black Haven: Only space station in orbit around the planet Arcturus. Considered a black market paradise and generally one of the most dangerous places in the Star Empire. This is due to the fact that Arcturus has become economically insignificant after a hundred years of blockade by the Solar Union fleet, and there are no monetary interests there.

Glossary

Black Nebula: Former mercenary corporation and non-permanent member of the Corporate Council, which had to declare bankruptcy in 2253 after many scandals and its expulsion from the Council. Its role in the Secession War of the 2200s is considered pivotal.

Bone Eaters: Former Invitro gang of the world of Kerrhain that saw itself as a rallying point for escaped clones from across the Star Empire. After long hiding in the jungles of Kerrhain and repeatedly committing attacks on the colonial authorities, they were offered exile in the system's asteroid belt, which they accepted. Since then, they have become notorious for smuggling Assai grass.

Bragge: Largest moon of the gas giant Kolsund in the Andal system.

C-555-X: Plundered asteroid in the Kerrhain system.

Caledonia: Colony in the Taarth quadrant. Its capital, Delize, is known in the Star Empire for a serious terrorist attack on naval personnel that killed over 200 sailors in 2384.

Carvis: Name of a planetless system and its only celestial body, the asteroid Carvis A, where a truce is signed by the Solar Union, Frontier Worlds and Corporate Council in 2258.

Castilliana: System and planet in the Sigma Quadrant. Famous for its heavy export of high-end cosmetics and smart-tattoo ink. The system gained sad notoriety for the Ceus-III disaster.

Cazacone: An organized crime syndicate with presence throughout the Star Empire, commonly and incorrectly called the 'Mafia'. Considered extremely well-connected up to the highest levels of government and infamous for its cruelty.

Ceus-III: Former mining asteroid in the Castilliana system, now deserted. In 2367, the Ceus-III catastrophe occurred when a reactor accident leaked radiation and killed the entire human work force, while the eighty Invitro clones who had been deployed were able to escape to safety via escape pods. The tragic event is generally considered the initial spark that later led to the Invitro Wars.

Com Barque: Communication buoy capable of receiving and transmitting signals at designated jump points within systems

Glossary

and relaying them to drones equipped with jump thrusters, which relay their messages to target system com barques.

Credstick: Personalized data carrier on which all the owner's banking information is stored, including his or her identity data. Central means of payment in the Star Empire.

Datamotes: Nanocomputers that can form complex neural patterns in the form of nanite swarms in the brain tissue of their users and support neural computers in their work. They are capable of accelerating thought processes and organizing them like a file system.

Dataverse: The Dataverse is a complex virtual network consisting of a pure data plane, accessible via external devices and resembling the Internet of the 21st century, and a virtual plane consisting of the sum of all its users and connected devices, which can be experienced as a parallel reality using neural computers. The third is the AR layer, a kind of virtual overlay of reality by means of which digital elements can be superimposed on the user's field of view.

The Forbidden Planet: Planet on the edge of the Omega Quadrant, discovered in the 22nd century by one of the first prospector ships, and famous for its *Saphyra* trees, of which only two have been discovered on the jungle world. One was later taken to the Rubov Habitat of Terra as a gift to the Emperor, the other is being cared for on the forbidden planet. Conspiracy theorists believe that secret Science Corps research facilities are located there, studying technologies of the extinct alien civilization that once inhabited the planet. The entire system is a restricted military area and is closely guarded.

The Black Night of Khorwana: A name given to the genocide of the population of the planet of the same name by its robot workers (Servitors) in 2238. The reason was a software anomaly that is still unexplained today. All 80 million colonists were murdered. The Black Night of Khorwana is considered the trigger for the so-called circuit genocide, as a result of which all Servitors and most work bots were banned and destroyed.

Diffundator: Diffundator: Medical device and successor to hypodermic needles. By means of high pressure and active

Glossary

substances atomized to minute particles, the drugs contained therein are 'pushed' through the patient's skin.
Dust System: Fiefdom of the younger brother of Emperor Haeron II, Jurgan Hartholm-Harrow. His eponymous colony is considered economically insignificant, hosts several training centers of corporate Protectorate mercenary companies due to its remoteness and strict local privacy laws.
E-15 Clearance: security clearance for enlisted personnel who have completed at least fifteen years of service. Considered the highest security clearance for crew ranks and is relevant for access to sensitive ship areas, such as mechanics.
***Einherjar* Orbital Ring:** Orbital ring around the planet Andal, completed in 2350 and used primarily for military and trade purposes.
Evac Bubble: Rescue device for operations in a vacuum. A self-deploying cocoon that protects its occupant from the vacuum for up to forty-eight hours, providing oxygen, heat, and water. Its shell is extremely durable and protects against the impact of debris - up to a certain kinetic force.
Flynites: Nanites for spacefarers programmed to line the endothelium of vessels and harden or widen as required, for example to prevent strokes under extreme acceleration forces.
FXTP: One of the two most important exchanges in the Star Empire. The FXTP (*Free Exchange Trade Platform*) is located on Alpha Prime in the Corporate Protectorate and is considered a counterweight to the mighty JFTSE around Jupiter.
Gamorah: Colony in the Taarth Quadrant that is a popular vacation destination for guests from throughout the quadrant.
Gleuse: Gas giant in the Kerrhain system.
Gridlink: Traffic guidance system for autonomous driving used throughout the Star Empire and controlled by highly sophisticated but weak AIs. Connection to the system is mandatory for every car owner.
Grove: Gas giant in the Kerrhain system.
Hatzach Deer: Rare antlered deer of the cloven-hoofed genus found only on the colony of Lapiszunt and resembling Terran deer. Named for its discoverer, zoologist Montgomery Hatzach.

Glossary

***Hermes* Reconnaissance Drone:** Advanced drone for deep space reconnaissance that has its own jump engines and a radar cross-section that is difficult to locate due to its shape and special paint job.

Hofzacher Plaza: Luxury hotel in the Zurich arcology.

Imperial State Bank: State bank of the Star Empire, responsible for interest rate policy and budget management, among other things.

Invitro Wars: The Invitro Wars are a period between 2372 and 2380 in which brutal purges of the clone population occur as a result of the CEUS-III disaster and preceding mass unrest. Most clones become victims of the police and Navy or the death squads of Emperor Haeron II, whose existence he denies until today.

IIA: Imperial Intelligence Agency, the most important secret service of the Star Empire. Reports directly to the Emperor.

Inferno Rifle: Standard rifle for the Star Empire's space forces. Optimized for use in microgravity, fires ammunition with its own rocket engine, keeping the weapon recoilless.

JFTSE: The *Jupiter Free Trade Stock Exchange* is the Star Empire's most important and largest stock exchange by transactions. It is located on the Jupiter habitat of Remus and is controlled by the Jupiter Bank.

Jupiter Bank: The Jupiter Bank is a powerful institution in the Star Empire that has special status as a separate political and economic entity, similar to the Corporate Protectorate. Formally, it does not report to the Emperor and is independent. Its banking secrecy and the high volume of deposits it manages are considered a kind of shield against any form of interference and threat to its sovereignty. Along with the Imperial State Bank, the Jupiter Bank is the Star Empire's largest lender.

Karadan: Rural colony in the Omega Quadrant. Famous for its wines and whiskeys.

Karadian Whiskey: Extremely expensive, peated whiskey from the colony of Karadan.

Karpshyn Sector: Frontier World sector consisting of five systems and three inhabited colonies. Fiefdom of the Andal

Glossary

family. Wealthy and known for its defense industry and wood products.

Notched Tooth: Predator at the top of the food chain on Kerrhain Colony. Females engage in sexual cannibalism after mating by eating the respective male.

Kerrhain: Neighboring system of Andal and part of the Frontier Worlds. Ruled by High Lady Isha Kerrhain.

Kerhal: Kerhal is a former Solar Union colony that is completely devastated in 2204 by ships from the hostile colony Arcturus dropping antimatter bombs. Only a few descendants of the colonists are still alive today.

KH-1: Central star of the Kerrhain system.

Khorwana: Colony in the Sigma quadrant. See also 'The Black Night of Khorwana'.

Kolsund: Gas giant in the Andal system.

Kong: Core World of the Star Empire, where student protests occur in 2335, considered the beginning of the fall of the McMaster dynasty.

Lapiszunt: Sparsely populated colony in the Sigma Quadrant, considered a paradise for xenobiologists due to its complex and diverse biosphere.

Light Hauler: Class of light freighters consisting of a connector between the cockpit and the engine section to which standardized cargo containers can be attached. Most common freighter type in the Star Empire, built for over eighty years.

Luna Mining Corporation: Considered humanity's first megacorporation, *Luna Mining Corporation* specializes in mining resources in vacuum and microgravity. Member of the Corporation Council, veto power in the Corporation Protectorate.

Medidoc: Automated medical supply unit.

Medicasket: The Medicasket is a closed medical capsule whose interior can be kept sterile and is used for robotic operations or induced stasis states for severely injured patients who require more intensive medical treatments.

***Morning Star*:** The *Morning Star* is a former passenger liner. Destroyed by an unknown ship in 2401.

Myelination: Process on Seed Vessels in which minute clumps of

Glossary

biomass are encased by a thin but tough layer of polyp to protect them from atmospheric entry forces on Seed Planets.

Neuenstein: Core world in the Akrulu Sector. Major colony for Navy research and development, fiefdom of the Crown Princes of House Hartholm-Harrow. Famous for its film industry and the assassination of its governor, Gowan Harkin, whose murder by Invitro extremists in 2371 triggered the Invitro Crisis and ultimately the Invitro Wars.

Neural Computer: Miniature computer implanted on the brain stem that allows its users access to biological monitoring and bodily functions. A necessary interface to control other augments of the human body and nanites such as Flynites or Smartnites.

New California: Core World of the Star Empire in the Omega Quadrant. Famous for its movie industry and orbital shipyards.

New Eden: Humanity's first colony and now a major Core World. In addition to its considerable Science Corps facilities located throughout the system, New Eden is considered a popular vacation destination for high society.

Omega-Zero: Secluded colony in the Taarth Quadrant.

P3X-888: First terraforming world of the Corporate Council, colloquially known as 'Green Rain' after the first Seed Vessel, which was able to turn what was once a rocky world with an atmosphere but no biosphere into an Earth-like planet by jettisoning biomass.

Section 2, paragraph 1 of the Interplanetary Space Traffic Act: Section 2, paragraph 1 of the Interplanetary Space Traffic Act states that any ship is obligated to render assistance to another when it declares an emergency.

Pulau Weh: World discovered in 2393 in the 777-Goggins system, beyond the Tartarus Void. It is considered biodiverse and habitable, but devoid of usable resources and insignificant due to its distance from the Zephyros Quadrant.

Quantcom: Network of novel com barques that enable faster-than-light communications through non-local quantum effects within star systems.

Raptor Engine: Latest generation of compact fusion engines from the Yokatami corporation.

Glossary

Reaper Suit: Navy's lightweight, vacuum-capable protective suit consisting of an interconnected swarm of programmable nanites with their own oxygen supply, inhaled in liquid form.
Reface Mask: Nanonic face mask that conforms to the shape of its user's face and can alter characteristic features to disguise the wearer's identity.
Rejuvenation: Anti-aging treatment performed with a mix of telomere extension, pluripotent stem cell injection, and NAD+ enhancers.
***Rubov* Orbital Ring:** Orbital ring around the Earth, and humanity's first orbital ring. Seat of important institutions such as the Council of Nobility and the Council of Admiralty.
***Saphyra*:** Tree species of which only two specimens are known in the entire Star Empire. They come from the forbidden planet and, according to the findings of the Science Corps, are not of natural origin. They are believed to be chimeras of evolved and technological elements. The extremely complex structure of the trees and its internal processes still puzzle researchers today. Little is officially known about their creators or breeders.
Saturn Parliament: The Saturn Parliament is located on the Aurora habitat in orbit around Saturn and is the seat of the Upper and Lower Houses of Parliament: the House of Lords and the Senate.
Schofield&Brugger: Private bank. Located on New California.
Sigma Tiri: Core system in the Sigma Quadrant, which in 2254 becomes the scene of a major battle between a Pact fleet and the Solar Union, in which the Union forces suffer a major defeat due to the intervention of a Frontier World fleet.
Skaland: Capital of the Frontier World Andal and seat of the Andal family.
Smartnites: Programmable pluripotent nanites that circulate in the bloodstream of humans, giving them control over important bodily functions.
Southhain: Capital of the frontier world of Kerrhain.
Jump Node: Part of the engines of interstellar starships used to generate subspace vacuoles, which are used to enable jumps through subspace.

Glossary

S1-Ruhr: Seed World in the Seed Traverse, which is under the control of Ruhr Heavy Industries.

S2-Yokatami: Seed World in the Seed Traverse, which is under the control of Yokatami. Restricted Area.

Taarth Quadrant: Quadrant in interstellar southwest Sol.

Tarshan: Capital of the former colony Turan-II in the Turan system. Lost in 2236 in the course of a Never infestation.

Tartarus Void: Empty area in the south of the Zephyros quadrant where there are no star systems.

Terra One: Most important and widely watched news feed in the Star Empire.

***Titan* Motorized Armor:** Latest generation of motorized armor used by Imperial Navy Marines.

Trabantius: A whale world on the border of Orb territory.

Tranit: Colony in the interstellar northwest of Sol, bordering the Frontier Worlds and the fiefdom of First Secretary of State Lord Janus Darishma. Economically rather insignificant.

Transducer: Augment that allows its users (voice) communication via thought.

Tromso Electronics LLC: Major telecommunications company on Andal.

Turan-II: Former colony world in the Turan system that fell victim to the first Never infestation in 2236.

Turing Agreement: 2062 UN agreement outlawing strong AIs, later adopted and ratified by all members of the Solar Union and also became part of Imperial legislation.

Universal Connector: Universal connector in the Star Empire, also used synonymously for universal connectors compatible with the same.

***Ushuaia*:** Former *Light Hauler*-class freighter. Destroyed by the *Glory* in 2401 in the Andal system.

Vactram: High-speed passenger train that travels in frictionless vacuum tubes and is the primary means of public transportation throughout the Star Empire.

Vaults: Former gang of the Frontier World of Kerrhain, which expanded rapidly through the profitable smuggling of Assai grass.

Glossary

Now considered one of the most important criminal conglomerates in the Frontier Worlds.

Warfield Armored Reconnaissance & Security: Insignificant mercenary group in the corporate protectorate.

Science Corps: The Science Corps is a major institution that coordinates all of the Star Empire's research and development projects. Maintains offices in virtually every university in the human-controlled territory and is the most important scientific institution in the Star Empire.

Zenith: Former alias of Lord Janus Darishma.

Cerberus Station: Secret space station in the asteroid belt of Kerrhain. Seat of the Broker and major transshipment point for Assai grass and other black market goods.

Zulustra crabs: Seafood specialty on New Eden. The native crabs are eaten alive there as a delicacy, usually with an expensive champagne sauce.

CHARACTERS

Adam Goosens: Administrator of the Cerberus Station.
Admiral Heusgen: Fleet Admiral and member of the Admiral Council.
Admiral Takahashi: Fleet Admiral and member of the Admiral Council.
Agent Walker: Agent of the IIA. Specializes in undercover operations.
Akwa Marquandt: Captain of the Imperial Navy and daughter of Fleet Admiral Dain Marquandt.
Artas Andal: Eldest son of High Lord Cornelius Andal.
Broker, the: Mysterious information broker in the Kerrhain system.
Cornelius Andal: High Lord of the House of Andal and Governor of the Karphshyn Sector.
Dimitri Rogoshin: COO of the Warfield Armored Reconnaissance & Security mercenary group. Former Colonel in the Marines.
Dyke Keko: Captain of the ice tug *Alabama*.
Elayne Hartholm-Harrow: Youngest daughter of Emperor Haeron II. Holds the title of Princess.
Elisa Andal: Daughter of High Lord Cornelius Andal.
Filio Jericho: Fleet Admiral and member of the Admiral Council.

Characters

Giulio Adams: Courier of the Senate President Varilla Usatami.
Gowan Harkin: Former governor of Neuenstein, killed in an assassination attempt by Invitro extremists in 2371.
Huelga Ferreira: First officer on the *Ushuaia*. Wife of Manuél Ferreira. Physicist.
Ikabot Nurheim: Head of the Seed Vessel *Demeter* with the rank of First Executive at Ruhr Heavy Industries.
Isha Kerrhain: High Lady of the House of Kerrhain.
Janus Darishma: First Secretary of State to Emperor Haeron II. Lord and Governor of Tranit Colony.
Jean Sapin: Mayor of the Arcology Paris.
Johanna Teunen: Captain of the passenger liner *Morning Star*.
Jurgan Hartholm-Harrow: Younger brother of Emperor Haeron II. Lives in exile on Dust.
Manuél Ferreira: Captain of the *Ushuaia*. Husband of Huelga Ferreira.
Mariella Andal: Daughter of High Lord Cornelius Andal.
Mirage: Code name of an unknown agent.
Nancy: Secretary of Janus Darishma.
Narun Grassimus: High Lord of the Star Empire.
Nova Ladalle: Fleet Admiral and member of the Admiral Council.
Orlon Kerrhain: Former High Lord of Kerrhain Colony and father of Isha Kerrhain.
Pedro Bachelet: Fleet Admiral and member of the Admiral Council.
Peraia Hartholm-Harrow: Eldest daughter of Emperor Haeron II. Declared missing since the disappearance of the research vessel *Persephone* in 2381. Princess.
Sophie Andal: Wife of High Lord Cornelius Andal.
Varilla Usatami: President of the Saturn Senate and highest civilian politician of the Star Empire. Former xenobiologist of the Science Corps.
Xavier Bennington: Alias of Gavin Andal.

AFTERWORD

Dear Reader,

After The Last Battleship, I knew there was more to come. During the writing process, I came up with so many other ideas that would require a new universe that it was clear to me: there will be a second series. A sister series, so to speak. But this time there will be a surprise: The Last Fleet 1-3 will conclude the first trilogy, then be followed by a few stand-alone volumes by authors (Brandon Q. Morris will kick things off on May 1) you know and whom I hold in high regard. Their contributions will complement the main storyline as completed novels. This will be followed by a second trilogy of mine, again self-contained and continuing the main storyline. And so it goes on. Not as an endless series, but as a big universe that is allowed to grow, but always concludes storylines in trilogies and single volumes, and then continues from there. I sincerely hope you enjoy it as much as you did The Last Battleship. As always, if you

Afterword

support the series and want more, feel free to review on Amazon and let me know if you enjoyed it.

If you'd like to contact me directly, feel free to do so at joshua@joshuatcalvert.com - I still answer every email. As always, I would love a review for this book on Amazon.

If you subscribe to my newsletter, I'll regularly chat a bit about myself, writing, and the great themes of science fiction. Plus, as a thank you, you'll receive my e-book Rift: The Transition exclusively and for free: www.joshuatcalvert.com

Best wishes, Joshua T. Calvert